PRAIRIE PARADISE

EMMA HARRINGTON

D0123284

ZEBRA BOOKS
KENSINGTON PUBLISHING CORP.

ZEBRA BOOKS

are published by

Kensington Publishing Corp.
475 Park Avenue South
New York, NY 10016

First printing: November, 1988

Printed in the United States of America

The fiery brilliance of the Zebra Hologram Heart which you see on the cover is created by "laser holography." This is the revolutionary process in which a powerful laser beam records light waves in diamond-like facets so tiny that 9,000,000 fit in a square inch. No print or photograph can match the vibrant colors and radiant glow of a hologram.

So look for the Zebra Hologram Heart whenever you buy a historical romance. It is a shimmering reflection of our guarantee that you'll find consistent quality between the covers!

PASSION IN THE MOONLIGHT

When Blue Feather lifted her arms to smooth back her hair, half standing in the shallow water, it was more than Adrian could bear. He surged abruptly to his feet and dropped his rifle, then stepped into the stream, startling her.

"Ohhh!" she cried.

Suddenly aware of her nudity and the moonlight and the strange expression in Adrian's eyes, Blue Feather grew very still. She had been waiting for him to admit that she was a woman, and now he would. She waited silently for what she was certain would happen.

Ignoring the water that lapped around his knees, Adrian pulled Blue Feather to him. His fingers were warm and strong, his mouth hot and hungry as it closed over her parted lips. Shivering, not with cold but with passion, Blue Feather closed her eyes. The cold handles of his knife and pistols pressed against her naked flesh. But she was aware of only his mouth moving against her lips, then her cheeks and the soft swirls of her ear as he whispered words she didn't understand.

"God, Blue Feather, I need you so badly," he groaned.

She knew he loved her, though his lips never formed the words. No other man would treat her so tenderly, with such sweet caresses and burning kisses, and she would do whatever she could to have him always love her. . . .

FIERY ROMANCE
From Zebra Books

AUTUMN'S FURY   (1763, $3.95)
by Emma Merritt

Lone Wolf had known many women, but none had captured his heart the way Catherine had . . . with her he felt a hunger he hadn't experienced with any of the maidens of his own tribe. He would make Catherine his captive, his slave of love — until she would willingly surrender to the magic of AUTUMN'S FURY.

PASSION'S PARADISE   (1618, $3.75)
by Sonya T. Pelton

When she is kidnapped by the cruel, captivating Captain Ty, fair-haired Angel Sherwood fears not for her life, but for her honor! Yet she can't help but be warmed by his manly touch, and secretly longs for PASSION'S PARADISE.

LOVE'S ELUSIVE FLAME   (1836, $3.75)
by Phoebe Conn

Golden-haired Flame was determined to find the man of her dreams even if it took forever, but she didn't have long to wait once she met the handsome rogue Joaquin. He made her respond to his ardent kisses and caresses . . . but if he wanted her completely, she would have to be his only woman — she wouldn't settle for anything less. Joaquin had always taken women as he wanted . . . but none of them was Flame. Only one night of wanton ecstasy just wasn't enough — once he was touched by LOVE'S ELUSIVE FLAME.

SAVAGE SPLENDOR   (1855, $3.95)
by Constance O'Banyon

By day Mara questioned her decision to remain in her husband's world. But by night, when Tajarez crushed her in his strong, muscular arms, taking her to the peaks of rapture, she knew she could never live without him.

SATIN SURRENDER   (1861, $3.95)
by Carol Finch

Dante Folwer found innocent Erica Bennett in his bed in the most fashionable whorehouse in New Orleans. Expecting a woman of experience, Dante instead stole the innocence of the most magnificent creature he'd ever seen. He would forever make her succumb to . . . SATIN SURRENDER.

Available wherever paperbacks are sold, or order direct from the Publisher. Send cover price plus 50¢ per copy for mailing and handling to Zebra Books, Dept. 2504, 475 Park Avenue South, New York, N.Y. 10016. Residents of New York, New Jersey and Pennsylvania must include sales tax. DO NOT SEND CASH.

This book is dedicated to

PAULINE CHURCH HARRINGTON

*a loving and wonderful mother
who wanted this book to see print as much
as the authors did.
THANKS MOMMA for bringing home your
stories of Wind River.*

and to

DOROTHY LEATHERS LIPSEY

*THANKS MOTHER for being kind and patient,
and for having enough faith in me to buy me
my first typewriter.
Your helpfulness enabled me to touch my dreams.
I haven't forgotten it.*

Book One

The Wind
1834

There is a great dark wind on the edge of every
storm . . . a wind of prophecy. It can sweep you
away. . . .

Wind River
Prologue
The Wind

Montana Plains, Spring 1834

Proud, copper-skinned horsemen rode swiftly down thick-forested slopes. A storm was raging, and they were the lightning — red flashes in the night. Muffled screams were silenced under the weight of stones, sticks and shafts of steel. Blood fell like rain, and the prey scattered like leaves, falling, falling.

Soon there were smiles amid the screams of victory. Loud laughter rolled through the steamy air as the Crow warriors danced around licking blue flames. War games were a way of life.

Rushing waters of the nearby stream gurgled over flat, smooth stones, circling around the fetlocks of a Crow pony. Astride him, a young Crow warrior watched with narrowed eyes the silent slice of slim brown arms through the dusky waters.

It was a young maiden. She had heard the pained screams, the voices of death, and numbing fear had sent her fleeing to the blue shadows to hide and watch. Now she knew the victor. She heard the celebration, the sounds of drums and dancing. The air was thick with the stench of death, the gamy odors of singed animal hides, sumac leaves and dried bark. More important, she understood the shrill voices of the Crow warriors as they chanted passionate songs of courage and victory over their enemy.

Inside, a small, flickering voice cried, "Blue Feather, you are safe. . . ."

Gathering courage as she did firewood, one small stick at a time, Blue Feather rose from the soft dark waters and moved cautiously toward the muddy slopes of the stream. Wet hair clung to her face, mantling her slender shoulders in a black velvet cape and molding the firm thrust of her breasts. A night breeze gushed upward out of the valley, and she shivered. Hugging herself tightly, she crouched in the water reeds near the shore. Pinpoints of red lights winked like sullen eyes through the night, and she stood, a tiny silhouette against the light of an icy moon.

The silent Crow watched, his pony motionless, blending with the trees and muddy slopes. The maiden was slight of body, a girl trembling on the edge of maturity, with small breasts like ripe apples and still-childish hips. She half turned, and he saw an oval face with delicate features, the high cheekbones of her race softened somehow, less pronounced. Something in him stirred, and he knew this had to be the maiden whose tipi he had found. She was Shoshoni, maybe even a shaman, and a very good prize for a young Crow. Still he waited, watching, half fearful because of the signs of powerful magic that had been in her tipi.

Blue Feather edged forward, water caressing her slender thighs, the current urging her farther.

10

Thoughts tumbled as wildly through her head as the mountain waters leaped over rocks. Should she run? All her instincts urged flight, yet to abandon caution could be fatal. She tried hard to recall all the lessons she had learned from the old woman.

"Blue Feather," she could almost hear Old Woman saying in her thin, crackling voice like dried leaves, "the rabbit thrives because he is clever. Be clever like the rabbit, Blue Feather, and hide when you sense danger." Oh, Old Woman, where are you now? I need you, Blue Feather thought desperately, fear pumping through her veins like the icy waters of the stream. But Old Woman would never hear her again, would never peer at her through wise old eyes like the owl's. Old Woman had taken that last journey through the mountains of death. . . .

Blue Feather shivered, her flesh prickling against the cold kiss of the wind. She was the only survivor, the only one who could tell what had happened to her people, how the Crow had come screaming down the slopes to slay them with clubs and sharp-edged blades. She was still alive because she was taboo, set aside in a tipi of her own, away from the others because of her menses. In spite of the awkwardness of her childlike body, she was a woman now. The sacred stones were still stacked inside her tipi, the feathers and bits of animal hide — *aiii*, Blue Feather wailed silently, stricken with grief. Who would tell her father of her fate?

An early spring had lured the Shoshoni from their winter range toward the mountains. It had been nearly twelve moons since Blue Feather had

11

seen her father, and she had eagerly anticipated sharing his time again. Even though he was not one of The People, he was respected. Pierre Duvalle was a friend of the Shoshoni and had taken the chief's daughter to wife. Blue Feather's mother had died two years before, a victim of smallpox, and Pierre Duvalle had retreated into his own sorrow for a time. Now he waited for his daughter to join him in the mountains.

Determination seized Blue Feather, giving her courage, and she took several steps forward, closer to the shore, closer to the mountains where her father waited. She had powerful magic, didn't she? Hadn't she, out of all her people, been spared the club or knife? The Great Spirit smiled upon her—

A shrill cry escaped her as harsh, hurting fingers clamped around her ankle like the bite of a great cat, almost crushing her fragile bones and sending her face-first into the dark waters. Life-giving water clogged her nostrils, choking her, making her gasp for air. All around her was dark, a world of water in her eyes, nose and mouth as she clawed at her assailant. Plundering hands felt bare flesh as she flailed, floundered and found him, tugging to free her leg from his grasp. The fingers only tightened. Mud spurted between her splayed fingers as she tore at the bottom of the stream, and tiny pebbles like silver fish scraped along her palms. Choking, gagging, Blue Feather was hauled toward shore.

Finally, in a sweet surge, she was able to fill her starved lungs with air. Her body twisted in the same moment to claw at her captor with curved nails. The young Crow muttered a curse, feeling as if he was gripping a snake in his arms, struggling to maintain his hold. Streaks of fire slashed his cheek in four furrows of pain as her hand raked him. Blood flowed in crimson rivulets, mingling with water from the stream and the streaks of warpaint on his face. Angered, a brown fist lifted and struck, slamming against the side of her head with a wet thud. Lightning flashed before her eyes, and the world grew dark, spiralling into oblivion.

Panting from the struggle, the Crow gently loosed her limply sagging body into the damp, dank-smelling reeds along the bank. He hunkered down on the balls of his feet, staring at his prize. Reaching out with the same hand that had dealt death to the Shoshoni only a short time before, the young warrior lightly searched the smooth curve of the girl's cheek with the backs of his fingers. She was beautiful. During their struggle he had seen the wild flash of her eyes, eyes that were the color of the summer sky. Yet, she was Shoshoni. She was with the Shoshoni, was dressed as a Shoshoni, and was obviously someone of importance. The buckskin dress she wore was studded with porcupine quills and glass beads, a mark of wealth and rank.

Black eyes narrowed thoughtfully, his gaze travelling up a slender body bared to the waist where the dress bunched around her hips. Only one moccasin remained on her small foot, the other lost to the swift-moving waters of the stream, and she wore a curious amulet around her neck. He hesitated, wondering about his captive. She would be worth much as a bargaining point with the

13

Shoshoni, and surely his reputation as a great warrior would be enhanced. He rocked back on his heels.

Lightning crackled in the treetops, outlining pine, fir and cedar against the sky, and the Crow warrior lifted his head to smell the cool gust of wind blowing across spiny ridges. The wind blew down from the mountains, bringing a change in fortunes for the Crow; Young White Buffalo could sense it as the wolf senses the unseen herd of deer.

A satisfied smile quirked his lips upward as he lifted his prize in smooth-muscled arms. A jagged bolt of lightning speared an ancient oak, and the dying tree seemed to scream as it slowly cracked in two. Rain hissed against birch leaves and plopped onto thick beds of pine needles as Young White Buffalo walked steadily toward the fires of his brothers.

Chapter 1
Storms

England, County Cornwall, Spring 1834

Splinters of white fire sliced through folds of indigo sky, illuminating green meadows and jutting rocks with blinding flashes of light. Rain clouds boiled across the Cornish coast to the rumbling applause of thunder and wind, and the sea crashed against jagged slate cliffs. Adrian Herenton, younger son of Lord Thomas Herenton, fourth Duke of Hertfield, stared through the leaded glass panes of mullioned windows, feeling as intense and restless as the approaching storm.

He pushed open the window and waited, letting the salty tang of the sea fill his nostrils, breathing deeply of wind and rain and the renewal of life. It was spring, a time when lambs frolicked beside their mothers, bleating innocent, milky cries; a time when birds built their nests in sturdy oaks to raise their families, and a time when the entire world roused itself to appreciation of just being alive.

Adrian noted with a faint grimace of surprise that his knuckles were white where he gripped the smooth wooden window frame. It must be the storm, the wind. Or perhaps . . . perhaps it was the knowledge that his future balanced as precariously as a boulder on the edge of the slate cliffs below. Downstairs, a faint ripple of laughter threaded the tinkle of music from the pianoforte, blending, drifting in and out with the melody. In spite of the mellow tune, Adrian found himself gritting his teeth.

Why? He had fought this uneasiness the entire day, had been as tense as if preparing to don armor and ride into battle, yet it was only a small, impromptu dinner party to celebrate his brother's engagement. It was an announcement he had been eagerly anticipating for some time. Richard was finally going to marry Elizabeth Shelley, and in so doing, Adrian would be free to marry Nell.

A gush of wind tangled in his thick blond hair, spattering Adrian's face with rain, and he put out his tongue to taste a teasing droplet resting upon his upper lip. More raindrops clustered on his thick lashes like liquid silver, diamond spangles to frame eyes of gunmetal gray, luminescent eyes, eyes that could be as clear as the fine Cornish mists of a morning, or as dark and stormy as the clouds sweeping over the crags and towers of Hertfield castle, sensitive eyes that could see through artifice to the pettiness beneath. Adrian shut the window and watched the rain hiss against the glass, then slide down in rivulets.

Dark brows knit into a frown at the bridge of his straight nose, but the lips compressed into a tight line still betrayed hints of sensuality in the shape of his mouth. High cheekbones and the firm sweep of his jaw gave strength to a face that could easily have been effeminate. But one glance into Adrian's eyes banished any hint that he might be weak. All the firm promise of manhood rested in those eyes, waiting for the temper of life to form and strengthen him. He was tall and had filled out in just the short space of a year, it seemed to his family, losing most of those awkward, gangly movements so common to adolescents. Years of fencing lessons had given Adrian a lean, taut body, supple yet well-muscled, and he carried himself with all the unconscious grace of an athlete.

A muscle twitched in his jaw as he stared out the window without seeing the broad sweep of green lawns, the neatly manicured bushes that edged the curving drive and several miles of intricately laid stone paths. Even the driving storm receded from his conscious thoughts as Adrian reflected on his older brother's marriage. It had taken so long for Richard to finally declare himself, when everyone in Cornwall knew that the Herentons and Shelleys always married each other. And once Richard married his precious Elizabeth, it left her younger sister free for him.

Finally a hint of a smile lifted the chiseled mouth. Nell—Eleanor—Shelley with her shining eyes, her wet, laughing lips and rich, promising curves that beckoned to him to touch and caress. . . . He stifled a sigh. Surely there would be no objection to his wedding Nell, but a small worry still nagged at the back of his mind. No one in either family had any idea they were more than childhood friends, and Nell had insisted upon keeping it that way.

"At least until Beth is married," Nell had said.

Reluctantly, Adrian had agreed to keep silent, even though the clandestine meetings, cleverly written notes and hidden letters had become more of a

17

nuisance than exciting. Soon it would be resolved.

A loud rumble of thunder shook the house sprawled atop the cliff, rattling windowpanes and doors and shaking Adrian from his reverie. As the thunder died, he became aware of a familiar tune drifting up the wide, curving staircase and smiled. *Für Elise* by Beethoven, his favorite. Nell was playing it just for him. Adrian straightened his snowy, starched cravat and smoothed nonexistent wrinkles from his impeccably tailored frock coat, glanced into the long mirror to be certain his trousers were wrinkle-free, then crossed the room to the door in three long strides.

Eleanor Shelley's slim fingers caressed the ivory keys in light, quick strokes. One small foot reached out to tap the pedals amidst a rustle of silk skirts. As usual, she was garbed in a soft mint color to match her glowing eyes and complement the golden sheen of her hair. At Adrian's entrance, she lifted heavy-lashed lids and smiled demurely, then returned her attention to the fresh page of music her brother was turning over. Only the sidelong glance from beneath those heavy lashes indicated that she was still thinking of Adrian, and he gave a smile of satisfaction.

Hands clasped behind his back, Adrian strode toward his father. Lord Herenton was deep in conversation with Sir Shelley, both gentlemen warming their backs in front of a cheerily crackling fire and their stomachs with potent French brandy. Adrian eyed his father warily, hearing the familiar bass tone of his voice alter to an indignantly higher pitch, and decided to change course at the last moment. He swerved to where his brother sat upon a small chaise lounge with Elizabeth.

"Richard," he greeted him with a nod, "and the

lovely Elizabeth!" He gave her outstretched hand a perfunctory kiss as his brother returned his greeting, gray eyes narrowing upon her pale, pinched face. Was it his imagination, or was she even paler than usual? Her golden eyes were dull, her hair lifeless and lackluster, and Adrian felt another twinge of disquiet.

"Adrian," she said so softly that he had to strain to hear, "it's so good to see you."

"It's always good to see you again, Elizabeth. Are you keeping my wayward brother in line?"

Elizabeth smiled, but did not reply, and Adrian was left to wonder over her unusual languor. Probably one of those female ailments young women were so prone to have, he decided. No one else seemed to find fault with her behavior, but still, it was a bit alarming to see her so pale and quiet.

Richard began a dissertation on the merits of working such long hours that there was no time to be "wayward," his flat, humorless voice quickly raking his younger brother's already restless mood. Adrian forced a polite smile, eyes scanning the parlor for an excuse to escape.

Distraction was provided in the form of a gentleman's disagreement between his father and Sir Shelley, a hot discussion on the merits of their prize stallions.

"I say, Adrian," his father expostulated loudly, "tell Shelley here what a beastly fine stallion Excalibur is!"

"Thomas," Henry Shelley cut in, "I ought to know, because I was at Tattersall's with you when you purchased the bobtail—"

"Bobtail!" Thomas Herenton's face flushed a bright red. "Bobtail," he said in a strangled tone, "is a flattering term when applied to that sorry nag you have the audacity to suggest is even remotely comparable to Excalibur—"

"If I recall correctly," Adrian broke in when it appeared as if his father and Sir Shelley were in danger of falling out completely, "you both have excellent animals. I would think that the only way to settle any question in your mind, is to pit one against the other in a race." A dark brow lifted questioningly as Adrian glanced first at his father, then at Sir Shelley.

"Just the thing!" Thomas Herenton agreed. A beatific smile replaced his disgruntled expression. "Right, Henry?"

Sir Shelley was slower to warm to the idea, finally nodding his head and muttering that if it was the only way to convince Thomas he'd do it.

Adrian edged away from the pair, who immediately pounced on time, place and rules as points to argue. His father's portly form, replete from years of fine French brandy and good English food, threw a long shadow, reaching to the loveseat where Elizabeth's and Eleanor's mother, Lady Anne, sat doing her needlework. A fragile woman, with soft eyes and pale skin, Lady Anne looked up with a fond smile.

"Adrian, you handled that marvelously," she said, her needle darting in and out of the linen like the rapid beats of a hummingbird. "You should sit in parliament."

He laughed. "Oh, no, Lady Anne! You're not getting rid of me that easily! I shall stay here in Cornwall and under your feet awhile longer, I think."

Lady Anne flicked a quizzical glance at the tall, fair young man smiling down at her. She had long suspected that her younger daughter bore tender feelings for Adrian, and could hardly blame her. He was very handsome, very charming and educated, and had travelled extensively on the Continent the year before. One day, Adrian would inherit his mother's lands, and she knew he would be as prosperous as a younger son can be. A fine match, if Nell would be willing. . . .

"Did you summon the rain, Adrian?" she asked with a playful smile. "I cannot recall having seen such a wet spring in some time. We were forced to stay a bit longer when the downpour began again, and now your father has been so kind as to invite us for dinner."

"No, no, Lady Anne. You do us an honor by staying," Lord Herenton cut in, moving to stand beside his son. "And I've no doubt Adrian has attempted to summon the rain before. Why, only last spring he ordered all these ridiculous textbooks with scientific experiments in them—I was certain we would all be blown to pieces before a fortnight was past! Chemicals! Bah."

Before Adrian could extricate himself from the unhappy turn in the conversation, his father added, "But enough of that, my boy. I have a splendid surprise for you."

"Surprise?" *That* was a surprise, Adrian thought with a familiar trace of cynicism. Lord Herenton was not given to surprises. Nor was he given to bestowing gifts, for that matter. The last gift Adrian could remember receiving from his father had been at Christmas when he was still a schoolboy at Eton.

"Yes, surprise," Lord Herenton was saying. "Arrived this afternoon while you were out working on that . . . that contraption of yours."

"Contraption?" Sir Shelley boomed, staring at Adrian with an expression of confusion. "What have you done now, lad?"

"His boat—"

"Boat?"

"Boat," Lord Herenton confirmed with all the nuances of an indulgent parent. Adrian fumed silently, hating being patronized. He managed a matching smile when his father's lips stretched into a grimace like a satisfied cat, inwardly cringing as Herenton continued, "Yes, I don't know which is worse, that wretched boat or his new laboratory. Adrian's always creating some new scheme or project—why, do you recall last year? He and some of his cronies went on a walking tour of the Continent. Walking tour! They even," he said with a moué of distaste, "camped out with a ragtag band of Gypsies."

"I never heard that," Shelley observed, gazing at Adrian with new interest.

"Tut! It's hardly something one talks about over horseflesh and tenant payments. And then there was that escapade two years ago, when a group of his friends attempted to swim the channel. Ended rather horribly, I thought. Young Geoffrey Hampton nearly drowned, and the rest of the fools were neatly pickled. You must recall when the Hampton lad was laid up for more than two months?"

"No, Thomas, not really. . . ." Sir Henry replied weakly.

"Have another brandy, Henry."

Henry Shelley gulped down a healthy amount, his considering gaze straying to Richard, his soon to be son-in-law. Herenton correctly read his thoughts.

"Richard is nothing like his younger brother,

Henry, but is a sober, steady lad with his head on straight . . ."

Adrian struggled for control, furious with his father and furious with himself for even caring about Lord Herenton's opinion. Matters had not changed in all the past twenty-two years, had they? Why change now? Thomas Herenton had always considered him a lack-wit, impulsive and radical. Richard's projects were studious experiments; his were wild, harebrained schemes. Richard's decision to crossbreed certain strains of sheep had ended disastrously and never been discussed again; Adrian's attempt to cross-pollinate different types of barley had been labeled "folly, moronic and rattlebrained," and had dominated the dinner conversation for several months. Like now, when all *his* boyhood peccadilloes were being paraded before Sir Shelley and his family like a list of crimes, Richard's were kept silent. Even future projects were being trotted out for inspection and ridicule.

". . . believe the group has formed some sort of club," Lord Herenton was saying with a broad wink. "S'pose it does keep them away from muslin and cards though, hey?" Adrian managed another polite smile at their amusement, his irritation growing as his father continued, "And this boat Adrian is building is intended to sail across the channel and down the coast of France to Rome, Italy. Seems they're all determined to visit the grave of some mad, forgotten poets in Rome. Can you imagine? And on a boat they're building themselves. I just hope it doesn't sink while crossing the channel!"

Sir Shelley eyed Adrian with a gleam of respect in his gaze. "I must admit, young man, that in spite of the eccentricity of the plan, I am much

23

impressed."

"Thank you, sir." Adrian glanced from Sir Shelley to where Nell was still singing softly and playing the pianoforte, and was relieved she hadn't heard his father's disparaging diatribe on his past and future schemes. After the planned voyage to Rome, Nell was his next project. He had a brief vision of Nell, her soft, satiny skin bared to his exploring hands, those glorious green eyes gazing up at him and shining with desire, and her lips parted and waiting for his kiss—

"Well," Lord Herenton prompted his youngest son, "aren't you going to ask about the surprise?"

Startled, jerked from much more pleasant reflections, Adrian's brows rose as he faced his father.

"Surprise?" he echoed, then, "Oh, yes . . . yes . . . where is it?"

"Walking into the room right this very moment" came the answer.

And it was. Adrian was delighted to see the elegant gentleman strolling through the parlor door with a dark, fashionable woman on his arm.

"Uncle Timothy!"

"Adrian!" was the enthusiastic reply, and both men smiled with genuine pleasure.

"Uncle Tim, Aunt Claire," Adrian said, taking his aunt's hand and kissing the smooth flesh, "dear friends! When did you get here?"

"Just before the rain," Claire Herenton said. "We were so exhausted from bowling along at such a pace, that we had to nap before seeing you, dear boy. You will forgive us?"

"I would forgive you both anything." Adrian seated his aunt beside Lady Anne on the loveseat, smiling down at her with such pleasure that her eyes filled with tears. This was her dear, dead sis-

24

ter's youngest boy, and the one most like poor Catherine. Richard was a stuffed shirt and deadly dull in Claire's opinion, much like his father with whom she'd never gotten along. Claire was a Shelley, and her husband Timothy was Thomas Herenton's younger brother, his position identical to Adrian's. Fortunately for Timothy, he'd never cared much for position nor title, while it mattered overmuch to Thomas. Claire worried that it might matter to dear Adrian, and that was one reason she maintained her contact with the family. Heaven knew, Timothy was usually in some cerebral world of his own and would forget that he had an older brother at all if it was left up to him. But they were here, and Adrian appeared to be well and was certainly more handsome than ever. So she turned to Lady Anne to make small talk while Timothy pulled Adrian to a corner to describe a new experiment of some nature.

Adrian was openly grinning now, already deeply involved in the complexities of a chemical equation that was puzzling his uncle, and thinking how much he preferred Timothy's simple, straightforward attitude to the more devious twists of his father. Timothy Herenton was both scholar and scientist to the extreme dismay of his family, who had wanted him for the Church. It had been Uncle Timothy's observations that had most influenced Adrian's childhood and mental growth, and he had emulated him.

A man of strong physical nature who swam regularly and kept a boat moored along Cornish shorelines waiting for the perfect wind, Timothy epitomized the spirit of eternal thirst for knowledge. Nothing was to great or too small to interest him. He sought out the curious, the oddity in the human social evolution, and somehow maintained the correct balance for his obsessive nature.

Timothy and Adrian were still deep in a discussion of electromagnetic rotation when the butler's austere frame appeared in the parlor door.

"Your other guests have arrived, Lord Herenton," Jenkins intoned, and Timothy leaped forward immediately.

"Oh, I say! I almost forgot they were coming, Claire, did you?"

"No. I was just relating a little about their background to Lady Anne, Timothy dear. Do see them in, Jenkins," she said to the waiting butler.

Politely curious, Adrian turned to greet these two visitors. Two women stepped into the doorway, both slim and dark, seeming to vibrate with intensity. One appeared to be a generation older, though there remained a sparkle of unextinguishable youth in the shrewd look of her eye. Adrian felt an odd sense of déjà vu and, confused, turned toward her companion. Much younger, the girl was almost a mirror image of the older woman, her face just as dark and sensual, her movements as graceful. His interest must have shown in his face, because the girl smiled at him, gazing into his eyes with such intensity he felt as if she knew his inner thoughts.

"Thomas, Sir Shelley," Timothy was saying, dragging Adrian's attention from the slim girl to his uncle, "permit me to introduce to you Madame du Jessupe and her daughter, Mademoiselle Josette du Jessupe. They are here visiting with us from Martinique."

Adrian could feel Nell move to his side, her slender fingers curling over the taut muscles of his forearm as if claiming him for her own, and more introductions were made. A strange tension seemed to vibrate, an almost tangible uneasiness that affected more than just Adrian. He lifted his eyes, accidentally meeting the deep, dark eyes of Madame du Jessupe, and recoiled slightly. She was gazing at him as if he was an inanimate object to be observed, studied and dissected. He repressed a shiver.

". . . and this is Adrian, my favorite nephew," the irrepressible Timothy was saying, disregarding the possibility of Richard's injured feelings. "Is he not a fine young man?"

Madame du Jessupe smiled, and some of the harshness faded from her gaze as she said in a throaty voice almost as deep as a man's, "I'm so pleased to finally make your acquaintance, *m'sieur.* Your *tante* has told me many good things about you."

"Aunt Claire has always been magnanimous—"

"Not so. She has been truthful." Madame du Jessupe inclined her head toward the slender girl at her side. "My daughter, Josette."

Adrian bowed over her proffered hand, aware that Nell was boring holes in the back of his head with her stare, and murmured, "Bon jour, *mademoiselle.*"

"Bon jour, m'sieur." Her voice was prim and proper, but with a delicate hint of the Americas in her accent. Her gaze lingered on Adrian, as hot and simmering as a steamy cup of thick, dark chocolate before long lashes fluttered down to hide her eyes.

It was unsettling, as the entire afternoon had been, and Adrian wondered wildly if it was the storm or if the entire household had somehow slipped into insanity. Desperate for an innocuous conversational topic, and not quite trusting his uncle not to choose something controversial, Adrian said, "Do you enjoy music, Madame du Jessupe?" He gently released Josette's fingers, sensing Nell's quivering anger as she stood speechless beside him. Appeasement was definitely in order.

"Oui, Monsieur Herenton . . . very much so."

"Bon! Mademoiselle Shelley plays quite beautifully, doesn't she Uncle Timothy?"

"Heh? Oh. Yes. Quite, quite." Timothy's wandering attention strayed from Nell's amply displayed bosom back to the subject at hand. "I wonder, though, if she could transfer her knowledge of the pianoforte to the flute, or the violin, or the tuba. It would be quite convenient if someone were to invent a method of universal transferral from one musical instrument to another, don't you think?" He stared at the crescent of blank faces gazing at him in bewilderment. "What I mean is, if one could play *all* instruments by just learning *one* particular instrument —"

"Timothy," Claire observed, "you are a blockhead. Do play for us, dear," she said to Nell. "We would love to hear you."

Mollified, Nell flashed Adrian a hesitant smile, then moved toward the gleaming pianoforte in the corner. Her silk skirts rustled like crisp autumn leaves as she stepped daintily across the plush rug. Just as she sat down and her cupped hands poised over the ivory keys, a clap of thunder exploded, vibrating throughout the house. Rain rattled against the windowpanes like a fusillade of bullets, and Nell jumped nervously.

The storm was making everyone nervous, but when Adrian turned to soothe Madame du Jessupe, he found her smiling enigmatically at him. It was most disconcerting.

"Madame, are you not frightened of the storm?"

"Non. Quite the opposite. I like a storm." Shadows curled in her black eyes, and she stepped closer, lowering her voice. "On Martinique we have many storms. Some bring much wind and water, and lightning so powerful it sets many trees afire." Her smile deepened. "This storm is special, m'sieur, for it is an omen."

Adrian stared at her, his flesh prickling. It was only a moment—or maybe it was several, he didn't know—before he dragged his eyes from hers to look around him. No one else seemed to be listening. They had all crowded close to the long windows at the opposite end of the parlor and were exclaiming over the fury of the wind and rain.

"Oui," Madame was saying, "I knew this storm would come. Nature often announces the future. . . ."

A sudden desire to laugh bubbled in the back of his throat, and Adrian swallowed hard. The future? This woman had lived too long in the Americas . . .

"Are you saying the storm is for only those of us in this room, madame?"

He forced his twitching lips to a straight line, not quite willing to insult a guest in his home, especially one brought by his Uncle Timothy.

"Nature is for all people, but *oui,* this storm speaks to your house and the people in it."

Adrian couldn't suppress a tight smile. "Ah. I see."

"What do you see?" Timothy asked, joining them and smiling at his nephew and Madame du Jessupe. "Did you see that last flash of lightning? Fearful it was, simply fearful. Now if one could

29

just harness all that power—"

"You never told me you were acquainted with a fortune teller, Uncle Timothy," Adrian interrupted. The slightly cynical smile curled just the corners of his mouth, inviting mockery.

Timothy Herenton did not respond in kind. "Madame du Jessupe is not a simple Gypsy, Adrian. She is an amazingly gifted woman, and possessed of a great deal of knowledge. You could learn a lot from her." The quiet rebuke snared Adrian's attention, wiping the amusement from his face.

"I beg your pardon, Uncle," he said quietly. "And yours too, madame. I meant no offense. I simply find it difficult to accept the idea that one can read messages in the wind and rain."

"Oh? Have you never anticipated a storm in the scent of the wind? Or known from the chill of rain that it would soon change to snow?" Madame du Jessupe shrugged. "I simply read more than most. . . ."

While Adrian fumbled for a reply, sensing his uncle's disapproving gaze resting on him, dinner was announced. A feeling of relief flooded him, and as he turned to escort Nell into the dining room, he caught the knowing glance between Madame du Jessupe and her daughter.

Two by two they walked into the dining room: Nell and Adrian, Uncle Timothy and Aunt Claire, Nell's brother John accompanying Josette, Lord Herenton and Madame du Jessupe, Sir Shelley and Lady Anne, and trailing slightly behind, Richard and Elizabeth. Candles flickered, and outside the wind roared like a caged lion.

For Adrian, dinner was strained and uncomfortable. There were nuances he didn't understand and didn't like, hovering above the long, linen-clad table like an ominous black cloud. China gleamed and silver glistened, and huge candelabra shimmered brightly at each end of the table, softly illuminating the dozens of dishes. Obsequious servants anticipated each guest's desire, replacing cutlery or emptied dishes, refilling drained wine glasses or furnishing clean linen. The flow of conversation hummed around Adrian's ears like the buzzing of summer bees, droning on and on, with only occasional phrases leaping out at him.

". . . these stewed eels are delicious . . ."

". . . but the Reform Bill of thirty-two gave increased parliamentary representation to the cities . . ."

"I say, those new steamships will be crossing the ocean soon, you mark my word . . ."

"You're so fashionably pale, Elizabeth. Do you use Venetian talc?"

Adrian's attention focused on Richard's intended, eyes narrowing as he noted once again that her complexion appeared even paler than usual. Her fingertips fluttered upward, and she smiled prettily.

"Oh, no, Lady Claire. I don't use much paint or powder. Just a little lampblack around the eyes."

"Good thing," Lady Claire observed. "I once used Balm of Mecca. Highly popular in twenty-two, you understand, but frightfully expensive. Four guineas an ounce, if you will believe that, but an imitation could be had for twenty-fives to thirty-fives. Hmmph. Timothy dissected it for me—"

"Distilled," Timothy corrected.

"Very well. Distilled. And he found that it contained various resins, turpentines and aromatic oils, along with a vast assortment of other horrors," Lady Claire finished. "I stopped using it at once."

"You stopped using it because your face swelled and your skin turned red," Timothy pointed out, "not because of any moral aversion to the ingredients."

"Be that as it may," Lady Claire continued doggedly, "I am pleased to see a young lady who needs no artificial devices to keep her skin fashionably pale."

Adrian gazed thoughtfully at Elizabeth. Fashionably pale? Her complexion suddenly reminded him of a death mask, with no color, and her cheeks were so hollow as to be almost sunk in. Was he being overly critical? Did no one else see what he did?

Madame du Jessupe, seated directly across from him with Elizabeth on her left, caught his eye. She gazed at Adrian steadily, fathomless shadows in her black eyes, and it was as if she had spoken to him aloud. He shifted uneasily in his chair, fingers tightening on the stem of his crystal wineglass, and sought relief in the comforting vision of Nell's quietly averted profile.

Eleanor Shelley would soon be Eleanor Herenton; her blond beauty would grace his home. Already he could visualize her dainty feet trodding the wide, curving staircase, the familiar rustle of her silk skirts trailing an enchanting invitation to follow. Adrian's imagination took a broader leap, going beyond the bedroom door into the honeymoon bower. Nell had let him touch her once, had let him bury his face in the lush curves that were even now peeping above the low décolletage of her gown. All his boyhood fantasies had swayed in an agony of suspension, his dreams of one day holding Nell in his arms finally realized, yet he had been unable then to do more than touch her reverently. At first embarrassed, then confused, Adrian had finally realized that his inability was caused by his great respect for Nell.

There had been many women in his life, casual women who meant no more than a night or two's dalliance, because he had always loved Nell. Once she was truly his, he would hold her as a man holds a woman. Until then, he could only chafe and yearn for the future to move on swifter wings.

Adrian's intensity must have reached out to Nell, for she looked up from her plate, glowing green eyes caressing his face, a smile curving the tempting fullness of her mouth. Soon, he promised her silently, soon. . . .

After-dinner chit-chat was anything but stimulating. Lord Herenton, Sir Shelley, his son John and Richard managed to corner Timothy and begin a detailed discussion of parliamentary events — which bored Adrian to the point of yawning — and the ladies retired to the parlor, a warm fire and small tumbrils of sherry. Rain beat insistently at the long windows, and a howling wind demanded entrance through the tiniest cracks, fluttering even the heavy velvet drapes.

Adrian, staring pensively into the flames of the library fire and cradling a large snifter of brandy, was pulled from his contemplation of the brass fire dogs by Jenkins' somber tones in the doorway.

"My lord," he said, addressing Richard, "Lady

33

Elizabeth wishes me to inform you that she is feeling rather ill and has retired early."

Richard's broad face creased into a worried frown. "I say, what a beastly disappointment. Thank you, Jenkins." As the butler nodded and backed out the door, Richard, taller than his father but not quite as tall as his younger brother, turned anxious eyes on Sir Shelley. "Do you suppose we should send for a physician?"

"A physician? Nonsense," Sir Shelley blustered, fearing his daughter's physical frailty might somehow hinder a marriage between the Shelleys and the Herentons. Such an alliance was particularly needed at this critical stage in his fortunes, and there was always the disturbing chance that Richard would develop a quirk that would defy family custom. Modern young people did such things nowadays, and he—but no. Richard Herenton would not flaunt family custom. Adrian, perhaps, but not Richard. Adrian was the adventurous one, the risk-taker, while Richard was good and stolid and always did what was expected. Sir Shelley relaxed slightly.

"It's the weather," he explained. "Storms frighten high-strung gals like Elizabeth."

Seeing an opportunity to escape the heavy political discussion in the library, Adrian said, "Quite right, Sir Shelley. I think I shall soothe any strained nerves that may be in the parlor. If you gentlemen will excuse me? Father, Uncle Timothy, Richard, John . . ."

Adrian backed out of the library in much the same manner as Jenkins had done, swiftly and gratefully. What a deadly dull bunch they could be, droning on and on about Whigs and Tories. Even Uncle Timothy, usually much more stimulating, had been engrossed. How ridiculous a custom, this separation of the sexes after a meal, men one way and women another; feminine companionship was much more pleasing to the eye, if not always the ear.

Madame du Jessupe and Lady Claire were deep into a discussion about the Americas when Adrian entered the parlor, a topic that he found especially fascinating.

"But have you ever been there?" Lady Claire was asking the French woman. "Have you seen the natives?"

Madame du Jessupe smiled. *"Oui,* and I found them most interesting. My cousin, Pierre Duvalle, still lives out there in the wilderness, lost in some remote mountain range where none can find him. He even married a Shoshoni girl, half-breed daughter of an Indian chief."

"He married an Indian?" Lady Claire's brows lifted, and even Lady Anne leaned forward with her mouth forming a round little O of horrified interest. "Is it true they wear no garments, only feathers and beads, madame?"

"Non, non, they are very modest most of the time. It is only certain—how do you say—tribes, who appear half-clothed. The feathers and beads are ornamental, and some of the women are very lovely."

"You are talking about America?" Adrian interrupted, moving nearer the small couch seating Lady Claire and Madame du Jessupe. "I understand there are marvelous wonders in that great land. Huge, shaggy beasts like wild cows, ranging so thick one can walk across broad meadows on their backs and never touch the ground, and trees—trees so tall they rise higher than the spires of Winchester Cathedral!"

"Oui," Josette said, rising from the little stool by the hearth, "there is all that and more, *m'sieur.* It is a land free from soot and crowds, free from religious and political persecution—"

"Not entirely," Madame du Jessupe corrected with a wry smile. "There are always those who will try to impose their will and beliefs upon others. But in the West there is country where you can travel for days—weeks—and never see another living soul. Only the mountains, trees and animals will hear your cry if you are lost. . . ." She leaned forward, staring intently at Adrian, and for the first time he did not look away. Somehow, meeting her gaze, he could see the things she had seen, could smell the fresh white gush of wind from snow-capped mountain ranges, could hear the piercing cry of an eagle floating amidst wisps of cloud, and he was lost in the rapture of discovery, lost in that unknown world across the Atlantic.

The present was brought back with a jolt when Nell said petulantly, "Well, *I* think it sounds horrible! All that empty space and those ravening beasts. . . ."

For the first time that he could ever remember in all the time he'd known and worshipped Eleanor Shelley, Adrian felt a trace of anger at her limited vision.

"Empty space? Ravening beasts? Don't you see the opportunities, Nell? The . . ." He paused, recognizing in her blank gaze that she did not see.

Madame du Jessupe observed softly, "The storm rests," and Adrian's fumbling attention grasped the conversational straw she offered.

"Yes, finally. You were saying earlier that the storm is an omen, madame. Could you explain

36

what you meant?"

"*Certainement*. Josette—bring me the cards."

"Cards? I can have a servant bring them," Lady Claire began; but Josette was already out of the parlor, and Madame du Jessupe waved away the suggestion.

"*Non*. It is not necessary. No one but Josette or myself touch the cards. Unless, of course, I am doing a reading."

"A reading?" Lady Anne and Nell echoed in unison, then Nell laughed.

"Do you mean you're a fortune teller, madame?" She rustled closer, curving a possessive hand over Adrian's forearm. "I can already tell you my future, and I don't need a pack of cards as props."

Madame du Jessupe did not return Nell's challenging smile, but turned to face Adrian, her serious gaze resting upon his clean-cut features for several moments.

"It is *your* future, m'sieur, which interests me the most. In a way, you are what brought me these many miles; you are the key to the mystery and the answer to unanswered questions. Already I know much since meeting you. After tonight—I shall know all."

Adrian shifted uneasily and disentangled himself from Nell's clutching fingers. He smoothed the wrinkles from his coat sleeve, gazing at Madame du Jessupe and further infuriating Nell.

"Well, really!" she snapped. "I think this is all very theatrical, and very silly! If I wished to see a play, I would travel to London, Madame du Jessupe."

The Frenchwoman ignored Nell, and the others exchanged uneasy glances. A small table was brought in and set up near the fire, and two

37

chairs were placed on opposite sides. Madame du Jessupe motioned for Adrian to occupy the chair opposite hers.

"Adrian," Nell objected, "don't do it. I . . . I would like for you to show me the new conservatory—"

"Oh, bother!" Lady Claire's silk fan closed with an irritated snap. "Leave him alone, child. I want to hear what Madame has to say, and I believe your mother does, too."

"Yes," Lady Anne agreed, "I do, but Adrian should make the final decision. It's his future. . . ."

Adrian smiled, recalling an incident with Gypsies in Italy the year before. He'd never had his fortune told, but had been singled out for special attention by a ragged crone. The old woman had hobbled close, then thrown a shower of what appeared to be dried leaves on him. Startled, Adrian had retreated, half-laughing, brushing the herbs from his pale hair.

"Cima di ruta," the Gypsy had muttered, *"cima di ruta . . . la notte sa star buona da per se."*

"What did she say?" he'd asked a companion, and it was translated to mean, "Wear the herb of grace, then it will be a good night."

He'd thought it was odd at the time, and odder still when a silver amulet filled with the same herb, rue, was mysteriously left draped over his bed. And now, once more, he had been singled out by a Gypsy for attention. Adrian shrugged, pulled out the chair opposite Madame du Jessupe and sat down.

Chapter 2
The Spread

"How unusual. What kind of cards are these, madame?" Adrian studied the patterns on the backs of the painted pasteboard cards as they were being shuffled, thinking the design resembled a nine-headed Chinese dragon.

"Tarot."

"Oh? I seem to recall more cards in the deck."

"You have seen tarot, m'sieur?"

"Once, years ago. A friend of mine, Sir Skeffington, had a collection of them. One of the decks was supposed to be the cards which Napoleon used to confirm his war strategies. I was always convinced Skeffie had been duped into buying them. Anyway, there seemed to be a lot more cards in his decks—almost eighty, I think."

"Seventy-eight to be exact, m'sieur." Madame smiled serenely, placed the cards on the table in a neatly aligned pile and closed her eyes.

Adrian's eyes narrowed as she placed her right hand upon the deck, fingertips resting in a light caress on the top card for a moment, then pressed firmly. The parlor was quiet, with only the sounds of the crackling fire, the steady ticking of the ornate French clock on the mantle and Lady Anne's slightly nasal wheeze.

Madame du Jessupe bowed her dark head as if she was praying, and Adrian felt an odd stir of excitement.

When she lifted her head and opened her eyes, her fine-boned hand spreading the cards into a row from left to right, he slowly exhaled and was surprised to discover that he'd been holding his breath. Adrian looked down. Twenty-two cards lay on the table, backsides up.

"Take my hands, m'sieur." Madame held out both her hands and he took them, noting her warm palms and cold fingers. He could feel her long smooth nails lightly scratching his palms, back and forth in a rhythmic motion that was oddly soothing yet exciting at the same time; it was not a sensual excitement, but a more abstract feeling that conjured up visual images. Adrian was almost disappointed when she dropped his hands and instructed him to pick up the cards in any order. "And give them to me one at a time, *'sil vous plait*."

As Adrian reached out for the first card he was struck with a sense of the ridiculous. A witch hunt! This was absurd, and he was letting himself be drawn into the spirit of the reading as if he were the credulous lackwit his father had always named him.

"Ah," he said, lifting the card, "here it is! What shall it mean? Death? Fortune? A woman?" Here he leered toward Nell, who giggled delightedly. "Tell me the meaning, madame!"

Madame du Jessupe did not smile. She stared down at the card Adrian had turned, her voice a husky timbre as she said, "The omen. It is tomorrow. It is the day after the storm. When the sun rises in tomorrow's sky, this card shall take literal meaning—for you have sought to ask so specifically." One hand quickly flipped the top card over and placed it in the left-hand corner.

Josette's in-drawn breath hissed, *"La mort. . . ."*

Adrian frowned. He recognized that single card if he didn't know any other—the skeleton, red scythe, blood . . .

"Death," Madame explained unnecessarily, and Lady Claire blanched.

"No . . ."

"But, madame," Lady Anne cried, "surely you don't mean. . . !"

Nell's voice drowned out her mother's. "I can't believe you would claim someone in this house is going to die tomorrow! That's a bit too much, isn't it?"

Unperturbed by the varied reactions, Madame du Jessupe said, "Sometimes the card means rebirth, change; but not here. Because he asked, I answered. Death it will be." Now her dark eyes met Adrian's. "Do not ask more of me now."

Shrugging, Adrian replied carelessly, "Certainly. Go on to the rest, madame." He slid an indulgent smile toward his aunt and Lady Anne, gray eyes crinkling at the corners with amusement. They were scared to death! Even Nell seemed shaken, and he bit back a grin. But when his gaze drifted to Josette, some of his humor faded. The dark-haired, dark-eyed girl sat stiffly, her eyes wide and fixed upon the card, staring at it with undisguised fear.

The clock ticked on the mantle, sounding loud in the silence, marking the passage of time. Madame du Jessupe pulled out the next three cards. The Empress, Temperance, and La Maison Dieu, only vaguely familiar to Adrian. There was a whisk as the last card was turned face up: the Tower of Destruction, the House of God struck by lightning. Adrian could not still his sudden shiver.

No one spoke, and the clock ticked on as Madame

du Jessupe turned over each card, studying them intently. Several cards were upside down, facing Madame instead of Adrian, and he asked, "What do these mean?"

"You've asked one specific question. It brought the death card. Ask no more. . . ."

Rebuffed, Adrian leaned back in his chair, forcing himself to relax. They were only cards, and cards did not decide one's destiny. Man decided his own destiny, was ruler of his own fate.

Long, lean legs stretched out under the table as Adrian let his gaze drift from face to face and the variety of feminine expressions: horror, scorn, interest and concentration. Gray eyes lingered on Josette, appreciating her slender, dark beauty. She was different from Nell, with a *café au lait* complexion and ebony curls that made such a striking contrast to the pale English beauty, but it was more than that. Josette was as mysterious as night shadows, and seemed to vibrate with an intensity that Nell had never possessed. A slight smile curled his mouth as he looked from the cards to Josette, then to her mother. They ignored him, looking at each other in that way people do when they share a secret knowledge, and he felt suddenly uneasy.

"Tell me what you see," he demanded. "What do the cards say about my destiny?"

Madame's eyes glittered, black lights conveying guarded excitement, closed in behind pursed lips. Just when the silence grew too heavy, too lengthy, she said in an even deeper tone than usual, "The first row is fulfillment of the omen. It is tomorrow and the next three weeks until the new moon. The second and third cards on that row could name the person who is to die. Do you wish the name?"

Startled by the question, and the calm assumption

42

that it was unavoidable, Adrian glanced to his aunt as if for guidance. She sat still and quiet, her face unusually grave, her fine eyes troubled. Adrian met Madame's watchful gaze.

"No."

"You are wise, m'sieur." Her dark head inclined slightly in his direction, the hint of a smile hovering upon her lips.

"Proceed, madame."

"La Maison Dieu. The lightning has come and the House of God is struck down. One man falls. Another lies upon the hard ground, streaked with blood. I see ruin and misery." Dark eyes moved from the pasteboard cards to Adrian. "I see a house divided— old trust destroyed."

Gray eyes gazed back unflinchingly, masking the quiver of laughter welling in his throat. Melodramatic pap, he told himself, wondering why he wasn't as convinced as he should be, melodramatic pap.

"The last card, m'sieur, is the Chariot. It is placed upside down. When the new moon arrives, you will be overwhelmed, and reality will be very difficult for you to face." A lengthy sigh curled into the heated space between them. "Then, m'sieur, there is a fool to be dealt with. All men are fools at one time in their lives—here destiny warns you." She leaned close, closing the gap between them, her intense face only inches from his, and whispered, "The cards can change."

Adrian swallowed hard, forcing a normal tone free from amusement or mockery. "Are you saying that I can change my destiny, madame?"

"Oui. Every man has the freedom of choice in his life. Yet, the fool is weak. Beauty tempts him. He yearns for something deep within himself, yet places that responsibility on something or someone else. In

43

your life, I see deep emotions placed in the arms of ignorance. You are deceived by others and yourself, but it is your own shallowness and conceit that brings you into temptation. You will abuse your power, and because of that, lose faith. For this, I am truly sorry. A man must have faith. Unless the cards change, you will lose your faith, and the Hanged Man you will be for a long time to come."

"Hanged Man?" Nell blurted, fascinated in spite of her earlier ridicule. "What do you mean?"

"The Hanged Man is suspended from a wooden beam between two living trees. His right foot is tied, bound with heavy cord as are his hands behind his back. He is suspended between two destinies, and on his forehead is the mark of repentance. Sacrifice and rebirth are necessary in order to reach redemption." Madame's somber tone was punctuated with the tap of a long fingernail upon the cards, accenting each word as though every syllable brought her genuine sorrow. Another sigh coiled into the air, and she closed her eyes as if suddenly weary, leaning back in her chair. Then she snapped forward as if jerked with a string, stared at the second half of the cards and smiled.

Madame's smile eased the tension that had become almost unbearable, and Nell heaved a great sigh of relief and giggled. The tempest outside the house had passed as well, and Adrian's tensed shoulders relaxed.

"Tell me, madame, do I detect optimism in your smile? Could it be that my destiny is not so grim? Perhaps the Hanged Man shall find some peace. . . ."

"You mock me, m'sieur, but I do not mind. It was you who chose the cards, not I. There will come a time when you will not scoff, when you will find yourself reflecting upon every word uttered this stormy night, scratching your brain for some hint, some flicker of an eye or toss of a hand—"

"No, no, madame. It was your smile. I do not mock you. I only think it wise to laugh at sorrow, for what else can we do? 'When sorrows come, they come not single spies, but in battalions,'" he quoted. "Shakespeare's *Hamlet*." Adrian leaned forward. "Tomorrow, if the cards are true, there will be time enough to cry. You yourself have said that someone in this house shall die. I do not—cannot—let myself take you seriously. If so, I would demand the victim's name in order to see his destiny changed. Humor us a little, madame. Pity us if you feel the cards are true, and show mercy. We," he said, his arms moving to include his aunt and the others, "are not accustomed to such visions. But you . . . you and your cards seem to be indivisible."

Madame's stiff features gentled as she reached out to lightly touch Adrian's hand. "Mercy you have requested, mercy you shall receive. The next card chosen is that of *Le Pape*."

"The Pope?"

"*Oui.* Forgiveness. The sacred eagle . . ." Her eyes closed tightly as she whispered, "*Oui . . .* I see an eagle soaring high over the mountains. There is snow. Peace." Her eyes opened, shiny mirrors reflecting her soul. "It is a long journey, m'sieur."

"But with forgiveness at the end? Forgiveness for what?"

"The next card is *Le Soleil*. It is turned. The sun shines in another direction. Clouded . . . the road to peace, or forgiveness of one's self, is clouded. Skies are gray, and the heart is lonely. Do not fear. The strength of the Pope is great, and next lies *La Roue de Fortune*. Near the Wheel of Fortune grows a bed of beautiful roses—progress, m'sieur. Through the dark

45

clouds you shall see hope, for in spite of your petty weaknesses you are delivered. *La Bateleuer* will save you—as it has always done."

"La Bateleuer?" Lady Claire echoed. "A magician?"

"Oui. Your nephew, Lady Claire, is the magician. He is clever, and with his hands he can rearrange many things. Like the magician, he is magic. He can make things disappear. Behind his smile is great knowledge and inner strength. It will give him great power. Does his past—his boyhood schemes and projects—not reflect this? I see in him a great ability to choose and make the right decisions . . . oui . . . to see events through to the finish. Your nephew is the magician, and will alter his own destiny."

"See," Nell pointed out with a laugh, "Adrian will be happy in spite of all the gloomy prophecies. Why didn't you just get to the point at once, madame, instead of trying to frighten us all to death?" She leaned against Adrian's shoulder, a possessive hand lightly caressing the collar of his gray coat, fingertips tickling the pale hair lying neatly over his ear.

Adrian's hand reached up to cover Nell's and he wondered if the cards meant he was to be happy with her. It had been so much on his mind lately, this longing for Nell, that he was beginning to wonder if he was obsessed.

He started to rise, murmuring his thanks for Madame's time, when she said, "It is not over, m'sieur. Your journey to destiny has just begun."

"But I thought all journeys ended when one found happiness." A dark brow rose mockingly. "Don't most fortunes end at that point?"

"Some. But not yours. Not yet."

"Oh?"

"Oui. There is the moon—*La Lune.* Your magic

46

will drive you to the goddess of the night. She is full of anxiety, wild obsessions. She will clutch you to her breast and pull you into the dark as she climbs into the night sky—"

"Really!" Nell cut in sharply. "Isn't this a bit much? A goddess, moonlight—when will this interminable reading end?"

Ignoring her, Madame continued, "This will be a troubled time for you, m'sieur, but fear not. It will be a time for growth. *L'Hermite* stands beside you. He will hold straight your magic, and you will learn the most. Self-denial will teach you wisdom and tolerance. Judgement will lead to rebirth, a new life. I see clouds of the gods, a new house in a new land, and a powerful white wind. . . ." Madame du Jessupe leaned close again, her face wreathed with a smile of pleasure. *"L'Estoille."*

"The Star?"

"Hope, m'sieur. I see a great land . . . the Star . . . a young girl pouring the waters of life. Here you will find true love. It is a good omen. But beware, m'sieur, of the Devil—*Le Diable* awaits your lady of the lake. With the Star you will regain your faith in the human race and with yourself, but the Devil is nearby. He is evil, truly evil. I see black magic. Death, disaster and misery follows him wherever he goes."

"Wonderful," Adrian responded rather testily. "I begin with death and end with death. Is this supposed to be a good life?"

"Oui. Do not despair. There are two cards left— one is *La Justice,* the other *Le Monde.* It is the final goal unto which all other cards have led you. You are truly a magician, Monsieur Herenton, for justice and success are your attainment."

Madame du Jessupe smiled, deftly sliding each row of cards into a neat pile and drawing them into her

47

lap. They were quickly deposited in a velvet bag embroidered with odd symbols, and the reading was over. Adrian felt a curious relief, as if he had been battling a storm and had escaped unscathed.

He stood as the Frenchwoman rose to her feet, and she reached out to touch him lightly on the chest.

"Take heart, m'sieur. Life is full of pain, sorrows. No one lives who is not touched by one of these, but the good things, m'sieur—the good things come only to a few. You will know great happiness under the moon with the stars . . . one very bright star." She paused, her body sagging wearily, and murmured to Josette, "Come, my daughter. It will be a long day tomorrow and we must rest. Excuse us, *'sil vous plait*."

"Of course," Lady Claire responded immediately. "This has been a most fascinating evening, madame, and we all thank you for your . . . informative . . . entertainment. Shall I send a maid to you?"

"Non. Josette will help me as usual. And it was not so much entertainment, Lady Claire, as it was a warning. *Bon nuit*."

Silence settled in an insidiously disturbing fog as Madame du Jessupe and her daughter left the parlor, and those remaining gazed at each other uneasily.

"How . . . unusual," Lady Anne finally observed, "and how frightening. . . ."

The clock on Adrian's fireplace mantle struck two, echoing through the night shadows of his bedchamber. Hazy images danced in his head as he tossed and turned in fitful slumber. Pasteboard cards had come alive, weaving through his dream in the form of a naked devil with wild, crimson eyes and a hooked nose, horned ears and clawlike hands with long tal-

48

ons. The beast held a two-pronged pitchfork in his left hand, and he was laughing, his blazing eyes filled with mockery. Adrian turned, kicking off his satin coverlet as he wrestled with his nightmare.

Then it altered subtly, a great, dark wind blowing up a cloud of dust to hide the grinning devil. In its midst was a young, exotic woman with long dark hair, but as she stepped forward, the devil reappeared. He motioned to her, beckoning with his long talons for her to come forward, but she fell at his cloven feet. Pressing her hands to her face to hide her features, she wept loudly. Again the wind blew, sweeping before it a horde of half-naked, painted men that descended upon the weeping girl. They were howling, and the girl cried out in fear as they carried her up and bore her away on the wind.

Jerking awake, Adrian sat up in a sweat. It was quiet now. The wind had stopped, and there was only the gentle dripping of the rain from the eaves of the house. He was breathing harshly; his heart pounding, and as he realized that he was in bed and it had only been a nightmare, he relaxed. The chaos of the outer and inner world gradually faded away.

Chapter 3
Death

No hint of yesterday's storm remained the following morning. Bright, bright blue skies stretched, cloudless, over emerald fields dotted with buttercups, foxglove and heather. Gray stone fences quilted the land all the way to the edge of majestic slate cliffs, framing a perfect spring day.

The day after the storm, Adrian thought, gazing out his windows. In just a quarter hour he would be meeting Nell at their rendevous spot in the south garden gazebo. Stone pathways meandered through the grounds to the shaded nook where the gazebo would afford them some privacy. Nell would be there at ten o'clock, and Adrian was already anticipating the sweetness of her luscious kisses.

"Will this cravat meet your approval, my lord?"

His manservant's correctly modulated tone dragged Adrian's thoughts from Nell to the business at hand.

"Yes, Harry, I think it will. Did you starch it yourself?"

"Of course." Harry's brow rose. "One cannot trust those incompetent ninnies who claim to be laundresses to understand the intricacies of a gentleman's cravat. Now stand still, my lord, and I will arrange the folds for you."

A wry smile tugged at Adrian's lips, but he meekly obeyed Harry's command. Harry had been his man-servant for too long, and was entirely too familiar and cheeky in Lord Herenton's opinion, but Adrian could not imagine life without him. Harry was more than valet. He was a friend.

"There. You are impeccably attired for a tryst in the bushes with your lady-love," Harry observed, patting the last fold into place.

Adrian sighed. "You don't care for Nell, do you, Harry?"

"It's not my place to care or not care, my lord. You may do with the little lady what you please. I am more concerned with the shocking state of your ward-robe. Your trousers and coats—"

"Harry. It's no good. I can tell what you're thinking."

"Can you? My, my. You're so clever, my lord." The older man's serene expression never altered, and he continued brushing imaginary lint from Adrian's coat with the utmost concentration.

"You pompous old goat," Adrian said affection-ately, and Harry inclined his head as if accepting a compliment. He was of medium height, with a bald-ing pate and wise old eyes that noticed every little detail, and his uneven, almost aristocratic features were creased with lines of character. Harry. Often a teacher, sometimes a confidante, always a friend.

Turning, Adrian inspected his image in the oval cheval mirror and nodded with satisfaction at the in-tricate folds of his neckcloth. "I'll be back shortly, Harry."

"I'll see that the church bells are run in wild cele-bration" was the reply, and Adrian chuckled.

Nell was waiting, posed prettily with the early sun-shine streaming through latticed walls checkering her

51

silky hair and skirts with gold. Birds quarrelled noisily in the eaves, chirping displeasure at the intrusion into their world as Adrian skipped lightly up the steps.

"Nell . . ." He grasped her hungrily, pulling her into his arms, trapping her hands in the warm space between their bodies. Nell's lips opened without hesitation, soft and yielding, her tongue flicking at the corners of his mouth in swift, erotic pulsebeats that sent Adrian's blood flowing through his veins like molten lava. He groaned, pressing even closer as if he would merge their bodies, his breathing rough and ragged.

"Ummm," Nell murmured when his lips left hers for a moment, "did you miss me, Adrian?"

"You know I did. . . ."

"No, I don't. I thought perhaps you had already met your mysterious moon goddess." She nipped playfully at his lower lip, sharp little teeth nibbling like a terrier, and Adrian pulled away, smiling.

"Minx," he said fondly, gazing into emerald orbs as he studied her lovely face. Blond ringlets lay carefully on a high forehead that had needed no plucking to be fashionable, and small dimples bracketed her sensuous mouth. Nell had that famous English complexion so much admired by the rest of the world, and her feminine attributes were lush enough to arouse any man's attention. Nell's beauty was considerable, yet it had been her spirit that had kept his interest. She was a lady, demure but fiery, bold enough to admit to desire and passionate enough to give herself completely if he would take her.

Adrian struggled to keep a tight rein on his self-control. Nell was to be his wife, and he respected her. He must try not to shame her before marriage even though she would allow it, and he loved her even more for her sweet yielding.

"I love you," he said into the fragrant tendrils of silky hair spilling down the nape of her neck.

"And I love you," Nell responded immediately, her arms rising to wind around his neck, pulling him closer, closer, until he felt the imprint of her curves burning into his lean frame like a fiery brand. Adrian muffled a groan in the satiny texture of her skin, feeling the shallow pulse in the hollow of her throat flutter wildly, like a trapped butterfly. Time slowed, shuddered and wheeled to a halt as Adrian jerked her to him so tightly she could feel the press of passion against her belly. "Adrian . . . Adrian . . . do not stop now," she murmured softly, and he didn't. His lips scorched a trail from her smooth wing of cheekbone to her mouth, lingering, then moving lower. Lace tickled his jaw as he kissed the soft mounds thrusting up out of her bodice, and Nell's rhythmic breath escalated wildly.

Adrian's control slipped as she moaned and arched closer, filling his cupped palms with that rounded sweetness that lured him to free them from confinement. The dress slid down, and twin mounds begged for his attention, the peaks hardening to beckoning rosebuds of flesh. Tasting, teasing, he explored the valley between until Nell was gasping with frustration.

Slender hands reached out, explored and found him, fumbling with the waistband of his trousers.

Common sense attempted to intrude, and Adrian muttered thickly, "We shouldn't . . . not here . . . someone is certain to find us. . . ."

"It would be worth it! Don't stop now or I shall die," Nell moaned, finally succeeding in releasing him from his trousers. "I love you, Adrian," she said, slim fingers circling him.

All restraint fled then, and Adrian swept her up and carried her to the long benches lining the gazebo walls, gently lowering her to the surface and burying his face into lavender-scented flesh. The cushions shifted slightly beneath them as he lay beside her, tugging at the hem of her skirts until they were bunched waist-high. One hand skimmed up the heated flesh of her thigh, and he realized she wasn't wearing stockings. For a brief moment he was shocked; then coherent thought fled as Nell's searching hands found him again, instinctively knowing the right rhythm, and he surrendered to sensuality.

She was ready, warm and wet and wanting him, her creamy thighs parting to accept him, but still Adrian held back, wanting her first time to be special. He kissed her again, exploring her mouth with his tongue, fencing lightly, letting his body nudge as close as possible without consummating. The danger of being discovered heightened the excitement, until Adrian could finally hold back no longer. He tossed Nell's skirts higher, poised over her, then cursed as he heard Harry calling him.

"My lord?" Harry called. "His Grace desires your presence in the drawing room immediately."

Nell's muffled comment was lost in the folds of silk and lace over her face, and Adrian struggled for control of his breathing.

"My lord?"

"Yes, dammit, Harry, I hear you!" Adrian's tight voice betrayed anger and frustration, but he didn't care. It would do no good to try to hide from Harry's shrewd eyes anyway, for he was certain to have already guessed at the activities behind the lattice walls.

"Don't let that wretched man come in here," Nell snapped. "He already despises me, and I've no desire to be ogled."

54

Rolling from atop his intended bride, Adrian replied, "I hardly think Harry is given to ogling, sweet. And he is an intelligent man and not unaware of our . . . uh . . . fondness for one another."

"How did he know where to find you?" Nell demanded, sitting up and swinging her bare legs over the bench to tug irritably at her mussed hair. "Did you tell him?"

"Yes, of course."

"Well, that will have to stop. I refuse to have the man follow us about like schoolchildren."

"My lord," Harry intoned from outside the gazebo, "I believe it is a matter of utmost urgency, requiring your hasty attendance—"

"I'm coming, Harry!" Adrian tucked his shirttail into his trousers and buttoned them, slanted a frowning glance at Nell's unpleasant expression, and pressed a quick kiss upon her forehead. "Don't be angry. We should wait until we are wed anyway, sweeting. It's not that far off now that Richard's and Elizabeth's marriage has been announced."

She flashed him a sullen, defiant glare. "Oh, don't be such a stuffed shirt, Adrian!"

"What—"

"My lord," Harry prompted from the lawn, "I was instructed to bring Lady Eleanor also, if you will so inform her."

"Damnation," Nell muttered in a most unladylike fashion, and Adrian's brows lowered.

"Hurry up, then, Nell, and make yourself presentable," he said stiffly. "Let us go and see what all the fuss is about."

"Father?" Adrian advanced into the drawing room, one hand cupping Nell's elbow. "What has happened?"

Richard, sandy hair ruffled and standing almost on end, answered for the duke, blurting, "It's Elizabeth!" His eyes were wild, red-rimmed and swollen, and Adrian felt the first faint, stirrings of alarm.

"Elizabeth?"

Nell shook loose Adrian's protective grasp and stepped forward. "What about my sister?"

"She's ill. . . ."

"Oh, pooh! She's always ill," Nell scoffed. "Give her some hartshorn and she'll be around within minutes. I think she only does it for attention."

"You don't understand!" Richard cried, and Adrian moved to stand beside his brother. "She's . . . she's . . . dying. . . ."

"No, Richard," Adrian denied. "Father, have you sent for her physician?"

"Of course, do you take me for an idiot?" His Grace shouted, quite overcome with impotent rage.

"I don't believe it," Nell said flatly. "She's only had one of her spells again. Where is my mother?"

"With . . . with Elizabeth," Richard managed to whisper.

Adrian's heart went out to his older brother, seeing Richard's forlorn expression, the misery in his eyes, and he put a comforting arm around his shoulders. They'd never gotten along really, but it still pained him to see his brother suffer.

"Take heart, Richard. Perhaps her physician will agree with Nell."

"I'm going to see for myself," Nell was saying coolly, her skirts lifted in one hand to keep from tripping over the long hem. As she turned to leave, Lord Herenton's gaze fell upon her bare ankles and the small brown leaf still trapped in her blond hair, and his eyes narrowed suspiciously.

56

"Yes, Eleanor, you go up to be with your mother," the duke agreed. "Richard will join you shortly." He escorted Nell to the door, opened and held it for her, then shut it quietly.

Rounding on his sons, Lord Thomas Herenton, fourth Duke of Hertfield, surveyed them with a wrathful glare. "You," he began, pointing a quivering finger at his youngest, "are a disgrace to the family!"

"I beg your pardon?" Adrian said. What bee did his father have in his bonnet now? His lips twisted wryly. "Have I displeased you once again, Father?"

"You young puppy! Have you no shame? Do you intend to treat a lady of quality as if she were a strumpet? I've no doubt you are more accustomed to the seedier side of—"

"Father," Adrian cut in quietly, and something in the steely tone of his voice made the duke pause. "I will not remain here and listen to one of your tiresome harangues, when upstairs lies a young lady who might be dying. There is a time and place for everything, and this is neither. I will be at your disposal when Lady Elizabeth has recovered. Now, I am going to escort Richard upstairs, for he does not look as if he could manage the stairs by himself. Good day."

Lord Herenton watched silently as Adrian propelled his brother to the door, opened it and angled him through, then listened to the sound of fading footsteps on marble floors with a half-smile slanting his mouth and a gleam of respect in his eyes.

"How did it happen?" Adrian asked Richard. They waited outside Elizabeth's chamber for her mother to open the door.

"She was feeling a bit tired, so I decided to send for Nell to come and read to her while I joined Father and the others for a ride. Elizabeth was . . . was sitting on the little stool in the parlor—do you know the one?—when she just clutched at her chest and screamed as if in terrible pain! I . . . I didn't know what to do, Adrian! Then she fainted, fell right at my feet, and nothing would bring her 'round. We've tried smelling salts, hartshorn. . . ." His voice trailed into miserable silence.

"Be heartened, Richard. I think I hear the physician's carriage arriving."

By the time Dr. Fenworthy arrived, Richard and Adrian were standing at Elizabeth's bedside. She lay, still and cold as death, her eyes closed and face as pale as milk, Adrian thought. Dr. Fenworthy stepped up and, with professional efficiency, ordered Richard and Adrian to the back of the room to stand with Nell and John.

"I daresay she's suffocating from all the attention," he said tersely. "Give the lass some air!"

"I say, a bit brusque isn't he?" Richard complained, but meekly moved to the back of the room, leaving only Lady Anne to stand beside her daughter.

They stood, Richard, Adrian, Nell and John, an anxious half-circle waiting for the doctor's verdict. The half-circle swelled when Lady Claire arrived, breathless, panting that she had just heard and what *was* the matter with poor, pale Elizabeth?

"We don't know, Aunt Claire. Richard was with her when she fainted, fortunately." Adrian leaned back against the wall, conscious of Nell's proximity, her body sandwiched between him and his brother who stood protectively close, his sharp features blurred with pain. Nell stood stiffly, arms hugging her chest, features composed except for the slight, betraying quiver of her lower lip. Adrian thought of her callous remarks in the drawing room and forgave her all, seeing the anxiety etched into her flawless features. She hadn't meant to be cold; she just hadn't realized that her sister was truly ill.

Another light tap sounded on the door, and Timothy Herenton appeared in the opening.

"What is happening?" he demanded, drawing back in alarm when Dr. Fenworthy rounded upon them with a sharp exclamation.

"Out!" the good doctor raged. "I will not have you crowding about like this is a dog and pony show! Out, I say!"

They were rudely ushered out the door, which slammed shut with a bang, leaving all of them standing in the hallway feeling foolish.

"Bit of a temper, what?" Timothy remarked, blithely unaware that his noisy and inopportune arrival had precipitated the doctor's reaction.

"Beastly," Richard agreed feelingly.

"Well, come, come, old boy. Let's repair to the library and pour us a bit of brandy. I daresay Lady Anne will advise us the moment she knows something. Come along, John. You look like you could use a bit of the hair of the dog, too."

Timothy shepherded Richard ahead of him, and Lady Claire tucked a hand through John's arm, leaving Adrian alone with Nell.

"Nell," he began, when they were alone, but she gave a sharp shake of her head.

"I'm going to my room, Adrian. Tell Mother if she asks."

Adrian watched her retreating figure rustle down the wide corridor, a wry smile on his lips. The bright promise of the spring day had dulled, though outside the weather was as beautiful as ever. The day after the storm. . . . He frowned, remembering Madame du Jessupe, the storm howling outside the house and the cards lying so innocently upon a gleaming table top. *La mort,* Josette had whispered, and he could still hear the hint of horror in her tone.

Pivoting, Adrian strode swiftly down the hall, brushing past a cluster of wide-eyed, whispering maids gathered with their feather dusters and polishing cloths.

"Get back to work," he ordered. "No one is dead . . . yet." And no one would die if he could stop the inexorable march of destiny. . . .

"But I never *said* it was a woman, m'sieur," Madame du Jessupe said calmly. She stared at him with a quiet, level gaze, hands folded in her lap.

"Yes, you did."

"Non. You had drawn the Empress card, but when I asked if you wanted to know, you refused."

Frustrated and angry, Adrian paced a small circle on the Aubusson carpet in Madame's guest room. "Well—is it? Is it Elizabeth who is to die?"

"Oui."

The simple, direct answer knocked the breath from his lungs, and he just stared at her.

"My God, madame, do you realize what you're saying? Do you have any idea what this means—what this could mean?" The implications struck him forcibly. "I cannot believe that a pack of . . . of . . . *pasteboard* would predict death. . . ."

"The cards are only harbingers, m'sieur, like the robin is the harbinger of spring."

"Damnation! You're mad!"

"Perhaps. But, you know what I have said is true." She leaned forward, her needlework forgotten, black eyes fixed intently on Adrian. "You know that it will all come to pass, just as I have said, don't you?"

He was mad, too, because he found himself nodding, his eyes meeting hers and knowing somehow that she was right.

"Yes. And there will be more—"

Footsteps rattled in the hallway, sounding like a herd of running deer, and Adrian whirled in alarm. Faint cries sounded, then a high-pitched wailing, and without glancing back at Madame du Jessupe, he was out the door and racing toward Elizabeth's room.

Dr. Fenworthy, a harried expression on his countenance, stood in the open doorway.

"Hurry, or you will be too late," he muttered, and Adrian shoved past him into the room.

Richard was already there, kneeling beside the high bed, tears trickling down his cheeks and Elizabeth's small hand clutched in his much larger one.

"Elizabeth . . ." he choked, "don't! Please don't!"

Lady Anne wept softly, nodding when a servant reported that Harry had gone after Sir Shelley.

"He went hunting before . . . before Elizabeth grew ill," Nell explained quietly. "Your man went to fetch him."

Adrian acknowledged her explanation with a short nod, sympathetic eyes glancing briefly at John, then went to stand beside his brother. Where was Lord Herenton? He should be here with his son. . . .

"Richard, I'm here," Adrian murmured softly, and his heart wrenched at his brother's ravaged face.

"She's dying. . . ."

A rattle sounded from the bed, and Adrian started, seeing Elizabeth's pale eyes fixed on a shaft of light slicing through a crack in the velvet drapes, her gaze reaching out determinedly toward the warm morning sun. All her conscious will was focused on that last glimmer of life, clinging, searching as the moth searches for the flame. It was over.

61

It was Richard who placed loving hands upon Elizabeth's still-open eyes, gently closing the warm lids.

"She's gone," he said, and like that long-ago King David who had grieved for the sick child yet ceased at his death, Richard wiped away his tears and said calmly, "I would like to be alone with her for a few moments."

Chapter 4
The Empress

A fortnight limped past, slow days and slower nights drifting by in a pattern of quiet meals and muted household sounds, the muffled voices of servants, wisps of black draped over furniture and doors, and still Elizabeth lay unburied. Richard was numb with shock from his loss, moving through long corridors with the slow, feeble steps of an old man, his eyes blank. Most of the time when Adrian spoke to him, it was like speaking to someone wrapped in a protective shroud of cotton wool. Richard hardly seemed to hear him.

The Shelley family remained at Hertfield Manor, and it had been decided, oddly enough, that Elizabeth would be buried in the cemetery on the Hertfield estates.

"She would have been a Herenton soon," the duke explained to his puzzled family, "so her father and I decided it was for the best."

A jarring note, Adrian privately thought, reluctant to voice his view to anyone else. And other, less significant things left him uneasy and puzzled. For five days after Elizabeth's death, while her mother lay in a darkened room drugged with laudanum and her sister made the few burial preparations, Sir Shelley and

Lord Herenton had been shut up in the library. Their few brief comments dealt more with the effect of Elizabeth's death on the family plans than they did with any expressions of grief. A week had passed before it was announced that Elizabeth would be buried in the Herenton cemetery, and then had come the edict that only immediate family would be present. No one else was to come, and no public announcements had been made. Certainly a most curious way to behave. . . .

It was the night before Elizabeth's interment that Adrian felt compelled to visit the tiny chapel where she lay on a flower-strewn bier. A Shelley servant stood respectfully by the bier. Two candleabra burning at Elizabeth's head and feet were the only illumination. The sickly-sweet smell of death permeated the entire chapel, and even the exotic blossoms did not dispel its distinctive odor. Adrian couldn't help a small start when the chapel bells tolled the midnight hour, long mournful peals that seemed especially oppressive in this close, dark room with soaring arches ribbing the ceiling.

Forcing himself to step close, Adrian looked down at Elizabeth's body, at the shapely hands folded across her chest, the spray of pink rosebuds tucked beneath them, and the pale, peaceful features that would never be animated with life again. Poor, quiet Elizabeth, now forever stilled, lying in a wedding dress she'd never worn.

Walking back to the great house, down dark stone paths shadowed with shapes formed by an overactive mind, Adrian reflected on the uncertainties of life. Death had come too early to gentle Elizabeth who had never harmed anyone in her brief, sweet existence. How much more swiftly could it come to one who thirsted for life? — thirsted for adventure and love and knowledge? Perhaps . . . perhaps he was tempting fate by refusing to acknowledge his own mortality.

No. He would not stand idly by and wait, but would rush out eagerly to greet life. Now was the time to grasp what he wanted, to secure his future by marrying Nell. As soon as this was over, he would approach his father and hers. The time for waiting was over.

Six black-clad men trod through the fine, cool mist, bearing upon their shoulders the mortal remains of Elizabeth Shelley. Up on the rutted road the ebony-draped hearse rolled slowly off, the quiet stamp of horses' hooves muffled and somber in the early morning air. Muted sounds of weeping escaped through fine linen handkerchiefs to mingle with the warble of robins and thrushes, drifting heavenward in a strangely discordant symphony.

The coffin was lowered to the ground beside that black, yawning void where it would soon rest for all eternity, and the mourners filed to each side of the grave. Adrian named them silently — Sir Shelley and his wife, John and Nell, then Lord Herenton and Timothy, followed by Claire and Richard — and he was left to stand between Josette and Madame du Jessupe. Madame du Jessupe . . . a silent mourner of a girl she had never met until a few weeks before, yet had known well enough to predict her death on a dark, stormy night. It was too macabre, too — coincidental.

Anger, unreasoning but fierce, surged through him. Why was the woman still here? True, she was a friend of his aunt's and uncle's, but in the face of the family tragedy, it would have seemed more appropriate for her to very quietly leave.

Clouds roiled overhead, and the pastor spoke more quickly, reciting familiar Bible passages that were intended to comfort the bereaved. As the first, faint drops of rain spattered down, he ended the service, and all the mourners scurried toward the waiting carriages. Only Richard remained, and Adrian, who couldn't bear to see his brother suffer alone.

Two servants lowered the coffin into the open maw of the grave, then picked up their shovels.

"Richard," Adrian said then, not quite certain his brother should remain, "why don't we go back to the house? The others will begin to worry."

Flat, final: "No."

Sharp-edged shovels plunged into the rich smelling dirt with a *shunk*, then poised briefly over the hole before tilting Cornish earth onto what remained of Elizabeth Shelley. Even Adrian winced as another *shunk*, and another, ending with the hollow rattle of dirt clods on lacquered wood.

"Richard . . ."

Whirling, Richard Herenton glared at his younger brother, half snarling, "Leave me be!"

Surprised by the unusual violence quivering in Richard, Adrian managed to say calmly, "You can't stay here forever. She's gone. Elizabeth is gone."

"Don't you think I know that?" Anger and violence trembled in him, sharpening his tone and even his facial features, until Richard seemed a stranger. He forced a more civil tone. "I have known that fact for years, Adrian. She's been dying for some time, you know."

"No, I didn't." Adrian felt a twinge of guilt for all the times he'd ignored his brother, when he had been so engrossed in his experiments, his travels on the Continent or just his reading. He'd never really paid

66

attention to anyone else's problems or concerns unless directly confronted. Quietly, he said, " No one ever told me, Richard."

Clasping his hands behind him, Richard rocked back on his heels, head up, face lifted to the wind and the rain that mingled with the salt of his tears. His untidy cravat — how unlike Richard! — fluttered wildly, and dull blond hair of a more delicate shade than Adrian's tangled in blue-gray eyes. The burgeoning promise of life was all around them, in the sweet scent of the grasses and soft rain, in the whisper of tree limbs dancing in the sky, yet Elizabeth was gone.

When Richard spoke his tone was conversational, almost normal, the words soft. "The doctors had warned of this for years, but I never wanted to believe. It was so easy not to, to pretend that she would live forever, and that we would be married and have children. . . ." He paused and turned to look across the bare, bleached bones of the ancient markers in the cemetery, gazing toward the distant meadows where lambs frolicked in the soft spring rain. "I always loved her," he continued, and Adrian had the eerie feeling Richard had forgotten his presence. "Even as a young girl, when we used to ride our ponies across the meadows, I was in love. There was only Elizabeth . . . and . . . and when I knew I would one day have to marry a Shelley it didn't matter. I already loved and wanted Elizabeth. She was my match . . . we were two sides of a coin. . . ."

Adrian was silent for a moment. It would be so easy to speak meaningless words of comfort, but he couldn't bring himself to offer such trite fare to his brother. Not now, not now when the pain was so intense, so powerful.

Richard's gaze dropped to where the last shovelful of earth was being tamped upon the fresh mound, his expression grim. "And if losing her is not bad enough, now I'm being forced to wed the next eligible Shelley, a poor replacement for my girl, a brood mare to spew forth an heir for the Shelleys and Herentons. Oh, God, Adrian—what shall I do?"

Freezing, Adrian's gaze was riveted upon his brother's anguished face. The words echoed in his sluggish brain, floundering in a pool of denial. There was only one other eligible Shelley female . . . Nell.

Chapter 5
The House of Destruction

Backing away, shaking his head in disbelief, Adrian pivoted, walking blindly away from his brother. No. His father would not do that. Or would he? The closed doors, the whispered meetings, the muttered secrets in dark corridors and the unusual manner of Elizabeth's funeral. . . .

Yes, the duke would certainly do that very thing if it suited him. And who would defy him? Adrian had never declared his intentions toward Nell, never betrayed by a single word that he wished to marry her, and now she was to wed his brother. This was madness, utter madness.

Adrian stalked past the carriage waiting to take him back to the main house, past the neat stone fence surrounding the little family cemetery where generations of Herentons lay in neat order, pigeon-holed for eternity, their aristocratic remains joining the centuries of common folk before them. All now lay moldering in the grave, the inevitable end for privileged and common alike.

Leaves crackled underfoot, and Adrian dimly realized that he'd entered the patch of woods that separated house from cemetery: oak, yew, pine and birch — centuries of trees standing strong and silent,

69

branches lifting heavenward. New growth budded, and the delicate, sweet fragrance of honeysuckle teased his senses.

He was on his knees now, staring in confusion at the latticework nature had woven with vines and tender, winding tendrils of green leaves and fragile, honeyed flowerets. Twigs snapped, and mysterious plops echoed in his ears, softly at first, then growing louder and louder until it seemed as if he was to be overpowered with noise.

In spite of the cool rain, Adrian found himself breaking into a sweat, huge patches wetting the sleeves of his coat, his shirt, and he tore at the confining folds of his neckcloth, gulping in air.

"Adrian!" Richard, thrashing through underbrush, limbs breaking underfoot, called again, "Adrian! Where are you?"

He didn't answer, just knelt on the damp ground, fingers splayed on the dirty knees of his trousers, contemplating ivy, honeysuckle and a thick mattress of fallen leaves. His brain struggled to align the words he'd heard with facts, and failed. Nell was his. *He* was in love with her, not Richard. Richard loved Elizabeth, poor frail Elizabeth, so cold and still in her satin and lace gown. Reality intruded again, Richard's troubled voice closer, right behind him.

"Adrian —" a gasp and wheeze, then a rustle of damp leaves beside him — "Adrian, why did you run from me?"

Why. Why, indeed? He had never run before. Why now? Adrian's head lifted, shocking Richard with his ravaged features.

"What . . . what is the matter, Adrian?"

"You can't marry Nell, Richard," he stated simply.

Richard's broad face reflected his momentary confusion, then an expression of dawning knowledge coupled with dismay. "Oh, my God . . . you're in love with Nell. Why . . . why didn't you tell someone?" A delicate pause, then: "Does Nell know that you love her?"

"Of course. We were to announce our engagement as soon as you had finally declared yourself with Elizabeth." Adrian's head, his pale hair plastered close to his skull by the fine, misting rain, wagged slowly from side to side. "I hope she does not hear of this from other lips. She might think I have betrayed her."

Silence descended, broken only by the sounds of nature subdued by rain. Richard's ragged breath expelled in a heavy sigh.

"Adrian—there's . . . there's something you must know." He seemed to struggle for words, his unusual intensity snaring Adrian's attention. "Nell . . . Nell already knows. . . ."

"Dear God. . . ."

"And Adrian—she has agreed."

Time and space cartwheeled slowly into unreality again, and Adrian stared at his brother's miserable face.

"No," he denied, weakly.

"I know it's difficult to accept, but it's true. What choice have we? Shelleys have always married Herentons, ever since that first truce between the warring families during the War of the Roses. It's a custom generations old—"

"A custom that will be broken this time!" Adrian surged to his feet. "No—it will still be honored. *I* am a Herenton, Richard, just as you are. Nell will still be in our family, and—"

"You know better, Adrian. She must wed the heir. It's the—"

"I know, dammit, I know!" Adrian glared, fists clenching at his sides. "It's the custom! Well, I say

71

damn the custom, and so will Nell! She cannot have agreed willingly, and when she learns that I do not mean to let her go—"

"She will wed me, Adrian, though I wish it were not so. Nell is aware of the family obligation and will do as she must." Richard stood, reaching out, fingers curling around Adrian's taut-muscled arm. "Please, Adrian—we are brothers. I want no strife between us."

"Then don't wed the woman I love!" Adrian snapped, jerking free.

Richard's arms dropped to dangle at his sides, and Adrian knew his answer. There was no point in further discussion with a mere instrument of his father's machinations. He would confront the duke, beard the lion in his den, and the ancient stone walls of Hertfield Manor would rattle with his fury.

"Father?" Adrian strode into the library, his garments muddy and damp, feet leaving a trail of dirt and leaves behind him. "Father. I must speak with you immediately. In private." Adrian's eyes cut meaningfully to Sir Shelley.

"Oh!" Sir Shelley puffed uneasily, plump cheeks blowing out like a chimpmunk's as he promptly set down a half-empty glass. "I was just leaving. Just leaving. Later, Thomas. Must see to . . . to . . . my new mare. Yes, that's it. New mare. Until later. . . ." The library door clicked shut behind him.

The duke's iron-gray brows rose as he surveyed his disheveled son. "And what," he inquired, "are you doing in my library in this disgraceful state of attire?"

Adrian ignored his father's attempts to sidetrack into a mundane discussion of his rumpled appearance.

"What is all this about Richard marrying Nell?"

The duke's lips twisted into a wry grimace. "Just as tactful as ever, I see. Did you ever flirt with diplomacy instead of bluntness, Adrian?"

"I see no need for mincing any words. Please answer my question."

"I take it you have some sort of objection to Richard marrying Nell?"

"That would be putting it rather mildly. I have a violent objection." Adrian leaned forward, knuckles pressing against the smooth wood of his father's mahogany desk, his eyes boring into the duke. "Why was I not consulted?"

A short bark of laughter, then: "You? Why should you be consulted? You have nothing to do with this at all—"

"I love Nell, and she loves me. I have everything to do with it!" Passionate rage quivered in his voice, and Adrian's eyes narrowed to icy slits as the duke fixed him with a slightly amused smile.

"Lady Eleanor has already agreed to the marriage. It seems that her affections are not so heavily engaged as yours. . . ."

"That's a lie!"

The duke's whisky glass slammed to his desktop, and he spat, "You impudent, blind pup! Don't dare speak to me in that fashion! I am still your father, and . . ." He paused, struggling for control of his rage, then continued more calmly, ". . . and if you dispute what I have to say, then ask the lady in question. She can do nothing less than agree with what I have told you, whether she wished it different or not."

Adrian's mind focused and grasped on his father's last sentence, and his tensed muscles relaxed. Nell had been coerced into agreement. It was not as he had feared.

He barely heard his father's following words, the observations that Lady Eleanor would wed Richard to cement the ties between their families, that heirs were needed to carry on the bloodlines and no interlopers could be tolerated on the adjoining lands of the Shelleys and Herentons.

"Love has no place in the arrangement of a marriage alliance, my boy, none at all. Even your precious Lady Eleanor is not so scattered as to believe that . . . just ask her."

"An excellent idea, Father. I shall ask Nell who she prefers—a man in love with a dead woman, or a man who loves her."

Lord Herenton shook his gray head, a faint sneer of contempt curling his lip. "You would do much better to take my advice, young man, and travel to London for a few months. Hell, I'll even provide the capital for your little venture if you'll be sensible. There are plenty of actresses searching for a sponsor, and hundreds of warm, available young women who would love to be under your protection. Think on it, Adrian," he said when his son backed off a step, fists clenched at his sides. "The alternatives aren't very promising."

"Is that a threat, Father?"

The duke shrugged. "Call it what you will. We're all familiar with the Cheltenham tragedies about penniless younger sons being cast off."

"But I'm not penniless. . . ."

"No, but how long do you think the monies from your mother's estate would last you if that was all you had? Be reasonable, Adrian. Young Eleanor is not going to choose penury over luxury. Being a lady instead of a duchess? Come, come, how ridiculous! Doesn't the future duchess of Hertfield sound much better than simply Lady Eleanor Herenton, wife of

Lord Adrian Herenton of Montagu?"

"Nell's not that impressed with a title, and besides, she's in love with me, not Richard—"

"Bah! Have it your way, Adrian! Only don't say I didn't warn you. . . ."

The duke's final words followed Adrian as he strode furiously from the library, adding more clumps of mud to those already streaking the exquisite Aubusson carpet. A red haze of anger clouded his vision as Adrian took the curve of stairs two at a time, and at that moment he detested his father and Richard with equal intensity. The duke, so poised, mocking and certain, would be in for a shock soon. It would seem that the only answer would be an elopement. After her first inevitable aversion to such a scandal, Nell would agree that it was the only way. And in time the furor would subside and their families would mellow.

"My lord?" Harry said as Adrian exploded into his bedchamber with unusual force. "Are there a pack of slavering dogs close behind you?"

"Almost, Harry, almost." His crumpled, filthy cravat snaked through the air to land haphazardly over the arm of a chair, earning a stern glance of disapproval from Harry. "I need clean garments . . ."

"That's obvious."

". . . as quickly as possible. And hot water, please."

"Certainly, my lord. At once, my lord. Shall I ring for more servants, my lord?"

Fumbling with the buttons of his shirt, Adrian slanted Harry an annoyed glance. "Dammit, Harry, I'm in no mood for your sarcasm! Nor your interference," he added when Harry's mouth opened to reply.

Nodding stiffly, Harry selected clean clothes and provided a basin of hot water, all done in silence. It was a silence thick with reproach, but Adrian did not take the time to explain. There would be time later. Now he had to see Nell, had to hear from her own lips that she would flaunt society and her parents' wishes and marry him as soon as possible.

Eleanor Shelley was admiring her reflection in the long cheval mirror of her guest room. Though she was still swathed in the hated black or mourning, she was already imagining the fine gowns she would one day possess, the fabled Hertfield emeralds that would complement her eyes and fill her jewelry coffers. She preened, pulling back the silky curls that framed her oval face, turning this way and that, trying to decide on a more sober chignon or flirtatious curls.

A duchess . . . ! She embraced the knowledge, delighted that she would rank among the highest nobility. Poor Elizabeth, she would miss her, she really would. But fate had cast her in the role of duchess now, and she considered it a most fortunate turn of events. And to think how she had ridiculed that pompous, dark Gypsy, who—she was now convinced—had been trying to prepare her. Well, after her marriage to Richard, she would give the creature some sort of gratuity. Nell smiled at her reflection. "Duchess of Hertfield," she whispered softly.

"Nell?"

Starting, Nell gave a small cry and whirled around to find Adrian standing in the open doorway. She hadn't even heard the door open and spared a dark curse for her absent maid. Recovering her composure, she managed a bright smile, recalled that Elizabeth's funeral had been only a few hours before, and altered it to reflect sorrow.

"Adrian . . ." She held out her hands and he

crossed the room to her, taking her long cold fingers into the broad warmth of his palms.

"Nell, sweeting . . ." He pulled her closer.

"No, Adrian —" she pulled away, —"it's . . . so soon." Pale fingers pressed to her eyes and her lower lip quivered.

"I know, love I know, and I apologize for the intrusion upon your mourning. It's just that I've . . . heard some disturbing things, and I need to talk. . . ."

"Not now, Adrian, please!" Nell whirled and walked to the long windows looking out over the south gardens where the gazebo sat in solitude. She recalled the day Elizabeth had died and Harry had been sent to find them, and the memory of Adrian's passion sparked anew. Turning, she met his troubled gaze. Ah, if only Adrian were the eldest, the one who would inherit the title of duke instead of stolid, dull Richard. But — perhaps she could still have both for a small time.

"It can't wait," Adrian was saying, and Nell wondered if he had any idea how handsome he was, how utterly masculine in the snug-fitting trousers and jacket that outlined his lean physique. Adrian brushed impatiently at the hair that fell into his eyes, a gesture Nell had always admired, and strode close to grasp her by both hands.

"Nell, Richard told me about our fathers' plans. I have quarrelled with my father about it, told him that we were in love —"

"What did he say?" she demanded sharply, drawing away to stare up at him through narrowed eyes. "Did . . . did he change his mind?" This last a bit breathlessly, waiting for his answer.

Adrian shook his head reluctantly. "No, but that doesn't have to matter." He never noticed how her tense features relaxed and her strain-taut muscles

77

sagged with relief.

"Oh, Adrian." She took his face between her palms and stood on tiptoe to press a kiss to his mouth, a kiss that he quickly returned. He jerked her so close that the breath was squeezed from her lungs. Long-starved passion flared high, and she hardly realized when Adrian had backed her against a wall until the molding was pressing into her tender skin.

"Adrian," she managed to gasp between hot, searching kisses, "the maids! Or my mother . . ."

"I locked the door, and your mother is prostrate in her own room, attended by your father." He nibbled at the soft skin just below her ear and was rewarded with a shiver. Reason fled, leaving only this driving urgency to possess her, to make her his so no one could ever take her from him, and Adrian scooped Nell into his arms and bore her to the high bed in the corner.

Heavy velvet draperies shrouded the mattress with welcoming shadows that beckoned to two lovers, and Nell made no protest when he gently lowered her to its surface. She lay looking up at him with wide, shining eyes, parted lips moist with desire. It was madness, but the past weeks of frustration and anxiety goaded him into recklessness, and Adrian pulled at her black garments with feverish haste. She would be his. . . .

Bare breasts pressed close to smooth-muscled flesh, mouth to mouth, tongues dueling hotly, hip to hip, and swollen passion nudged against a firmly-rounded belly. The atmosphere in the drapery-enclosed bed shimmered with heat, crackling with static excitement and steamy desire. Cool, lavender-scented sheets grew damp from the moist press of the entwined lovers, and the air was thick with throaty mur murs of passion.

"God, Nell . . . you're so sweet . . . so soft and warm. . . ."

"Umm, for you, love. Just for you. . . ."

Exploring hands searched for and found each other, and they reveled in the mutual discovery. Pale, firm breasts thrust proudly at Adrian, and his mouth teased, tasted, trailed paths of fire from one proud peak to the other until Nell was writhing helplessly beneath him. She twisted, long fingers circling him, urging Adrian closer.

He groaned, lifted his lean body and slid between her thighs. Poised at her velvety entrance he paused until Nell squirmed, devouring him with her greedy mouth and eyes. Her voice was a breathless little moan.

"Please hurry, Adrian! Please . . ."

"I don't want to hurt you. . . ."

"Now! I can't wait any longer."

Lunging forward, Adrian slid smoothly into her ready body, and at her sinuous movements was quickly lost in the rhythm of love. They soared on pulsing waves of passion, finally crashing to fulfillment like the roar of the incoming tide against Cornish cliffs.

Adrian recovered first, raising to prop himself on one elbow and gaze into Nell's face. Her eyes were closed, long lashes lying like dark wings against her pale cheeks, her mouth slightly parted and still bruised from his kisses. She was his. . . .

"Sweeting." He kissed the tip of her straight nose. "I dare not linger too long. We need to make our plans quickly."

Lashes fluttered up to reveal eyes still smoky with passion. "What plans?" she murmured lazily, reaching up to trace the outline of Adrian's sensual mouth with a fingertip. "What are you talking about?"

"Wedding plans, love, *our* wedding plans."

Now he had Nell's full attention. Her eyes opened even wider, all traces of passion evaporating like morning mist. She listened tensely as Adrian outlined plans to escape Hertfield Manor in a coach, racing the length of England to Scotland to elope.

"You must be mad," she said coldly when he paused. "I would be ruined!"

"But we could outface the scandal. . . ."

"I'm not talking of just the scandal, Adrian! Your brother would never marry me then."

Adrian's voice was tight, his gray eyes narrowed. "I thought that was the general idea," he said dryly. "We were to be married instead of you and Richard."

"But Richard is the heir."

That one, short sentence said much more than Nell realized, but Adrian was still unwilling to believe it.

"Are you saying," he began carefully, "that you do not wish to marry me, Nell?"

"Of course I'd rather marry you! But don't you see? Richard is the heir. Unless I marry Richard, I cannot be duchess . . ." Sensing at last that she trod upon delicate ground, Nell added hastily, ". . . and . . . and my father will be furious! He'll disown me, or worse!"

"You would not risk it for love of me, Nell?"

"Oh, Adrian, don't! It would not have to be the end of us. Why, after the wedding when things have died down a bit, we could still see each other like this. No one need ever know, and we can—" She shuddered to a halt, shrinking from the naked fury in Adrian's eyes.

A muscle twitched in his jaw, and it was obvious he was struggling for control of his temper. Angry white lines bracketed his mouth with deep grooves, and his mouth, that sensuous mouth that could spark such passion, was thinned to a straight, taut line.

"Marks of my lovemaking are still on your body," he ground out, "and you sit there talking of wedding my brother? — of making a fool of him as well as me? I swear, Nell, by all that's holy, I ought to strangle you!"

"Adrian—" She stopped and licked suddenly dry lips, swallowing hard to fight her panic. "Adrian, my love, I'm just so confused . . . so bereaved . . . all that's happened. . . ."

Rolling from the bed, he gave her a glance of contempt. "You're not confused, Nell. You know exactly what you want and how to get it. You want to be a duchess. Fine. But I intent to tell my poor brother what's happened tonight so that he won't be so shocked when he finds you tumbling in the hay with a groom or stableboy." He gestured to the bed where she sat, the imprint of their bodies still on the mattress, and said, "Where is the proof of your virginity, Nell? There are no blood stains." A harsh laugh erupted into the room. "And I, the fool, tried to be so careful not to hurt you. . . ."

Adrian shrugged into his clothes in spite of Nell's fumbling attempts to stop him, her incoherent pleas to keep silent rattling against deaf ears. When he stalked to the door, she flung herself at him, nails raking, the silk wrapper she'd pulled on sliding half off one shoulder.

"I'll make you sorry, Adrian. . . !" She beat at him with her fists, bare feet kicking at him shins. "I swear you'll regret this."

Grasping both her wrists in one strong hand, Adrian looked down at her with distaste. "I already regret this, Nell. I shouldn't have soiled myself with a dirty piece of goods." He yanked open the door and gave her a shove back into the bedroom. "Stay inside unless you want everyone in the house to know what a slut you are."

"Slut?" she screeched, eyes wild, blond hair straggling into her face. "You call *me* slut when you've been with every whore in London?"

"But at least they were honest whores, Nell, and didn't pretent to be ladies." He fixed her with a steady gaze. "I think they were more lady than you'll ever be, even with the title of duchess."

She lunged forward, stumbling into the hallway, and Adrian tried to wedge her back inside. Nell fought him wildly, cursing under her breath. It was such a fierce commotion the frightened maids summoned Richard.

Stunned, Richard stood with a horrified expression on his face at the sight of a half-naked Nell wrestling with his brother in the corridor of the guest wing.

"What . . ?" he began, and Nell, catching sight of him, cried, "Help me, Richard! Oh please . . . your brother's tried to . . . to. . . ." Her lashes fluttered, and with a soft cry she sagged to the floor.

Fury enveloped Richard, and he lunged for his brother. "How could you?" he bellowed. "Did you think I would not marry her if she was soiled?" One arm slashed at the much quicker Adrian, and he ducked it easily.

"Richard, now listen to reason. It's not at all like it looks. . . ."

But Richard, unhinged by the past few weeks, was beyond listening to reason. He stormed and bellowed, creating such an uproar that the hallway was soon choked with bug-eyed spectators. Maids gawked and footmen muttered uneasily as they ringed the struggle, and it wasn't until the duke's familiar voice was heard that they recalled other tasks in faroff regions of the house and scuttled away like beetles.

His Grace, the Duke of Hertfield, was no fool, and he had few illusions about the younger daughter of Sir Shelley; but neither was he willing to cancel his plans. It seemed as if there was only one solution, though he had resisted the idea until confronted by Adrian earlier.

"Stop it, both of you," he said to his battling sons, "and get up off the floor. Do you have any idea how ridiculous you both look? Dolly—" he gestured to a scared ladies' maid—"take your mistress into her room and tend to her. And tell her not to leave it until she has spoken to me."

"Yes, Your Grace. At once, Your Grace." Dolly bobbed a quick curtsy and scurried to Nell's limp form. She was a sturdy Cornish farm girl and had no problem lifting Nell and carrying her back into the bedroom.

Richard, his face covered with blood from cuts over his eye and on one cheek, stood glaring at his brother. His Grace turned back to his sons.

"Adrian, you come with me," the duke said tersely. "Richard, please go wash your face and go to bed. I will talk privately with you tomorrow. And under no circumstances, do I want this . . . incident . . . mentioned to anyone."

Casting a last, angry glance at Adrian, Richard swung around and left the hallway without speaking. The door to his bedchamber slammed shut with extra force.

Adrian followed the duke downstairs to his study, and they shut the door behind them. Silence fell. Waiting, Adrian considered offering a denial and explanation, then thought better of it. Best to hear what his father had to say first.

The duke was abrupt and to the point. "I've thought about this for several days—I think it best

83

that you leave Hertfield, Adrian. There is nothing to be gained by your remaining, and matters can only worsen. You have the misfortune to be the second son instead of first and must seek your fortune where you will." His voice was weary, his face lined with strain.

"When do I leave?" Adrian asked stiffly.

"I've already made arrangements, and Harry is packing for you. You will leave," the duke said, "tonight."

Chapter 6
The Chariot

Fog rolled in from the swelling seas on silent cat feet, smothering ships and Plymouth dock in a fleecy blanket. Adrian gazed at the wisps swirling playfully around tall masts that swayed gently to and fro, not really seeing any of his surroundings. The sounds of a busy harbor teased his senses; the muffled chant of seamen tugging at hemp lines, the muted clank of chains being hauled, and the shrill, tinny bo'sun's whistle mingled with the rich, throaty cries of gulls.

He lifted his head to the wind blowing from unknown lands across the Atlantic, and breathed deeply. He was excited in spite of the circumstances. The ripe pungency of salted fish, the sharp tang of exotic spices, fresh-cut woods and decaying produce only added to the lure of the salty sea. For a brief moment, Adrian considered purchasing a sailing vessel and taking to the high seas, then smiled ruefully at the idea of a merchant in the Herenton family. His father would die of apoplexy.

Tugging the edges of his coat closer together, Adrian shivered as cold, searching fingers of damp wind crept beneath. He was suddenly impatient to have it over with, to board whichever vessel that the duke had chosen and sail for sunny Italy. It wasn't quite the manner in which he'd thought he would be travelling to Rome, but that didn't matter now. Very little mattered now.

"I certainly hope we have excellent accommodations, my lord." Harry stood beside him. His face was gray in the early morning light, his lips pinched with the cold. "And a warm brazier filled with coals," he added.

Adrian grinned. "Where's your adventurous spirit, Harry?"

"Hugging a warm furnace, I'm quite certain, my lord. I never thought it would be so cool at this time of the year."

"It's the ocean. Don't you ever think about where this wind came from, who it has touched before crossing the ocean to us?" Adrian leaned on a rough rail, then grimaced at the smear of tar on his coat sleeve.

"No. Not at all," Harry replied, producing a clean square of linen from one of the huge pockets of his greatcoat. He gave it a snap and proceeded to scrub at the tar on Adrian's sleeve, adding, "Judging from the . . . *distinctive* odor, I'm not at all certain I care to know where the wind originated."

Adrian's mouth slanted into a smile of affection, and while Harry dabbed at the tar, he gazed out over the older man's balding head to the line of ships. There were vessels from Spain, France and Italy, and he recognized Portugese and Dutch ships as well. Their names were as varied as their countries; the *Señora de la Merced, La Bon Voyage, Santa Lucia,* the *Molly Glynn* . . . Adrian's eyes narrowed. A trim ship with clean lines and gleaming brass, the *Molly Glynn* flew an American flag—the Americas.

Words spoken on a stormy night echoed in his head, and he recalled a vision of snow-capped mountains and fresh white winds, the image of a soaring eagle still imprinted on his brain.

"Ah," Harry was saying, having successfully removed most of the tar from Adrian's coat sleeve, "here comes your father now, my lord. I believe he has secured our passage upon the *Santa Lucia,* bound for Rome."

"Our passage, Harry? You're going with me?"

"But of course. You did not expect me to let such a helpless lad travel to Italy alone, did you?" Harry gazed at him with mild reproach. "Who would see that you were properly dressed, my lord?"

A surge of affection swelled Adrian's throat. Dear Harry—who recoiled at the thought of displaying any emotion other than disdain—was probably his truest friend.

"I might be gone for some time, you know, Harry. I suspect Father will not want me returning to the family fold in the near future." He hesitated, then said, "You never wanted to travel with me before, Harry, and I know how you hate ships and the sea. . . ."

"It's all that water—I don't swim, you know."

"Yes, but you should have learned."

Harry shuddered. "How undignified, splashing about like a mackerel, with water dripping into one's eyes . . . no, no. I quite detest even the idea of it." He paused, then added, "But the idea of sunny Rome, Florence and Naples will more than compensate for the necessary voyage. My bones long for warmth these days."

"I must say, Harry, that I'm most glad you're coming along. It would be deadly dull without you."

"Naturally. My sparkling wit and scintillating conversation enlivens any social gathering, my lord." Harry stepped aside as Lord Herenton approached, nodded to His Grace and said that he would have their luggage unloaded from the carriage now.

The duke's unsmiling face betrayed no emotion as

he regarded his youngest son. Damn, but he hated this. Silly little chit had caused more than enough trouble, but he'd nipped *that* in the bud. She'd been warned of her place, and had bloody well better remember it.

"Adrian," he said aloud, "I have secured your passage on the *Santa Lucia*. You are scheduled to arrive in Rome on the twenty-fifth of the month. There are funds available in Rome and Florence, and all the details"—he held up a large square envelope—"are in here. This other envelope contains a letter to my solicitor." He cleared his throat. "If, for any reason, you need to contact me, do so through Señor Pallo."

The implication of his words struck Adrian almost physically, and he reeled. "I am not to write my family directly?"

"No."

"You are disowning me, then." Adrian stared at the duke, who met his gaze without flinching. His father the duke—rigid, inflexible, omnipotent—was casting him from the family.

Gulls wheeled overhead, rending the air with raucous screeches, and water slapped against the buttresses of the dock as Adrian and his father gazed at one another, neither knowing quite what to say. There didn't seem to be any words left, nothing to express tangled emotions. Finally the duke thrust out a leather satchel.

"Take this. There are . . . some sentimental things . . . that you might wish to have, as well as useful items."

Nodding, Adrian took the soft, weathered bag, kneading the leather between his hands as he said, "Am I to stay away forever, or just a few years?"

Lord Herenton rubbed the deep crease between his eyes and sighed. "Ten years should ease the tension."

"Ten years . . . !" Bitter anger choked Adrian, and he clutched the leather bag so tightly his knuckles were white against the deep sable.

"Yes. In ten years there should be enough heirs, and perhaps you will have married by then." Hooded eyes shifted to stare past Adrian, resting upon the sleek Italian vessel that was to carry his son away. There were regrets that would have to remain unvoiced. To express them now would only make the parting more bitter. Squaring his broad shoulders, the duke faced Adrian and took a step forward. "Farwell, Adrian. . . ."

Adrian's brows rose and his mouth twisted. "Do you intend to embrace me, Father? Why now, after all those lost years? Any show of affection can only be a mockery to a life already filled with empty arms." Turning, Adrian stared across the slip at the *Molly Glynn* riding the harbor waves.

The duke's arm dropped, and he seemed to age ten years in that instant, his haggard face seamed with new lines. Then, nodding, he spun on his heel and walked away, footsteps echoing down the wooden planks of the pier. Adrian listened to his father's staccato steps until they blended with the jumbled noise of the harbor and disappeared forever.

Time passed in a blur of salty wind and unfamiliar sounds, and he didn't move until he heard Harry's voice.

"The *Santa Lucia* will be leaving shortly, my lord. Our luggage is ready to be loaded now."

"No."

"Pardon? But . . . but are we not to leave . . . ?"

"Oh yes, Harry, we're leaving, but we're not sailing on the *Santa Lucia* to the crowded cities on the Continent. . . ." Adrian's tone was firm, his eyes filled with purpose. "You don't have to go, Harry, but I am determined to do so."

"But the sun," Harry protested, thinking of liquid gold pouring down on baking cities, "it's warm in Italy. . . ."

"We are off for a real adventure, Harry my man! Do you see that ship?"

Weakly he asked, "The Molly Glynn?" followed by a despairing moan when Adrian nodded. "But my lord, that ship is bound for the Americas!"

"I know that."

"And there's no evidence the sun even shines in that barbaric land. . . ."

"It shines, Harry, it shines so brightly the mountains are gilded with gold, gold that solidifies and lies in clear, sparkling streams just waiting for someone to come along and . . ."

". . . and he murdered by savages . . ."

". . . and pick it up. Don't you see? There are no crowded cities in America!" He ignored Harry's heartfelt moan. "The air is fresh and clean, and no one cares if you're a duke or a butcher as long as you're honest."

"I do believe, my lord, that I am going to do something I have never done before," Harry said.

"What is that?"

"Weep profusely. . . ."

Book Two

1835
The Storm

And the wind swept out across the prairies toward the mountains high in the sky

Chapter 7
The Wheel of Fortune

Unorganized Territory, United States, Summer 1835

It was happening again! Dark hair whipped behind her as Blue Feather ran from her tipi. Shots rang out, and screams filled the air. Ducking behind a rack of buffalo meat left to dry in the sun, she crouched fearfully.

It was hunting season, and most of the men in the Crow village had gone to hunt the great, shaggy buffalo that roamed the plains. In their absence, the village was being attacked by the Piegan-Blackfeet — the most feared tribe on the plains.

Swallowing the fear that sat like a huge lump in her throat, Blue Feather shivered. Her new Crow husband, Young White Buffalo, was gone with the others, but due back shortly. She had no one to protect her, no one to fight for her. His other wives, no doubt, were happy about her situation. Half-crouching, she crept back toward the tipi she shared with Young White Buffalo. Still inside was the rifle he had captured from the raid months before, the raid on her Shoshoni camp when she had been taken. A woman was not supposed to touch a brave's weapons, she knew, but she had to defend herself. Perhaps she could use it.

But when she had ducked back into the tipi and found the rifle, it was useless. There was no powder or bullets to load it with, and so she tossed it aside. All she had was her skinning knife for protection. Almost frantic with the pressing need to hide, Blue Feather flung cooking utensils and blankets into a heap in the tipi as the screams and shots outside grew louder. She could smell the sharp, acrid scent of burning hide and knew the tipis had been set on fire. Fear choked her, and she knew she must flee.

It was then that the flap to the tipi flew up and a tall brave ducked inside. A small scream burst from her mouth before Blue Feather realized it was her young husband. She put her hands over her mouth and sagged with relief.

"Hush, foolish one!" he said swiftly in the Crow tongue. "Come with me. . . ."

He reached out for her, yanking her with him, and she followed willingly, grateful he had come for her. She did not ask how he had known of the attack, or why he had chosen to come back for a female captive, or where his other wives and children were, but went with him silently.

Instead of leaving the way he had come, Young White Buffalo slit a long opening in the rear of the tipi, and they fled through it. The village was in chaos, with horses running madly about and the camp dogs barking furiously. Children screamed and cried, and mothers called out for them as howling, painted warriors dashed about on their horses. They killed indiscriminately, smashing heads like ripe melons with fierce war clubs, skewering old men, women and children with their lances.

Blue Feather bit back a sob as she stumbled behind

her husband. The Piegan were fierce and savage warriors. They had come to kill, to massacre and perhaps take captives, and would leave no one alive. Young White Buffalo pulled her with him, not thinking about how he had been too late to save the rest of his family. Only Blue Feather still lived. His long legs leapt over fallen meat racks and smoldering fires without pause, jerking Blue Feather over or through them without regard to injury. A wound could always be treated, but a lance or arrow through the heart would be fatal.

Other survivors also fled, running panic-stricken to the woods behind the village. Few Blackfeet pursued them now. It would only be later, when the killing in the village had ended, that they would search for the living.

"Stop," Young White Buffalo called to some of the others when they had come to a huge pile of boulders set in the mountainside. "Let us wait here and hide. We cannot run far or fast enough to escape. We shall have to fight . . ."

"No, I say run," a bloodied old man argued. His hands and legs were trembling with age and fright, and blood ran down his face. His woman was with him, an old crone in a shapeless tunic, and she agreed with her husband.

"I say we flee," she echoed in a tremulous voice.

Blue Feather pressed close to Young White Buffalo's side. A glance over her shoulder showed her the entire village in blazing ruins, and the screams and shouts were beginning to fade. Soon they would pursue; soon the painted Piegan would follow them up this mountainside, and they would overtake them if they tried to flee. She tugged at her husband's arm. "Let us stay and fight," she whispered.

He nodded. "I have a gun," he said to those who

had stopped. "Some of you have guns. If we run, they will only catch us. Let us die fighting. It is a good day to die."

At this there was a general murmur through the dozen people gathered on the mountainside. Finally they agreed. They would stay and fight. Logs, brush and large stones were dragged to the shelter of boulders to form a rough breastwork behind which they could hide.

Thick, black smoke boiled up from below, drifting on the wind to where they worked, bringing the stench of death with it. Blue Feather shivered as she piled brush on top of the stones, heedless of the fine garments her new husband had brought her only a moon before. The blouse and skirt were now ripped and stained with sweat and soot, but at least she was alive. Soon the Piegan would be upon them, and then even that could change.

Time passed on the wings of anxiety and fear, great swooping wings that cast shadows across the group waiting in their hiding places. Kneeling close to her husband, Blue Feather remembered the time he had pulled her from the cold stream and how she had fought him then. It had been only a few months since she had been taken from the Shoshoni—the tribe known to the Crow as the Snakes—and she had come since then to feel a certain affection for the young brave who had taken her. He had been kind, if maybe aloof, and treated her with more gentleness than many warriors treated their female captives.

Blue Feather was his third wife, and she had not been demanded upon to give him a child yet. He had several children already and had been away hunting for almost all of the time they'd been together.

She put a hand on his arm, and he looked down at her.

"You have been good to me," she said in halting Crow.

Young White Buffalo smiled. His black eyes moved from the girl's finely chiseled features to her brilliant blue eyes. It had been easy to be kind to her. She asked for little and did not nag like many women. She was easy to please and obedient, and she performed her household duties without complaint. Many of the braves he hunted with had remarked that they, too, would to to a Snake village and get a wife, and didn't Young White Buffalo want to part with his new wife? He had many children for so young a man already. He had laughed at them, and now he thought how fortunate he had been that day. Reaching out, he stroked back the tangled strands of his wife's hair. It was a tender gesture, and she closed her eyes.

When she opened them again, she saw the stealthy approach of warriors through the forest below their breastwork. Shadows flitted from tree to tree as they drew near, now quite certain of their quarry.

"They come!" she whispered to her husband, and he gave a grim nod of his head.

"It is better to die now — quickly — than to die slowly as they prefer." He pressed her skinning knife into her palm and met her gaze. "If you must — use it upon yourself."

Understanding, Blue Feather nodded. She had heard how the Piegan preferred killing captive enemies very slowly, with ingenious and cruel methods of torture. They could keep an enemy alive for days, ignoring his screams for mercy and death. Shuddering, she looked back at the forest.

The Blackfeet had seen their fortress of stone and logs and had paused. They were grouping for attack, and Blue Feather steeled herself. There was no turning back now, no hope of escape. She could see that there were too many of them.

The old woman in their group whimpered softly, and her man hushed her. Several other women muttered to themselves, and the few braves exchanged knowing glances.

"It is a good day to die," one of them said slowly, echoing Young White Buffalo's brave words, and they all gripped their rifles tightly.

Then, rising from the comparative safety of the rocky shelter, they broke into howls of challenge and defiance. Scaling the rocks, the Crow warriors brandished their weapons and began firing. Arrows were notched and lances were flung, and the air was thick with deadly missiles. The action took the approaching Piegan by surprise, but they recovered swiftly.

Hand-to-hand combat raged as they grappled, war clubs and sharp-edged axes flashing in the shadows of the trees. Cowering behind the rocks, the women watched. If there had been enough weapons, they might have fought beside their men, but there had not been. Now they waited and watched.

Her heart was in her throat as Blue Feather watched her young husband clash with a painted Piegan. Sweat streamed over their copper bodies as they strained against one another, each trying to kill the other with a knife. Their arms were raised, fingers gripping wrists, lean body against lean body, muscles taut. The Piegan had covered his body with oil to make it slippery, and Young White Buffalo was losing his grip. His hand kept sliding over the slick skin of his opponent.

Dimly realizing that her fingers were digging so deeply into the hard shale of the rock that they were scraped and bleeding, Blue Feather abruptly released her grip and stood up. If she was to die, then she would die with her husband. It was never good to die alone with one's enemies. . . .

A fierce howl burst from her throat as she saw that she was too late. The Piegan's blade had slipped easily into Young White Buffalo's unprotected side, piercing his heart. He slid lifelessly to the ground, and Blue Feather flung herself over the top of the rock. Her skinning knife was in her hand, and she paid little heed to the amazed glances of the Piegan as she raced across the ground toward the man who had killed her husband.

Seized with blind hatred, she had no room left to fear. And perhaps it was that hatred that saved her life. If she had not behaved like a crazy woman, throwing herself upon the warrior and stabbing at him with her knife, the others might have killed her instantly. Instead, astounded and amused, they merely took away her knife. Blue Feather had done the warrior little damage, and he held her away with contemptuous ease.

Killing was over for the moment. The slain bodies of the Crow warriors lay sprawled upon the leaves and stones, their blood slowly draining into the Earth Mother. Blue Feather could not look at them. She waited numbly for the Piegan to decide what to do with her, and prayed that it would be quick or that she would die bravely.

Screams shrilled down from the rocks where she had hidden, and she knew that the enemy was gathering more captives. Perhaps they intended to trade them, she thought, with a ray of hope. That was not unheard of. Many times a strong squaw of childbearing age was worth much, and a man-child worth even more. Perhaps the Piegan would not kill them or mutilate them, but trade them to another band such as the Mandans or Minnetarees. They used captive slaves to do the hard labor.

But when the Piegan warriors came back down the hill from the hastily-built fortress where she had hidden, Blue Feather knew that they would not wish to trade these captives. The old man and woman still lived, cringing in fear as they were shoved brutally ahead of the enemy. The other captives were women and old men also, and Blue Feather felt her last hope die.

Keeping her chin lifted, Blue Feather stared straight ahead. As her hopes died, so did her defiance. She could not fight the Piegan, could not hope to win. Only numb acceptance would placate them. She could do that without losing her dignity.

When the warrior who had killed her husband came to Blue Feather, grinning with pleasure, she ignored him. He stepped close, peering into her face, and she looked away. A chill shivered down her spine when he reached out to lift a heavy strand of her hair in his hand, letting it spill over his palm. He exclaimed something she didn't understand, dropping her hair and gripping her chin as he turned her to face him. Yellow zigzag marks to imitate lightning bolts streaked his face, and his black eyes narrowed as he gazed into her startling blue eyes. Half-turning, he called something over his shoulder, indicating that his companion should come and look.

Blue Feather tried to jerk away, but he held her fast, his fingers gripping her chin so tightly that she had to press her lips together to keep from crying out. She sensed that they were remarking over the strange color of her eyes, and felt another flutter of fear.

Speaking to her with crude hand signs and snatches of Crow, her captor asked if she was Crow. Blue Feather shook her head, anxiously scanning the faces crowding around her for a sign of mercy. There was none evident in the ruthless painted faces staring at her. Nudging her with a rough elbow, her captor was obviously asking her what tribe she belonged to, and Blue Feather hesitated. Should she tell them that she was Shoshoni? The Blackfeet had often warred upon the tribe known to many as the Snake, and she paused so long he hit her with the heel of his hand.

Then, rationalizing that the Blackfeet warred upon all tribes, she made the sign of the Snake with her hand and arm, waggling it backward as if it were a snake crawling through the grass. The Piegan nodded and said something to the others, then said in crude Shoshoni, "How is it you have eyes the color of the sky?"

Blue Feather swallowed the surge of fear in her throat. To tell these men that her father was white would be to die. The Blackfeet had hated the white men ever since Lewis and Clark had explored this territory. After an incident involving Lewis in which one Blackfoot was stabbed to death while stealing rifles and another shot, they had made war on every white man they saw. The fact that her father was French would be her death.

A triumphant whoop erupted from the throat of the warrior as he saw his answer in her face. Turning to his companions again, he spoke rapidly. Blue Feather waited. He turned back to her, and she knew her fate. She would soon die. . . .

But it seemed that the death of the blue-eyed captive was to be a special occasion shared with the rest of their tribe. It would be big medicine if they killed her slowly, and to deny the others would not be good. They would take her back to their village.

Pushing the captives ahead of them, the Piegan began the long trek back to their camp. They were in a good mood, laughing and boasting of their prowess in battle as they hurried through the forest. They had succeeded, cleverly striking the Crow village while the warriors were hunting. Now they had counted many coup, killed many Crow, and taken captive a Snake with blue eyes. They had to retreat before the warriors returned, and many a jest was made about the reaction of the returning hunters when they saw their ruined camp and dead families. Yes, it was a great joke, a great raid, and many among the Piegan had gained glory this day.

Blue Feather kept her head high, understanding only part of what they were saying. She only knew that she was to die. Perhaps death should not frighten her, for hadn't her mother and brother died? She had no family left. There was no one but her father, and she had not seen him in years. Perhaps death would be comforting, she consoled herself. Many of her loved ones had already gone to the Land of Everfeasting. . . .

Chapter 8
The Hanged Man

It was the soft time of year, when summer skies and tender green shoots of new grass should have softened the harsh, forbidding angles of rocky crags and steep summits. It did not. The wide land shimmered beneath the burning orb of the sun; cool winds blew ceaselessly, and eagles soared on the air currents in great, wheeling patterns. Puffs of clouds checkered the distant valley with lazily drifting shadows, and a breeze gushed upward from the lower rock ridges to the crest where Adrian Herenton sat on his horse.

In spite of a certain worldly cynicism, he was awed by what he saw. The past months of traveling across the waste of the Dakotas had not prepared him for this grandeur, this wide, endless panorama spread before him in wild, primitive beauty. There had been the open plains and the constant howl of the wind. Miles and miles of empty grassland had stretched before them with no trees, no hills, nothing but flat, rippling plains, and of course, the ever present wind. Now he stood on the precipice of the world and it took away his breath.

Dragging one sleeve across his face, Adrian wiped away the beads of sweat dotting his forehead. Even in the misty cool of the morning he was hot and sticky, not so much from the heat of the sun, but from exertion. He had spent most of the last week in his saddle, and he could feel it in his aching muscles and joints. There had been moments, such as the night before when they had paused for a few hours rest, that Adrian had wondered if he'd made the right decision.

Crouched beside a small fire and sipping hot, bitter coffee, Adrian had gazed at the starlit sky and pondered upon his decision to leave the huge hunting party he'd accompanied to the rugged Dakotas. He had left them to join a group of strangers headed to a legendary rendezvous in the Green Mountains of Wyoming Territory. It had seemed like the right thing at the time, but now, in view of the hardships already suffered and more promised, he began to doubt his impulsive decision.

Tilting back his head, he grimaced at the bright burn of the sun and closed his eyes. But — why not? The past year since leaving the bustle of New York City had been spent drifting anyway, with no purpose or destination in mind. He had found himself drifting westward in his travels, toward the lure of uncharted territories that had rarely before seen a white man.

So here he was, perched upon the very brink of a great adventure with his servant Harry as companion — two dapper Englishmen in a group of eight rugged trappers who Harry had aptly remarked were, "of dubious descent."

Adrian half-turned and glanced at the group behind him. And that they were. The trappers were all hard men, hard men in a harsh land, a land that was more enemy than friend, a land capable of killing and swallowing up a man without a sigh or sound from the rest of the world. In the past weeks this was a land Adrian had come to respect, and maybe even fear. Yet he had wanted danger, craved excitement, anything that could erase from his mind — even for just a moment — all that he needed to forget. And it had succeeded.

Now his days were filled with schemes for survival, with new dangers always yawning just ahead of him. Only the night before he had listened with a prickly scalp and barely concealed shudder to the tales of men's throats slit and bleeding, of frozen bodies found in the mountains, blue and crusted over with ice so that they looked almost alive. It was only when they began to thaw that they resembled long-dead men. . . .

"Hey, *Duke!*"

Turning at the shout, Adrian grinned when he saw Broken Arm break away from the rest of the group and ride toward him. He could not have suppressed a grin at the sight of the rugged, fur-draped trapper who had befriended him. Even Broken Arm's off-hand, careless manner and the moniker of "Duke" that he had hung on Adrian could not detract from the trapper's congeniality. Broken Arm meant the name as a gesture of acceptance and friendship, something Adrian could not have afforded to overlook even if he'd wanted to do so.

Sweeping out one arm to indicate the valley below, Adrian said when Broken Arm rode close, "Quite a view from this mountain, isn't it?"

Broken Arm guffawed and slapped a meaty hand against his thigh with glee. *"Mountain?"* he echoed loudly. "Hell, Duke, this isn't a *mountain!* These are hills! The Rattlesnake Hills, to be precise! The mountains are still ahead of us."

Adrian knew his face revealed his incredulity, and his grin became sheepish. He glanced back at the jutting crags and sweep of sky that seemed as large as the universe, and shook his head.

"I say, then — I do hope you are about to inform me that we are stopping to rest for a day or two. I feel as if I have become bonded to my saddle, and it's deuced un-

105

pleasant at times!"

Chuckling, Broken Arm gave a brief tug to the edge of his furry hat, and Adrian could hear the muffled clank of wolf and bear teeth that were strung on leather strips around the old man's neck. His buckskin shirt was decorated with feathers and shells in places, but most had long since fallen off or broken. A bizarre hat covered the crown of his gray head, a hat that was made of part of an animal skin that had a long, dark-ringed tail, Adrian noticed. The fur tail fell over one of Broken Arm's shoulders like a braid, giving him an oddly lopsided appearance. The trapper's weathered face was stitched together with deep lines and creases, and his eyes were a soft, rich brown, eyes that were glittering with laughter.

"You should have slept last night, Duke," the old trapper was saying. "In the mountains, when a man can sleep, he doesn't waste time sitting and looking at the stars. Star-gazing is for poets and dreamers. A wise man closes his eyes at night. This is not merry ole England, my boy, and tonight we may get no sleep at all!"

The amusement threading Broken Arm's voice eliminated any irritation Adrian might have otherwise felt at his implied rebuke, and he nodded. After all, the old trapper was right, and it didn't really matter how many hours he had spent in an unaccustomed, hard saddle. Broken Arm knew well that Adrian and Harry were not seasoned hunters or trappers. What mattered was that he realized how important were the little things in the wilderness. Out here where few men had ever gone before, a man quickly learned to worry about only the things he could control. It was a waste of time to fret over a past decision. . . .

Forcing a smile to lips burned by the sun and chapped by the wind, Adrian said, "Then tell me something that has a ring of hope to it, Broken Arm! Such

106

as — we will soon be able to stop and rest for the night."

The old trapper grinned, then slowed his big chest-nut gelding to a pace matching Adrian's smaller mare and looked the younger man straight in the eye.

"See that steep hill up ahead of us?" he asked with a wave of one gnarled hand.

Adrian squinted in the direction he pointed, then shifted in his saddle and looked back at him. "How could I help it? I have been staring at those hills for the past hour. Those are the mountains you've been telling me about — "

Broken Arm snorted. "No mountains — hills. The mountains I told you about are even farther ahead. They are tall, and almost graze the sky in places, so that you feel as if you can reach up and touch the face of God." He smiled, a simple pure smile like that of a child, and added softly, almost reverently, "When you see them, there will be no mistaking them, Duke."

Slowing his mare, Adrian pushed his hat — a sensi-ble, flat-crowned fedora — to the back of his head. Without the shadow on his face, he looked his age, much younger than the men with which he traveled. His pale English skin was now windburned and toasted a light brown from the days in the sun. With his long blond hair curling down into the collar of his shirt, and his tanned face, he might have looked the part of a rugged trapper if not for his garb — Harry insisted that Adrian allow him to tie his cravat every morning in the height of fashion, and the young Englishman's impec-cably cut coat and trousers were of the finest cloth and fit. The gleaming Hessian boots still bore their tassels, and Harry still kept them highly polished so that one could see the reflection of the sky in the gleaming leather toes. This ritual elicited admiration from some of their group, amusement from some, and contempt from the rest.

107

Bracing a palm against his thigh, Adrian glanced ahead at the hills indicated by Broken Arm. He could discern no path up the apparently impenetrable slope.

"Have you been this way many times before?" he asked the old trapper.

Instead of answering, Broken Arm said, "Bessemer Bend is where the first white man built in this territory. It was Robert Stuart and some of his men who first settled there. Good men . . . some of them are gone now, dead or back East somewhere. Ahh, times are changing." Adrian glanced at him curiously, hearing a trace of something in the old man's voice that caught his attention. Before he could comment, Broken Arm continued in the same reflective tone, "Yes, I've been this way many times before, and I intend to make it one last time before some man or beast does me in, my boy." He sucked in his breath in a deep, mournful sound that reminded Adrian of a wild beast, and added, "It won't be too long before that happens. . . ."

Adrian would have protested, but the old trapper fended off his words with an upheld hand. "Ah, I've been on this old earth for many years, Duke. Good years. Years of good fortune." His dark eyes cut over to the younger man's troubled face. "I don't much mind dying. It happens to all of us sooner or later. Sometimes it's the living that's hard." Again that peculiar, primitive sound that usually preceeded one of his profound remarks, then Broken Arm said softly, "'Times have changed. I belong to the past.'"

In a way, maybe we all do," Adrian said, thinking of England and the life he'd left behind. He'd left England to escape the system in which he'd been trapped, the way of life his family followed, and had come to a new land full of hope. Yet here in America he had found nothing to make him feel as if he belonged. The land was strange and he was alien.

"No, not you," Broken Arm was saying. "You're young and strong, Duke. You didn't come here to hunt the beaver or dig for gold."

"Is that why you came, Broken Arm?" Adrian asked curiously. "For the beaver pelts and gold?"

Both men reined their mounts to a halt and eyed one another. "No more so than you," the old trapper said, and smiled.

Adrian smiled back at him. How well the trapper understood men and what made them search for the unknown. He knew that Adrian did not know what he was looking for or even why, and apparently, he had felt the same way at one time. Slanting the old fur-swathed trapper a curious glance again, Adrian wondered what lure had brought him to this wilderness, and why he felt the urge to return in his final days. Broken Arm had mentioned a place along the Wind River several times, and spoken longingly of a small tribe of Shoshoni Indians. This trapper was different from the other men who wandered the mountain peaks and forested ridges in search of the beaver, wolf and otter. Broken Arm was more educated, and Adrian had been astonished to hear the old man quote passages from Shakespeare at great length, as well as Chaucer and even Dante — it as an image at odds with the rough character he portrayed as cunning, tough old Broken Arm the all-wise trapper. But whatever or whoever he was, the trapper could deftly handle whatever trouble came along, even Ramone Jardin, the surly Frenchman in their group who could not look at Adrian or Harry without scowling fiercely.

Adrian nudged his mare alongside the trapper's gelding again as they rode back toward those waiting. "Tell me," he began conversationally, "if a man came out here for more than just pelts or gold, what would it be, Broken Arm? The open sky, maybe? Or the solitude? What lures men to this primitive wilderness?"

Shrugging his broad shoulders, the old trapper gave Adrian a quizzical glance that somehow inferred he should know without asking, but said nothing. They had reached the others who were waiting, and the Frenchman Ramone was glaring at Adrian with his customary scowl.

"Tout droit, monsieur!" Ramone snapped at Broken Arm with a thin veneer of civility that did nothing to conceal his dislike of the Englishman.

"Straight ahead," Broken Arm replied shortly, and his dark eyes narrowed.

The Frenchman nudged his mount into a trot on the rocky path leading almost straight up the side of a hill. The stocky, black-mustached trapper did not glance back at Broken Arm or the Englishman, but muttered to himself in French. A tight smile tugged at Adrian's lips as he heard Ramone call down a thousand Gallic curses upon the heads of all foolish English boys who pretended to be men.

Turning to Broken Arm, Adrian asked, "Does Ramone always ask you for directions?"

A wide smile slanted Broken Arm's mouth, revealing yellowed teeth stained with char lines and tobacco. "He has to" was the blunt answer. "He doesn't know the way."

"You are the only one who does?" Adrian asked in surprise.

Broken Arm's grin widened as he nodded. "You see, these men are new to this part of the country. They've never come this far before. Besides—they are fools searching for a future where none exists."

Baffled, Adrian shook his head. "I thought they were all trappers like you."

"Oho! Trappers yes, but not like me, my friend! These men have never been south of the Platte until

110

now. None of them have seen the Green Valley or gone to a rendezvous." His voice lowered so that the wind would not carry his words to the others. "They are a weaker kind of man, one who fears going higher and higher into the mountains to catch the beaver. They do not know or like the Indian, or even the land upon which they walk; they will not stay away too long from the safety of St. Louis!"

"Then we are alone—stranded—if something should happen to you," Adrian mused aloud.

"Yes, but you would go ahead without me."

A frown furrowed Adrian's brow. "Now I understand why Ramone is civil to you when it it obvious he does not wish to be, but what will happen after we reach the rendezvous and he no longer needs you?"

"Ah, then that is another matter, another day" was the cryptic reply.

Shifting in his saddle, Adrian let his gaze drift ahead to the burly Frenchman who had forged up the path. "I do not like the man," he murmured thoughtfully.

"And well you should not. He is mean, sly, but very clever," Broken Arm said.

"And he hates Harry and myself," Adrian returned with a glance toward his long-suffering servant. Harry was slumped in his saddle, his spotless bowler still atop his balding head and his shoulders drooping. Poor Harry. He had not enjoyed this journey, but he had refused to be left behind.

"You will watch Ramone, Duke," Broken Arm was saying. "He would like to kill you and maybe take your scalp. The French like to take scalps. They are the ones who taught the custom to the Indian, and I heard terrible things about Ramone while I was in Quebec."

"I assure you that I am watching him," Adrian replied. "I don't know much about scalps, but several times I have felt the shadow of cold steel on my back

111

and thought of Ramone."

"It would be done with his knife," the trapper confirmed. "You are right. The Frenchman carries a big one, the kind of blade that could easily carve your liver from your body before you realized you'd been cut."

Adrian's mouth twisted in a wry smile. "That's comforting information. I've seen it. I think he likes the notion that I have seen him use it, and he fantasizes about using it on me." Glumly, he added, "I saw him shave with it once. The blade is sharp as a razor. It was a terrifying sight."

"No more terrifying than the skinning of a rabbit," the trapper teased, then took pity on Adrian. "Do not look so alarmed, my boy. Not all men who come this way are mad."

"Present company included, I suppose?"

Broken Arm grinned. "Present company included. I come because I love the land and enjoy the hunt."

"But why do you stay?"

Tilting back his head, the old trapper surveyed the blue bowl of the sky and the eagles riding the air currents with outspread wings. His gaze drifted downward, to the tips of evergreen trees that rose like church spires against the horizon. Leaning forward again, his gaze moved to Adrian.

"I suppose it's the land that draws me," he said slowly. "In the end, it's the land that matters. It stretches to eternity, my boy, reaching forever. The Indians, now, they respect the land, even worship it. They live so close to it that they are an integral part of the land. Maybe that's the reason I like to live among them. Once I thought of returning to the white men to live among them . . . I was so foolish. The dirty, crowded cities where the air is dark and stale and factories belch up clouds of soot that crowd out the sky . . . no, my friend, that was not for me. I was wrong."

112

His dark eyes burned with the memory. "This land should be protected, respected. When the land goes . . . nothing remains."

Adrian was silent in the face of the trapper's fierce intensity. There was nothing he could say. He did not know enough about the land to make a judgement, but he did know enough about Broken Arm to respect his opinion. And the old man was right. Even in England with its cultivated fields and rolling green hills and the wild moors, he had felt that the land should not be defiled with factories or the ugly scars of copper mines.

Adrian's mare shied and he almost lost control as Broken Arm jerked sharply on his own mount's reins. The trapper's soft exclamation hissed through his teeth, and he punched his gelding into a gallop with his moccasin-clad heels.

"The damn fools are taking the wrong path!" Broken Arm snorted before he disappeared over the ridge just ahead of them. The dangling foxtail from his hat slapped against the thick-set trapper's back as he rode after those ahead, and Adrian grinned as he calmed his mare with a steady hand.

"I say, sir" came Harry's voice at his elbow, "is something amiss?" The servant rode close, managing to steer his recalcitrant animal near Adrian's mare.

"No, not really, Harry. It just seems that Jardin has taken the wrong path. Broken Arm will set him straight."

"I daresay. A pity he will not set Jardin straight on the wrong path while we take the other. Do you suppose it possible, my lord?"

"As much as I hate to dash your hopes—no," Adrian replied. His glance took in Harry's painfully flushed face and the bands of perspiration dotting his shirt and coat. In spite of the sun's rays, Harry refused to garb himself in more comfortable attire, insisting upon remaining in his customary coat, trousers, high-collared shirt and waistcoat. "Have you considered removing even your collar, Harry?" he asked kindly, and was rewarded by an expression of horror.

"Good heavens no, my lord! I would feel . . . undressed!" Harry exclaimed.

"Oh. Well, we couldn't have that," Adrian agreed.

After a moment of silent riding, Harry asked in a faintly plaintive tone, "Do you suppose we shall be stopping soon, my lord? Or does the French bandit insist we ride another twenty miles before pausing?"

A faint smile tugged at Adrian's mouth. The Frenchman's enmity toward Harry had resulted in Ramone's insistence they push on without rest, earning him a well-deserved dislike from the servant. The pace was an easy one for the seasoned trappers, but the two Englishmen were finding it difficult to keep up, especially the much older Harry.

"I don't know, Harry. Perhaps we shall," he answered after a moment. "We are past the halfway point, I believe, so it is quite likely."

Lifting his eyes to Adrian's, it was apparent that Harry had a pressing issue weighing on his mind. His eyes were troubled, and deep furrows were etched across his usually smooth forehead.

"I wonder," Harry began slowly, "what would happen if our redoubtable friend and guide were to be . . . fatally injured on his journey into no man's land, my lord. Do you have any notion of what would occur if such a dire circumstance were to come about?"

Adrian had to shake his head, but he tried to reassure his servant. "I am certain that the others know enough about the land to get us to safety, Harry."

"Oh, I am also certain of that, my lord," Harry returned, "but I am not so certain that one particular

114

Frenchman would feel kindly disposed to doing such a thing."

"Then we would do it ourselves," Adrian said firmly and confidently, earning a considering glance from his servant.

"Perhaps we would, my lord," Harry said after a moment's contemplation of Adrian's tanned face and self-assured posture. "Perhaps we would." His gaze turned back to those ahead of him, and he could not stifle a sudden groan. "Oh, my heavens! Must we climb that sheer precipice? I should much prefer going around it. . . ."

Adrian successfully suppressed a laugh at Harry's dismay. Harry always took matters so seriously, but there were times when Adrian couldn't help but wonder if the bland-faced servant was having a subtle jest at his employer's expense.

"Go around it?" Adrian echoed, surveying the folds of rock and impenetrable brush that bordered the relatively clear hillside ahead of them. "That would be rather difficult and time-consuming, but I suppose Broken Arm knows what is best. Have no fear, Harry—we have England's reputation to uphold!"

Harry's drooping shoulders straightened, and he gave Adrian a withering glance. "I should not dream of betraying my country with even the slightest hint of cowardice, my lord. However, I did not deem it cowardly to wish for a brief respite from our arduous journey—"

"Nor I," Adrian cut in with a grin. "I shamefully admit to pleading miserably for a rest, and Broken Arm has assured me that we shall soon do so." He felt no regret for boldly deceiving Harry, and was rewarded by the faint flicker of relief that crossed the servant's face before he nodded.

"I see. I gladly anticipate such an occurrence." A

115

taut smile curved Harry's lips as he added, "For your sake also, of course. You must be as weary as I, my lord."

"Probably more," Adrian conceded graciously.

"I think I shall ride ahead now, if it pleases you, sir. This fractious animal seems much more energetic than I am."

With that, Harry bounded ahead as his jug-headed mount took the bit between his teeth and leaped over a shallow cut in the path. The horses somehow sensed that forage and fresh water lay ahead, and they were eager. Adrian watched Harry's progress up the rocky ledge shelf that curled around the sloping hill, and he felt a soggy wash of affection for the older man. In his own way, Harry was a noble man, full of high ideals and a rigid code of what was proper and what wasn't. There were moments when Adrian felt an unaccustomed sense of responsibility for bringing Harry along on what could be an extremely dangerous journey. This land was savage and harsh, treacherous at times, just like life.

A cruel smile flickered on his mobile lips for a moment as he recalled England—and Nell. Hadn't she taught him how faithless and treacherous life could be? He briefly wondered where she was now, and if she and Richard were wed and producing the children the duke wished for. After all, it had been over a year since he'd departed England's green shores—quite adequate time to produce a child.

Wrenching his thoughts away from Nell, Adrian suddenly recalled Madame du Jessupe and the spread of paper cards on the drawing room table. A storm had raged outside the house, perhaps echoing the one inside. It had been a house divided within such a short time after that eerie night. . . . Could he ever forget?

They had crossed the hills that day. The rocks on the trail skittered from beneath the horses hooves as they climbed the slope, granite chunks often shooting over the edge of the narrow, winding trail. Sunlight beat on their heads during the day, finally fading to the soft rose of dusk, and to Adrian's immense relief, Broken Arm gave the order to halt and camp for the night.

Adrian stifled a moan as he dismounted, fully aware of every muscle in his entire body. They were easy enough to identify, he thought with a grimace, because they quivered and ached with excruciating intensity. A single glance at Harry confirmed that his suffering was just as acute, and Adrian spared a moment's envious admiration for the other trappers who apparently experienced no discomfort whatsoever.

Later, when the sun had gone down and a scant meal had been prepared and eaten, Adrian laid down in his bulky blankets and stared up at the vast ebony sky pressing down in thick folds. It was peppered with thousands and thousands of tiny twinkling lights, glittering icily above, so far yet seeming so near. He felt as if a gigantic blanket had been spread over him, surrounding him with an emptiness that was almost palpable. The universe was so large, and he was so small and insignificant, lost in the cosmos.

A smile pressed the corners of his mouth as Adrian reflected for a moment upon his formal education. *Cosmos,* a word derived from the Greek word *kosmeo,* means to "order" or "arrange." *Kosmos,* he had learned, meant "the world," or "the universe" because it is perfectly arranged. It *was* perfectly arranged, he thought, arranged in great, wheeling patterns of which he was an infinitesimal part.

God, how completely alone he suddenly felt, lost in the great empty bowl of the universe, a single, silent being whose cry in the wilderness would never be heard. . . . For the first time in his life, Adrian Herenton understood what it meant to be truly alone even in a crowd.

For weeks he had listened to Broken Arm's talk of the land and what it meant in the great plan of the universe, and now he understood. There would be no more land. This was it. This planet with its sun and moon and thousands of stars was the last frontier, and once it was gone there would be no more land to be had. Now he understood Broken Arm's attachment to the land, his fierce love for the wild crags and wide blue skies.

There was nothing, nothing but the solitude and the silence and the stars, and Adrian felt an inexorable pull toward them. What was happening? Where would it all end? This was such a savage, harsh land, and so much could happen.

"Duke?" a voice called from the shadows just beyond Adrian's blankets.

Jerking at the sound, Adrian sat up to see a formless face swimming in the dark, seemingly disembodied but quite familiar. His heart slowed its abrupt, rapid pace, and his breath began to come easier as he recognized Broken Arm.

"Are you all right, Duke?" the big trapper asked, and stepped into a shallow pool of light afforded by the moon.

Managing a weak grin, Adrian nodded. "Yes . . . yes. You just caught me asleep."

"Asleep?" Broken Arm frowned. "Not true, my friend. I have been watching you for an hour or more. You are afraid, perhaps. . . ."

"No."

"Yes. I think you are."

Adrian turned irritably away from the trapper's

knowing gaze and stared into the dark. Harry's blanket-wrapped form was close by, and he could hear the servant's deep, rasping breaths and muffled snores.

Hunkering down on his heels, Broken Arm said reflectively, "It's the land." Adrian turned back to stare at him as the trapper continued, "It was the same for me when I first came this far west."

"When was that?" Adrian asked.

"Many years ago. I paddled a canoe up the Platte, and hunted the beaver."

"You were recruited for one of the fur companies, then?"

"No. I came to . . . to leave my past behind, just as you do now," Broken Arm answered slowly. A shifting patch of moonlight lingered on his face, revealing the weathered map of creases and furrows that the years had etched upon its surface.

Stiffening, Adrian said, "What? You know nothing about me. Nothing!"

"I know enough. You and I are alike, Duke. I knew it when first I met you." He grinned in the dark, and the beams of moonlight reflected from his teeth. "Escape is a powerful reason to go anywhere, my friend."

"And what were you escaping from?"

Broken Arm shrugged. "A man escapes from many things. We are all prisoners of one thing or another . . . for me, it was the past, to escape from what I had become. For you, I think it is much the same thing. Only—it is more difficult for you. To lose yourself is hard. A man can leave his past behind if he goes far enough, long enough, but he can never leave himself behind."

Leaning back on his elbows, Adrian surveyed the old man silently for a moment. "Did you escape?" he finally asked.

"Ah, that remains to be seen," Broken Arm replied,

and Adrian grew even more perplexed. The younger man's mouth opened to ask another question, but the trapper was saying, "I shook for nearly three months on my first trip out here, shivered in my boots! I travelled in the company of another man who knew the land well, where I did not. We were good friends, and we parleyed with the Indians for beaver. No traps. We set none. The Indians would have killed us if we had, so we used trinkets and guns to buy the beaver from the Indians who trapped them. Pawnee, Arapaho, Shoshoni. . . ." He grinned, and Adrian could barely see the glitter in his eyes.

"I was afraid, Duke, and I thought of myself as a coward, a weak man. My friend—he was so brave, and the Indians feared him. He had many coups, you see. I wanted to be as him—"

"What is a coup?" Adrian asked then.

"A coup? It is a test of courage. Coup is a French word, and the Indians use it to denote the first touch or wound upon an enemy. The trick, you see, is to touch the enemy without killing or being killed, then ride away in triumph. That is a true test of bravery."

"I thought it was scalps," Adrian said.

Broken Arm shook his head, and the foxtail flapped beside his ear. "No. Not for most. One day I saw my friend face a Crow brave. This Crow warrior was dressed in fringed leggings and wore wolf tails on the heels of his moccasins, a mark of a great warrior. Ermine skins and a gun-snatcher decorated the front of his shirt. Oh, he was a fierce one, and I knew this Crow wanted more than just a coup. He wanted blood. I knew that it was important, for you will never hear of a Crow boasting about his scalps. Those are not important to him, as he would rather have a gun. When I saw the look on this warrior's face, I was afraid, for I knew that he wanted to kill my friend."

Broken Arm paused and shifted position slightly, certain of his audience's attention. The pause lengthened to just the right tension before Adrian demanded, "Well? What happened?"

"They went at each other with their knives, and the Crow fought savagely!" the trapper said with obvious relish. "Oh, it was a sight to behold, I can tell you that! But my friend, he fought well and bravely, and the Crow was vanquished, slain upon the bloody field. I thought all was well, and that my friend must be the most fearless man alive, but when he stood up over the slain warrior, he suddenly toppled to the ground."

"Dead?" Adrian asked incredulously.

"No. Fainted. Fainted dead away, my friend, as sure as I'm sitting here!"

"Fainted!"

"Yes. I had never seen a man faint before, and I could not believe my eyes. Later, my brave friend told me that he had counted many coup, made many enemies, but until that time he had never killed an enemy. And when he did—he fainted from the task!"

A chuckle rippled into the night, and Adrian could not help a smile at the trapper's obvious enjoyment of the tale.

"From then on," Broken Arm continued, "I was never ashamed of my own fear again. I've killed, and emptied my stomach from it. I've trembled with the thought of being alone for months and not hearing the sound of another man's voice. I've been afraid that I would die alone, and no one would ever know it or mark my passing. Then I look at this land and I know that it is only right that I am afraid. It is a mark of respect, as the land is awe-inspiring and powerful." He glanced at Adrian's rapt expression. "That is what you are feeling, my friend. The power of the land. It can make a man feel small and weak."

"Yes," Adrian murmured, "that is it. I look around me and I know that for miles and miles there is no one else, that I am alone except for my few companions."

"We are all essentially alone. It is the greatest lesson to be learned."

Silence enveloped them again as Broken Arm's voice faded, and Adrian once more stared up at the night sky. He relaxed, and the old trapper smiled.

"Go to sleep, Duke" came his gentle voice, "for tomorrow we ride hard again."

Chapter 9
The Fool

It was almost light when Adrian rolled over and opened his eyes. A quick glance around made him frown as he saw the empty blankets where the others had been. No fire had been lit, and as he sat up with an expression of confusion on his face, he saw his companions.

They were lying flat on their stomachs on the edge of a crest that jutted out over a dense thicket. There was a slope that dropped sharply down into a small basin, and it seemed to be this basin that had gained everyone's attention. Instinctively, Adrian knew not to call out. Instead, he grabbed for his loaded pistol and slithered over to the others on his belly, pulling himself along by his elbows. He peered through the thick blades of grass.

"What is it?" he whispered to Harry, who lay alongside Broken Arm.

Harry's glance was strained as he whispered back, "Savages, my lord. A dozen of them."

A cold knot formed in Adrian's throat as he scooted closer to the crest and parted the blades of grass edging the rocks. He could barely see through the lacy covering of tree limbs and grasses, but finally made out the forms of several Indians below in the basin. Some were lying prone, obviously bound, and some were towering over them with gleeful prances and noisy, triumphant whoops. Two of the figures on the ground appeared to be women, but it was difficult to tell from that great distance. Adrian edged closer to Broken Arm.

"What is happening?" he asked softly.

"Killing."

Stunned, Adrian felt a shiver ripple icily down his spine, and he tried to swallow the lump in his throat.

"But . . . who are they?" he managed to ask, and the trapper shrugged.

"I'm not sure. Pawnee, maybe."

"Non, je ne crois pas," Ramone shot back in a whisper. "Piegans . . . Blackfeet."

"What did he say, my lord?" Harry asked nervously.

"He said he didn't think they were Pawnee, but Piegan."

Broken Arm frowned, and mused aloud, "Hmm, I just did not think . . . they are too far down, perhaps lost . . . the Blackfeet do not like coming this far south. . . ."

"Piegan," Ramone insisted, and the old trapper looked at him quizzically.

"You are sure?"

"Oui!"

"But what are they doing?" Adrian asked then, still staring at the scene below.

"They are killing their captives, it appears," Broken Arm said slowly.

"Killing . . . but why?"

"I do not know. Perhaps they are of no use to them."

Adrian's fists bunched on the sharp edges of the grass, but he did not feel the tiny little cuts inflicted on his bare palms. "But . . . but some of them are women!"

Again, a shrug from the old trapper. "That means little to them. They will be killed."

"Can't we do something?" Adrian demanded in a

rising voice that gained him a harsh glance from the others.

Scowling, Ramone hissed, "English swine! Fool! They will kill us, too, if we try to stop them! I will not risk my life for an Indian's, woman or not!"

"He's right," Broken Arm said warningly when Adrian would have protested. "They will not stop just because we go down and ask them to do so. . . ."

A sudden, horrible scream sliced through the early morning mist, and Adrian's head jerked around. One of the Blackfeet warriors had taken his knife blade and slashed it across the throat of a captive. A gurgle sounded in the silence, and Adrian could see the gush of crimson blood before he turned away.

"Horrible!" Harry muttered hoarsely.

"True enough," Broken Arm said quietly, "but a way of life here."

"De quoi parlez-vous?" Ramone mocked with a sneer. "Indians—they kill other Indians all the time, English. You are weak and womanly!"

Cocking a brow at the Frenchman who was mocking him, Harry said, "I am not womanish. I am *civilized.*"

Ramone's answering snicker was cut short by a sharp movement from Broken Arm.

"Stop it," the trapper said softly. "We must leave quietly, so that the Blackfeet will not know we are here. We are only eight, while their number is an even dozen, and it appears that they have guns."

There was another scream, and Adrian could not keep from glancing back at the Blackfeet and their victims. One of the women had been struck, and while he stared in sick, fascinated horror, one of the male prisoners was killed and scalped. His stomach lurched, and he looked quickly away.

"The . . . the Indians who are being killed . . . who are they?"

125

"Crow," Ramone supplied, squinting down into the basin, and one of the Stanfill brothers disagreed.

"Naw, that girl ain't Crow," he said. "She's Shoshoni, if you'll notice her headband — Hey! Lookit her clothes! She's wearin' white man's clothes."

Craning his neck, Adrian could barely see the girl Chris Stanfill was discussing, but he caught a glimpse of a cotton skirt. He must be right, because the slender girl cringing away from one of the warriors was wearing a skirt and blouse.

"We can't let them kill her," Adrian said with sudden decision, "no matter who she is."

"Aw, they ain't likely to kill her," Stanfill replied. "She's young enough to have many braves. . . ."

Adrian's attention was diverted by a blur of movement as the girl under discussion broke away from the warrior who held her. A brutal fist slashed out, knocking her to the ground and stunning her.

Disregarding everything he'd been told, Adrian surged to his feet. All his instincts compelled him to come to the aid of a helpless female, but Ramone snatched a fistful of Adrian's shirt and yanked him back to the ground.

"Do not be a fool, English!" he grated. "Would you kill us all? Get down!"

Jerking away, Adrian rasped, "I do not intend to sit here and calmly watch while a young woman is murdered by a band of savages! If you are all too afraid to help, so be it. I intend to try and stop them. . . ."

Broken Arm's attempt to stop Adrian was futile, and so was the Frenchman's drawn knife. Harry, with a cool aplomb that surprised his employer, levelled a drawn pistol at Ramone Jardin and brusquely ordered him to sheath his knife.

"You wouldn't dare," Ramone muttered tightly. "The shot would alert the Blackfeet. . . ."

126

"Which is a circumstance that his lordship will soon bring about anyway," Harry put in coolly.

As Jardin hesitated and Broken Arm stared in amazement, the Indians in the basin finally became aware of the commotion above them. There were quick, excited shouts, and Adrian was the first to leap over the edge and slide down the slope with a drawn pistol.

Broken Arm gave a delighted laugh and catapulted to his feet and down the slope behind Adrian. Those left behind exchanged uneasy glances. The Stanfill brothers, Chris and Michael, shrugged and muttered that they might as well join the fight, while the other four men looked to Ramone Jardin for an answer.

Jardin scowled fiercely. "Perhaps the Blackfeet will kill the English for me," he said. *"Cela m'est egal . . ."* he added, then translated for the Stanfill brothers, "It is all right with me!"

"I say we fight," Chris Stanfill said stubbornly, and began loading his fifty caliber Hawken rifle with swift, efficient motions. Michael followed suit, and then Ramone capitulated and signalled to the others to go also.

By this time Adrian had reached the bottom of the basin and was met by a howling, painted warrior. They grappled, and Adrian caught a glimpse of the young woman who lay just at their feet. She was obviously stunned, yet was struggling to avoid being trampled in the fight as she inched away. Distracted by the sight of slim golden legs and thick mane of ebony hair framing an oval face of exquisite loveliness, Adrian almost lost his hold on the Blackfoot warrior. They twisted and turned as Adrian held desperately tight. A knife blade flashed, glinting in the soft sunlight filtering through the brush and trees, and he managed somehow to grip the sinewy arm that held it high.

Behind him Adrian could hear shouting and recognized Broken Arm's bellow, though he could not decipher any of his words. His concentration was now trained on the warrior who was inching the knife blade closer and closer to Adrian's body. There was no more time to think about the girl or wonder if he had made the right decision by impulsively leaping into the basin. There was only time to fight, to survive this grim encounter in a wooded glen.

Gunfire popped and roared. Men were screaming with pain and excitement, and Adrian still felt as if the world contained only himself and this black-eyed, painted bronze warrior who glared at him with such hatred. Adrian's muscles were taut and strained, and he flexed one knee to gain leverage against the taller man, then straightened his body with a swift snap, throwing the warrior off balance. With this slight advantage, he pressed forward, sending the enemy sprawling on his back with Adrian straddling him. The knife was still clutched in the warrior's fist, the deadly point only inches away from Adrian's cheek. He hesitated, never having killed a man in combat before, and wondered if he should allow the Indian to live.

But the warrior erased Adrian's hesitation. A quick jab with the knife and it dug into the Englishman's flesh, stinging and spurting blood, and Adrian reacted instinctively. He leaned his weight on the arm holding the knife, forcing it slowly down until it pressed home in the warrior's squirming body. Adrian held it there, panting with exertion and rage until there was no more struggle. The bronzed features were contorted in a death grimace, and Adrian stood, the knife now in his own hand.

Harry came to his side and wordlessly handed Adrian the pistol he had dropped in the struggle with the warrior.

"You're hurt, my lord," he said anxiously, and

128

reached up to touch the streaming slash on Adrian's cheek.

Jerking away from his touch, Adrian shook his head. "No, I am all right, Harry. It is only a scratch." His glance lifted to Harry's face, and he managed a smile.

"May I say, sir, that you were perfectly splendid!" Harry approved, and Adrian's glance moved around the small basin.

He realized with a vague sense of amazement that the fight was already over, and that the trappers were now in possession of the battlefield. Slain Blackfeet lay sprawled in the grotesque postures of death, as well as the unfortunate captives they had not been able to save.

"We lost no lives," Harry was saying, "but Michael Stanfill was wounded by a gunshot in one arm. It is not serious, however. The other Indians seem to have fled the area, so I suppose that we are the definite victors, my lord."

"So it would seem," Adrian murmured, and suddenly recalled the girl. He turned and noticed Ramone Jardin straightening from a body and lifting a bloody scalp high in a gesture of triumph. "Does he have to do that?" Adrian demanded with an expression of revulsion on his face. He started forward, but Broken Arm blocked his way.

"There's nothing wrong with the taking of a scalp out here, Duke," the trapper said firmly, and Adrian paused.

"But we are supposed to be civilized men," he said, and his nostrils were flaring wide with anger. Broken Arm's hand was heavy on his arm, but the trapper was staring at Adrian with a new respect.

"It's the way of the land," he said then.

Adrian would have argued the point further; but a

sudden soft cry interrupted him, and he pivoted to see that the Frenchman had turned his attention to a new target — the girl. Wrenching away from the old trapper, Adrian strode forward just as Ramone reached the supine form cowering on the ground.

When the girl threw back her head and faced the burly Frenchman, Jardin shouted, *"Ellie a les yeux bleus!"* He was grinning, and his dark eyes glittered as he bent to grab the girl.

Rising painfully to her feet and ducking beneath his outstretched arm, the Indian girl threw herself against Adrian's chest, surprising both of them as his arms instinctively closed protectively around her. He looked down into her pleading face and felt his throat tighten. Ramone was quite right — this girl was obviously part white, and had the most beautiful deep blue eyes he had ever seen. She was young — very young — and had the smooth, unlined skin of a girl perhaps just out of puberty, though the hard, firm breasts pressed against him definitely indicated a certain maturity. Adrian was shocked at his body's reaction to the frightened woman/child he held in his arms. Passion, something he thought he had forgotten how to feel, stirred within him, its spark startling him so he felt time had stopped, and he wondered briefly if she, tattered and frightened as she was, felt it, too. But the odd reverie was shattered by the sound of Ramone's voice sputtering with frustrated rage. He reached out brusquely for the girl, but was stopped cold by the icy stare he saw when Adrian lifted his head and looked him straight in the eye.

"Do not touch her," the Englishman said, and Jardin paused.

"Who is going to stop me?" he blustered, but his dark eyes narrowed in defeat at the strange look he saw on Adrian's face. His glance flitted to the pistol held in one hand and the knife in the other, and he backed away a step. "What do you want with a squaw, Englishman?" he asked in a reasonable tone. "She would only be a burden to you, while me — I have others to help me care for her. He indicated with a sweep of one arm the four men who were his constant, silent companions.

When Adrian paused to consider his next reply, the girl obviously thought he meant to relinquish her, for she burst out frantically, *"Non! Non, monsieur! S'il vous plait . . ."* as her small fingers tightly gripped the lapel of Adrian's coat.

"Voila!" Jardin said quickly. "See? She is French, like me, so should come with a countryman. . . ."

"She is also obviously Indian, and should perhaps go back to her own people," Adrian cut in coldly. He gently disentangled the girl's fingers from his coat, but allowed her to continue to huddle protectively beneath his arm.

Broken Arm stood silently to one side, and he spoke now for the first time since the girl had flung herself at Adrian.

"Why don't you let the girl choose?" he asked calmly. "Jardin, if you would quit blustering and scaring her, she might just decide to go with you. And you, Duke, why don't you let her go and stand on her own two feet?"

Somewhat reluctantly, Adrian pushed the girl slightly away from him so that she stood at arm's length. She shook her head, tossing back sable waves that curled to her slim waist, and fastened huge blue eyes on Adrian's face. He gazed at her for a long moment, feeling once again the stirring of passion that he thought long dead, as he took in her slender curves, smooth bare feet and strong legs. She wore a tattered long cotton skirt that reached to just above her ankles, and her loose blouse was almost torn from around her

131

slender frame, revealing far too much of her youthful bosom than could ever be considered proper. Much to Adrian's discomfort, he felt his gaze linger too long on the fabric pulled tightly over her breasts; thinking how if he were younger he might blush and be enslaved by the thoughts this half-white/half-Indian female aroused in him. Her features were not the flat features of the few Indians he had seen, but were sharply defined, with high cheekbones and huge, wide-spaced eyes framed by thick, curling lashes, eyes of such a deep blue it was as if pieces of the sky had been captured in her gaze.

"Parlez vous anglais, mademoiselle?" Adrian asked after a moment, pulling himself out of his reverie. He should know better he told himself, after Nell. She did not answer him.

Her heart was beating rapidly, like the wings of a hawk trapped in a net, and her throat dry from fright and thirst. Yet she could appreciate the tall, fair man who stood before her and spoke quietly. He was the most handsome white man she had ever seen, unlike her swarthy father and the Frenchmen she had known. This man had hair as pale as the moonlight, with sun-kissed skin many shades lighter than her own. Clear gray eyes like quiet mountain pools held no hatred or contempt in them when they gazed at her, only an aloofness and confusion that she didn't understand yet but knew was not life threatening. Blue Feather knew that the gods had answered her prayers and petitions at last. The last few months of tribulation, of being traded from tribe to tribe then captured by the Piegan, had been a time of seasoning so that the gods would know if she was worthy of saving. Maybe this fair-haired man who seemed gentle in a way she just knew was different from anything she had experienced before could take her back to her father in the mountains.

132

"My name is Adrian," her deliverer was saying in English, "and yours?" He pointed to his chest and repeated his name, then pointed to her.

Transfixed by her good fortune when she had thought she was about to join her ancestors at the cruel hands of the Piegans, she stood staring at him for another moment.

"See?" Ramone sneered. "She knows no English! She is French—"

Flinging him a defiant glance, the girl said angrily, curtly, "I speak French and a little English. . . ." Her English was perfect, and only faintly accented.

Relaxing slightly, Adrian half-smiled at her. Even in anger, her voice was as melodic and lovely as she was, and somehow—he wasn't quite certain why—whe reminded him in some small way of Josette du Jessupe.

"What is your name?" he asked her, then pointed to his servant. "That is Harry, and this gentleman garbed in fox fur and wolf pelt is Broken Arm."

Proudly, she said, "My name is Blue Feather," then looked expectantly at the others.

One by one the men introduced themselves, some amused, and others annoyed by the entire affair. Females meant trouble, and one female—especially a pretty one alone with eight men—could mean disaster. Even Broken Arm was gazing at the girl doubtfully and uneasily, and Adrian could sense his thoughts.

"Are you Shoshoni? Where are your people?" the old trapper asked her finally. His breath wheezed in faint imitation of a wild animal again, but he was staring at her seriously as she nodded.

"Yes, I am Shoshoni, but I have not seen my people in some time."

Frowning, Adrian asked, "How did you become separated from them?"

Delicate eyebrows lifted in faint surprise at the

strange question. It should be obvious, but perhaps he did not know that such things were common occurrences. "The Crow came and killed all those in our hunting party some moons ago. I was . . . apart . . . and they took me with them."

"Then how did the Blackfeet get you?" Adrian pursued, and Blue Feather's brow furrowed.

"The Blackfeet fell upon us, and I was taken," she explained patiently. It was apparent that this trapper did not know the land well.

Snorting, Jardin interrupted rudely, "Well, enough of this! I will take her with me now, since we do not have the time to stand and talk. . . ."

Adrian's narrowed glance stopped him, and the Frenchman turned persuasively to Broken Arm for interference.

"What should we do with her, then? Take her? Leave her? I say she should go with me. She is part French, and it should be a Frenchman who warms her pallet on cold nights."

Broken Arm shook his head and reached out for the girl. She resisted him at first, but, at an encouraging word from Adrian, allowed the old trapper to draw her to his side.

"I am certain that this is an unnecessary waste of time, but I intend to allow the girl to choose. There will be no argument later. The decision will stand, and she will not be allowed to change her mind." He paused and slanted the girl a half-smile. It was plain that she had already chosen, but he would go through the motions.

Ramone Jardin forced a smile to his thick lips, and ran a meaty hand through his uncombed, greasy hair.

"I would be nice to you, cherie," he said in French, "and I could protect you better than this beardless English boy who pretends to be a man."

Adrian said nothing, but merely waited. After Nell, did he really want this girl? But in his heart he knew the die was cast — it was too late. Blue Feather cautiously avoided the lecherous Jardin, her blue eyes flashing with a weary hatred before stepping forward to stand at the fair man's side.

"I choose," she said softly, and Broken Arm nodded.

"It is done," the trapper said. "Let's be on our way before the Blackfeet return with more warriors. I've no desire to be caught in this basin like we caught them." He sliced Adrian a hard gaze, then added, "She is your responsibility, Duke. You will provide for her, and protect her."

Glancing down at the girl, Adrian asked, *"Ou vos parents demeurent-ils?"*

"I have only my father," she answered in stilted English. "I wish to be taken to him."

Glowering, Ramone Jardin snarled, "We do not have time to take *un petit fille* to some faraway place if we are to be at the rendezvous in time! She can find her papa by herself. Or, perhaps the brave Englishman can take her by himself!" he added with a bitter laugh. "We have a ways to go before we reach the Green River."

"Green River?" Blue Feather echoed excitedly. "I know the Green River. It is not far from my home, from my people!"

"Then you are from Wind River?" Broken Arm asked, and she nodded.

"I know your people. That is my destination," Broken Arm said reflectively. "I have a good friend among them."

"A white man?"

The trapper's eyes narrowed on her piquant face, and he studied it closely for a moment, then smiled. "Yes. Pierre Duvall, whom I have not seen for many years, but who has piercing blue eyes —"

"My father!" Blue Feather cried delightedly.

Expelling a long breath, Broken Arm murmured, "Little Margarethe Duvall . . . and to think I almost let the daughter of my old friend die at the hands of the Blackfeet. Where is your father now?" he looked up and asked her.

"You know her?" Adrian was asking incredulously, and frowned at a teasing memory. Pierre Duvall . . . a common enough name among the French and Canadians — why did it sound so familiar?

But then the trapper was grinning and saying, "Yes, or I knew her as a small child. Her mother was the daughter of a great Shoshoni chief and a white captive, and Blue Feather has a brother who is probably the chief now. . . ."

But Blue Feather was shaking her head sadly. "No," she whispered, "my grandfather is still alive, but my brother is dead. He died during the raid by the Crow who took me away many moons ago."

"And your mother?" Broken Arm asked.

She made a waving movement with one hand and said, "Gone also."

"And my old friend Pierre?"

"Gone into the mountains. No one knows just where, for he hides his secret place well."

This last snared Ramone's attention, and he stepped closer to them, but they fell silent. It was only after the burly Frenchman had walked away that Blue Feather turned back to Adrian and smiled.

"Are you like the others?" she asked softly, almost to herself, too tired to guard her thoughts, hoping she chose wisely.

"Am I?" he raised one eyebrow. She looked at him quizzically, her head tilted and her hair rippled in gleaming waves that made him want to reach out and touch it. It curled softly, temptingly, not like the coarse hair of the Indians he had seen, who kept it well-oiled and rarely washed.

"No," she was saying, sleepily, and her head lowered slightly.

Adrian stared down at her, noticing once again how much of her was exposed by the torn blouse, the creamy swells of breasts barely hidden by the material. Passion aroused, but this time it was mixed with a tenderness for the woman/child who had undergone so much. He could see the baby-fineness of her cheek where it curved down into her small, firm chin, and the long sweep of eyelashes that shadowed apricot-tinged skin. And because he was thinking of her as such a young girl, he was doubly stunned by her next words.

Peeping up at him, she said in a voice that surprised him with its strength. "I chose you but I am not your woman, A-dri-an. I am part white and know the white man's ways are not the same as the people."

"My woman?" he almost gasped. "Believe me . . . you are not my woman! Have no fear on that score."

She flinched slightly. She had wished only to protect herself, not be rejected so openly. Recounting, she said quickly, "Did you wish me to go with the old man? My father's friend?" She mocked him now and he knew it.

"No! No . . . I didn't mean anything of the kind! It . . . It's just that . . . that . . . well, I'm certain I don't know what it is you are saying!" Adrian finished helplessly, caught up in the spell of her stunning blue eyes and shinning hair.

It was Harry who eventually rescued Adrian from his racing emotions as he floundered beneath Blue Feather's steady regard and Broken Arm's amusement.

"My lord, if I may be of assistance, I shall be happy to help the . . . the young lady. She obviously needs clean and mended garments, and I can be of use there."

Relief flooded Adrian's face as he backed away from

Blue Feather. "Yes! Yes, Harry, that is wonderful. Perfect. Thank you."

"You wish me to go with him?" she asked with a frown, and Harry made a shocked sound as he recoiled from her.

Adrian moaned. "No, no, you misunderstand! You are your own woman. You belong to no one."

The frown lines deepened in her smooth forehead and then relaxed. "Good," she said, "then we understand each other." But a part of her tired body and soul knew that with time this could change, and he would want to possess her. They always did.

"You will be cared for," he assured her. "Do not misunderstand—you will be cared for until we return you to your father. I promise you I will do that, but you will . . . will sleep alone in your blankets. Now do you understand?"

Pleased by this answer, Blue Feather nodded. *"Oui. Merci."*

Her step was light and her smile joyous as she walked between Adrian and Harry to their camp, and she ignored the Frenchman's scowl as they passed him.

Standing in the basin, he watched as they climbed the slope. "Fools," he muttered darkly. The girl was slender and pretty, and it had been a long time since he'd had a woman; but there was a glint in the fair Englishman's eyes that boded ill for any who tried to take her. Ah well, there was time enough for anything to happen along the trail. . . .

Chapter 10
The Pope

"Ou estes-vous ne?" Blue Feather asked softly as he knelt close to the campfire. A pot of thick, strong coffee bubbled merrily, its aroma filling the early morning air, and Adrian paused as he reached for it. His glance went directly to the girl's face. It was still flushed with sleep, and her eyes were bright and sparkling. A smile touched his lips.

"I am from far away," he answered as he lifted the pot and poured a stream of hot coffee into his tin cup. "It is very far away from here." The coffee pot clattered against the hot stones as he set it back on the fire, and Adrian peered at the girl over the rim of his cup. She was watching him so closely, so intently, with an expression of grave interest on her face as if nothing else mattered in this world but his answer.

Plopping down on the ground, she regarded him for a moment and thought again that this man must be the most handsome she had ever seen. He seemed so serious for a white man of so obviously different a background. How would he ever survive out here in the wilderness, and how could he be so smug to think he could protect and care for her? She might as well be with an injured brave. Did he know what she was thinking? The Blackfeet could smell blood, and together they'd be a fine target. Blue Feather hugged her knees and rested her chin atop them.

"How far? Is it near . . . St. Louis?" she asked.

"You have heard of St. Louis from your father?"

She nodded. "And others. Trappers like to talk." She added with disdain, "And drink. And trap. You are from St. Louis, then?" she probed.

Shaking his head, Adrian said, "No, I came from much farther away than that. A great distance, Blue Feather, across the great water. I came from a land known as England."

"England?" Blue Feather rolled the word on her tongue slowly, trying to recall if her papa had ever mentioned such a place. "Across the great water—then it is near France?" she asked. "My papa lived in France long ago."

Smiling, Adrian said, "Yes, England is close to France. Perhaps like the Green River is close to the mountains where your grandfather lives."

"And you will go back to this place called England?" Blue Feather asked. It would be a good thing for him to plan to leave the wilderness before it ate him up. Her gaze rested on his face, on the features she could still see even when her eyes were closed. Despite her caution, she was drawn to this man, and this surprised her. So when she saw the faint flicker of a shadow darken his gray eyes, she was concerned. Had he read her distrust of him, her fear that he was incapable of surviving out here? That she felt herself more equipped for survival than he?

Then Adrian was shaking his head, and his voice was low and soft as he said, "I don't know if I will ever go back." Blue Feather's reaction startled him, dispelling his momentary melancholy.

"Good!" she resolved. "You can stay with my people." If they made it there, he would be safe. *If* they made it, that is. "My grandfather will surely reward you for bringing me back to him."

"No, I don't want a reward," Adrian said so quickly that the girl's head jerked up and her smile faded, fearful that he might have decided against returning her after all.

"I have offended you?" Blue Feather asked with a little catch in her voice, suddenly sad at the thought that gentleness and strength seemed to not exist at the same time in a man. Sad that maybe she would see him die before the end of their journey. Her eyes were huge, liquid pools, startling in her dusky face.

"No, no," Adrian assured her. "It is just that I need no reward for taking you safely to your grandfather, Blue Feather. My reward would be seeing you returned to him. I need nothing else."

Relief flooded her strained features, and Blue Feather nodded again. With an abrupt change of subject, she strayed to safer ground, asking, "Do you hunt the beaver?"

"No," Adrian said again, shaking his head and sipping at his coffee. "I do not hunt the beaver."

Puzzled, Blue Feather tilted her head and gazed at him as she tried to think of a proper reason for this man's presence in her country. All the white men she had met had hunted the beaver, all but one, she recalled suddenly. But that man had been more spirit than mortal. He had ridden with the wind and disappeared into the forests without a trace. No one had dared search for him, as the young men of her people had considered him crazy. Blue Feather could remember that her father had called him Cheney, but no one else dared say his name. He was thought to have an evil spirit, and of course, now that he was thought to be dead, his name could not be spoken. No one ever said the names of the dead, but left their names to rest with them.

Blue Feather regarded the lean man who sat cross-legged by the fire. "Then, why do you go to the rendezvous, if not for the pelts?" she asked.

Rising in a smooth, fluid motion, Adrian flung the dregs of his coffee into the fire and watched as it hissed against the hot stones. A slight smile pressed against the corners of his mouth, and Blue Feather noticed that he had once more scraped away the fair bristles of a beard from his smooth jaw.

"For adventure," he answered her, and put out his hand to help her rise.

"And that is all?" Blue Feather countered as she took his hand and stood beside him. The top of her head reached only to his shoulder, and he put one hand atop her hair to ruffle it gently.

"Why do you ask so many questions?" he teased, but his eyes were not angry. They were slanted in laughter at her, and she smiled cautiously.

"You will keep me with you at the rendezvous?" she asked then, and could tell that her question made him uneasy. "I would be no trouble," she added quickly. "I would sew for you, and cook for you, help you, teach you about the land. . . ." She stopped, worried that he might imply she would give herself to him and had been about to reiterate yesterday's discussion about warming his blankets, but recalled this man did not exhibit any interest in her in that way. Maybe that surprised her more than she liked to admit. So she finished, "You are a stranger here."

Adrian cupped her chin in his palm and stared down at her. "Are you afraid to go to the rendezvous, Blue Feather?"

Biting her lower lip, she nodded once, then said, "You may call me Margarethe if you like. My father does."

His hand dropped away, and his eyelashes, which

were long and curly, lowered over his pale eyes. "I like the name Blue Feather, too. It is a very pretty name."

Blue Feather was stunned by this. Few white men liked Indian names, more often preferring their own names. Even her own father preferred Margarethe to the more lyrical Shoshoni name of Blue Feather.

Before she could tell him that she too preferred being called Blue Feather, and then impulsively add that she felt, despite everything, safer when near him, she was distracted by the arrival of the man called Harry.

"My lord, the horses are now ready. Everything is packed, and I believe that Mr. Broken Arm is preparing to mount. Is there anything else you require before we go?"

Blue Feather glanced curiously from Adrian to the man who so obviously admired him. She very much liked Harry. He had shared his garments with her quite willingly, giving her the shirt she now wore to replace her torn one. He had chatted amiably with her the night before, and made her feel welcome even though she had sensed how awkward he too felt about the whole situation. Though perhaps she should be used to it, having spent much of the last year being shuffled about from captor to captor, none of them quite knowing what to do with her yet unwilling to kill her.

"Coming, Duke?" Broken Arm asked as he rode close to them, breaking into her reverie. "That damned Frenchman's straining at the bit. He's surly as a sore-tailed grizzly this morning, and wants to leave early." The trapper grinned. "I don't think he likes being bested, Duke."

"I daresay," Adrian answered, and reached for the black fedora Harry was handing him. "One must suffer grave disappointments at times, it seems."

"I daresay," Broken Arm mocked with an even wider grin. "Well, tally-ho, Englishman!" Nudging his geld-

143

ing, the trapper trotted away through the brush.

"I shall assist the young lady, sir," Harry was saying, "while you mount. And I will see that this fire is put out and the utensils gathered."

Adrian seemed to accept this as normal and simply nodded his fair head. "Very well, Harry. But I refuse to leave until you have finished, so do make haste."

Blue Feather listened to this exchange with growing concern. If Harry took care of Adrian so well, what would there be left for her to do? How could she make herself useful—no—indispensable to him, thus assuring his continued cooperation? It was a problem that nagged her during the rest of the day, even while suffering heat and thirst and off-putting glares of Ramone Jardin.

Camp was made early that night, and Adrian was relieved to be able to dismount once again. Perhaps it would grow easier as time passed, but he had been riding hard and steadily since joining Broken Arm's group, and had yet to become accustomed to it. Oddly enough, the day's ride had somehow been made easier by the company of the slender, bare-legged girl who had ridden behind him on his mare. As they climbed a steep incline, Blue Feather's arms around his middle and her small body pressed close to his back had been a constant reminder of her presence.

Adrian glanced over at her. He had spent a restless night dreaming about Blue Feather, haunted in his sleep by images of her long hair—which had been full of snarls and tangles—blowing in the wind. He felt the pressure of her arms around him as they rode, holding him tight and touching him in a way that made him sure she wanted him; it was driving him wild with desire. But when he turned to try and steal a kiss, her face was Nell's. Now in daylight, her hair was brushed to a glowing skein of silk that flowed down her back like a ribbon. She was animatedly telling Harry how she preferred to leave it free and wild to let the wind tangle it, and he was shaking his head in dismay.

"No, no, that is defeating my purpose," Harry was saying with a groan. "You must use it, and if it becomes broken, why we shall get you a new one!"

"You have many of these?" Blue Feather asked dubiously, glancing at the hairbrush.

"No, but I am certain — oh, that is right. I suppose one cannot just pop off to a shop to buy a new brush, can one?" A wry smile stretched his lips, and he shook his head and sighed. "Quite vexing, quite."

Adrian was amazed by the exchange, and he shook his head and removed his fedora. It did little to keep the sun from his face, and he had thought more than once about getting a new hat. Perhaps one like Broken Arm's would be a bit too much, but a wide-brimmed affair like the one worn by Michael Stanfill would do nicely. There should be many different styles of hat at the rendezvous according to the old trapper's account, and he should be able to select a proper one for himself.

Glancing down, Adrian frowned slightly at the dust and dirt marring his once-clean trousers. Though Harry washed them at every opportunity, his garments were in sad disrepair, a state that did not bother Adrian nearly as much as it did poor Harry. The servant never paused to consider that no one really cared about appearance in this wild land, but cared much more about survival. It was Harry's task to see to Adrian's garments and needs, and that he would do, regardless of time or place.

Since Blue Feather's arrival in their camp, however, the servant had been challenged in what he considered his God-given right to care for Lord Adrian Herenton. The girl, who Harry felt could not be more than fifteen or sixteen at the most, obviously felt indebted to Adrian for his rescue of her. Perhaps he should not have painted the details of Lord Adrian's role in her emancipation quite so *glowingly*, Harry thought as the girl ruffled his patience with her determined efforts to assist Adrian.

"But I will help you cook his meal," she said to Harry when he had a campfire going and was rummaging through a pack for dried beans. "I am a good cook." As Harry—ignoring her—pulled out a small packet of beans and opened them, Blue Feather gave him a scornful glance. "That is not good! There are fresh things all around us, and I shall gather them for a delicious meal. . . ."

Harry never had a chance to utter a sound before Blue Feather leaped to her feet and scampered into the thick brush around them. Using her skirt as a basket, she picked several new stalks of *yampa*, wild carrots, some wild onions and grass seed, serviceberries, wild turnips, and chokeberries. When she arrived back at the camp, she set them aside and filled a huge kettle with fresh water from a nearby spring. Harry was disgruntled as the slim maid cheerfully chopped up the vegetables and pounded the grass seed and berries into a powder, but he grudgingly offered a freshly killed rabbit for the pot. The powdered grass seed and berries were mixed with water into some form of paste, then kneaded vigorously and patted into round balls, flattened and placed between two huge wet leaves, then shoved into the coals of the fire.

Sitting back with a smile of satisfaction, Blue Feather said, "Soon we eat!"

"Well, I must say, it certainly smells delicious," Harry admitted.

Coming to stand beside them and stare down at Blue Feather with amusement, Broken Arm said, "It will be delicious. I have eaten Shoshoni stew and bread before, and it suited me well." Then, pointing to Blue Feather's feet, he observed, "Your feet are bare. Have you been wearing Blackfeet, Crow or Shoshoni moccasins?"

Scathingly, she said, "No Blackfoot would make moccasins for my feet! I have moccasins from The People—Shoshoni—but they are not mine. I took them from another captive who had no more use for them."

Nodding sagely, Broken Arm commented, "Dead, huh. Well, I don't blame you. The living must go on. How many moons has it been since you left The People?"

Reflecting for a moment, Blue Feather wondered how time had passed so quickly and unremarked. She had just lived from sun to sun, not worrying about the day before and thinking only of the present. The future had not existed for her, and the past was a painful memory. There was only one burning ember inside that urged her to think of escape, and that had been the knowledge that her papa was somewhere in the mountains, perhaps searching for her. That she had allowed herself to recall at times, late at night when she was lying on her sleeping couch and listening to the bellow of frogs and the call of nightbirds, or the howling of the wind during the season of Deep Snows.

Finally, holding up both hands then closing them and showing two fingers she said, "Seven moons have passed . . . or maybe eight."

Hunkered down by the fire, Adrian stared at the slim girl in disbelief. She was so young to have been taken from her home! And to have lived with the cruel Blackfeet for so long!

147

"You have been with the Blackfeet that long and not suffered?" he asked in amazement, but she was shaking her head.

"No. The Blackfeet came less than a moon ago. They took me from the Crow, along with the others. I have lived with the Crow a long time."

It was quiet for a moment, with sounds from the others in camp filtering over to where Adrian and Harry had thrown their blankets several yards away. Broken Arm's breath wheezed loudly, and he picked at his yellowed teeth with a long twig. Blue Feather watched him intently, sensing he was about to ask more questions about her.

"You had a Crow husband, perhaps?" Broken Arm inquired. "Or children?"

"Husband!" Adrian expostulated. "Children! Why, she is no more than a child herself, Broken Arm! Look at her!"

Sharply, the old trapper said, "I *am* looking at her, Duke, and you should, too! She may be young, but she is not a child. Indian women marry and bear children young, when our girls are still in short petticoats and playing with dolls. It's a fact of life out here, and one you might remember before it leads to real trouble."

Sensing Adrian's shock and disapproval, Blue Feather shifted uneasily, looking from man to man.

Turning back to her, Broken Arm said, "Your people must think you gone forever."

She nodded, her eyes still lingering on Adrian's tight-lipped face. "*Ai*, I am sure of it. My grandfather was ill when I was taken. He will think me dead or the wife of a Crow warrior."

"And were you?" Broken Arm probed gently.

"*Ai*," she said again, this time with a trace of sadness. "The brave who took me from my home became my husband. He died when the Blackfeet came."

148

"No children?" Broken Arm asked while Adrian let out his breath in a slow rush of air.

Blue Feather's gaze fell to her hands, which were twisting the material of her ragged cotton skirt in agitation. Her answer, when it came, was so low all three men had to lean closer to hear.

"There was little time. He was away on the hunt, and when he came back, the Blackfeet came. He had two other wives."

Irritation washed over Adrian, and he said roughly, "I do not think we should be asking her these questions. It's not proper. She's just a child." He annoyed himself because he did not want to think about her with another man, especially a young Indian. While he pondered his strange reaction, Blue Feather gazed at him in faint confusion, the old trapper shaking his head and saying, "You know nothing about Indians, Duke, or the life out here. A woman is meant to have sons. The tribe must have them as warriors and hunters."

Broken Arm's brows lifted in amusement. The grass blade wiggled in his mouth as he chewed on it and stared at the suddenly hot-headed young Englishman. Blue Feather stared at him, too. Even Harry, who thought his lordship was rarely in the wrong, gazed at his employer with a measure of surprise.

Turning back to the girl, Broken Arm asked her a question in rapid Shoshoni, using his hands for many of the words in a crude, but effective manner. She answered just as rapidly, with no embarrassment. Matters of nature were treated casually, as matter-of-fact as a discussion of the weather. The old trapper was grinning when he turned back to Adrian.

"Her husband was young, strong and lusty, Duke," he began, and Adrian surged angrily to his feet.

"This entire conversation is ludicrous!"

149

Blue Feather quickly interrupted Broken Arm's next reply by standing and saying softly, "Thank you, A-dri-an." Her blue eyes sparkled with the reflection of the fire.

Adrian's anger faded, and he took a deep, steadying breath. Broken Arm was right. This was a new land, and people he did not understand. Their customs baffled him at times — harsh, seemingly cruel rituals that appalled him. He had thought at first that the old trapper was only trying to shock or frighten him, but now he sensed that all the tales he had been told of an evening must be true. A rueful smile curved his lips.

"You are welcome, Blue Feather," Adrian said. "And I look forward to your cooking this evening," he added politely. "Harry's last effort tasted remarkably similar to an old moccasin — " Struck by the memory of Broken Arm's unusual question he paused. "Why did you want to know the origin of her footwear?" he asked then, turning to the fur-draped trapper still crouched by the fire. "Is there some custom that decrees what she shall wear while a captive?"

Chuckling at Adrian's ignorance, Broken Arm shook his grizzled head and the foxtail slapped against his cheek. "No, no, Duke! There are moccasin prints close to Ramone's campfire, faint but recognizable. I only wanted to see if our little 'captive' here had made them."

Disliking the reference to Blue Feather as still a captive, Adrian scowled but said nothing.

"I wondered," Broken Arm was continuing as if he did not notice Adrian's scowl, "if they were made by Blue Feather when she dismounted from your horse, as there were also hoofprints. Most of the prints had been rubbed out, but there were a few left, enough to know that they had been made by Blackfeet moccasins. . . ."

"And however are you able to deduce that?" Harry

150

asked in surprise. "Do the Blackfeet carve their initials in the leather sole or some such thing?"

"No, the moccasin was shaped to fit the left foot. The Shoshoni and Crow make moccasins that will fit either foot, but the Blackfeet have left and right, see?"

"Oh. Yes, I see," Harry said thoughtfully, and looked around as if expecting to see a raging horde of Blackfeet warriors emerge from the brush around them at any moment. "Do you suppose they are near?"

"Maybe." Slapping his hands against his knees, the old trapper rose to his feet. He eyed Adrian for a moment, then grinned and shook his head. "Enjoy your dinner, Duke!" he bellowed, then laughed hugely. The old trapper was still laughing as he returned to the others, who had grouped around their own campfire several yards away. His amusement was not shared by the big Frenchman, however, for Ramone Jardin sat and glowered sullenly. He took long pulls from a half-empty bottle, gazing in the Englishmen's direction.

Blue Feather slanted Adrian an oblique glance as she bent to tend the cakes in the embers. They were covered with a fine ash, but cooked to perfection, and as she removed them she was aware of Adrian's presence behind her. He was standing and watching her, and she wondered if he was angry or just curious. Half-turning to look at him, she met his clear gaze and thought there was a faint glow in the depths of his eyes. Her heart thudded rapidly, and she dropped one of the cakes back into the ashes without realizing it. There was something so familiar in his eyes, a warmth that often presaged coming together, and she felt a tightening in the pit of her stomach. Did he want her?

Did she want him? What would become of her and this strange Englishman who had another man to serve him? How could she trust him? White men, including her father, had always let he down. The magic of the

151

moment vanished.

Blue Feather gently retrieved the cake from the ashes and scraped it clean before placing it with the others. The stew bubbled and simmered, and she squatted beside the pot and crushed small bits of sage between her fingers, letting it crumble into the mixture of meat and vegetables. A pinch of salt from Harry's supply, a dash of ground peppercorn, and it would be ready, she decided. She took a long metal spoon and stirred the stew, thinking of the many nights she had done this same thing, sniffed the same hot aroma coming from her cooking pot at her father's home. A stew simmered constantly on a Shoshoni fire. Each day more meat or vegetables or whatever was available were added, and the pot stayed over the fire the entire winter before it was ever cleaned. Of course, during lean times the stew was little more than melted snow and dried roots, but it would stave off the worst hunger pains. Though her father had been a good hunter, the meat would only last so long.

Blue Feather's efforts were rewarded when Adrian ate every bite of the food she had prepared, and three of the cakes. Even Harry praised her cooking, and she basked with pleasure at their lavish compliments. No man of the Shoshoni would praise a woman for doing what she was expected to do, and even her French papa had considered it as his due. He hunted for the meat, his daughter prepared it.

Flushing in triumph, Blue Feather's gaze rested on the fair-haired Englishman. His hands were soft, and his back, she'd noticed as they rode, was not as strong, or as finely muscled as one of an Indian brave. He was a skilled rider, though, but not hardened to the trail. She admired the way he toughed it out, though she was sure he was aching all over. He was not totally at ease in the wilderness, and maybe he was running from something. Even the fabric of his clothing was fine and soft. Everything about him but his attitude made her think he had led a pampered life. He was leaning back against the trunk of a tamarack, smoking a thin sheaf of paper-wrapped tobacco, blowing smoke rings into the air. She watched in fascination for a moment, letting her rapt gaze drift from the sharp angle of his cheekbones to the way his mouth formed to make the smoke rings. He was a beardless man among many bearded ones, and she liked that. Even though her father wore a beard, the Shoshoni did not. Their women pulled out any hairs with the sharp edges of two rocks. It was not seemly to wear body hair so that one resembled the bear, she thought, and she was glad Adrian did not. What did it matter to her? she asked herself. Afraid to give herself a chance to answer impulsively, Blue Feather reached out to touch Adrian's pale face, letting the pads of her fingers skim over his smooth skin. Though faintly startled by her gesture, he smiled.

"My color fascinates you," Adrian commented, thinking that her dusky complexion was much more pleasing to the eye than his pale skin.

"*Taiva-vone*," she murmured, and let her hand fall away from his face.

"You're speaking Shoshoni?" he guessed, and she nodded.

"*Ai*. It means 'stranger' in my tongue. You have the whitest skin I have ever seen, much fairer than my father's skin, and I thought him more pale than any man. You are very different, A-dri-an."

"Not so very different, Blue Feather. I am a man, like the men of your tribe or your father. Only my speech and customs are different, my outward appearance. Inside" — he touched his chest — "I am the same. I have feelings similar to those of other men, desires, emotions . . ." Pausing, he reflected that he was treading

153

on dangerous ground here. He did not even understand the strange urges that were pricking him, so how could he relate them to this young girl looking at him with such wide, oddly innocent eyes? She had been married — a galling thought — yet she seemed so vulnerable, innocent when he knew she was not.

She was looking at him with her head tilted to one side and a smile curving her soft mouth. The bear oil she used to make her hair gleam had worn off, and the stiff-bristled hairbrush had removed most of it from her long tresses so that they had begun to slightly curl. One of the trappers had taken out his fiddle and was playing a plaintive melody that drifted to where they sat, and Blue Feather swayed with the music.

"Is that . . . English . . . music?" she asked after a moment.

Adrian shook his head and crushed out his half-smoked cigarette on a stone. "No, that is American. Englishmen and Americans are very different."

"English," she repeated slowly, savoring the word. "You are English. Why does the big man call you Duke? Do you have more than one name?"

"I have many names, Blue Feather, like you. You are called Margarethe by your father, Blue Feather by The People. Do you have others?"

Laughing, she nodded. "I was called She Who Talks Too Much by my Crow husband. He once said that I was like dried seeds in an empty gourd, always rattling for no reason. I asked too many questions, which is unseemly for a female. A good wife is quiet and obedient, which I was not."

Adrian grinned, well able to believe it of this irrepressible girl with the dancing blue eyes. "Why are you called Blue Feather?" he asked.

"All names should have a reason," she explained, "and when I was born my father was away hunting. My

154

mother did not name me until he returned, and by then my eyes had become the color they are now. My poor mother was worried that my father would be angry because I was a girl, but he was not. He picked me up, she often told me, and said I was a feather in his cap — a blue feather because of my eyes." Cocking her head to one side, she predictably asked, "What does A-dri-an mean?"

As he'd been expecting this question, Adrian had his answer ready. "Adrian is really a family name, passed from one member of the family to another, in this case, from my uncle to myself. It will probably confuse you to know that it does not fit me at all." Meeting her direct blue gaze he continued, "Actually, it is from the Latin language meaning dark one, or a brunette nicknamed by a fair-haired person. I could dissect the name for you and explain how it is derived, but I do not think you would really be that interested."

Thinking that she was vitally interested in every little detail concerning this man, Blue Feather merely smiled. "If you think not, A-dri-an," she agreed. "I was named for my father's mother, as you were named for your uncle. It is a strange thing for one of The People; for a name is private and sacred, and one is not usually named for another person. But in the way of the white man, it seems to be common."

"What was your mother's name?" Adrian asked idly, and Blue Feather shook her head.

"It must not be spoken aloud, for she is dead and has gone to the Land of Everfeasting," she explained patiently, and he nodded.

"Harry, would you mind brewing us a bit of tea?" he called over his shoulder to the Englishman, who he saw through the corner of his eye, loitering within hearing distance.

"I am *thrilled* at the prospect, my lord," Harry returned, and Adrian glanced at him in surprise.

Fumbling in one of the leather pouches for a packet of tea, Harry said politely, "I am at your disposal for whatever useless task you find amusing."

Adrian regarded Harry quietly. The servant was jealous of this slip of a girl for some reason. Did he think he would be replaced? How odd of him, but Harry had always been a bit protective of his place at Adrian's side, so it was not entirely unexpected.

"Tea?" Blue Feather was saying delightedly, clapping her hands together, then reverted to French. "I know that word! I have not had tea since I was in my father's lodge in the mountains."

"He no longer lives with your mother's people?" Adrian asked, leaning back against the tree trunk again. Harry was clattering the copper tea kettle noisily, and Adrian's attention was only partly on the girl's answer as he regarded his servant with a trace of annoyance.

"*Ai*," she was saying. "Years ago my father went high into the mountains to search for the fattest beaver. For a whole season of deep snows he did not return. My mother thought that perhaps he had been hurt or was dead, and she sent my brother after him. When that one found my father, he had changed. He no longer wished to come down from the mountains to the valleys, even in the season of the big leaves when the hunting is good and the grass is high. He would not come down with my brother, and has not since that time."

Though he wanted to ask about her parents again, Adrian knew that she would not answer. It was forbidden to speak her mother's name, yet when Blue Feather had spoken of her earlier, there had been a softness in her voice and a light in her eyes that had revealed the great love she'd felt. It was an image that did not conform with the one he had once visualized, of the Indians as barbaric savages living in a land of equal savagery. This gentle-eyed girl with the slanted blue eyes and full, pouting mouth that was so quick to smile or laugh was an enigma. A welcome surprise. She was like no Englishwoman he'd ever known, and certainly not like Nell, who had been greedy and grasping, ready to suck the life from a man and leave him an empty, useless husk. Adrian knew that this girl, this Shoshoni/ French girl who would be regarded as a mindless, ignorant savage by most civilized white men, had more kindness and decency in her than anyone he'd ever met.

His smile was so warm, so unexpectedly tender, that Blue Feather could not help the sudden surge of emotion that washed over her. Her lips parted slightly, and her breath came in a sudden rush of air, but Adrian was only asking her another idle question that had nothing to do with his smile or the soft light shining in his eyes. She tried to concentrate on his words instead of the simmering stew of different emotions she felt.

"When did your father come to this land from France?"

Gathering her thoughts, Blue Feather reflected for a moment then replied, "I do not know how to say the time as you would know it, but it was before the time of my birth, which was fifteen warm seasons ago."

Adrian stared at her, aghast. "Fifteen . . ." he began, then paused. She was younger than he'd thought!

"*Ai, ai,*" she answered, unaware that he was surprised by this information. "This season of the Big Leaves will be my sixteenth. I was born early in the season, I was told, so perhaps I have already passed that time. My papa had come and met his wife, and they already had a son before I was born, but he had not been here long—"

There was the loud pop of a tree limb and a crackling

of undergrowth that snared Blue Feather's attention, and she mentally berated herself for not paying proper attention to her surroundings as Ramone Jardin staggered into the circle of light thrown by their campfire. Instinctively, the girl withdrew into the shadows, blending in with the dark forms of trees and fallen logs.

Ramone swayed drunkenly, his face a mask of belligerence and animosity as he squinted at Adrian through piggish little eyes.

"English . . . I want the squaw!" Jardin said, his words slurring together.

Quietly, contemptuously, Adrian rose to his feet and gazed at the Frenchman. "You are drunk, Monsieur Jardin," he said after a moment where there was no sound but the crackling of the fire and Jardin's rasping breaths. "I suggest you return to the company of your companions."

Drawing himself up to his full height, Jardin said loudly, "And so I shall! But I shall take the Indian squaw with me when I do—"

"I think not," Adrian said coolly. His right hand rested casually on the wide leather belt around his waist so that Jardin could see the butt of the pistol and the bone handle of the knife he always carried with him. A show of weaponry seemed advisable at this point, especially as Broken Arm seemed disposed to stand back and watch for the moment.

Jardin's blurred gaze slid from Adrian's weapons to the beardless face, and he sneered. The man was tall and lean, but he wore the clothes of a city man, a dweller in soft ways who would not know how to properly use his weapons. He, Ramone Jardin, had watched the Englishman fight and knew that he was too soft. There was a rustling in the bushes and Jardin knew that the girl watched. Straightening, he threw back his broad shoulders and let out a chilling bellow meant to terrify his enemy, then took a step forward.

"No, English! We fight for the squaw!" His hand dipped downward in a movement surprisingly fast for a man so drunk, and the long, wicked blade of his knife flashed in the firelight. Grinning evilly, Jardin turned it so that it caught the reflection of the fire and pinpoints of light danced along the razor-sharp edge. "Come and taste my steel, English," he taunted, half-crouching, and in the shadows, he looked remarkably like a shaggy she-bear.

Harry, white-faced and shaking with angry fear, stood up also, reaching inside his coat pocket for the small flintlock pistol he always carried. It was cumbersome and did not always work well, but he carried it religiously, believing in being prepared for the unexpected. This occurrence was not completely unexpected, but it was, however, an explosive situation.

Levelling the pistol at the menacing Frenchman, Harry cleared his throat and said in a quavering voice, "Stand back, you dastardly fellow. Stand back at once, I say!"

Jardin was more amused than threatened, and he laughed loudly at the small Englishman.

"Ho! Put away your toy, *bâtard!*"

The pistol point wavered but did not drop, and Harry shook his head and said, "I shall not."

"Put your pistol away, Harry," Broken Arm said, stepping forward at last. "I see I shall have to settle this dispute over the woman."

Ramone Jardin flexed his brawny arms, and his dark eyes glittered in the pale light afforded by moon and fire. His gaze remained on Adrian, who had not flinched from him nor moved a step away but remained quietly watchful.

"Me, I shall kill this scrawny gamecock!" Jardin

159

boasted. "He will be as the rabbit for the kettle!"

"You shall have your fight," Broken Arm agreed, "but not to the death. You will fight only until one man decides to forfeit his claim. If one of you kills the other, then that man shall die also," the trapper added when Jardin sneered. "Is this understood?"

The Frenchman gave a terse jerk of his head, and his teeth gleamed in a wide grin beneath his straggly mustache as he said, "I comprehend, monsieur. Now, let us fight!"

Protesting, Harry said loudly, "I thought you were a friend of the girl's father, Mr. Broken Arm! Surely you cannot allow such a thing as this to happen! How can you even consider letting the child go with this . . . this monster of a Frenchman!"

Weaving his knife blade in a circling pattern and darting an occasional jab at Harry, Jardin cooed, "Maybe Ramone will kill you, too, little Englishman! *Oui*, and maybe I kill the girl after that —"

"Enough," Broken Arm snapped fiercely, and gave a signal to the men behind him. They ringed the scene with drawn rifles trained on the Frenchman. "I told you — no one will die this night, Jardin, unless it is you for disobeying my orders."

Blue Feather, still cowering in the bushes, skimmed a glance at Adrian. He stood easily, with both hands propped on his hips, his eyes narrowed on the shuffling Frenchman. Her heart was pounding like a frightened rabbit's, and she closed her eyes for a moment. Would it always be like this? Would men always fight over her, pulling her back and forth between them like two camp dogs quarrelling over the same bone? It had happened before in the camp of The People, and after her capture, in the Crow village. Then had come the Blackfeet, and two of their warriors had bickered over possession of the Shoshoni captive. But those had been fighting men, men trained to war, while this man was not. How could he fight the big, burly Frenchman and win? He was too lean, though she had seen men of his stature best bigger men before.

Hearing Broken Arm's next words, her head jerked up and her eyes widened.

"You will fight in the manner of the Indian," he was saying, "with knives and ropes."

Blue Feather's eyes darted to Adrian, who obviously did not understand what was required. How could he? He did not know the Indian way. . . .

Shrugging carelessly, Adrian said, "I'll fight you, Jardin. I'm tired of the sound of your voice which sound like the empty honking of a goose—"

"*Goose!*" the Frenchman howled, enraged. "I will spit you like a goose, English, and roast you over a slow fire!"

"No killing," Broken Arm reminded sharply, but Jardin was not listening. He leered at Adrian and gestured with the knife, his eyes glittering. His feet shuffled in the dirt and fallen leaves as he did an impromptu dance, and Broken Arm stepped between the Frenchman and Adrian.

"You will wait now, while I explain the rules to both of you," the trapper snapped, and gestured to one of the Stanfill brothers to hand him some rope.

While this was going on, Blue Feather crept from behind to be close. Trembling, her gaze locked with Adrian's, and he saw her anxiety and fear and smiled reassuringly.

"Don't worry, Blue Feather. Everything will be fine," he said. "You won't have to go with Jardin."

She nodded briefly, and lowered her head. When his hand reached out and one finger gently stroked a corner of her mouth, trying to coax a smile from her, she reached up, her small brown fingers closing over his strong hand.

Blue Feather was almost frantic with apprehension, though it did not show outwardly. Unlike the others, she had little faith in Broken Arm's ability to keep one man from killing the other. She hated the idea of Adrian being forced into a fight with the Frenchman. Men like Jardin were hard and devious; they never fought fair, yet were more often than not the victor in such an encounter. But of what use was it to protest? If Adrian lost or was killed, she would be given to the ugly Frenchman anyway. And she would eventually kill him before he killed her.

Slowly releasing his hand, she said haltingly, "I will go with the Frenchman, A-dri-an. You do not have to fight."

Startled, Adrian stared down at her in the dim, flickering light from the campfire. This small snip of a girl with nothing to look forward to in life had selflessly offered to go with a beast like Jardin just to keep him alive. How many women would offer such a thing?

For a moment he couldn't speak, then he managed to say, "I must fight Jardin. It is a matter of pride."

Blue Feather understood pride. The People were very proud, and this was a thing she knew well. She nodded and said, "I will ask the Great Spirit to keep you from harm."

Even in the dark, with the light from several campfires glimmering and glowing, Harry could see the strain on Adrian's face. In spite of the cool night, beads of sweat glistened on his brow. There was a tight set to his jaw, and his neck muscles were taut. The two men had been stripped to just their trousers — a barbaric custom, Harry thought — then tied to each other by means of a rope wound about each one's left ankle.

A knife was gripped in each man's fist.

Glancing from his knife blade to Ramone's face, Adrian narrowed his eyes. He had never fought a man in this manner before, nor even seen it done, but Ramone had given him no other choice.

They stood facing one another, muscles tense, jaws clenched. Adrian watched Jardin warily, wondering if he should strike or wait. He could hear the Frenchman's harsh, rapid breathing, the crackle of burned twigs in the fire, a faraway wolf howling at the moon, and the whirr and buzz of night-flying insects. There was the creak of leather as one of the watching trappers shifted from one foot to another, then a muffled snort from a horse, and a shadow flickered at the edge of Adrian's vision. The slight distraction was just enough to make his gaze waver, and Jardin lunged.

It was the moment the Frenchman had been waiting for, and he took full advantage. The slice of his knife skimmed through the fleshy part of Adrian's upper arm, and blood gushed, dripping down his side to stain the waistband of his trousers.

Though it hurt, Adrian did not have time to react to the pain. He leaped backward the length of the rope tied around his ankle, then swerved sharply, keeping the rope taut. Before the big Frenchman could guess his intentions, Adrian slashed out with his knife, catching him by surprise and gashing a long streak across Jardin's hairy stomach. The rolls of fat rippled, and Ramone grunted heavily with pain but did not slow. Instead he jerked sharply on the rope and pulled Adrian off balance so that he stumbled toward him. Adrian could smell his opponent's foul breath on his cheek as he twisted to keep from falling on Jardin's knife blade.

When the Englishman fell to one knee, Ramone lifted his knife high, but missed when Adrian rolled away. Adrian came up with the rope in one hand, and gave a hard yank to bring Jardin down. By now they were both smeared with blood and breathing heavily, sounding, Adrian thought, like two bulls squaring off. They grappled in the dirt, rolling over and over in the dust and leaves, even into the fire before Broken Arm reached out with a foot and shoved them free. There was the acrid smell of burning hair and buckskin in the air, and Adrian found himself straddling the burly Frenchman.

Ramone was panting and wheezing, his eyes bleary and filled with dust and bits of leaves. He had dropped his knife in the struggle, and stared up at Adrian with mute hatred.

"Kill me!" he rasped when Adrian did not move but kept a tight grip on Jardin's wrists. His knees were digging into the Frenchman's shoulders, holding him down. "Kill me, *bâtard!*" Jardin snarled again when Adrian did not move but remained still and quiet.

Blue Feather watched with her heart in her throat. He was wounded but alive, and she waited for Adrian to kill the Frenchman and be done with it. In spite of Broken Arm's edict not to kill, everyone there had known it would be a fight to the death. The Frenchman had made that obvious. So she waited for Adrian to do the expected, to end the life of the man who had taunted him and who would have killed him with no compunction whatsoever.

Shifting from one foot to another, Harry watched just as anxiously as Blue Feather. He had never seen this side of Adrian Herenton, never guessed that so close beneath the thin veneer of civility lay a man as savage and harsh as the crude Frenchman. Was this the elegant, languid Adrian Herenton, son of a duke? If so, he was an entire world removed from that life.

When Adrian deliberately shifted his knife to his

164

right hand and drew it across Ramone Jardin's chest to leave a long, crimson slash, Harry closed his eyes. He knew this could not be the same young man who had left England a year before, bitter, disillusioned and adrift, but still quiet and bookish. This Adrian Herenton had altered drastically, and Harry was not at all certain it was for the better.

Pushing away, Adrian surged to his feet and gazed down at the fallen Jardin. The slash would leave a vivid scar from his collarbone to his breastbone, a constant reminder of the time he had been bested.

"Don't look at the girl again," Adrian said quietly, and his eyes did not leave Jardin's face. "She is not for you."

Ramone did not answer, but his mouth tightened and his jaw dipped once to signify that he heard and understood. Then Adrian bent with a smooth, easy motion and slashed the rope still binding them together. Wiping his knife blade on his trousers, he turned to face the others.

They were silent, and Broken Arm stared back at him for a long moment before turning away. The trappers filed quietly back to their campfire, and only one man paused to help Jardin to his feet. No one spoke for several minutes, and the sounds of Adrian's rapid breathing filled the air.

"Here," Blue Feather finally said, and handed Adrian a water pouch. She watched as he tilted his pale, sweat-drenched head and drank deeply, the water trickling from his mouth and over his chin to splash upon his wide, lithe-muscled chest. His body was not soft, Blue Feather decided, impressed with the way he bested Jardin, eyeing the smooth muscles that flexed with his movements and the light brown hairs that curled down to his stomach. She liked the way the bands of muscles were hard instead of soft, and didn't even mind the fact that he had hair upon his body like a bear. This one did not have too much hair like the others. She was beginning to believe that there was much more to this Englishman than met the eye.

Finally lowering the water pouch, Adrian handed it back to her and turned to Harry.

"I had my pistol ready, my lord," Harry said to Adrian, and his face betrayed nothing of his thoughts.

"Fortunately, I did not need you to help me, Harry. I do appreciate your willingness to do so, however."

Gesturing toward the other campfire, Blue Feather murmured, "He will not forget this insult to his ability, I think. You must always watch your back now, for the Frenchman will not give you another chance to shame him."

Frowning, Adrian slid a glance toward Jardin. He was tending his wound and had not uttered another sound since the fight. Perhaps Blue Feather was right. A quiet Ramone Jardin was much more dangerous than a blustering one.

Then Blue Feather stepped close to him, taking his arm and examining his wound, clucking her tongue and muttering in her own language.

"What are you saying?" Adrian asked with a smile.

"I am saying that you shall need this tended and I shall do it," she said firmly. "It is still bleeding, and I must find an oak and scrape the bark for medicine to stop it."

"I think we have medicine for that," Harry began, but the girl shook her head.

"No," she said emphatically. "I will tend him."

Harry, watching as the girl spoke softly and tenderly to Adrian, gently cleaning his wound with hot water and a soft cloth, could sense the attraction between them. It wasn't just a certain jealousy of his position that made Harry doubtful; it was the knowledge that nothing could come of a relationship between the son of a duke and the daughter of a Shoshoni. It just wasn't done. When Adrian returned to England to take his rightful place, he could not be burdened with a woman, even such a lovely, exotic creature as Blue Feather. . . .

Chapter 11
The Sun

Two days passed without incident, and they camped at a spot not far from the Green River. Blue Feather was excited as she recognized familiar landmarks: a tall, lightning-split tree, a wide fork in the path, a racing stream with a headrock shaped roughly like the head of a dog, and peaks that towered against the horizon like the jagged teeth of a bear. She tried not to show her excitement, for it was never good to let another know what inner thoughts were stirring; but she found it increasingly difficult. Home. She had not let herself think of her people in almost a year. Now they were near. So much could happen in such a short time — did she dare dream of a homecoming?

Squirming with such a delicious promise just ahead of her, Blue Feather let her mind drift to the Englishman. He promised nothing, yet she felt the most happiness when she was with him. Her heart raced at the sight of him every morning, and she thought of many excuses to be near him, or to touch him, or even just prepare him a bowl of food. She listened for the sound of his voice and watched the way the sunlight glinted in the depths of his thick, pale hair. She liked to watch the fine-spun strands blow in the wind, seemingly like thin hairs of gold that made her want to reach out and touch them. And at night, when they lay within easy distance of one another, she listened to the sound of his deep, even breathing.

Sighing, Blue Feather admitted to herself that her feelings toward the Englishman were dangerous. She could not bring herself to forget the way she had been treated before. Perhaps it was meant to be, for hadn't her mother loved a white man? Her mother had met Pierre Duvalle, loved him and married him. Could she not do the same? — could she not love and marry a white man? After all, Pierre Duvalle had come to the country of the beaver when few had seen a white man before, and he had been accepted.

Looking up from the pot she was stirring, Blue Feather slanted Adrian a bold glance. She should not confuse his gentleness with weakness. He had fought the Frenchman for her, and won. Yet he had not taken advantage of the prize he had won. And Blue Feather shook herself with the thought that she wished he would. But how could she convince him that she was not a shy child he obviously thought her to be? Would being his woman make him feel bound to take her to her family. Blue Feather thought of way to show him she was not a child. . . .

They made camp earlier than usual the next day because of the weather. By noon dark clouds raced and rumbled across the sky. Jagged tongues of lightning pierced the horizon in blinding flashes, illuminating the heavens and making the animals skittish.

Harry worked swiftly to pitch a tent, choosing a spot partially sheltered by an overhang of rock. There were two tents, and Adrian helped him erect the other not far from the first one.

"This one is yours," Adrian told Blue Feather, and

gestured to the small canvas shelter. "Do you like it?"

Gazing at it rather dubiously, for it did not appear as sturdy as brush shelters or tipis made of buffalo hides, she did her best to seem pleased. Perhaps she could improve on it quietly, without risking insulting him.

"It is very nice," she said. "Is this for you also?" She had to speak loudly to be heard and leaned closer so that the wind would carry her question to him. Waist-length strands of hair whipped wildly about her face as she waited for his answer.

Startled by her question, Adrian held tightly to his hat and shook his head. "No, this tent is just for you. I am to share the other one with Harry."

Blue Feather nodded and tilted her head to the sky to watch the clouds race swiftly over the mountain peaks. Her skirt blew around her ankles, pressing close to her slender legs, and she put one hand down to hold it. A bolt of lightning cracked overhead, and she trembled, suddenly recalling her capture by the Crow warrior and how the winds had howled and the thunder and lightning raged in the sky.

Noticing her movement, Adrian said awkwardly, "You better get inside before the rain begins to fall. There'll be no fire tonight, but I will see to it that you get food." Then he was gone, stepping across the wind-swept ground to help with the horses.

Blue Feather paused to glance at the other trappers who were hastily throwing up brush for a shelter, then ducked and crawled inside the small tent. Harry had thoughtfully placed an oil lamp and several blankets inside, and she sat atop the stack of soft wool and peered through the triangular opening. This was a different tent from those her people used, quite small with two poles at each end to hold it up. There was only room for perhaps two people inside, so it was not very practical, she thought.

Large drops of rain began to fall, spattering against the canvas tent and making small craters in the dust outside. Blue Feather watched with interest as Harry scurried about, reminding her of a chipmunk with his quick, agitated movements. When the older man appeared in the open flap of her tent, out of breath and asking if he could enter, she nodded in surprise.

"You are welcome here," Blue Feather said, and scooted over to allow more room.

"I apologize for barging in uninvited," Harry said as he shook the raindrops from the front of his coat, "but it was unavoidable. His lordship's tent is so small, and he is so large, that I thought it best not to intrude upon his comfort." A smile curved his mouth as Harry gazed at the girl for a moment. "You seem much smaller and more comfortable in such a small space."

"You always care for him," Blue Feather said after a moment. "Are you his slave?"

Taken aback, Harry said, "Oh my, no! Not in the sense you mean. I have been with his lordship since he was very young, and I care for him because . . . because it is my duty and I enjoy it."

Nodding, Blue Feather smiled. In the gloomy gray light from outside she could see the fine lines at the corners of Harry's eyes, the soft folds of skin that draped on each side of his mouth. He was much older, yet he followed Adrian to this new land because he wanted to be with him. It seemed that her Englishman inspired great love from those around him. And in spite of Harry's occasional caustic comments to Adrian, it was obvious that he loved him.

"I have not properly thanked you for the shirt," Blue Feather said after a moment. "But I have nothing to give in return. I will when we reach the camp of The People."

Smiling, Harry shook his head. "It is a gift," he said.

171

"Do not worry about reciprocating."

Blue Feather stared at him. Her mind worked swiftly to define the peculiar English word, and she finally decided that it must mean *riposte*. She watched with silent interest while Harry began to unload a small leather pack he held in his lap. There were long, thin wooden sticks that he said were lucifer sticks to light a fire, several small packets of fragrant tobacco, a book, a compass—Blue Feather had seen one before and been fascinated with the quivering needle which seemed alive—a packet of tea and the familiar strips of jerky that every trapper carried and which the Englishman told her he detested.

"Why?" Blue Feather asked. "It is good. It will keep the stomach from growling like a she-bear when one is hungry."

"I detest it because it is as tough as shoe leather and tastes remarkably similar," Harry replied as he handed her the jerky. "You may have mine."

"My father has a book," Blue Feather said after several minutes of enthusiastic chewing on the jerky. "He reads from it when the winter snows are piled high against the lodge."

"I don't suppose you read," Harry said as he fumbled with the oil lamp. A match hissed and flared, and he held it gingerly to the wick of the lamp until a steady flame appeared. Successful, he sat back and held the lamp up high. It threw a soft pool of light in the small tent, illuminating the girl's features. Adrian was quite right in not staying with her himself, Harry decided. Of course, he'd had a part to play in that decision. He did not want those two young people thrown together any more than necessary, and had offered to sit with the girl until the storm had abated.

"She looked frightened, Harry," Adrian had said with a troubled expression, "and I think she is recalling something unpleasant."

"I shall sit with her until the worst is over, my lord," Harry had said quickly, so quickly he had drawn an amused glance from his lordship.

Ah well, Harry reflected now as he hung the lamp on a small hook on the tent pole, it was for the best. Besides, he rather liked the girl. She was open and honest, and quite lovely. She was also very clever, and there were moments when he felt that she could see through his every motive. As she would only be hurt by Adrian's inevitable return to England, his interference was required.

Smiling, Harry turned his gaze on Blue Feather and was startled by her silent regard. She was looking at him quizzically, with her head tilted to one side and her mouth curved in a knowing smile, and he felt suddenly exposed.

"You do not think I should like A-dri-an, no?" she asked.

With an Englishman's innate sense of dislike for any kind of emotional scene, Harry began to explain himself in order to forestall such an appalling occurrence.

"Oh no, my dear, it is not that at all! Or rather, I suppose that it is in a way, but not because of anything you have done. It is just that you are from such different backgrounds, and Lord Herenton will soon return to the land of his birth, and I am not at all certain you would like it there. . . ."

"He is leaving soon?" Blue Feather asked quickly. "But he has not even reached Wind River yet, so I do not see how —"

"Oh, not that quickly," Harry hastened to say. His tone grew kinder as he added, "But he will go back one day, Blue Feather."

Sitting cross-legged with the strip of jerky still held in one hand, Blue Feather regarded him thoughtfully.

He was trying to help, but he did not know of the spark that ran between her and the Englishman. It could be felt, like the lightning that slashed through the night outside their tent and threatened to tear apart the sky.

Blue Feather was silent as Harry began to talk to her, telling her things in words she could not understand but only sensed their meaning. He talked of nothing important, as white men were often prone to do, but chattered like the blue jay in a tall pine as he lit another small lamp beneath a tiny pot and threw in a handful of tea. It began to brew, filling the air with yet another fragrance, this one sharp and subtly sweet.

The air already smelled of fresh rain and wet earth, of damp leaves and leather and wet wool. An occasional gust of wind through the tent flap brought a whisper of raindrops inside to dampen their garments and make the lamp flicker. Blue Feather smiled as Harry poured a small amount of tea into a tin cup and offered it to her.

Shaking her head, she said, "No, I do not want it."

"Then I shall take some to his lordship," Harry decided, looking up in surprise as Blue Feather rose to her knees.

"I will take it to him," she said swiftly, and before he could protest she took the tin cup from his hands and left the tent.

Harry stared after her with an open mouth. How had that happened? he wondered. One moment he had been here with the girl, the next she was gone. And drat it all — she had adroitly managed to do that very thing he'd tried so hard to avoid — she was alone with Adrian.

When Adrian glanced up at the rattle of his tent flap, he saw Blue Feather crouched in the opening. She was wet to the skin, with her long ebony hair hanging in soft curtains around her face and her skirt and

174

blouse stuck to her skin. In one hand she held a tin cup, and the other hand was cupped over it protectively as if to keep out the rain.

"I brought your tea," she said, and waited expectantly.

Rousing himself, Adrian said, "Come in, come in! What are you doing out in the rain?"

"I brought your tea," she said again, and held out the cup. The movement shifted the loose blouse she wore, and it gaped open slightly, exposing her smooth, tawny skin. Adrian took a deep breath.

He'd been writing a letter to his uncle, and the pen and paper he held slipped in his grasp as Blue Feather entered the tent and sat cross-legged on a blanket. Light from the lamp flickered over her face, and he put aside his letter as he took the tea and handed her a blanket. The wet shirt was evidence that Blue Feather was not as immature as he'd wanted to think she was, and he fought against the sudden impulse to reach out and touch her. It had been a long time since he'd been with a woman — too long — and he had to steady his hands and try to slow his pounding pulses.

Then Blue Feather destroyed his self-control as she said, "You are a brave man, A-dri-an. With the Shoshoni, bravery is much admired. Tell me, A-dri-an, what do men do in England when they admire a woman. I'd like to know."

Feeling as if he had just been kicked in the chest by a wild horse, Adrian stared at her, hardly able to draw in a breath. She was gazing at him intently, her eyes wide and blue and filled with smoky shadows.

"Blue Feather . . . I told you before, because you are under my protection does not give me the right to take advantage of you. In my country a man does not take a woman without courting her — or he's not supposed to, anyway."

"I do not understand. You have been with a woman before, yes?"

"Yes, of course, but—"

"Many women?" she pursued.

"Well . . . more than one or two," he admitted with a scowl.

"And you courted all of them?"

"Well, no I didn't, but—"

"Did any of them offer themselves to you?" Blue Feather asked, trying to ignore his darkening scowl.

"For God's sake!" he exploded. "Can't you understand what I'm trying to say nicely? When a man cares for a woman or wants a wife there are certain rituals that they perform before . . . before they are married." He could not bring himself to say "make love." Staring at her, Adrian's hands bunched into fists on his knees as he strove for just the right words to use without stirring up his own feelings or the girl's. He cleared his throat and continued, "If a man wishes to wed a certain young lady, his parents often arrange the marriage for them. . . ."

"Ah!" she exclaimed. "It is so with The People! My father paid my grandfather many ponies and a silver-studded saddle for my mother—"

"No, no," Adrian said hastily. "That is not how we do such a thing. There are estates involved, you see, land and titles that often exchange hands. . . ."

"But is that not the same thing?" Blue Feather inquired. "One pays for the bride with land instead of horses, but it is all the same. She is purchased."

Rocking back on his heels, Adrian stared at the slim girl facing him. His gaze shifted from her lovely face to her wet garments, and his clear eyes darkened. The blanket had slipped from her shoulders to her waist, and he could see her firm breasts beneath the transparent material of the shirt she wore. The full cotton skirt clung to her slender legs, wet and soggy and outlining them perfectly, and his gaze travelled reluctantly back to her face again. She was watching him, and he flushed.

"A-dri-an," she was saying huskily. "You saved me from death. My life is yours now."

She was so close, within arm's reach so that he could have just reached out and touched her, let his fingers trace the smooth line of her cheek, down her neck to her collarbone and the rapidly beating pulse in the golden hollow of her throat, then lower to those firm, thrusting breasts beneath the wet shirt. With a groan of surrender, Adrian pulled her to him, revelling in the feel of her rain-damp skin next to him, the beat of her heart pounding against his chest and the soft fragrance of mint in her hair. She must have washed it with herbs, for the scent clung to him, filling his nostrils each time he inhaled, and he wondered if it had the power to stimulate him. There must be a good reason for his surrender, he reasoned as his lips found hers.

Aching with need for her, Adrian kissed her fiercely, deeply and hungrily, his mouth moving from her lips to her arched throat and the rapidly beating pulse. His hands splayed across her back, moving down over the damp garments to her gently rounded hips, holding and caressing her, pulling her so tightly against him it was almost as if they were one creature sharing a single heartbeat. They clung to one another on the canvas floor of the tent, half lying and half sitting, forgetting the storm outside and only aware of the raging tempest inside.

For Blue Feather it was a revelation, an awakening to the true emotions a man could arouse. She wanted this man, this fair Englishman who had piqued her interest and curiosity, despite her reservations. This man could be hers, without violence, anger or fear. Maybe this was love, she thought, as this one embrace released a thousand different emotions inside her. Even if it wasn't, she would ride this wave and learn. It was time she did.

Passion was answered with passion as Blue Feather opened herself to him aching with true need. Circling him with her arms, she was as eager for him as he was for her. Adrian pushed her back against the rumpled wool blankets, still kissing her, his lips searing a path from her throat to the gentle swell of her breasts. He gently moved the wet shirt aside to bare the tempting, flushed mounds. They thrust proudly out, filling his palms, and when his mouth moved to a dusky peak, he heard Blue Feather sigh with pleasure.

Whispering to her in French and English, Adrian moved feverishly over her, pressing his hard length against her supple body, melding flesh to flesh, pausing only to fumble with the buttons of his trousers. He wanted her, ached with the need for her, and he yanked impatiently at the last obstruction to his desire.

Thunder rolled and lightning cracked loudly while the wind whined through the pine boughs overhead and made the canvas tent ripple. The lantern flickered and died, and they were plunged into darkness. Adrian didn't care. All that mattered now was the moment, the soft, yielding woman in his arms and his raging desire.

Holding her closely, the last button surrendered to his efforts, and Adrian pushed free of his confining trousers. He tugged at the cotton skirt bunched around her hips and tossed it to one side, then stretched over her, fully aroused and wanting her. Thunder rumbled loudly again. The swish of pelting rain and the moment inexplicably carried him back to the year before, to rain against mullioned windows and a blond woman in his arms.

"Nell!" he half-moaned as his mind played tricks on

178

him, and when the lightning slashed across the sky again, briefly illuminating the interior of the tent, he saw not Nell's fair hair and pale face, but ebony hair and dusky, innocent features.

Jerking away as if stung, Adrian rolled away from Blue Feather and sat up. He raked his hand through his hair, then pulled his fingers over his face, wiping away the perspiration that dotted his features.

"A-dri-an?" a soft voice asked doubtfully, almost fearfully, and a small hand touched his arm. "What is wrong?"

"Nothing." Shoving her skirt toward her, he told her to put it on, then picked up his trousers.

Confused by his rapid change from lover to stranger, Blue Feather did as he bade her. Shaking hands tugged the still-damp skirt up over her legs and hips, then fastened it around her tiny waist. She reached for her shirt and pulled it over her arms and shoulders, then finger-combed her long sable hair before gathering enough courage to speak again.

"Have I done something to offend you?" she asked, but he shook his head.

"No. It is not you. You must return to your tent now," he said roughly. Lightning flashed again as he fumbled for a match, found one, and lit the lantern. A soft glow grew to light the tent, and he glanced at Blue Feather.

Though she said not a word, her gaze was reproachful, and there was a suspiciously bright sheen in her eyes. Adrian could offer no words of comfort, for he did not know what to say. Did one apologize for halting in the act of making love to a girl he wasn't wed to? Was there a precedent in protocol for such a situation? And what could he say in explanation? Tell her that he had been thinking of another woman? That would certainly wound her, and he had no intention of doing so

179

any more than he already had. . . .

Staring at him, Blue Feather sensed the inner struggle but could not guess the cause. Perhaps it had to do with the fact that she was Shoshoni and he was English. She'd faced enough prejudice to know about such matters. Perhaps it was due to his pampered background and the fact he wasn't a real man, she thought bitterly.

Quietly and with dignity, Blue Feather left Adrian's tent and disappeared into the driving rain and shadows outside. When she ducked into the tent where Harry was waiting, he wisely asked no questions, and she gave no hint of what had happened.

Dawn burst over the mountain ridges with an explosion of color, washing the sky with bright pink and yellow. The air was fresh and clean after the night's storm, and the wind was brisk. Blue Feather lay curled in her blankets and listening to the sound of the men breaking camp. Harry had not yet come to her tent, but she could hear him talking with Adrian. Squeezing her eyes tightly shut, she tried not to recall the night before when Adrian had rejected her. It was too painful and had haunted her sleep.

But it was difficult to forget how his lean body had fit to hers, and the feel of his smooth skin beneath her exploring fingertips. She could still see him in the pale light that had shadowed the contours of his body with interesting hollows and planes, could see the smooth flow of his muscles as he moved, and her throat tightened. He had held her so tenderly, kissed her until a coiling fire had burned deep within her belly, then pushed her roughly away. Why? Did he sense she had thought to ensnare him to get him to do what she wanted? But in her heart she knew her actions came

180

from feelings that were honest and real.

The question still tormented her after she left the tent and crouched beside a densely smoking fire to drink from a tin cup Harry gave her. The wood was damp, creating smoke that billowed into the air in thick clouds that stung the eyes and burned the throat, and Blue Feather rose abruptly.

Broken Arm paused beside her, giving the girl a shrewd glance, then shifted his gaze to Adrian. The fair Englishman stood several feet away, his attention apparently absorbed in the repair of a bridle as he ignored them.

"Too smoky for you?" the old trapper asked Blue Feather in Shoshoni, and she nodded.

"*Ai*. Does no one know how to build a fire that will not smoke?" she added irritably, rubbing at her reddened eyes.

Broken Arm grinned. "If I recall it right, your papa was never that good at finding dry wood, either. I spent an entire winter in his lodge trying to find fresh air."

A reluctant smile curved Blue Feather's mouth, and she tossed the dregs of her coffee onto the ground with a flick of her wrist.

"Where did you meet my papa?" she asked as she placed the empty tin cup into an open pack. "You are not French, and you're not one of The People."

Switching to English, Broken Arm answered, "I came many years ago, not long after two great American explorers known as Lewis and Clark had found a route to the Pacific Northwest. Your father had been with them, but left to trap with a man called Cheney. By the time I met him, he needed a new partner, as Cheney had disappeared into the mountains and never returned. In the wilderness, it is best to have a partner with you in case of accident or trouble, so I was glad to go with Duvalle."

181

"And Cheney?" Blue Feather asked curiously. "Whatever happened to him? I recall Papa mentioning him."

Shrugging, Broken Arm said, "Don't know. I heard he was still alive somewhere in the mountains, but that was many years ago." Pausing, he scratched at his grizzled jaw, then asked, "Did your papa ever talk of me?"

"He may have, but I do not remember."

Nodding, the trapper said reflectively, "Ah, Pierre Duvalle was a strange man. A good trapper, but full of crazy ideas at times."

Listening to their conversation while he repaired the leather bridle strap, Adrian frowned. He hadn't meant to eavesdrop; but they had not bothered to lower their voices, and Broken Arm had switched to English so that he couldn't help but understand what was being said. Now he heard the name Pierre Duvalle again, and it played upon the chords of memory in a familiar chime. Pierre Duvalle . . . a raging storm and fair Nell . . . pasteboard cards spread upon a table and the dark Madame du Jessupe. . . .

A chill shivered up his spine as Adrian suddenly recalled more than just the name. He recalled the reading that he had scoffed, the words of Madame du Jessupe as she told of her cousin who had travelled to America and married. Could this be the same man? It was so unlikely a coincidence that he should meet the daughter of a man whom he had first heard discussed in an elegant English drawing room, that he was inclined to dismiss it as merely similar circumstances and name. It could not be otherwise.

Adrian thrust the thoughts of that night firmly from his mind. He did not want to think of Madame du Jessupe nor her ludicrous prediction.

"My lord?" Harry was asking, and Adrian turned with a start.

"Yes, Harry?"

"Well, I just wondered if you were unwell. You seemed rather . . . intense."

"I'm fine. I was listening to the conversation between Broken Arm and Blue Feather," Adrian answered easily, though he wondered how much Harry knew of what had happened the night before. The servant had returned from the girl's tent shortly after her abrupt departure, but nothing had been said. Of course, nothing would be said, as Harry was not a man who would question his employer's *amours*.

Harry, too, had been listening to the conversation, and he wondered how much Adrian recalled of that night with Madame du Jessupe. He knew all about it, of course, and had been told of the destiny she had predicted for Lord Herenton.

"I see, my lord," was all Harry said, however, and he turned back to the task of taking down the tents and packing them onto their animals.

Broken Arm chose that moment to approach Adrian and Harry, ambling over in a friendly fashion and asking if they were almost ready to leave.

"We've got some ground to cover," he added. "At least two days of hard riding before we reach the Siskadee."

"Siskadee? I thought you said Green River," Adrian protested with a glance of disbelief. "And why so long?"

Nodding, the trapper said, "That *is* the Green River, Duke! The Crow name for it, anyway. Hell, two days, ain't nothing out here!"

"I'm beginning to slowly realize just how vast a country this is," Adrian replied, and Broken Arm laughed as he moved away. Adrian's gaze flicked past the trapper to the girl covering their campfire with dirt. He'd not spoken to her since rising, but now he felt the urge to ask how her night had been, and if she felt well.

He had the opportunity when Blue Feather shyly approached with a food pack Harry had left for her.

"I have finished," she said, and Adrian took it from her.

"Did you sleep well?" he asked then, awkwardly, wanting to begin a conversation but not certain how. He was relieved when she nodded, apparently as eager as he was to talk.

"*Ai,*" she lied, unwilling to admit that she had tossed and turned most of the night, recalling Adrian and his arms around her. "I slept well."

Adrian smiled down at her, and while for a moment to Blue Feather it seemed as if the sun had broken through a cloudy sky and she felt warm all over, she did not forget his rejection of the night before. She would fight to forget her strong feelings for this man. The fact that he was now speaking to her kindly would not affect her, she swore. She would use him as he would her.

"Good," he was saying. "I wondered if you would be able to sleep on such a stormy night. Your tent cannot have provided much shelter."

Tilting her head to one side, Blue Feather reminded him, "But I have slept in such shelters all my life."

Taken aback, he said, "Oh. That's right. Well, I guess I forgot." He *had* forgotten. He should have remembered, should have recalled that this girl was different from any other he'd ever known, much different from haughty, icy Nell who had cared more for a title and money than she had for him. But he hadn't remembered, had thought instead of Blue Feather and her sweet nature.

"Would you care to assist me over here, Margarethe?" Harry called, and Adrian turned with a start of surprise to see who he was talking to. Smiling, Blue Feather nodded and said she would be right there.

"Is there anything you need of me?" she looked up at Adrian and asked, and he shook his head.

A smile slanted his mouth as he asked, "When did Harry begin calling you Margarethe?"

An enchanting dimple flashed at one corner of her mouth as she replied, "Last night, when he told me I needed to be more civilized like the women you have known. . . ." Her smile disappeared immediately when Adrian's brows lowered in a fierce scowl.

"No!" he snapped. "Harry was wrong, my dear. You do not need to be like the women I've known at all. Not at all!"

Pivoting on his heel, he stalked away, leaving Blue Feather staring after him.

"He'll get over it," Harry comforted her, approaching with a smile. "I know what he means. Perhaps I can find a way to explain it to you. . . ."

Blue Feather, head bent and her expression puzzled, followed Harry, wondering why Adrian had reverted to his dark mood again.

Though the sun beat down warmly, it was cool with the wind at their backs, seeming to push them closer and closer to the Green River and their destination. Adrian regretted his outburst, and often glanced at Blue Feather. She rode her pack mule easily, keeping it close to Harry, but would not look in Adrian's direction. Sighing, Adrian wondered aloud if Blue Feather was feeling the effects of the wearying ride.

Broken Arm guffawed, adding, "She can hold her own, Duke! Do you think her Crow husband ever asked her how she felt? Hell no! Indian women have to be strong, and this gal seems to be just as strong as you and me. Or me, anyway." he said with another laugh.

It was hard for Adrian to think of Blue Feather as the

185

wife of a Crow brave, though he knew she had been. He just could not conjure up the vision of dainty, fragile-looking Blue Feather in the copper arms of a fierce warrior. It was a galling thought, and he shoved it from his mind.

They rode all day without stopping. At one point, Broken Arm seemed preoccupied, riding slowly and staring at the still-soggy ground. He was frowning as he motioned for Ramone to join him, and the two men rode ahead of the others. Adrian shifted uneasily in his saddle, wondering what was afoot.

"I do hope the Frenchman has not slain our leader and guide," Harry remarked nervously when it grew dark and neither man had returned.

"I hardly think Broken Arm is fool enough to turn his back on Jardin for a moment, Harry," Adrian replied. "It's more than likely that they have gone hunting, or perhaps are scouting a new trail."

Harry nodded, but his face betrayed his doubt as he glanced around them nervously. They had halted to wait on the old trapper, and the others were nonchalantly going about the business of setting up camp, building fires and erecting a makeshift corral for the pack animals and horses that waited to be fed. Even Blue Feather was busy, skinning and gutting a freshly-killed rabbit as she prepared to roast it over their fire.

Adrian watched in detached fascination, thinking how horrified a proper Englishwoman would be at the thought of doing such a thing. It was one thing to eat food already prepared and arranged enticingly on a silver platter, but quite another to behead and clean the night's dinner. Blue Feather's hands were marvels of efficiency as she worked and soon had the rabbit ready for cooking.

Instead of roasting the rabbit, Blue Feather swiftly cut the meat into small pieces, coated the chunks with herbs, browned them in sizzling fat, then added some water to a deep-bottomed pan. Deftly positioning the pan to cook atop a rack fashioned of wet green wood, she placed a lid over it and sat back on her heels to wait.

"Won't the rack burn?" Harry asked curiously, unable to resist questioning the girl's proficiency. He pointed to the wood sticks surrounded by high flames.

"*Ai,* but not before the food has cooked," Blue Feather answered with a smile. "And when it is done, the rabbit will be very tender."

Harry nodded in satisfaction, once more reflecting on the resourcefulness required to survive in this wilderness. The Indians seemed to have mastered that trait well; indeed, it was necessary in order for their ultimate survival.

As Blue Feather had promised, the rabbit stew was tender and tasty, with the gathered herbs adding more spice and flavor than they were accustomed to having.

"Too bad Broken Arm has not returned in time to share dinner with us," Adrian observed aloud, glancing around the small area for what must have been the fifteenth time in as many minutes.

"Indeed," Harry agreed warmly. "This stew is superb, Margarethe . . . exquisite!"

"Exquisite?" she echoed with a gurgle of laughter. "Do you mean *délicieux?*"

"Of course. I am pleasantly surprised at your culinary accomplishment, though I should imagine that you are quite proficient at this sort of effort. Do you have a speciality that you prefer cooking, perchance?" Harry was asking when he heard a faint rustle in the bushes behind them.

All three turned in one movement, their tension easing when they recognized Broken Arm in the shadows.

"It's about time!" Adrian began loudly, but the old trapper leaped forward to seize him tightly by one arm.

187

In an urgent tone Broken Arm whispered, "Put that fire out! Get your guns ready—quickly!"

From one corner of his eye, Adrian could see that Ramone was making motions and speaking softly to the others, and he began moving even before he knew why. Harry also was moving quickly, and Blue Feather—more accustomed to danger—had already begun to kick dirt onto the fire. Rifles and powder were snatched up and passed around as the campground was plunged into darkness.

The only light came from a fitful moon riding drifts of clouds, faintly wavering patches that gave the world an eerie air of gloom. Harry lay on his stomach with his pistol cocked and ready, and the others lay ready around him.

"What is it?" Adrian finally whispered to Broken Arm.

"Blackfeet" was the chilling reply. "Around twenty of them."

"Do they know we're here?"

"I'm sure they do," Broken Arm answered wryly. "If I could find you, they sure can. Besides, they tried following me and Ramone earlier this afternoon."

"Dammit," Adrian muttered tightly. His glance moved to Blue Feather, her darker shape barely silhouetted by the dim glow. If he concentrated, he could just make out her fine features, the dark shape of her brows and her high cheekbones and full mouth. He hated the thought of her as a prisoner again, another Blackfoot captive. His fingers tightened around the smooth wooden stock of his rifle, and he pressed his cheek against the cold metal barrel. He would do his utmost to protect her.

When Adrian moved closer to her, Blue Feather looked up at him with anxiety knitting her features. "Do you think they will come?" she asked softly.

Shrugging, he said, "I don't know, but if they do come, we intend to be ready." Their gazes met and locked, and he repeated her name aloud. "Blue Feather." A soft whisper in the night wind, a gentle promise. "Blue Feather," he said again, softly, remembering the night before when he had sent her abruptly from his tent. "Blue Feather . . . forgive me for what I said last night. . . ."

Sensing his sincerity, she whispered back to him in spite of herself, "It is forgiven as if it had never been said." When he started to speak, she put two fingers over his mouth and said, "No, do not say any more about it. There will be time later."

He smiled in the dusky shadows, a soft curving of his lips matching the glow in her eyes, gently promising. Giving her hand a squeeze, Adrian turned his attention back to the sounds of the night around them. Everything was still—too still. No nightbirds called; no owls gave their questioning cry. Even the buzz of insects had ceased as if waiting for danger. They all waited in the long dark hours, waited and watched.

It came suddenly in the hour before first light pinkened the sky. Only a pale, misty glow brightened the horizon when the Blackfeet surged through the underbrush and trees with unearthly yowls and piercing screams. They were met with a blistering fusillade of rifle fire, fell back, then charged again. There was the sharp, acrid smell of gunpowder in the air, drifting puffs of smoke that stung the eyes and burned the nostrils. Bursts of orange fire split the indigo shadows with brief flashes, and loud pops seared the eardrums.

Blue Feather worked swiftly to reload the long-barreled rifles as they were shoved in her hands, and had tiny blisters on her palms and fingers from handling the hot weapons. She was vaguely aware of a brave's crash into the bushes beside them, and of the struggle between him and Ramone. There was a grunt of pain, and the Blackfoot slid to the ground while Ramone brandished a knife in triumph.

"Spend less time gloating and more time fighting!" Adrian shouted as more braves followed the path of the first. Their protected area was being swamped with howling Blackfeet. Slicing Adrian a sneering glance, Ramone turned back to the fight just in time to have to swerve to avoid a warrior's heavy club. He ducked, then slashed upward with his knife as he grappled with another opponent.

In the thick of the fray stood Broken Arm, bellowing a challenge to one of the frenzied warriors. Blue Feather watched with widening eyes as a warrior leaped atop the fur-clad trapper and bore him to the ground. She couldn't tell one from the other as they rolled on the grass in the shadows. Adrian, who was busily fighting off another club-wielding warrior, had no time to help the old trapper. It wasn't until he had succeeded in dispatching his own enemy that he was able to make his way to Broken Arm.

The old trapper lay unmoving on the ground, but he was still alive. Rasping noises gurgled from Broken Arm's throat as the warrior lifted his war club to finish him off. Adrian leaped for the Blackfoot at the same time as a pistol sounded close by. The warrior half-turned in stunned surprise, then slumped to the ground, the club falling from his loosened grasp as he died.

Adrian looked around to see Harry standing with his pistol in one hand, and he grinned at the older man. "Good shot, old boy," he approved.

"Rather, wasn't it?" Harry agreed with a slight smile.

Blue Feather was already kneeling beside Broken Arm, anxiously peeling back his eyelids to check for signs of life. "He's alive," she reported with relief as the old man's lids flickered and he grimaced.

"Hell yes, I'm alive!" Broken Arm snorted irritably. "It'd take more than one of them pesky Blackfeet to get rid of me. . . ." A groan followed this last statement as he tried to sit up, and Blue Feather pushed him gently back down.

"Be still until we tend your wounds," she advised, but he was shaking his head.

"I ain't hurt bad, just stunned. He gave me a good lick with that club of his, is all."

Only a few shots were being fired now, and it appeared that the worst of the fight was over. The trappers had won for the moment, and the Blackfeet were retreating. One of the trappers had died, a companion of Jardin's, and the French trapper was furious.

"It's all the girl's fault," he railed. "If we hadn't rescued her, Emile would still be alive! The Blackfeet did not bother us before, now look!"

Adrian fixed him with a steely gaze and said softly, "I do not care if the entire Blackfoot nation decides to descend upon us, Jardin. I would not stand idly by and watch as they took her."

"Better her than us," Jardin countered harshly.

Stiffening, Adrian grated, "You are a selfish brute, Jardin, and I should expect no better from you. Why expect a jackal to become civilized?"

Jardin spat at the ground, then wiped his mouth on his stained shirt sleeve. "Now the Blackfeet know us, and they will remember that we are the ones who killed their braves and took their captive. Mark my words, English—they will hunt for us. The Blackfeet do not forget."

"So let them remember," Adrian returned coolly.

"At the rendezvous, we part company with you and your woman!" Jardin shot at him as he pivoted and strode away.

"I hope he means that last bit, at least," Harry murmured, and Adrian smiled.

"I'm sure he does, Harry. Here, help me with Broken Arm," he said as he bent to help the trapper to his feet.

Chapter 12
The Moon

"What are you thinking so hard about?" Adrian asked Blue Feather with a smile. Her brow was furrowed into lines that marred her exquisite prettiness, and he was seized with a sudden desire to see them erased. "Pretty gowns? Ribbons for your hair?" he teased, and was rewarded with an answering smile.

"No." She shook her head, and black hair rippled like ocean waves down her back. "I was thinking of . . . of other things."

"Such as?" Adrian pursued in the soft silence after her reply. It was quiet in the camp as the others rested for a brief time before moving out. Even an hour's rest was welcome after the tense night and brutal attack. Now he lay beside the Shoshoni girl and waited for Broken Arm's inevitable order to mount and ride.

Sunlight glinted in Blue Feather's raven hair as she pushed it back from her face and slanted Adrian a curious glance. She thought suddenly of her Crow husband and how abrupt he had been—not cruel, just aloof and distant. There had never been any talk of love or the future together, only the day to day living that had occupied their time and minds. Until meeting Adrian, Blue Feather had not even realized there could be something else, an entirely different emotion that welled in her whenever she looked at the Englishman. Maybe this was love and passion — the kind she'd heard about in stories her mother had told her when she was a little girl. Maybe the feelings this Englishman was awakening in her were what she was supposed to feel instead of anguish, pain and emptiness. Maybe there was joy and love in life after all. Tears welled in her eyes, but when she saw that now he sat looking at her with a quizzical expression, she knew she must answer his question.

"I was thinking of the Crow warrior who took me as his wife," she answered honestly, and was startled by the grimace that flashed briefly on Adrian's face. "Oh, I only meant that he was so different from you, and how much maybe I could grow to like that difference," she tried again, and this time she could tell that Adrian was pleased by her reply. She was slightly uncomfortable that she had revealed that much.

"Yes," Adrian said after a moment, "I suppose I am a great deal different than most men you've known. Just as you, lovely Blue Feather, are quite different from any other woman I have ever known."

"You have loved many?" Blue Feather asked shyly, and he gave her a broad smile.

"I thought we'd taken care of that question before," he teased.

Blushing, she nodded and looked away. *"Ai,* we did. I was just being sure."

Taking her small chin in his palm, Adrian gently turned her back to face him. "That is the past. We shall not think of it any longer," he said seriously. "We cannot change it, nor can we forget it. But we can learn from it and go on."

"I shall try. When I was a little girl my mother taught me the true way of The People. The customs, the tales of The People are not written down in books. They are

194

carried within The People, and each family has its own tales of courage that are passed down. In this way, a family's life is always continued. From these stories one can learn that there is so much more to life than heartbreak and struggle. I think I understand them better now since I met you."

Sitting back on his heels, Adrian thought about his own father for a moment. It wasn't so very different in England after all, he mused. Hadn't his father wanted much the same thing from him and Richard? Even Richard had seemed to understand that more than he had. Richard . . . his brother and the husband of the woman he had loved for so many years . . . it seemed so odd now, another life, another world ago. Adrian found himself nodding and murmuring, "I understand, Blue Feather," because he finally did understand.

They smiled at each other again, comfortably and with a growing mutual respect, and Blue Feather realized how much she didn't know about Adrian. She would try to see him not as a white man, a member of a group who used and betrayed her people, but as someone she could love and be happy with. Then she wondered if she could ever bridge the vast gap between them.

Broken Arm was rising from his pallet and giving the order to mount up, and they all began to gather their belongings. The old trapper swayed slightly; but his voice was as strong as it had ever been, and he still had the same crusty edge to his words.

"Get on up, you lazy dogs! We're headed for the rendezvous!" he roared, gesturing with his bandaged arm.

"The man is invincible," Harry muttered more to himself than to anyone else as he bent to lift a loaded pack. "I daresay he will have us riding at a breakneck pace regardless of any wound he might have suffered."

195

"I daresay!" Adrian commented with a laugh, earning a dark glance from his servant.

"Well, you needn't sound so jolly about it, my lord!"

"Look at it this way, Harry—the sooner we ride, the sooner we get to the rendezvous."

"A delightful thought, I'm sure. I quiver with anticipation. It has long been my desire to consort with brigands adorned in animal skins like primitive man, and fairly reeking with the rank scent of stale whisky and unwashed flesh. I beg your pardon, miss," he added in Blue Feather's direction.

"Don't pardon him," Adrian ordered her with a grin. "He can be a cantankerous old growler when he chooses."

Blue Feather smothered a giggle behind her hand, not wishing to offend Harry as he had been so nice to her. The poor little man seemed so harassed, so out of place in this land with his funny hat and clothes that seemed so uncomfortable. Even Adrian did not wear such restrictive garments.

An hour later found them on the trail again, winding up rocky paths and through thick underbrush that often necessitated a man dismounting and hacking away tree limbs and brush so that they might pass. It was obviously a path used by men on foot, and only wide enough in places for a man to pass through. Jardin often wielded his long knife, slashing at the leafy branches that barred the trail. The Frenchman so obviously enjoyed such vigorous exercise that Adrian wondered if he was practicing with the knife for his future enemies. The thought must have occurred to Broken Arm also, because he muttered an observation that Jardin would no longer need his services once they reached the rendezvous site.

"And we'd best be on our toes, Duke," he added with a knowing tilt of his head. "That Frenchman hasn't forgiven either one of us for offending him."

"I know," Adrian said.

After a moment of silent riding, the old trapper asked, "What are your plans once rendezvous is over?"

"I'd planned to find some men travelling back toward Fort Williams, then head back east, I suppose. I promised Harry we would leave the wilderness before the winter snows hit."

Nodding sagely, Broken Arm commented, "Wise decision. It gets rough in the winter mountains for unseasoned men."

"So I heard," Adrian replied with a glance at Harry. Still wearing his bowler hat and an expression of stubborn acceptance, the middle-aged servant showed signs of weariness in the lines of his face. Blue Feather would be staying with her people at Wind River, and suddenly the thought of leaving her behind struck Adrian. How could he? Would he really be able to when the time came? He regretted his promise to Harry, yet knew he could not renege.

He was still thinking of having to leave the Shoshoni girl behind when they made camp for the night. It was earlier than usual, but they had to stop in order to rebind a wound suffered by Michael Stanfill in their first skirmish with the Blackfeet. It had been torn open in the last fray, and needed attention.

"How bad is he?" Adrian asked Broken Arm.

"Ah, he'll live, but he needs some caring for," the old trapper answered with a shrug. "How about Harry? He seems to have a flair for tending wounds."

"I'm certain he will be glad to take a look at it," Adrian said. "We have a decent supply of medicines in his little leather bag, and Harry knows how to use them."

"Thanks. I'll tell the Stanfill boy."

When Adrian turned around to summon Harry, he

caught Blue Feather's curious glance. "Is something the matter?" he asked her, and she shook her head.

"No, nothing is wrong. I was only . . . surprised . . . by your kindness to those who have not been kind to you," she explained.

Shrugging, Adrian said lightly, "It doesn't really matter. We're all in this together, and I just want to get to the rendezvous like everyone else."

"But not everyone else wants you to get to the rendezvous," Blue Feather pointed out with a glance in Ramone Jardin's direction. "You allowed him to live when you could have killed him, and now he will try to kill you one day."

"Perhaps," Adrian agreed.

"*Ai,* I am sure of it."

Looking down at her anxious face, Adrian let his gaze drift from her silky spill of ebony hair to her piquant features and startling blue eyes. She was so lovely, so sweet, gentle and caring. No Englishwoman he'd ever met had the endearing qualities he'd found in this one young girl. Reaching out, he traced the line of her high cheekbone with his fingertip, and a half-smile slanted the generous curve of his mouth.

"Are you so certain I am an easy man to kill, Blue Feather?" he asked teasingly. "Jardin has not been able to do so yet."

Blue Feather returned his smile, and her eyes sparkled with glints of blue fire. "I like you, A-dri-an, but I shouldn't," she said instead of responding to his teasing query.

"I like you too, even though I shouldn't," he said. His hand dropped away from her face, and his gaze raked over her skirt and soiled blouse. "Tomorrow morning we will arrive at the rendezvous, and I intend to buy you new clothes," he said suddenly. "I am certain they will have pretty trinkets, too."

198

Surprised and pleased at his generosity, Blue Feather shook her head. "New clothes, A-dri-an? And trinkets? I do not understand why. . . ."

"Because you deserve them. In my country, when a young lady attends a social function, she always wears a pretty new gown. You shall have one for the festivities at the rendezvous."

Her attention caught by this reference to the mysterious women of his land, Blue Feather seized on his words with avid attention. Vivid visions of vague females garbed in yards and yards of soft material and bright ribbons filled her mind. For a brief moment she envisioned Adrian with such a woman, smiling down at a soft, pale creature with hair like sunlight, and her heart lurched.

"Will I be as pretty as the women of your country?" she could not keep from asking shyly.

Adrian chucked her under the chin. "You will be much prettier than any girl I have ever seen," he said honestly. "And when you get older, you will be more lovely than any woman. But that will be a few years yet," he added with a condescending smile that jarred her.

When he turned to join Harry, Blue Feather watched, feeling oddly disconcerted. He had treated her as a woman the other night, but now he had just talked to her as if she were a child, with the vanity and emotions of a child. A feeling of frustration swept through her, and Blue Feather followed the tall Englishman.

Adrian and Harry had half-walked, half-carried Stanfill to a small stream nearby and were helping him remove his jacket and shirt when Blue Feather arrived. While Harry did the necessary cleaning of the festering wound, Adrian handed him the proper medicines.

Frowning, Harry muttered an observation that the

bleeding was hard to stop. He glanced up when Blue Feather crouched beside them.

"I can make medicine to stop the bleeding," she offered first in French, then switching to English so he could understand. "There is a potion made from the bark of a tree that will stop the spurt of blood. Wait. I will go get some for you."

Before Harry could reply she was gone, disappearing into the trees. After turning to look at Adrian, who shrugged his shoulders, Harry turned his attention back to cleansing the moaning Stanfill's deep gash. Within the space of a few minutes, Blue Feather was back, bearing several chunks of bark with her. She immediately set about building a fire and slinging a pot over the flames. Tossing the bark into the pot, she brought it to a boil and let it simmer for several minutes, then stirred it into a thick mixture that she gave to Harry to apply to the wound.

"Let it cool first," she warned as he took the potion she had prepared.

"I don't suppose you know how to make tea, too?" Adrian inquired with a touch of humor. Blue Feather turned to gaze at him.

"Thé?" she echoed. "Oui, I can make tea. . . ."

"I was just teasing you," Adrian added then, giving her a mischievous grin that made her smile. "You seem so capable of doing all manner of different things that I could not resist."

"You tease me a lot, A-dri-an," she retorted, "but I will still make you some tea."

"I'll unload the horses and find the tea if you'll gather the firewood," he said, "but hurry. It will soon be dark, and I don't want to have to look for you."

A light, tinkling laugh floated toward him as Blue Feather responded, "You forget that it is I who know this land well!"

"I know!" he shot back to her departing figure, and stood watching until she disappeared into the thick undergrowth, fading lightly into the trees like a wisp of smoke. A smile remained on his face for a long time as he unloaded the packs and tended the horses, setting aside the small packets of fragrant tea.

Blue Feather was still smiling, too, thinking of the Englishman and his humor as she ducked low-hanging branches and tree limbs, searching for small, dry twigs to kindle the fire and larger limbs to make it burn long and hot. She made a sling out of her long skirt, tucking the hem into her waistband as she filled it with oak limbs. Birds sang overhead, squawking and chirping merrily with the promise of spring in the air, and here and there was the rustling of a small animal as it scurried away. A chipmunk sat up on a fallen log to berate her loudly, scolding furiously until she got too close, then darting away among the fallen leaves and trailing vines.

Blue Feather paused beside the log to tie up her hair, using a smooth stick to knot it at the nape of her neck. A fresh breeze swept across her, cooling her bared skin, and she closed her eyes for a moment, breathing deeply.

"Jeune fille!" a harsh voice grated close by, and Blue Feather's eyes snapped open as she jerked in surprise.

It was Ramone Jardin, and he was standing only a yard away from her, his lips twisting into a cruel smile.

"De quoi avez-vous besoin?" she asked quickly, and began backing away from him.

"I need to help you," Ramone was replying as he took several steps toward her. "What else would I want? I come to help you search for the firewood. Perhaps keep trouble away, heh?"

"You are the trouble," Blue Feather responded. Her fingers clutched at her heavy skirt, and the firewood

201

slipped slightly, some of the limbs spilling to the ground.

"Aw, why you go and talk to Ramone in such a way, *jeune fille?*" he asked with a plaintive sigh that did not fool Blue Feather for a moment.

"Go away! *Vous allez!*" she hissed. Her muscles tensed to flee, and she darted a glance left and right for possible assistance.

Intercepting her glance, Jardin laughed softly. "There is no one nearby, little goose! Just you, and me —" With this last he sprang forward to seize her by one arm and jerk her close, and Blue Feather opened her mouth to scream. Jardin's hand clamped quickly over her mouth, and he grated, "You will do as I say, *jeune fille!*"

Her bare heels drummed against his shins with a rapid beat, and Jardin growled low in his throat and tightened his fingers around her mouth and nose until she was light-headed from a lack of air. The burly Frenchman lifted her easily from the ground, slinging her across one shoulder so that she bounced painfully over his back. The stick holding back her hair fell out, and a heavy curtain of hair swung down to obscure her vision. Dizzy now, Blue Feather watched the forest floor pass in a blur, only vaguely aware of where they were going. Any sounds she made were only slight pants and wheezes as the air was knocked from her lungs, and she realized with a sense of panic that Jardin was going deeper and deeper into the dense forest.

"Where is Margarethe?" Harry asked as dusky shadows deepened from shades of rose to purple. The air had grown much cooler, and he glanced around the shadowed campground.

Looking up with a frown, Adrian murmured, "I

202

don't know what could be keeping her. She only went to fetch some wood for a fire."

"It's getting rather dark for her to be traipsing about the forest alone, don't you think, my lord?" Harry asked with his brows creased in an anxious scowl.

"Yes, but she assured me that she was quite capable of taking care of herself," Adrian said. "And I had to agree, for this is her land and she does seem to know how to take care of herself under normal conditions. Look at the way she can cook, and gather healing plants and herbs. . . ."

"Yet we must take into consideration the circumstances under which we first found her," Harry pointed out.

"Ah, that's quite true, Harry!" Straightening his long legs, Adrian stood up and gazed thoughtfully around the campground. Everything seemed as normal, with the men working and taking care of their evening tasks. Yet as he gazed around him he was struck by something different; it was not the presence of a disturbing force that jarred him, but the absence of it.

Even as he opened his mouth to voice his discovery, Harry was exclaiming, "That Frenchman is not here, either, my lord!" But Adrian was already striding away.

Approaching Broken Arm where he knelt before a fire, he asked brusquely, "Where is Jardin?"

The old trapper rocked back on his heels and gazed up at the Englishman. "Jardin? I don't know, Duke. Is there trouble?"

"That I won't know until I find the Frenchman," Adrian answered grimly. "Have you seen him in the past hour?"

Broken Arm pushed his wolf-head hat to the back of his head and scratched his scalp, saying slowly, "No-o, can't say that I have, Duke." Bushy eyebrows knit in a frown as he asked, "What's the matter?"

"Blue Feather's gone, and now I don't see Jardin. I don't know that there's a problem, but I don't know that there isn't, either."

"I see. Well . . . why don't we see what we can find out before we jump to any conclusions, Duke?"

"Fine, but I intend to look for her, and if he has done anything . . . well, I don't need to say more, I think."

Broken Arm leaped to his feet as Adrian stalked away, and he made a quick gesture to Chris Stanfill. "Stanfill, keep your eyes on things here — I've got some tracking to do," he growled swiftly, then started after Adrian.

The forest grew dark more quickly than the open slopes, and already it was hazy with the cool air of evening. Faint rays of dusty light slanted through the towering trees, and Blue Feather was only vaguely aware of their direction, though she struggled to identify landmarks. Her ribcage was sore from the rough pounding of Jardin's shoulder against her, and she was still light-headed and dizzy from the struggle for air. The musty smell of damp and decaying leaves filled her nostrils, mingling with the rancid odor of beaver and bear that enveloped the French trapper. He must avoid the cleansing streams and rivers, Blue Feather thought as she twisted her head in an attempt to view her surroundings. Already he smelled worse than the choking musk of a beaver —

Then any rational thought was erased from her mind as Jardin finally paused, and there was the sickening feel of weightlessness as he tossed her through the air before the bone-jarring thud of her body against a grassy hummock. She lay there gasping for breath as Jardin stood over her, a darker silhouette against the forest shadows.

"Ah, *mon petit,*" he purred, "at last I have you alone. I have not tasted a woman since Quebec, and I know you will be as sweet as I have dreamed—"

"Non!" Blue Feather managed to gasp between pants for air. *"Non!"*

"Do not struggle. No one will hear your cries, and I will only think that you do not like Ramone," he jeered as he bent forward.

Blue Feather lashed out with both feet, catching the Frenchman in his paunchy belly, then she was rolling free. Freedom was short-lived, however, for he caught her before she had taken more than a half-dozen steps. One hand wound in the length of hair streaming behind her, and he yanked cruelly, bringing Blue Feather crashing to the ground again. A knotted fist slammed into her head once, twice.

"No more gentleness from me!" Jardin spat as he pulled her along with him, half dragging her over fallen tree limbs and rotting logs. He pushed her down on the grassy hummock again, one large hand splayed against her chest. Dazed, Blue Feather could feel the dampness of the earth and grass beneath her, the cushion of the ground too firm to allow her to sink away from him, and she cried out in Shoshoni for the Earth Mother to help her.

Jardin smothered her cries with the bruising force of his mouth, crushing her lips. Repulsed, Blue Feather tried to wrench her head away, but failed and felt the bile rise in her throat. Her hands were trapped between their bodies, and she pushed weakly at him as he ripped her blouse, exposing her breasts. Hatred and fear surged through her. No, not this evil man, this vile-smelling trapper who had tried to kill Adrian and now violate her, she thought as she twisted and turned beneath Ramone's weighty bulk. One dirty hand pawed her flesh as he pinned her down while the other hand groped to raise her skirt higher.

Lifting slightly away as he fumbled with the wide leather belt holding up his grease-stained trousers, Jardin gave Blue Feather the opportunity she needed. Filling her lungs with air, she screamed, a high, piercing cry that echoed through the forest and soared above the tree tops. Startled, birds roosting for the night rose with an alarmed flapping of their wings, and she screamed once more before Jardin's hand was over her mouth again.

"Sacre bleu!" Jardin grated. "Be quiet!"

The Frenchman's warning was too late, however, for there was a crashing in the bushes behind them and Adrian burst through. In the dim light his swift gaze took in the sight of the hefty man sprawled atop the bare-limbed girl, the purplish bruises on her face, and the cords in her throat where she strained against the smothering hand. With a low roar of fury, Adrian sprang forward.

Muttering another oath, Jardin rolled from atop the girl and surged to his feet. A faint glitter shimmered in the shadows, and Blue Feather cried out, "He has a knife!"

Jardin's fist slammed against her head again, sending her head snapping back. Lights exploded in front of her eyes, and there was a dull ringing in her ears, so that she never saw Adrian's agile leap.

The Englishman lunged forward and dove into the thick body of Jardin, sending him backward. They both crashed to the ground, and Jardin's long knife flew from his hand to soar through the air. It landed in the bushes with a distant plop as Adrian grappled with the Frenchman. There was the dull thud of fists pounding into flesh, and an occasional grunt of pain or expulsed air from tortured lungs as the men fought silently, viciously.

When Broken Arm arrived, huffing and out of breath, he found Adrian straddling Jardin, his fist slashing into the Frenchman's face again and again while blood spurted and gushed.

"Duke! Duke!" Broken Arm wheezed, and motioned with one hand for Harry. The servant was almost as out of breath as the old trapper, but he drew out his pistol and fired a shot into the air. The bullet severed a slender branch from a tree, and it fell almost atop the fighting men, gaining Adrian's attention at last.

He drew back slightly, gazing down at Jardin's battered face in the dusty, hazy light. Restraining himself with an effort, Adrian took in a deep, steadying breath. He wanted to kill Jardin, pound him into a senseless, lifeless pulp. Hot blood still pulsed through his veins, filling his ears with a roar and flushing his face. He slowly released the front of the trapper's shirt, letting Jardin fall back onto the grass.

Standing slowly, Adrian turned his head to where Blue Feather crouched, her eyes wide, her bruised face solemn. "Are you all right, my darling?" he asked tenderly, scooping her into his arms. Harsh sobs racked her slender body, though she made no sound, and he held her tightly yet carefully as if she would break. "I'm so sorry. Did he hurt you? I should have killed him when I had the chance," he said savagely, and held her closer. Then she flinched. Alarmed, he pushed her from him and said, "Where are you hurt?"

"It is nothing. Only bruises and scratches where I was thrown to the ground," she answered quickly. Her small hands held him back as she sensed his inclination to return to Jardin, and she urged, "Let us go back to camp now! *S'il vous plaît!*"

Yielding to her plea, Adrian gave a last glance at the

grunting Frenchman, who was sitting up cradling his bloody face in his hands, then put an arm around Blue Feather's shoulders.

"One of these days I will enjoy killing you, Jardin," he said quietly before he turned away.

"I wouldn't," Broken Arm drawled when Ramone Jardin made an attempt to rise. "It wouldn't be too safe for you right now, Jardin."

Sinking back to the ground, Jardin glared at the old trapper. "All this for a wretched Indian girl!" he spat.

Broken Arm gave him a glacial stare and leaned forward to speak softly. "Duke should have killed you the first time, Jardin, but it's not too late. I could have just let him do it now, you know."

"My men would have killed you!" Jardin blustered.

"You don't have that many men left, remember?" Broken Arm reminded contemptuously. "And it would take more than one or two skulking dogs to dispose of an old man like me, Jardin. You might remember that in the future. . . ."

Straightening, Broken Arm turned and followed the path Adrian, Blue Feather and Harry had just taken, leaving the Frenchman sitting on the dew-wet ground glaring after them.

"One day, old man, you will die by my hand," Jardin promised softly. "I shall see to it!"

It was Adrian who gently tended Blue Feather's cuts and scratches, while Harry watched closely, offering an occasional suggestion.

"Put some of this salve on that cut, my lord. No, not that one, it's too deep and requires another . . . yes, that's right," the harried servant observed with a shake of his head and a soft, clucking sound.

"You both fuss too much," Blue Feather protested,

but Adrian held her firmly on his lap and would not allow her to rise. "But for a few scrapes and dirt I am fine. If you would allow me to bathe in the stream . . ."

"You don't look that fine to me," Adrian said kindly but firmly. "We shall tend your injuries, and you, in turn, will be so good as to not wander off into the woods again."

Staring at him, Blue Feather was astounded at his concern. No one had ever said such a thing to her before; indeed, it was expected that she gather firewood and hunt for berries, herbs and roots. What was the Englishman thinking of? How could she exist without going into the forest?

"If you must go," he was saying, "either myself or Harry will escort you. I think it best that you not be alone until I have returned you to your father."

"Then you *do* intend to take me to my people?"

"Of course. Didn't I already tell you that?" he replied, though it was the first time he had been able to say it with conviction.

"But I thought you only meant to go as far as the rendezvous," Blue Feather said with a questioning look up at his handsome face.

"Yes, I had thought so, too, but now I have decided to see you safely home. I have a desire to see Wind River," he added, and slid Harry a careful glance. Wind River. It was much farther than the Green River, much farther than the area where the rendezvous was to take place. Wind River was also higher in the mountains. It was there the Shoshoni had their encampment. There they chose to live far from other tribes and the wandering white men. They were a private people who did not care for the white man, his diseases or his barter. They scorned the cheap trinkets he chose to trade them for luxurious beaver pelts, and preferred keeping to themselves. The Shoshoni chose to remain aloof from all outsiders.

Adrian's attention was turned from his servant back to Blue Feather as she sat up and pushed away.

"Please, Adrian—before you use more of your medicines, I wish to bathe in the stream. I am dirty, and I feel as if I must wash the touch of the Frenchman from my skin," she said. *"Si'l vous plâit."*

After a moment's hesitation, Adrian nodded. "Very well, you may," he said reluctantly. "Though I insist that either Harry or myself accompany you to the stream for safety."

"I can take a knife," she began, but he cut her off with a quick shake of his head.

"No. You must not risk being alone again. There are too many men like Ramone Jardin wandering about."

"Yes," Harry put in with a meaningful glance at Adrian, "and I shall lend the young lady a robe to wear. It is not proper for her to be prancing about without some sort of decent covering, even with you as her faithful guard."

Sitting back, Adrian gazed at Harry with amusement. The old dog, he thought Adrian could not be trusted with her! And he was very likely right, Adrian silently admitted as he nodded his head in agreement.

"Excellent notion, Harry," he said aloud. "I commend your notion of what is proper."

Grinning, Harry inclined his head slightly. "I was certain that you would, my lord."

So Blue Feather was loaned a long, soft cotton robe that she greatly admired, much to Harry's pleasure. It was too long, of course, even with Harry's short stature, but it was loose and comfortable, the hem reaching to her ankles and the sleeves flapping below her fingertips. She stepped into the concealing foliage of towering shrubbery and peeled away her dirty garments, changing into the robe so that she could wash her skirt and blouse. When she emerged from the bushes Adrian was waiting on her, a knife tucked into his trousers and two pistols dangling from his belt. A Hawken rifle was held in one hand.

"Are you ready now?" he asked pleasantly, noting her startled glance at his weapons.

She nodded and said the first thing that came to her mind to distract him from the events of earlier.

"Is this a man's dress I am wearing?"

Somewhat taken aback, Adrian smiled and shook his head. "No, it is a robe. One normally wears it over his night clothes."

"Do women wear them also, or only men?" she asked curiously, fingering the soft material as they walked through the night shadows. High overhead a silvery slice of moon hung in the sky, offering subtle light that filtered through the trees and gave a shimmering glow to the world. There was the muted murmur of nightbirds and an occasional stealthy rustle of dead leaves and underbrush as some forest creature made its way along.

Adrian glanced down at Blue Feather's bent head, admiring the curve of her cheek, the gentle sway of her hips. Her long hair which moved with each step was outlined against the pale material of Harry's robe like a dark ribbon. He resisted the urge to reach out and touch her, sensing Blue Feather's sudden shyness and knowing the reason. The last time they had been alone he had taken advantage of her. Did she think he had acted like the Frenchman? He would make every effort to resist such urges, he swore. So he smiled and made an innocuous reply to her question.

"Women have a different kind of robe to wear, Blue Feather. Usually of silk or satin, with rows of lace and yards of ribbons adorning the bodice. It is worn over a nightdress."

"Nightdress?" she echoed in surprise. "One wears a dress to bed every night?"

"Well, in my country it is the accepted thing to do. You see, one often . . . entertains . . . and it is better to have on concealing garments — shouldn't we talk about something else instead of this?" he asked with a tinge of desperation. For some reason, the mental vision of Blue Feather adorned in white satin and lace was most disturbing.

"*Ai,*" she said softly. "We have reached the stream now, anyway."

"Here," Adrian said, and handed her a slippery cake of soap. "Harry said you might prefer this to what you may be accustomed to using."

"What is it?"

"Soap. Lavender scented soap. It was somehow included in our order, and Harry being the frugal soul that he is, just never threw it away. Of course, I do not wish for my garments to be washed with such a sweet feminine fragrance, so he thought you might wish to use it."

Delighted with it, Blue Feather nodded. "Do the women of your country use this?" she asked, and her smile grew wider when Adrian said yes. "Then I shall use it also!"

When she stepped behind a tree and began untying the sash to the robe, Adrian discreetly turned his back. He rocked on his heels as he stared back down the path they had just traveled, thinking of the nude girl behind him and wondering what sweet mysteries lay beneath Harry's robe. Lucky robe, he thought enviously, to be so close to such smooth perfection, such a lovely body —

A tiny splash diverted his attention, and he knew she had entered the water. Closing his eyes, he imagined

212

her in the swiftly running stream with the moonlight silvering her body, her wet hair clinging like silk to her high, firm breasts and her skin glistening with crystal drops. Adrian stifled a sudden groan and damned his vivid imagination.

"A-dri-an," a sweet voice called, and he stiffened, not daring to turn about.

"Yes?"

"I am in the water now, so you may turn around," she called. "I would like to talk to you while I wash."

Half-afraid yet eager, Adrian slowly turned around, lifting his eyes from the ground to the glittering waters of the stream. Blue Feather sat in the water several feet from the grassy banks, a dark silhouette against the light-chipped swirl around her. Relaxing slightly, Adrian stepped closer and sat gingerly upon a flat rock that was still warm from the heat of the sun. He rested the Hawken across his knees and leaned back against the rough bark of a tree, crossing his legs at the ankles.

Finally, searching for a neutral topic of conversation, he cleared his throat and asked, "Is the water cold?"

"Oui, il fait froid." There was a splash and a squeal, then the hasty explanation that she had almost lost the bar of soap, and he relaxed again as she began to chatter. "Harry told me that in your country you have big pots you call bathtubs, and that you warm the water before you bathe in them. This is true?"

Smiling, he said, "This is true. There are some people who have entire rooms devoted solely to the placement of a tub."

"It seems wasteful," she commented, and idly skimmed the soap over one arm, sighing with pleasure. It felt so good, so slippery and fragrant, making her skin tingle with soft scent. Reconsidering her observation, Blue Feather amended, "Perhaps it would be nice

213

to have such a room, though. I have never washed in a big pot, *la bain* is always in a stream or lake."

"You must try it sometime," Adrian said, and was suddenly absorbed in the notion of the girl doing just that very thing. Why not? She was, after all, French as well as Shoshoni. Perhaps she could visit a town with him, and he could show her—no, Adrian scolded silently. She was an Indian, and he was only taking her to her father.

The night grew silent, filled only by the sound of the rushing stream and Blue Feather's movements, the tinkling patter of water as she washed her hair with the soap then wrung it out. Adrian cleared his throat and shifted position on the warm rock, his eyes growing accustomed to the play of moonlight and shadow. He was now able to see the girl more clearly, the gentle sculpting of her fine features and the high, proud line of her breasts just above the water. They jutted out, jiggling softly with her movements, waterspouts pouring over them, and he was fascinated by the scene.

Oblivious to the fact that he could see her so well—because he sat in the shadows and she could not see him—Blue Feather played contentedly in the water. Scooping up a double handful, she splashed it over her face, sucking in a deep breath when the soap stung her eyes. She still held it tightly in one hand, a precious possession. Occasionally, she would call out a laughing comment to Adrian, which he would usually manage to answer calmly, though it strained him to sit so far away and watch her cavort in the stream.

When Blue Feather lifted her arms to smooth back her hair, half standing in the shallow water, it was more than Adrian could bear. He surged abruptly to his feet and dropped his rifle, then stepped into the stream, startling her.

"Ohh!" she cried, dropping the soap and stepping

214

away until she realized it was Adrian. *"Quelle est-il?"*

"It is nothing," he assured her huskily, "only a foolish Englishman, cherie."

Suddenly aware of her nudity and the moonlight and the strange expression in Adrian's eyes, Blue Feather grew very still and calm. She had been waiting for him to admit that she was a woman, and now he would. She waited silently for what she was certain would happen. Water dripped over her in silent rivulets, skimming from her smooth amber shoulders over her breasts and down the curve of her ribcage to her flat stomach.

Ignoring the water that lapped around his knees, Adrian aggressively pulled Blue Feather to him. She had been a brave's wife. She was no innocent maid despite her age. His fingers were warm and strong, his mouth hot and hungry as it closed over her parted lips. Shivering — not with cold but with passion — Blue Feather closed her eyes. The cold handles of his knife and pistols pressed against her naked flesh, digging into her, yet she never felt them as he held her close. She was aware of only his mouth moving against her lips, then her cheeks and the soft swirls of her ear as he whispered words she didn't understand, his heated breath humming over her chilled skin.

Groaning, he husked, "God, Blue Feather — I need you so badly. . . ." And she understood what he meant.

Her heart soared with his words. His splayed fingers moved over her back, stroking the cool, wet skin as he lifted his head to stare into her eyes. Her answer must have been evident in the misty blue depths, for he was scooping her from the water, one arm under her knees and the other behind her back, carrying her to the grassy banks and laying her gently down.

Lowering his body half-across hers, Adrian pushed clinging wet strands of her hair from her face, gazing down at her with a faintly quizzical expression in his eyes. He said nothing for a moment but only held her. Tough grasses cushioned Blue Feather's lithe body, their sharp fragrance mingling with the sweeter scent of the soap she had used, and he buried his face into the hollow of her neck and breathed deeply.

Gently, tenderly, he began to kiss her again, his mouth roaming from her soft, trembling lips to her closed eyelids and then the tip of her nose. Did she tremble with desire, or with dismay? he wondered, and withdrew slightly. When her arms moved to circle his back and hold him, he smiled and knew the answer. She wanted him.

Lifting her hands, Blue Feather let her fingers touch his broad shoulders, exploring the play of muscles that flexed with his movements, moving up over his shirt to the soft pale hair that curled over the back of his collar. His hair was so soft, so fine, like slender threads of the summer flower, and she opened her eyes and smiled back at him.

Adrian shifted his body slightly, remembering the weapons he still wore in his belt, and began to remove them. His gaze held hers as he pulled out the knife and pistols and laid them within reach. They must have dug into her tender flesh, yet she had said nothing, he mused as he lowered his head and began to kiss her again. He kissed her softly at first, lingering over the honeyed taste of her lips, perplexed at the inexperience and shyness she exhibited, and understood with a sudden sense of triumph that no man had ever taken the time to teach her about love. Lust, perhaps, but not love.

Caressing her silken skin with deft, sure movements, he traced circular patterns with his tongue over her quivering breasts, watching her reaction. She was breathing heavily, turning restlessly beneath his hands and mouth, arching upward against his skilled fingers. Adrian explored her slender body until he knew every golden hollow, every succulent curve and fold of soft-scented flesh. His tongue blazed wet paths across the undulating muscles of her stomach and up the ridges of her ribs to the heavy swell of her breasts again, lingering sweetly and agonizingly until she cried out his name and tangled her fingers in his hair to hold him still. Writhing beneath him, she whimpered softly, aching for a release but not knowing how to achieve it. No one had ever brought her to the brink of such need before, and she was helpless before the onslaught of Adrian's teasing hands and mouth.

Now his hands dipped lower, moving between her velvet thighs, and she struggled against him.

"Non! Non . . ."

"Oui, oui, ma petite," he murmured. "You do not know yet what it is all about. Be still, and I will show you."

Shuddering, Blue Feather dug her heels into the soft earth and strained against his searching hand, her head tossing back and forth on the pillow of grass. How could she bear it? It was so sweet, so agonizingly sweet, and she had never dreamed of such a sweeping rush of ecstasy. She wanted to cry out, to shout to the wind whispering overhead that she had not known of such rapture. Wave after wave of pleasure rippled through her, leaving her weak and limp when it receded. Her eyelids grew heavy, and she nestled close to Adrian, nuzzling against him and murmuring in satisfaction as he smiled down at her.

"Now you shall do the same thing for me, cherie," he said softly, and rose to his knees. He unbuttoned his pants and shirt, shrugging swiftly out of them as Blue Feather gazed at his hard man's body with the pride of ownership.

He was hers. This tall, lean-bodied Englishman with his flat ridges of muscle and smooth skin was hers. He belonged to her as she had never thought to have a man, by the invisible bonds of love. She knew he loved her, though his lips never formed the words. No other man would treat her so tenderly, with such sweet caresses and burning kisses, and she would do whatever she could to have him always love her.

Adrian's skin gleamed in the moonlight, his sun-tanned face darker than the rest of his body, but somehow blending in without seeming odd. Perhaps it was the dark mat of curls on his chest, blanketing the smooth muscles, that kept the difference from being so noticeable. The springy curls narrowed to a vee at his hard, flat belly, and Blue Feather's eyes widened as he shed his trousers and stood nude before her. He was perfectly formed, a well-made man who was not ashamed of showing tenderness to his woman, and she reached out for him.

Lying back down beside her, Adrian took her into his arms and held her, admiring the differences in their skins. Blue Feather's was dark and golden while his was so much lighter. Her fingers moved lightly over his body, touching and exploring curiously, skimming over the bands of muscle. Pausing at the pelt of hair on his chest, she watched in fascination as it curled around her fingertip, then laughed softly.

"I have other, more interesting novelties to show you, my sweet," Adrian offered, and reached for her hand. "Here, love," he instructed, moving her hands to caress him, "like this."

Shyly, Blue Feather followed his hands, watching his reaction closely. Noticing that she was affecting him as he had affected her, she smiled. Her caresses grew bolder, and at last Adrian could stand it no more. With a desperate groan, he rolled atop her, spreading her thighs with his hands, slightly baffled by her resistance. *"Non, Non,"* she murmured as his hand found the place and his touch seared her flesh. Eagerly moving between her now parted thighs, he entered her velvety softness in one swift motion, shocked at the barrier he found there. Confused, he thrust deeply forward. His breath warmed her cheek, and she cried out in his ear, soft breathy moans that did not urge him on faster but begged him to stop.

"Mon Dieu," he groaned huskily, "I am the first. You feel so good! Hold me, I will make you feel as warm as the kiss of the sun, as cool as the first welcome spring rain . . . ah, Blue Feather," he ended in a sigh as he plunged deeper into her and felt her relax. There was no more pain for Blue Feather, or discomfort, only raging need. She felt as if she had always been empty but now was filled.

Words were no longer needed or wanted as he moved inside her, filling her with his hard man's body and making them one being, a creature of love. They both ached with the need for it, with the longing for that intangible meeting of two hearts and bodies. When the end came, bursting over them like a shower of stars, Adrian cried out, softly and hoarsely, his ragged words mingling with hers.

"Sweet love!" he cried at the same time as she clutched him fiercely and whispered her love.

"I am your love forever!"

Spent, drenched with a pearly mist of satisfaction and relaxing his body against her soft curves, Adrian lifted his head to peer down at her in the shadows. Moonlight gave her pure features a soft shimmer, a silvery glow that made Adrian think of angel wings and moondust, starlight and magic, and he smiled tenderly.

Adrian's eyes were shadowed, but Blue Feather

could still see the radiance reflected in them, the shine of love. Even if he could not say the words, could not voice his emotions, she knew it as surely as she knew the sun would always rise. He loved her, and it was enough for now to see it in his face, in the beloved features that she saw even in her sleep. One day he would realize it and would say aloud those precious words she longed to hear.

"Blue Feather," he said after a moment of exquisite silence where the nightbirds sang and the rush of water serenaded the lovers, "you are more wonderful than I had ever dreamed a woman could be."

Emotion choked her for a moment, then she managed to reply in a thick, prim whisper, "I am happy that you think of me in such a way."

Rising to his elbows, he let his fingers stroke the damp wings of ebony hair away from her face, his eyes soft with tenderness. "Perhaps I should not have yielded to the longing to hold you and love you as I just did, but I do not regret it for a moment. Why didn't you tell me your husband never touched you? Why did you let me believe it was so? I would never have—"

"I do not regret this—but, A-dri-an, I did not know this was what should be between a man and woman. Forgive me if you think I deceived you." There was another silence, not awkward but soothing, when Adrian murmured, *"L'etoile."* He thought how different she was from Nell who had truly deceived him, this innocent Indian girl who begged forgiveness after she had given him a precious gift.

Puzzled, she asked, "What star?"

He smiled. "You, sweet Blue Feather. You are my star. I know that now."

"There are many stars in the sky," she told him, and his arms tightened around her.

"Not for me," he said lightly, but his tone was serious

220

and his grip possessive. He kissed her on the tip of her nose and pushed away, sitting up beside her. "We must go back now before they think something has happened to us. Come." He held out his hand to her and she took it.

"I would rather stay here with you," she said then, and his expression softened.

"Ah, you don't have any idea how much I would like the same thing, sweet, but it is not possible now." Leaning over her, he reached for the robe she had left hanging on a nearby bush and held it out to her. "As much as I prefer the moonlight you wear, I suggest you wear the robe back to camp," he said, and she laughed as she took it.

"And shall you wear the moonlight?" she teased, and he grinned as he reached for his clothes.

"No, I don't wear it as well as you. . . ."

Chapter 13
Rendezvous

Morning came too early for Blue Feather and Adrian. They had spent the night in restless slumber, half-awake and thinking of the hours by the stream, a night of tossing and turning that left them heavy-eyed and restless. Even when they rode out from camp, sitting their mounts and riding side by side, they could not keep the memories at bay.

Harry had noticed at once, of course, his gaze troubled as he'd noted the lingering looks between them, the way they would reach for an object and accidentally touch hands. It was as plain as if written in the sky, and he'd sighed as he'd mounted his mare and followed them. Blue Feather would inevitably be hurt when Adrian left, and there was no help for it. What could he do? And what if Adrian insisted upon taking Blue Feather back to England or Italy with them? That would never do, either. Even being half French, the girl would be shunned and slighted and would never be happy in such an unfriendly atmosphere. This was her land. Here she belonged, a part of the forest and wind and sky around her. The only recourse that made any sense was for Adrian to remain in America, and that thought filled Harry with dread. His master did not belong in such a wild, uncivilized land. Adrian belonged in a world of his peers, of elegant homes and cultivated gardens, not this wilderness with tangled forests and wild, untamed mountain regions.

A frown furrowed his brow as Harry observed the wistful exchanges between Blue Feather and Adrian, the lingering, silent glances that fairly shouted of what had happened between them, and he stifled a groan of dismay. Adrian was so vulnerable now, having barely recovered from Eleanor Shelley's betrayal of him. What kind of happiness could he hope for in the shadow of such pain? And there was Richard to think of—the brothers who had once been close and were now hostile to one another. How could that ever be resolved if there was yet another wedge driven between them? Harry doubted if it could be done, and he thought pityingly of Richard, who had lost the woman he truly loved and been saddled with Nell Shelley as a bride.

Harry's morose thoughts were interrupted by a shout from Broken Arm as the trapper rose in his stirrups to point to a glittering ribbon of water just over the ridge.

"The Siskadee!" Broken Arm shouted, lifting his bandaged arm to indicate the wide sweep of river. "The Siskadee!"

Memory teased Adrian, and he turned with a questioning glance at Blue Feather. "The Siskadee?" he echoed, and she nodded happily.

"*Ai,* the Green River."

"Ah, yes, now I remember. It's the Crow name for it, right?"

"*Ai,*" she confirmed. "It is called Siskadee because of the Crow. It was their hunting ground. My people live there in the mountains," she added, pointing to the northwest.

Following her direction, Adrian felt a shiver of awe at the panorama spreading before him. He reined in his mare and stared, his gaze shifting from one splendid, snow-capped peak to another. Serrated mountain peaks gnawed at the sky with jagged teeth, tearing at the horizon in majestic splendor. A single eagle soared overhead, its cry spiralling down through the cloudless blue sky, an eternal, wildly triumphant cry of supremacy.

Adrian's eyes moved to Blue Feather where she gracefully sat her pony, her own eyes locked on the land spreading before them. For a moment Adrian was struck with the sudden memory of Madame du Jessupe and her pasteboard cards. She had told of his visit to a land of mountains and snow, had known that he would come to America long before he had. The star—she had told of a star, and it could only be Blue Feather. The girl was a bright, shining star in a dark, soulless night. . . ."

"See?" Blue Feather said then, one arm sweeping out to encompass all that lay before them. "This is my home."

"I know that you are glad to be back," he said softly, and she nodded.

"*Ai,* I have not seen The People in many moons. They will think me dead."

"You have many relatives?" Adrian asked, and she shook her head.

"No, not many are left. I have a cousin, Gray Eagle, and I hope that he will still be there. It is he who can go to tell my father that I still live, and tell him of my return to The People."

"Perhaps you should go yourself," Adrian suggested, but she shook her head again.

"No, it is forbidden. No one goes where Duvalle lives. He does not allow it, and The People fear him.

224

He is becoming as Cheney, who was before him."

"Cheney? I have heard you speak of him before. Who was he? Where did he go?"

Shrugging her slender shoulders, Blue Feather said, "He vanished like the morning mists. No one saw him go; no one knows where he went. He is like the spirits. . . ." Her voice trailed into silence, reverent and reflective, and Adrian wondered about this Cheney.

The mysterious man must have been imbued with a special quality to have inspired such fear and reverence from the simple Indians who were so close to nature. And for a mere man to have inspired an awe equal to this splendor and magnificence was a most profound mystery to Adrian.

His gaze moved again to the scene before him, and he thought that surely this must be the most beautiful place on earth. Nudging his mare closer, Adrian gave Broken Arm his reluctant attention when the old trapper beckoned him forward.

"Look, Duke," the old trapper said, pointing over the crest to the valley floor stretching below them. It lay like a green carpet, tufted with trees and stitched with a lazily winding ribbon of water. Innumerable cones of tan and brown sprouted from the valley floor, and Blue Feather gave a soft exclamation of delight.

"So many different tribes!"

Gazing at the tipis, Adrian asked, "How can so many hostile tribes live in peace?"

Broken Arm chuckled, and pushed back the wolf-head hat he wore. The gray and black wolf tail dangled over his left ear, giving him a comical appearance as he began pointing out the different tribes. Though old, his eyes were still sharp as he read the markings on the erected shelters.

"Pawnee, Arapaho, Crow, Utes, Nez Perce—"

225

"Shoshoni!" Blue Feather interrupted excitedly. She rose slightly on the broad back of her pony and peered into the distance, squinting at the familiar markings. "I see some of my people!"

"Your people are here," Adrian commented softly, almost to himself, and Broken Arm gave him a sharp glance.

Blue Feather was nodding happily, her voice bubbling as she said, *"Ai!* I am sure one of my kinsmen must be here also! Gray Eagle has attended a rendezvous before, and I heard him speak of it around the fires one night. Many people gather here for the rendezvous."

"A temporary truce must have been called, then," Adrian observed. "I see."

Blue Feather glanced over at him and tilted her head to one side. "That would not have happened before such a thing as the rendezvous," she said. "It is not the Indian who bothers to make peace with one another. It is the white man who shares his ideas. That is his strength."

Surprised by this observation from such a simple girl who was so young, Adrian stared at her for a moment. "This is so," he said slowly, "but there is something about the Indian that I feel the white man has lost, something vital and precious to the survival of the race."

Slightly confused by his words, Blue Feather just gazed at him with a puzzled expression. Though she did not understand his meaning, she did understand his tone. There was kindness and strength in him, a struggle to understand instead of condemn, and she smiled. The more she knew this man, the more she cared for him and trusted him.

Noting this exchange between Adrian and Blue Feather, the soft words and lingering glances, Broken

226

Arm frowned just as Harry had done earlier. He knew well the barriers that could come between a white man and an Indian girl, even a girl whose father was French. It would make no difference in either world as long as her parentage contained a drop of mixed blood. Before he could comment or say what was on his mind, there was a bellow of delight from behind him, and Ramone Jardin approached the trio.

"Mon Dieu!" the Frenchman crowed, lifting his rifle high. "We are here! It is the Green River!"

Broken Arm nodded. "Yes, it is."

"Then this is where we part company, old man," Jardin said with a sneer.

"And I cannot say I'm sorry," the old trapper returned coolly, "only relieved."

A dull flush spread up the Frenchman's thick neck, staining his cheeks above the straggly black beard he wore. His lips twisted in contempt, and his gaze reflected the same emotion as he looked first at Adrian, then to where Harry sat his gentle mare. It was only when he turned back to look at Blue Feather that his expression changed, altering subtly to a lascivious glower that made her shudder.

Intercepting Jardin's evil glance at Blue Feather, Adrian said icily, "I can express no sorrow at your departure, monsieur, only the length of time it is taking you to leave."

Jardin's eyes swung to Adrian and he grinned, his lips curling back to reveal his broken, decaying teeth. "We shall meet again, English, I swear it! And this time, your fate will rest in the hands of *le bateleur!*" Mockingly, he bowed from the waist, his dark eyes resting on Adrian's face.

Taken aback, Adrian gave a start at the title Jardin applied to himself, recalling the reading of the cards. He glared at Jardin with narrowed gray eyes, regarding him as more representative of *le diable,* the card that had depicted a naked devil with wild eyes, his wicked talons holding a tearful woman. Coincidence, he told himself, that he should think of those ridiculous cards and apply them to reality. It had only been chance, and Ramone Jardin was very real.

Breaking the tension between them, Broken Arm said, "I think we should ride instead of talk, gentlemen." His tone gave no room for argument, and he casually moved his Hawken rifle to rest across the pommel of his saddle.

Ramone Jardin gave a snort of sardonic amusement and remarked contemptuously that the trapper need not bother with the effort of keeping him from the weak Englishman, "for I shall not harm him now."

"I wasn't necessarily worried about you harming *him,*" Broken Arm replied with a lift of his bushy brows, and Jardin muttered a strangled oath as he wheeled his mount around. The Frenchman galloped away, shouting an order for his men to follow him. Adrian and the old trapper watched as they disappeared over the rise, leaving only clouds of dust behind.

Nudging her mare close to Adrian's, Blue Feather murmured, "You shall have to watch your back closely now."

"Because of him?" Adrian asked scornfully.

"You'd best take her warning seriously," Broken Arm said. "I would not trust that one at all."

"Oh, I don't. It's just that I think he will find it more difficult to kill me than he once supposed."

"I hope so," Broken Arm said, and Harry gave him a sharp glance. "I hope so," he repeated.

The closer they got to the sprawling encampment

below, the more the air around them changed. It was almost palpable with the odor of refuse and green-cured animal skins, the reek of whisky and of blood from freshly killed game, of smoky fires and browning meat. Dogs barked shrilly and men bellowed with drunken laughter. There were excited shouts in many different languages as several men engaged in a wrestling match, with the onlookers placing bets on the outcomes.

Adrian didn't know where to look first. Everything was new and fascinating, from the unkempt figures of the rough-clad trappers who had spent an entire winter in the mountains, to the red-skinned men who wore ragged blankets with all the dignity of a king in his royal robes. There were women, too, some not much older than the age of puberty, and all of them Indian. They were obviously slaves or captives and accustomed to being bartered, for they appeared to have no objections to being shoved from one man to another. He glanced anxiously at Blue Feather, who had ridden her mare so close to his that she was almost atop his mount with him.

Smiling, he said quietly, "Do not worry. You are safe with me, Blue Feather."

She looked up at him with wide blue eyes, the thick lashes shadowing the fear in them as she nodded. "*Ai*, I am much safer with you than with any other man here," she whispered, "but I would not like for them to decide to take me from you."

Glancing about him, Adrian wondered with a sense of uneasiness what would happen if that were to occur. After all, there was no law here in the mountains, unless one considered the law of survival.

"Somehow, my lord," Harry was saying, "I had thought this gathering would be more civilized. This is little more than a collection of vagabonds and footpads."

"Don't judge them so harshly," Broken Arm put in. "They have their own sense of justice and fair play, and this is the only time of the year they can relax, get drunk, have a woman, and talk to another human. The rest of the year is spent alone in the wilderness with only the beaver and grizzly bear for company."

"My word!" Harry murmured in distress. "Even the Indian?"

"No, not necessarily the Indian, but most of the trappers live a lonely life. Look at them, Harry, for they will be extinct one day," Broken Arm added reflectively. "More and more men are coming west every day, and soon the land will be defiled by towns and cities and civilization. The wild game will flee; the forests will be cut down for houses, fences and fires. Corn and beans will grow where wild flowers once basked in the sun. We move higher into the mountains, but more men come. This is the mountain man you see before you, a true knight in buckskin, the last of a breed. Soon there will be only men in frock coats and beaver hats roaming the ground we stand on now. . . ."

"No!" Blue Feather exclaimed in horror, thinking of her beloved forests and wild clean rivers flowing with boats and white men. "No, you do not speak straight!"

"But he does," Adrian disagreed sadly. "I think it will take many years, possibly several generations, but it will come to pass just as he predicts. Already there are men in New York — a big city — who talk of trading out west, of building forts and posts in which to trade and barter. It will come to pass," he repeated slowly.

"Perhaps rightly so," Harry commented. "After all, progress must be made."

Shrugging, Broken Arm said, "It doesn't really matter what we think. It will happen."

Dodging staggering drunks and stepping over snoring, unconscious men, they wound through the wide-flung confines of the camp until they found an area that had not yet been settled by a tipi or hut. It was on the fringes of the camp, not too far from the river and not too far from the edge of the trees.

"It's just us now, so we need to keep an eye on the girl," Broken Arm told Adrian in a low voice as they unsaddled their mounts. "Women here are considered fair game, so don't leave her unattended unless you want to lose her."

"They would take un unwilling woman?" Adrian asked incredulously, and the old trapper just stared at him.

"Indian women never have a say in the matter, Duke!" he exclaimed a moment later. "This isn't London or New York! Out here, if a man wants a woman he wins her in a game of chance, trades for her, or just takes her. It doesn't matter to him how he gets her, and her wishes are hardly considered."

"I see," Adrian said thoughtfully, and sliced a glance at Blue Feather. She was helping Harry set up their camp, cheerfully unloading supplies and staking out the tent, her small face alight with laughter at Harry's glum comments on the lifestyle of the trappers.

Resting his arm across the broad back of his gelding, Broken Arm said, "You think a lot of that girl, don't you, Duke."

Adrian nodded. "Yes, I do. Why do you ask?"

he shrugged. "Oh, no reason. Maybe you should remember that she's Shoshoni, though and not like you. She doesn't think the same way a white woman thinks, Duke. Girls like Blue Feather are brought up to think only of today, not tomorrow and *never* yester-

231

day. It's strictly survival out here, you see, and to long for the past or to wonder about the future could endanger her existence. One learns to accept, and to live."

"What are you trying to tell me now?" Adrian demanded, half exasperated yet knowing the old trapper was only trying to help.

"I'm trying to tell you that you've got more to worry about than whether that Frenchman wants to steal her. You may care about her, but she's not worth losing your life over."

"Don't worry about that, my friend. I'm not sure I even lost my heart."

"Ah, my honest friend, Blue Feather's grandfather is a great chief among the Shoshoni, and much respected by his people. He can take care of her much better than you can. But there is something else you don't know. I haven't mentioned it yet, and I don't want you saying anything in front of the girl, but . . ."

When he paused Adrian gave a gesture of impatience at his mysterious tone. "Well, what is it?"

"Years ago there was talk of gold in the mountains, of a Frenchman who had found it and hidden it. It was supposed to be Pierre Duvalle who found it, Duvalle who took refuge high in the mountains to keep the rest of the world away."

"Then why didn't you mention this before? Why wait until now? Does Blue Feather know?" Adrian demanded.

Waving a hand, Broken Arm sighed and said, "You don't much believe in letting me answer one question at a time, do you? I didn't mention this before because I didn't want the girl to hear me, and no, she doesn't know."

Bluntly, Adrian asked, "Why?"

"A wise man says little when it pertains to gold,

232

Duke. I didn't relish the idea of Jardin overhearing anything I might have said."

"And now?"

"And now I think he may already know. It's only my idea, of course. He never said anything, but there were times when he looked at the girl that I saw more than just lust in his eyes. There was a glitter that I have seen before, a glitter that always means gold and death."

Frowning, Adrian swiftly made the connection that the old trapper had already made. If Jardin had heard of Duvalle's retreat to the mountains with gold, and knew that this was his daughter, then it would be very easy to use one to gain the other. Lifting his head, he met Broken Arm's eyes.

"I understand."

Broken Arm nodded. "I thought you would. It's important that you get her to her people for her own safety."

"But I could keep her safe," Adrian mused aloud. "She need not stay with the Shoshoni unless—"

"Don't be foolish," Broken Arm said quickly. "You cannot protect her from gold-lust, Duke. It will take many more men than you could gather."

"Do you think Jardin would risk telling others about it?"

"He might. It depends on who he told."

Letting his gaze move around the sprawling acres of huts and tipis, Adrian said slowly, "And there are many men here from which he could choose."

"Right."

Adrian looked back at Broken Arm's weathered, seamed face. "Shall we walk around and see what we can see and hear?"

The old trapper's head dipped sharply. "That sounds logical to me, Duke."

Left in Harry's care and armed with not only a knife but a pistol, Blue Feather was told to stay out of sight in the tent. It seemed like a great deal of unnecessary caution was being used, but she was privately grateful for Adrian's concern. And even Harry seemed anxious for her welfare as he scurried about outside the tent, keeping up a continual flow of idle conversation so that she would not get lonely or bored.

"I say, Margarethe, there is an abundance of different woods here," Harry was saying as he returned with an arm-load of tree limbs and dead wood. "I've found oak, pine, birch, cedar, fir and others that I have no idea of what they may be. And even with all this commotion so near, I saw fat rabbits and several deer. Of course, there are so many people roaming about that I find it difficult to understand why the silly creatures don't flee, but there you have it. And . . . oh my, what do we have here?" he added on a note of dismay, and she stuck her head out the tent flap to see.

A man clothed in a breechclout and a robe of soft deerskin trimmed in ermine stood not far away, his arms folded across his chest and his copper face intent. He was not noticeably armed but for a knife in a beaded sheath at his waist, and he did not move a muscle as Harry cautiously reached for a loaded rifle propped against a nearby log.

"May I help you, sir?" Harry asked the man, who briefly inclined his head but did not move.

Staring at the man garbed in the familiar dress of a Shoshoni, Blue Feather's heart began to pound. It had been so long since she had seen one of The People, and this man had obviously recognized her, though she did not remember him.

Emerging from the tent in spite of Harry's frantic efforts to keep her hidden, Blue Feather paused.

"He is one of my people," she explained to the older man, "and I must speak to him."

Reluctantly, Harry allowed her to take a few steps closer to the man, though he pleaded with her to go no farther. Nodding, she spoke softly in Shoshoni, asking the man why he visited her tent.

"I was told to come," he answered.

"Who told you to do so?"

Instead of replying, the man asked, "Are you the one known as Blue Feather?"

"*Ai,* who are you?"

"I am The One Born After Rain. I am a friend of the great warrior Gray Eagle. Is he your kinsman?"

When she nodded, he said, "Your kinsman, Gray Eagle, told me to find you. He saw you ride in with white men, and wished to know if you did so willingly."

"*Ai!*" Blue Feather assured him quickly, and explained the tale of her capture by the Blackfeet and subsequent rescue by Adrian and the others. "They have been very kind to me and would return me to The People," she finished, and The One Born After Rain nodded.

"It is good. Gray Eagle will come to you tonight, to fetch you back to your grandfather, who waits for news of you. I will tell Gray Eagle what you have said."

Harry, who had not understood a single word, watched anxiously as the man turned and walked away with slow dignity. "What did he want?" he asked Blue Feather when he had gone. "Is everything all right?"

She nodded, but there was a pensive look on her face as she sighed softly. "I am well. He only wanted to tell me that my cousin is here and wishes to take me back to my grandfather."

"But that is wonderful news!" Harry exclaimed,

then paused. "It doesn't make you happy?"

"Yes, it does, but I . . . I . . . I will miss A-dri-an," she admitted with a sad smile.

"Ahhh," Harry said with sudden understanding. "I see."

"Do you? Do you understand what is in my heart?" Blue Feather turned and asked him.

"Yes, I do. But I also know that it is right that you be with your people, Margarethe. Think of how your grandfather has missed you."

"I think of that, but I also think of how I will miss Adrian," she said. "I had hoped that he would be the one to take me high into the mountains to find my father, not my cousin."

Harry perched upon a fallen log and regarded her thoughtfully. "His lordship may still wish to travel into the mountains with you," he said after a moment. "Do not be sad yet. There is still time to decide."

She shook her head, her dark hair whipping about her face as she stared down at the ground. "No," she said so softly Harry had to lean forward to hear, "Gray Eagle will come for me tonight."

"Well," Harry said, "I have no doubt that his lordship will make that decision for you. He can talk to this Gray Eagle person and tell him what he wishes done."

Blue Feather had to smile at Harry's assumption that Adrian's wishes would take precedent over anyone else's, but she didn't disagree. Perhaps it would be so. She would not worry until it happened.

"Come along," Harry was saying with forced cheerfulness, "scurry back into the tent until his lordship's return, and I will give you some bags to unpack for me. It should keep you occupied for a little while, and I will cook our evening meal."

Blue Feather spent the next hour unpacking strange

and diverse objects from Adrian's bags, examining curiously the soft garments and odd-looking footwear, and wondering what some of the items were used for as she laid them out. Harry had shown her a few things, such as the ink bottle and long feathered pen that Adrian used to write letters home to his Uncle Timothy. She knew little about that, though she had overheard Harry and Adrian talking about them one evening. Adrian seemed to miss his family, and had mentioned his brother — Richard — briefly and bitterly, a fact for which Harry had scolded him. It was strange, she thought as she neatly arranged a stack of blank paper upon Adrian's small wooden writing desk.

Adrian's appearance at the open flap of the tent immediately diverted her attention, and she smiled widely at him. His face was slightly flushed and his golden hair ruffled by the wind, but he was smiling back at her as he held out a paper-wrapped bundle. Blue Feather just stared at it for a moment, looking from Adrian's expectant face to the package.

"It is for me?" she asked at last, and he nodded.

"Yes. I bought it for you. Well," he prompted when she still did not reach out for it, "don't you want it?"

"Ai," she said, and put out her hands to take it. She just held it for a moment, turning it over and over in her hands and squeezing it slightly. When Adrian, impatient at her delay, threatened to open it for her, she laughed and pulled open the strings binding the crackling sheet of paper. A dress fell into her lap, a beautiful dress made of the softest doeskin and heavily beaded with hundreds of brightly colored quills and glass beads. Thick fringe hung at the neck, sleeves and hem, and Blue Feather knew it must have cost Adrian a great deal. She held the dress awkwardly, almost reverently, then slowly lifted her head to look at him.

"Well? Do you like it?" he asked when she still said nothing, and to his consternation she began to cry. Slow tears trickled over her cheeks, and she dashed them away with the back of one hand before they fell onto the beautiful dress. Rocking back on his heels, Adrian gazed at her in dismay. "You don't have to like it," he began, but she quickly shook her head.

"No! No, it is not that I don't like it, A-dri-an! The dress is more beautiful than anything I have ever owned before. I just . . . I just cry because of your thoughtfulness."

Helpless laughter welled in his throat, and he shook his head. "Just when I was beginning to think you were not like other women you surprise me," he said ruefully, and reached out to pull her into his arms, crushing the dress between them. Blue Feather immediately registered a protest at such harsh treatment of her gift, and Adrian released her with a laugh. "I suppose there are some things to which every female in the world reacts in a similar manner," he said fondly. "I am glad you like my present, little Blue Feather."

"Oh, I do! I do!" She held it up with delight, noting the fine needlework and tiny, even stitches.

"And what do I get in return?" he teased, shifting to sit cross-legged in the opening.

Faltering, and suddenly embarrassed that she had nothing to give in return, Blue Feather shook her head in dismay. Her head bowed, a curtain of ebony hair falling forward to hide her shamed face.

Adrian immediately sensed her dilemma and eased it by lifting her chin with his forefinger.

"I only meant this," he said, leaning forward to claim a kiss from her. Her lips parted beneath his searching mouth, and she gave a soft sigh of pleasure. Adrian's palm cupped her chin gently as his tongue probed searchingly, teasing, tasting the salt of the

238

tears she had shed. When he released her, she opened her eyes and gazed at him with such a yearning expression that he was taken aback.

Pushing her down on a pile of soft blankets he told her, "I'd like to see you put on the dress, but first you have to take this off." Delighted at his game, Blue Feather in one swift motion sat up and took her blouse off. She loved to watch the look in his eye as she sat revealing herself to him. Softly, he embraced her, kissing first her mouth and then letting a hot trail of kisses run down her neck, tracing a path between her breasts. He kissed each peak with tenderness, arousing such passion in her that she arched her neck back letting her breasts push against him and her hair brush past the floor. His hungry mouth released her as his hands worked to remove her skirt, delighting in the nakedness revealed. Again his lips showered her with kisses, sweet ones, lower this time till she could stand it no more and she cried out for him to stop.

Adrian let her undress him now — her hands, strong and determined as she worked his clothes off. Finally, with a daring that shocked him, her mouth found his secret place. She kissed and tickled and teased him until he pushed her away, gently lowered her on her back and entered her with sweet, wild abandon, riding until both lay sated and exhausted with their sweet love making.

"I shall hate to leave you," Blue Feather whispered with love swollen lips, not missing the questioning look in his eyes.

"Leave me? Who said you were leaving me?" he asked with a frown.

"My cousin is here and will come for me tonight," she answered simply.

"Your cousin? Here? But I thought . . . I was under the impression that your people were in the mountains at Wind River," he protested.

She nodded. "They are, but my cousin is here at the rendezvous. He says I must return to my grandfather."

"I can take you to your grandfather," Adrian began, but she was shaking her head.

"No, I am afraid that he will not allow it. Gray Eagle will say that I must go with The People, that I am an unmarried woman and not under the protection of male relatives. He will insist."

"I see," Adrian said thoughtfully. "I suppose that is easy to understand. It is the same in my country, you see."

"It is?" Blue Feather echoed in surprise. "Your women are not allowed to have freedom to choose, either?"

"Most of the time," Adrian replied darkly, thinking of Nell and how she had freely chosen a title for her husband instead of the man she had professed to love. Impatiently, he shook his head to clear it of the memories, adding, "But now I wish for you to stay with me. I do not wish for your cousin to take you."

Kissing his shoulder, she said, "And I do not wish to go without you! Then you will marry me?"

Taken aback with her honesty, Adrian was speechless for a moment, and Blue Feather sensed his hesitation. Her head lowered, tears of humiliation welling in her eyes at having spoken too soon. She glanced at the forgotten dress lying in a heap on the floor. It was only when Adrian reached out and once more lifted her chin so that she could face him and see that he was whispering reassuringly that she felt better. He wished it was otherwise, but he still could not bring himself to trust her totally. Could she have lured him with her innocence to get her home to The People?

"Perhaps we can come to some sort of an honorable agreement between us," he was saying noncommittally. "With Broken Arm's help, I may be able to make your cousin understand that I will not shame him, and that I would do nothing to dishonor you in the eyes of your people."

Carefully folding the dress and laying it aside, Blue Feather drew close to him and put her head against his shoulder. She drew in a deep, contented breath and said, "I will talk to him also. We were children together, and perhaps Gray Eagle will be as wise as our grandfather and understand my feelings."

Chapter 14
The Star

Stepping outside the tent, Blue Feather straightened and glanced around for Adrian. He was standing not far away with his back to her as he talked with Harry and Broken Arm. She began walking toward them. Her fingers raked through her long hair with a nervous gesture, and she wondered if he would like seeing her wear the dress he had given her.

She'd carefully donned the supple garment, then brushed her hair until it gleamed, leaving it long and free in the manner of The People. It hung around her shoulders like an ebony cape, lifting slightly with the gentle breeze that wafted through the air. Her hands smoothed the creases from the doeskin dress as she approached Adrian, her fingertips lightly grazing the beadwork that formed intricate patterns on the bodice and skirt.

Adrian turned and saw her before she could reach him, and he stared at her hungrily, thinking how Blue Feather looked as mysterious and exotic as any mythical goddess he had ever read about. She was so fresh and lovely, with her doe-shaped eyes and sable hair, her dusky complexion and alluring curves, and he swallowed a sudden lump in his throat as he stepped forward and took her hands.

"You are so beautiful," he said softly.

"It is the dress. . . ."

"No, it is not the dress, Blue Feather. You add grace and beauty to whatever you wear. You outshine the stars and the moon—even the sun!"

Blushing at his effusive flattery, Blue Feather looked down at the ground, lowering her lashes. She could feel the heat on her cheeks and dared not look back at Adrian lest he see the love and confusion in her eyes.

"*Merci*," she murmured.

"You're welcome, but can you not look at me?" he asked teasingly. His fingers tilted up her chin so that she had to look at him, and he was startled by the melting warmth he recognized in her gaze. His grip became a caress, only altering when Harry loudly cleared his throat.

"Hmm-hmm," Harry rasped. "I must say, Margarethe, that you are wearing a most becoming gown this evening!"

Glad of the interruption, and slightly flustered from Adrian's lingering gaze, Blue Feather smiled widely at Harry and said, "It is Shoshoni."

Adrian's hand dropped to his side. "I am pleased that I was able to purchase it for you. The man who sold it to me promised that it was Shoshoni, and I wanted you to have a dress that reminded you of home."

"A very thoughtful gift," Broken Arm commented.

"I have not worn such a pretty dress in many moons," Blue Feather said.

"I wanted her to have something lovely to wear when I take her home to her people," Adrian explained to the old trapper. "It has been a long time since she has seen them."

While Broken Arm nodded, Blue Feather was recalling the visitor earlier in the day and thinking of how her cousin might think differently. Gray Eagle had indicated his intention of escorting her home, but Adrian was the man she loved. She would do all in her power to see that he accompanied her to her grandfather. At first she had wanted to use him, but now she knew it was more than that. Her heart belonged to this fair man from across the wide sea, and she longed to be his. It was never far from her mind, and she thought often of that night beside the rushing waters, when Adrian had claimed her in the way a man claims a woman. This had shocked and surprised her. She had misjudged him once again; she never suspected him to be so virile, so aggressive, so at ease with passion. There had been nothing to prepare her for the way he had held her and brought such delight to her, shown her such pleasure.

A shiver rippled down her back, and Adrian glanced down at her, asking kindly if she was cold. Blue Feather had to shake her head, wondering what he would say if he knew why she had shivered. A slight smile curved her mouth at the thought, and Adrian smiled back.

"Do you think—" he began, but was interrupted by the arrival of a small group of strangers. The men paused at the edge of their small area, eyeing them for a moment before one of their group stepped forward.

"You are the one they call Broken Arm?" the bearded man asked, indicating the old trapper.

Cautiously looking them over, Broken Arm replied, "Who wants to know?"

"Jim Bridger."

Broken Arm aimed a stream of tobacco juice at the ground and snorted. "You're not Jim Bridger," he said flatly.

"No, but are you Broken Arm?" the man persisted.

The old trapper's wary gaze moved to the half-circle of men and his grip tightened on his rifle as he nodded. "I am."

"Then you are the man we seek. Jim Bridger asks to meet with you."

"Oh, he does, does he?" Broken Arm hitched up his pants with one hand, narrowing his eyes thoughtfully. "Well, where is he?"

"In his tent. He's not well, and there's a preacherman by the name of Whitman who's gonna cut on him" was the answer. "Bridger asks to see you before the doc starts cuttin' on him with a knife."

"I'll come with you," Broken Arm said after a moment's brief reflection. He glanced at Adrian. "You come along, too, Duke."

Nodding, Adrian stepped to lift his rifle, instructing Blue Feather to remain close to Harry until his return. "And you keep a sharp watch on her," he ordered Harry, who nodded.

Adrian and Broken Arm followed their escort across the littered camp of tipis, brush huts, sagging tents and refuse, earning curious glances at the distinct contrast between them. Adrian was garbed in his usual trousers, vest and elegantly-cut coat, with his boots retaining traces of Harry's efforts to keep them highly-polished. There were laughter and jeers as they passed through the camp, but Adrian ignored them with aloof dignity. He was well aware of the curious figure he must cut before these rough-clad, rough-mannered mountain men. These were men who had rarely seen another human being in the past year since the last rendezvous, and they were more accustomed to those like themselves. Most were garbed a great deal like Broken Arm. They wore tattered buckskins and had untrimmed hair and beards. Hats of coonskin or some other fur topped unkempt, unwashed heads, and Indian-style moccasins of elkhide or buffalo skin covered their feet. Adrian realized that in his expensive garments he must be a ludicrous sight to them indeed, and he felt a sense of relief when they finally halted before a large canvas shelter.

"Bridger's in there," the man said with a jerk of his thumb at the tent. "Yer to come on in."

Nodding, Broken Arm ducked his head and pushed aside the flap, motioning for Adrian to follow. When Adrian stepped forward, the bearded man put out an arm to halt him.

"Bridger didn't ask fer you," he began, but Broken Arm stopped and pivoted to face him.

"Duke goes where I go," he said flatly. Nothing was said for a moment as the bearded trapper regarded Broken Arm with narrowed eyes.

It was only after this silent exchange that the bearded man jerked his head once to indicate agreement and said, "I reckon it'll have ta be, then."

Without replying, Broken Arm turned back and entered the tent, with Adrian close behind him. As their eyes slowly grew accustomed to the dim, hazy light provided by a smoking oil lamp, they could see three men in the tent. One of them was stretched out on a pallet of blankets, and Adrian decided it must be Jim Bridger. He held a whisky bottle in one hand, and his bearded face was creased in lines of discomfort. When he saw Broken Arm's burly silhouette, Bridger grinned, holding up the bottle in a salute.

"Ahh, the great Broken Arm!" he said as the old trapper drew closer and knelt beside his pallet. "It's been a while since we hunted together, old friend."

"Indeed it has, Jim. How'd you end up on your back like this?"

"Ah, that was easy enough. About three years ago

I managed to stop a Blackfoot arrow with my back—you can probably tell from the location of the arrowhead that I was doing my best to get away at the time—anyway, it's still in there."

"Why?" Broken Arm asked in disbelief. "Couldn't you get somebody to pull it out for you?"

Shaking his head, Bridger grinned weakly. "Naw, my partners thought it might kill me if they tried. Now it feels like it already has . . . damned Blackfeet!" He shifted slightly and stifled a moan at the effort. "Today, when I was doing the dance of the yellow apron, the arrowhead must've moved over a bit. It feels like it's right up agin' my backbone."

"It is," said a voice from the smoky gloom beyond Bridger's pallet. "I'm Marcus Whitman," he introduced himself as he stepped forward. "I'm a competent physician, and examination shows that the arrowhead is going to have to come out as soon as possible."

"And how am I supposed to help?" Broken Arm asked with a glance at the half-drunk Bridger.

Grinning widely, Jim Bridger slurred, "Why, yer s'posed to help hold me down, Broken Arm! I knew you was here, an' I decided there wasn' anybody better fer th' job. . . ."

"That right?" Broken Arm responded with a glance at the doctor, and Whitman nodded.

"Yes, it is. If he moves even the slightest bit, it could be fatal."

Glancing around him, Broken Arm observed, "Well, with all this help you got around here, Jim, I don't know why you had to send for me, but I'm glad you did! This is probably the only chance I'll ever have to get the best of you."

"You old coot," Bridger responded in a weak voice, and Broken Arm agreed affably.

247

"Yeah, but I'm the one standing up, Bridger!"

Bridger laughed at that, then peered into the hazy shadows beyond the old trapper. "Who's that with ya?" he asked as he lifted the whisky bottle again. His gaze rested on the elegantly-clad, incongruous-looking man who stood quietly at Broken Arm's side.

"A good friend. I call him Duke, and he's just as fine as his name, Bridger."

Nodding, the bearded trapper slanted a glance at the doctor hovering over him. "Then let Duke grab a'hold of me too, Doc." Grunting with effort, Bridger turned over on his stomach, presenting his bare back to the physician. "Get on with it! Grab my legs, Duke!"

While Adrian complied, Whitman gave Broken Arm a nod as he lifted up a glittering scalpel. "Let us begin our work, gentlemen."

Several men crowded around the pallet, and Whitman told them to stand back and give him room. First he liberally swathed the area with a portion of whisky, then positioned his gleaming blade over the small puckered scar that hid the arrowhead from view.

The muscles flexed in Adrian's arms as he held down Bridger's legs, with Broken Arm at the man's head. Beads of sweat popped out on Adrian's forehead, and he looked away as Whitman sliced into the flesh with his scalpel. After a muffled cry of pain, Bridger thankfully lapsed into a faint, and Whitman swiftly and efficiently continued his work. Finally the physician held up a three-inch, barbed iron arrowhead in triumph.

"Here it is!" he cried, holding up the bloody trophy in his fingers. "A most famous piece of iron, indeed!"

An onlooker snatched it from Whitman's hand and fled the tent, crying aloud that he held the arrowhead that had been in Bridger's back for three years. There was a roar of confusion outside, and Adrian exchanged glances with Broken Arm, who shrugged and grinned.

"You can let go of his feet now, Duke," Broken Arm commented.

Rather sheepishly, Adrian released his tight grip on Jim Bridger and looked up at Whitman. "He'll be all right, Dr. Whitman?"

"Yes, he's too mean to die," Whitman responded with a relieved smile. "His heartbeat is strong and steady, and when he comes around he'll be fine."

"Thank God," Adrian murmured, and Whitman nodded as he wiped his hands on a clean scrap of cloth.

"Thank God, indeed," he agreed.

Broken Arm, ever resourceful, bent and scooped up the half-empty bottle of whisky from which Bridger had been drinking. Holding it up, he said, "No need to be wasteful, Duke!" When he'd swallowed a healthy amount, he held out the bottle to Adrian and urged him to do the same.

Feeling rather weak from all he'd witnessed, Adrian gladly took the whisky and followed Broken Arm's example. It slid down his throat with fiery warmth, reaching his stomach in a rush of heat. Half-gasping, he lowered the bottle and wiped tears from his eyes.

"That's good," he rasped, and Broken Arm burst into delighted laughter.

"So it is, Duke! So it is! And I have a notion that our friend Bridger may sleep awhile, so why don't you and I join the revelries outside?" Sweeping out one arm in a gesture reminiscent of a cavalier, Broken Arm motioned for Adrian to precede him from the tent. "Tell our patient that he's welcome to find us when he can, Doc," he called back over his shoulder, and Whitman laughingly replied that he would.

"Whisky sells for three dollars a pint," a smooth-shaven man said as he joined them outside the tent. "I have some for less."

Turning, Broken Arm asked, "And your name, sir?"

"Bowie—Everett Bowie," the man replied.

"Bowie . . . didn't you travel with Fitzgerald?"

Nodding, the trapper said, "Plenty of times until last year. Now it's not so easy to find the beaver, and prices aren't as good as they were. I trap alone, but Fitzgerald, Bridger and some others signed up with Chouteau. I want no part of that man. I don't work with a Frenchman!"

"You don't like the French?" Adrian inquired, and Bowie shook his head.

"No! The only Frenchmen I like are the dead ones. I've not been able to find one I trust."

Shrugging, Broken Arm put in, "Well, you can't hold it against Bridger for signing up with Chouteau. After all, trapping is getting harder, and there's less beaver and more trappers. A man does what he has to do."

Bowie agreed, then added, "Do you want the whisky?"

"British whisky?" Broken Arm asked, and Bowie's mouth split in a wide grin.

"Adventurer's of England twelve-year-old rye whisky, gentlemen!"

"We're right behind you, sir, right behind you," Broken Arm said.

As they trailed behind Bowie, the men found yet another distraction to interest them. A huge mountain of a man in shaggy buckskins was obviously drunk, had mounted his horse and was brandishing a loaded rifle over his head. He was challenging any and all comers—Frenchman, American, Spaniard, or Dutchman—to fight him in single combat.

"Is he crazy?" Adrian muttered skeptically, and Broken Arm laughed.

"Yes. That is Shunar, the bully of the mountains. He is a formidable opponent, Duke."

Nodding thoughtfully, Adrian was surprised to see a man step forward, obviously about to accept the challenge. He turned to Broken Arm with an expression of astonishment. "Is that man going to actually fight the drunken brute?"

Grinning, Broken Arm said, "That man is Kit Carson, Duke. I hear he's not a bad fighter."

Turning back to gaze at the scene with incredulity, Adrian could hardly believe what he was hearing as Carson calmly told the huge Shunar, "If you wish to die, I will accept your challenge."

Carson was half the size of Shunar, a slightly built man with light brown hair, but he exhibited no concern when Shunar defied him. The American mounted his horse and drew a loaded pistol, and as Carson maneuvered his horse into position, Shunar sneered. Both men surged forward at the same time, and almost at the same instant fired their pistols. While Shunar's ball passed harmlessly over Carson's head, he was not so fortunate, or perhaps just not as expert a shot. Carson's ball pierced Shunar's hand, exited at the wrist, then sliced through his upper arm just above his elbow. Still calm, Kit Carson went to fetch another loaded pistol in case Shunar expressed a desire to continue the battle. Shunar, however, seemed to lose his inclination to fight. He pleaded that his life might be spared while the onlookers roared with laughter and amusement.

"Is it over?" Adrian asked as the crowd drifted away to new amusements.

"Seems to be," Broken Arm replied, then sliced a glance at Bowie. "Lead on to the whisky, Mr. Bowie!" he boomed, and Bowie gladly complied.

They wound their way through clumps of men spinning yarns about their adventures or bartering, and passed several groups of white men and friendly Indians engaged in lively discussions. The mountain men danced about the campfires as much as the Indians did, and here and there could be heard music from a fiddle or mouth organ. Soulful hymns mingled with bawdy tunes, and there were shouts of glee as men bet on the outcome of a wrestling match or footrace. Contestants challenged one another at demonstrations of marksmanship, sometimes while riding at a wild gallop. It was a strange scene, and one Adrian was sure he would never forget.

Once more Adrian found himself sitting inside a dark, musty-smelling tent full of smoke. An oil lamp sputtered and flickered as Bowie pulled out a stone jug of whisky. It bore a Hudson's Bay label pronouncing it to be twelve-year-old rye whisky. The cork made a promising pop when pulled, and Bowie drank first before passing it to Broken Arm.

Adrian followed suit, leaning back against a stack of furs and listening to the two old trappers spin yarn after yarn, bragging impossibly and outright lying when they felt the urge. It was common practice and a highly entertaining diversion completely alien to Adrian. His interest flagged, then was piqued when he heard the two seasoned trappers begin to discuss the best method of trapping beavers.

"If'n you let 'em get up under their lodge, it's hard to flush 'em out," Bowie was saying.

"Naw, all you've got to do is use a chisel of some sort to break into the house, and you can catch them when they try to escape," Broken Arm disagreed. "Just use a net or a big stick to whack them with when they come out of their house."

"They're clever little critters," Bowie observed with a shake of his head. "Why, I've been up in a beaver lodge, and d'ya know, a man could hide there if he had to! When I come up inside it, holding my breath, I thought I was a goner. But there was this big pocket of air, stinkin' though it was, and I coulda stayed there as long as I wanted ta."

"Was it worth your while?" Broken Arm asked with a grin as he lifted the stone jug again, and Bowie laughed aloud as he admitted that it had been highly profitable.

"Those furry little things made me a bundle, but I spent it all on whisky and women!" he added with a gleeful chortle. "You know, that year I met some pretty interestin' folk at rendezvous. Why . . ."

Adrian smiled at their exchange; but his head was slightly spinning, and he began to feel queasy from the thick smoke and whisky. There was a churning in his stomach that had little to do with the fact that he had not eaten all day, and he struggled to concentrate on what they were saying.

". . .when I first came to the mountains," Bowie was saying with a shake of his close-cropped head. "Men used to talk of you and Duvalle and the other one—what was his name again?—Cheney! Yeah, that's it. Cheney. The crazy one, they said."

"It's hard to remember Duvalle riding with Cheney" was all Broken Arm would say, but the other men never noticed his reticence. Bowie was still musing aloud, occasionally drinking from the stone jug and talking as if accustomed to hearing only his own voice.

"Yeah, and I remember when you killed that man, too. What was his name? I can't recollect it rightly now, but I remember hearing about it. It was the same summer old Dacus was killed by that mama grizzly . . . do you recollect that?"

Broken Arm had grown very still, his eyes peering at Bowie through the thick smoke and gloom of the tent, and Adrian could feel the old trapper's sudden tension.

"I don't quite recall," Broken Arm said at last, casually as if it did not matter.

In truth, Adrian realized that it did not matter very much to most of the mountain men, though somehow he sensed it mattered a great deal to Broken Arm. Death was commonplace, something that happened or did not happen, and was not much considered. Survival was an instinct, and if a man was killed, he had not been careful enough.

The smoke began to choke him, and Adrian stood up abruptly, gaining both men's attention as his head grazed the low ceiling of the tent. Broken Arm peered at him in the hazy light, squinting against the smoke.

"Whatsa matter, Duke?"

"I need to get back to our tent," Adrian replied. "Care to come along?"

"There's no hurry," Broken Arm began to protest, but Adrian shook his head.

"Blue Feather mentioned something about one of her kinsmen coming to get her tonight. I need to be there."

"A kinsman?" Broken Arm echoed.

"Yes, a cousin, I think. Name of Gray Eagle."

Startled, Broken Arm jerked. "Gray Eagle? I've heard of him, Duke!"

254

"Well, he's at the rendezvous and sent word that he's coming for Blue Feather tonight."

Shaking his head, the old trapper commented, "Gray Eagle is not a man to trifle with, Duke. He's a powerful warrior and will soon be chief. I heard the old chief is dying."

"Dying?" Adrian echoed slowly. "I see. . . ." If the old chief were truly dying, it would be best to get Blue Feather to her people as soon as possible. It would be too bad for her to have come this far and be too late, and with that decision made, Adrian stepped to the open tent flap.

"I'll be along later," Broken Arm called after him, and Adrian merely nodded as he stepped out into the fresh air. He took a deep breath, letting his gaze travel from the humps of hills and the sharper outline of the high mountain peaks to the placid waters of the Green River. Sloping banks led to thick underbrush and towering trees, and the blue-green waters looked almost black in the twilight. A pale sky had darkened to purple, and distant ridges glowed with a translucent light. If one ignored the brawling inhabitants, the piles of refuse and temporary shelters that had sprung up like mushrooms, the Green River site would have been peaceful and tranquil. Adrian briefly wondered what it would look like when they were all gone, then turned in the direction of his tent. He had to talk with Blue Feather, had to decide his course of action.

Glancing up from the frayed ends of rope she was reworking into a lead line for the horses, Blue Feather saw Adrian approaching. A smile instantly curved her mouth, and she forgot the frayed rope, letting it fall unnoticed to the blanket she sat upon.

Not far away, kneeling beside the campfire, Harry also saw Adrian, and paused in the task of stirring a rich, bubbling stew he had prepared with Blue Feather's help.

Blue Feather was pushing to her feet, murmuring that she had worried about something happening to Adrian, and now here he was, looking as fine as he ever had.

"I doubt that any of these men would harm him with Broken Arm close by," Harry observed, earning a disagreeing frown from Blue Feather.

Peering down at the servant, she said, "There are many things that happen at rendezvous, Harry. I have heard it told over a lodge fire how men are crazed by the white man's firewater and do things they would not usually do. There are always killings at these things."

Horrified, Harry said, "My word! And to think that we came here willingly—"

"Came where willingly, Harry?" Adrian asked as he drew close enough to hear them.

"Here, my lord. Margarethe was just informing me of some of the more popular activities that normally occur at this function—activities that include murder among them."

Faintly amused by Harry's disapproval and distress, Adrian laughed aloud. "Turning coward on me, Harry old man?"

"No, not cowardly, my lord—just sensible. Perhaps we should not linger here too long." Harry looked across the campground now studded by blazing fires and silhouetted figures dancing eerily about. "It puts me rather in mind of a scene from Dante's *Inferno,* my lord."

"Does it? To an active imagination I suppose there is a certain resemblance, Harry, but I must say that I

256

am a bit surprised by your thinking so," Adrian stated with an uplifted eyebrow. "It seems rather out of character for you to be so nervous."

Confused by their conversation, and anxious that Adrian would leave without her, Blue Feather pressed close to him. She tucked her hand into the folds of his vest with the pretence of rebuttoning it, letting her fingers gently stroke the soft material of his shirt. His heart thudded against her fingertips, strong and steady, and she looked up at Adrian as he talked with Harry, letting her gaze move over his features. Only Harry's urgent tone distracted her attention from the study of Adrian's face, and she glanced over at him.

"Begging your pardon, my lord," Harry was saying, "but may I have a private word with you?"

"Private, Harry? There's only the three of us here. . . ."

"Yes, I know, but . . . but there is something I must say to you, and I am not certain it should be heard by tender ears," Harry replied.

Blue Feather looked directly at him. "What do you mean, Harry? And where is Broken Arm?"

Blinking in surprise as if he'd just recalled the missing trapper, Harry asked, "Yes, where is Broken Arm?"

"He's visiting with an acquaintance," Adrian replied. "Now what is all this about?"

"It's all about that gentleman standing over there in the shadows," Harry answered reluctantly, indicating the direction with a wave of one arm. "He's been hovering about our camp for the past hour. I had hoped you might discover his reasons for doing so."

Turning, Adrian stared in the direction Harry was pointing, but could discern no one in the dark shadows. He turned back to Harry with a puzzled expression. "I see no one," he began, but Blue Feather gave his sleeve a sharp tug.

"I see him," she said quietly. "It is The One Born After Rain. He is my cousin's messenger."

"One born after rain . . ." Adrian repeated, then paused and added, "Oh, I see. That is his name. Well, shall I invite him to join us?"

"No, he has gone now."

Exasperated by this, Harry put in, "I should certainly like to know what is going on, my lord! This is most disturbing, and I find it awkward that we have a constant trespasser encroaching upon our privacy!"

"Calm down a bit, Harry," Adrian reproved. "After all, this is not exactly our private estate. We are in the midst of many people and cannot expect that we shall attract no attention."

"Nonetheless, I find it most disturbing," Harry repeated with added emphasis. *"Most* disturbing!"

"Well, do not fret too greatly about it, for I intend that we shall leave early tomorrow. . . ."

"Leave?" Harry grasped eagerly at this hope. "We are returning to New York, my lord?"

"New York!" Rather startled by this, Adrian hated to dash Harry's obvious desire to leave, and shook his head slowly. "No, not New York, Harry. I had in mind the Wind River range, where Blue Feather's people are living. We need to take her home to them."

"Take Margarethe home? Tomorrow?" Harry looked from Blue Feather to Adrian, his brows lowering in a frown. "I had not considered that you might wish to do so quite this soon."

"Neither had I, but it now seems imperative, as her cousin has expressed a desire to accompany her instead of letting her travel with me. You know, Harry, that I have long wished to see as much of American wilderness as possible."

"Yes, my lord," Harry answered in a resigned tone. "I just had not considered how much wilderness there was until we arrived."

"Neither had I, Harry. It never occurred to me that this land would be so vast and unsettled. I find it most adventuresome," Adrian said. His gaze swept around them, taking in the high mountain peaks and virgin forest that stretched for miles and miles. Even in the dark he could sense the uncharted territory that lay waiting for man to explore it, and felt a sudden rush of excitement. This was the adventure he had craved, filling the empty void in his life, and Blue Feather was a most important part of that. "We shall leave at first light, Harry," he said then. "I have every intention of being the man to see our lovely companion home. If I allow her to leave with her cousin, I may never see her again."

"That is true, my lord."

"And if I were to never see her again," Adrian continued, turning his gaze back to the girl, "I would not be happy."

Blue Feather smiled at his words, and her heart swelled with happiness. Belatedly remembering her manners, the lessons she had been taught by The People, she looked down at her feet as any modest Shoshoni woman should do. It was not her place to respond to such comments in front of others, for it would be unseemly. Instead, she asked demurely, "Would you like some stew? I will go and prepare you a bowl."

When she had stepped away to the blackened pot hanging over the fire, Adrian lowered his voice, looking directly at Harry as he said, "I will expect you to sleep alone in her tent tonight, Harry."

Keeping his expression carefully blank, Harry replied, "Very good, my lord. Shall I begin packing our supplies?"

"Yes. I think that would be a good idea, Harry." Adrian put out a hand, touching his servant lightly on the shoulder. "You don't approve of what I'm doing, do you, Harry?"

"It's not my place to approve or disapprove, my lord. I'm only a servant, deaf, dumb and blind to my master's whims—"

"Oh, spare me, Harry! We've been too close too long for you to pull that master-servant relationship on me now! I'm not asking for your approval, just clarification of where you stand."

"Very good, my lord, for I believe you must know that I stand where I have always stood—at your side no matter the action or consequences." Harry met Adrian's opaque gaze directly, and a current of understanding passed between them.

Adrian's fingers tightened on Harry's shoulder. "I thought you would," he said softly. "Thank you, Harry."

"No thanks are needed, my lord. Shall I begin packing now?"

"Yes, that would be excellent," Adrian replied, letting his hand fall away.

After finishing his full bowl of stew, Adrian retreated to his tent, where he gathered his papers and pen. He had often been in the habit of writing notes of what he saw, describing the land and people and animals, but since having encountered Blue Feather, he'd ignored his journal. Now he intended to write a description of the rendezvous and the events that had happened in the past few weeks.

He was scribbling busily when Blue Feather crouched at the tent opening, peering hesitantly inside. Adrian put down his pen and smiled at her.

"Come in," he invited, and she smiled back as she entered.

"Harry sent me. I do not wish to disturb you," she began, but he shook his head.

"You could never do so, Blue Feather," he said gently. He patted a spot on the blanket beside him, and she happily positioned herself at his side. "Tell me," he began as she nestled closer, "what do you know of the rendezvous?"

After a short silence, she replied, "I know that it is good for the Indian because he can trade for things he needs, and I know it is good for the white man because he can cheaply buy furs that he sells elsewhere for much more money. Often the white man cheats the Indian by giving him only firewater or cheap trinkets for the furs, but that is the Indian's fault for allowing him to do so." She paused and looked up at Adrian. "Is that what you wanted to know?"

Ruefully, he replied, "More or less. You're right, though, Blue Feather. Even I, in my short time here, have found that my fellow intruders in your land shamefully cheat your people. We buy rich furs for little or nothing, and sell them in St. Louis at exorbitant rates. Of course, the rendezvous is an excellent alternative to getting the furs to market themselves, and also a good time for the mountain men who participate, so I do not foresee an end to it as does Broken Arm. Why should it end? It's quite profitable for the men who sponsor this yearly event, for they not only make money from the eventual sale of the furs, but from the mountain men as they linger here, buying whisky purchased in St. Louis for thirty cents a gallon and sold here for three dollars a pint. Then there's the average St. Louis price for tobacco, coffee or sugar at ten cents a pound, lead six cents, and gunpowder seven cents. I have noticed that it sells here for two dollars for each item." He glanced down at Blue Feather's upturned face and sighed. "And of course, there are the inevitable Indian girls like yourself who are exploited here. I find rendezvous a rather sordid business instead of the romantic adventure I had hoped to find." His arm curved around her shoulders and he held her closely. "You are the best thing I have yet found in this wilderness, sweet Blue Feather," he added as his lips brushed against the top of her head.

Shivering from his touch, she squeezed her eyes tightly shut, wanting this moment to last forever. She was here alone with Adrian, and though he had not yet declared his love for her, she knew he would. It was as inevitable as the rising of the sun, the path of the moon through the sky, and the fall of rain and snow.

The lamplight flickered and shadows danced around them as they sat close, Adrian's comforting arm circling Blue Feather's slender shoulders and her head nestled close to his chest. She could hear his heart beat beneath her ear, could hear the rhythmic cadence of his breathing, and she sighed with contentment. This was a closeness she had never before felt in her life, the special intimacy that she'd suspected existed, but had never dared dream might be hers. Now she shared that with Adrian and felt like her heart soared on the wings of an eagle.

It was only when Adrian leaned slightly away from her, his voice deep and husky, that she opened her eyes to look up at him. He was staring at her solemnly, and Blue Feather slowly returned from her pleasant reverie to pay attention to what he was sa ing.

"I have news of your family," he was saying, an she frowned slightly.

"My family? Do you mean Gray Eagle?"

"Only partly. No, I meant your grandfather. I wa told that he is . . . well . . . he is ill, Blue Feather and may be dying soon."

Sharp tears stung her eyes, and Blue Feather struggled against them. Hunching her shoulders, she put her face in her hands to hide her weakness. It was a moment before she could say anything and then she had to clear her throat. "I had hoped to see him before he took his last walk," she said, looking up again. "That is one of the reasons I have felt so strongly about returning to my people."

"I am sorry," Adrian sympathized.

"It is the way of the world, A-dri-an. One is born, one lives, one dies. There are tears and laughter in every life."

Reaching out for her again, Adrian took both her small hands in his larger ones and said earnestly, "I am taking you to your people, Blue Feather. We will leave in the morning for your grandfather's camp."

"But what of Gray Eagle? Will he not come for me tonight as he has said?"

"Probably, but you are with me now. I will talk with him myself and explain what I wish to do."

"He will not let me go with you."

"He may not have a choice in the matter," Adrian replied in a determined voice. "You are with me," he repeated.

Smiling, she said, "That is true," and leaned over to place a kiss on the tip of his nose. Adrian responded with a hungry kiss slanting across her mouth, his lips plundering hers with such intensity

263

that it took her by surprise and she gasped. He took immediate advantage of her half-open mouth to probe gently with his tongue, flickering in hot, darting jabs that left her breathless. She moaned, a soft sigh of surrender, and he pushed her gently back on the thick cushion of blankets and furs spread on the floor of his tent.

The air in the tent was charged with steamy moans and soft, half-whispers of desire, hot and moist and urgent. An oil lamp cast its glow across them with leaping light and hazy shadows, and Adrian's journal and papers were soon forgotten. The ink bottle lurched sideways as his foot bumped it, spilling an indigo pool onto a blanket, but neither of them noticed. They were wrapped up in each other and unaware of the world about them.

There was a rustling of clothes being shed, the soft murmurs of two lovers, and soon the sweet sound of surrender. Blue Feather's arms lifted to curl around his neck and draw him close, and her lips barely grazed his as Adrian moved against her.

Blue Feather could feel the heated length of him nudging her thigh, and instinctively she reached down to hold him. Adrian stifled a groan, and she knew she had pleased him somehow, so her inexperienced fingers circled and held him boldy. When Adrian sucked in a deep breath, she became more adventurous and began caressing him with increasingly rapid movements.

"A-dri-an," she said softly, so softly he wasn't quite certain he'd heard her at first, and his head lifted from the golden hollow of her throat and shoulder. Slate-gray eyes hot with passion narrowed down at the dusky girl in his arms, and Adrian stared at her. One hand lightly caressed the sable tendrils of hair spilling over her forehead into her eyes, and he traced the arch of her delicate eyebrows with a forefinger.

Love. It was not the first time he had thought of love when he thought of Blue Feather, and though he was in love with this girl, did he love her enough to marry her and cast his lot with her forever? Could he after Nell? Could he trust himself not to be wrong about her as he was about Nell? Instead of answering, he held her more closely, his mouth brushing against the high sculpting of her fine cheekbones, over the satiny softness of her skin to the tiny whorls of her ear. His voice was a husky whisper as he said, "You are my star, sweet, my shining star of love."

"And you are my sun," she breathed, cradling his face in her palms as his mouth moved back to tease the throbbing pulse in her throat. When his lips moved lower, tracing a fiery path to the soft swell of a breast, Blue Feather moaned aloud, arching her back as she liked to do. Straining to hold him closer, she gave a cry of regret when Adrian shifted away from her, and her eyes opened to gaze up at him. He was smiling slightly, a tender curving of his mouth that erased the questioning look in her eyes. Then Adrian's hands slipped beneath her to cup her hips and hold her still, his lean, hard body surging forward as he entered her.

Twisting, turning in his embrace, Blue Feather purred with delight, and Adrian lifted on his elbows to push back the tangle of dark hair from her eyes so that he could press small kisses along the line of her brow, over her nose and down to her lips. Tasting, exploring with the tip of his tongue, he could feel her trembling in his embrace. She quivered with the need for him, with the desire to hold him even closer, and her heels burrowed into the thick furs and blankets spread on the tent floor as she pushed against him.

"Slow, love . . . I want this to last forever," he murmured against her cheek. His arms spread outward, grasping each of her hands and holding them as his mouth moved along the path that his right hand had just travelled. His lips skimmed over her shoulder and arm to the soft skin of her inner elbow, pausing to taste and tease with the tip of his tongue, then moving along her softly rounded forearm to her wrist, then the heel of her palm. There he stopped to trace the sensitive creases of her palm with his mouth, lifting it slightly so that he could kiss each of her fingers in turn. When Blue Feather made a murmur of protest—or delight, he wasn't sure which— Adrian nibbled on her fingertips.

"A-dri-an," she whispered urgently, no longer able to deny the boiling fire deep within her, "now! Please . . ." She wasn't quite certain what she needed, didn't know if he could repeat his former magic and satisfy this swelling need that threatened to consume her.

The dim flame of the oil lamp afforded little light, just enough so that Adrian recognized the smoldering fire in her eyes, and he finally responded to her plea. Now he began to move against her, rocking with a quickening tempo that brought strangled cries from Blue Feather's throat. Her head thrashed to and fro on the cushioning fur, and her exquisite features were knotted in a look of concentration. Abruptly changing position, Adrian rolled over in a deft movement that put Blue Feather astride him. He had to laugh at her look of confusion and bewilderment, but a simple thrust of his hips left her in no doubt as to what to do.

Now she was in control, half lying atop him with her hands splayed on his broad chest. Swinging back a long fall of hair to drape over one shoulder, Blue Feather rocked forward and was rewarded by a subtle change of Adrian's expression. His silvery eyes glittered in the lamplight, and his mouth thinned to a taut line as he reached up to cup the firm breasts thrusting temptingly above him. Toying with the puckered tips that swayed just out of his reach, Adrian could feel his own build-up of desire. Blue Feather moved sensuously, her silken thighs clasping him around the middle in a light, clutching grip.

As the rolling sensations swelled in ever-rising tides, Blue Feather began to swing back and forth, her lithe body rocking sinuously against Adrian. Her eyes were closed and her head thrown back, long ebony hair spilling down her back to brush his thighs with each movement of her body, and he could not hold back a groan. His palms cupped her breasts, and he thrust upward, his sudden hard lunge making Blue Feather cry out, a soft sound that was muffled by the canvas tent over them. Together they moved in even strokes, striving higher and higher, faster and faster until she cried out again, a lingering cry of ecstasy that signalled her release. Adrian's hands briefly tightened on her breasts as he reached his own release, a shuddering explosion that shivered through his entire body.

When Blue Feather slumped forward, her hair falling across his face and shrouding both of them in fragrant sable clouds, his arms moved tiredly to circle her quivering body. The world had receded into a mist of magic and wonder, and he was lost, lost in thoughts of Blue Feather, bright stars, and the rapture they had just shared together. It was suddenly hot in the tent, too hot, and he longed for a cool breeze to sweep over his body. A fine mist dotted his skin, and he could feel the same sheen on Blue

Feather's tawny curves.

"I love you, Blue Feather," he surprised them both by saying into her ear, and she was still for a moment.

Holding her breath, hardly able to believe he had said those three most important words, Blue Feather drew back and gazed down at Adrian with misty eyes. Crystal tears shimmered on the long sweep of her lashes like diamond drops, and she blinked them away as she whispered, "Oh, A-dri-an! I love you, too!"

"I know," he murmured huskily, "I know. And we shall be together always."

"Always?"

"Always," he confirmed, nuzzling that special hollow where her neck curved into her shoulders. Taking her hand when she pulled slightly away, he turned it over and kissed her open palm. Blue Feather's fingers curled back to stroke the side of his face as he did, and she smiled down at him.

"I hope so. . . ."

"We *shall*," he said. "I love you and want to be with you always, be husband and wife. That means forever. You have rescued me from the depths of despair, shown me that there can be love and goodness where I thought there could be none. I no longer carry the burden I once carried in my heart."

"You *are* my heart," Blue Feather replied softly as she swallowed the sudden lump in her throat.

Adrian broke into a happy grin. "Tommorow I will take you to your grandfather and ask his blessing upon our union, sweet Blue Feather. I shall marry you in the Shoshoni way, so that nothing will ever mar our new life together."

"Then you will take me with you to your land?" she asked.

Adrian paused thoughtfully, then said, "No . . . I don't think so. Our home will always be here."

Pleasure glowed in her eyes as Blue Feather said, "Then I am truly happy, because I was afraid you would want to leave the mountains and cross the big water to your country instead of stay here. I am not certain I could be content there, though I would have tried for your sake."

"I know that," he said gently, "but now I have no need to return to England. I have found my heart's desire here. This is my home, here with you and Broken Arm and the wide blue sky and the mountains that rise so high I can almost reach up and touch God—" His words slowed to a halt and he frowned. Blue Feather touched the crease between his brows with her forefinger.

"What is troubling you, A-dri-an?"

Sighing, Adrian said, "Harry."

"Harry? But why? He loves you and serves you well." A matching frown touched her brow, and she added, "And you love him."

"That's just the point," Adrian replied. "Because I do care about Harry and he cares about me, I must do the right thing and send him home to England. He has family, you see, real family and not just an employer. I am certain he will want to see them again and not remain here."

Shaking her head, Blue Feather said, "Doesn't Harry belong to you just as I do? I don't understand. . . ."

"It's very difficult to explain, Blue Feather," Adrian said with a sigh, and pulled her to his side to nestle next to him. "I cannot explain hundreds of years of English social rules easily, but let it suffice to say that Harry—though much loved by me—is a servant to my family, and has been so since he was a very young man."

"Was he forced into service?"

Adrian shook his head. "No, it's his choice, his vocation in life. Harry has never known any other way of living, you see, but now his devotion to me had endangered his own well-being. I feel responsible for him and would rather see him return to my family than to remain here and risk being injured or killed."

Slanting a glance up at Adrian's troubled face, Blue Feather restrained the impulse to brush a damp strand of pale hair from his face. Instead she said, "Harry will not want to leave you."

"I know, but I must let him make that choice." Pausing, Adrian reflected on the fact that every day in this savage land brought new dangers, new risks that he could no longer subject the faithful Harry to without giving him the opportunity to return to England. Managing a smile, Adrian said, "Even if Harry decides to go, I will still have you to give me comfort, sweet Blue Feather. With you at my side, life cannot be too harsh."

Wriggling closer to him, Blue Feather put an arm around his chest to hug him. She laid her head against the smooth, broad expanse of well-muscled flesh and let her hand roam. The pads of her fingers explored the ridged bands of muscle with light, skipping movements, moving lower and lower over his belly until Adrian caught her wrist in a firm grip.

"Minx," he growled mockingly, and twisted so that she was beneath him again. "Insatiable, greedy, voracious minx! You are so impetuous and impatient. . . ."

Blue Feather gave an irritated shake of her head. "You know I cannot understand the meaning of all those words you use," she began, but he stopped her with his lips over her mouth.

"Perhaps not," he breathed a moment later. "But I think you can understand this, my sweet love. . . ." And his body lunged forward, removing all necessity for speech as he was ready for her again.

It was finally quiet on the banks of the Green River. The wind had ceased blowing, and the stars sprinkling the night sky were hidden by a cover of clouds. Shadows blended in with black silhouettes outlined against the paler background of the river, flickering with the suggestion of movement, but all the revelers were either asleep, in a drunken stupor, or closeted with the female of their choice. Campfires had burned down to smoldering embers or gray ashes. Only the most hardy had lasted until this final hour before the rising of the sun.

Alone in their tent near the thickly-wooded slopes, Adrian and Blue Feather had at last slipped into an exhausted sleep. She lay asleep in his arms, covered only by a fur, her bare body fitting closely to his. Adrian's warm breath stirred the back of her neck, and his soft snores filled the tent.

It was not Adrian's snores that woke her but some alien sound, something different in the night, a disturbance that penetrated her slumber to prick her. Heavy lids refused to lift in spite of her struggles, and Blue Feather slowly sank back into a light sleep. It came again, the stealthy sound like a purring animal, rousing her so that she rolled away from Adrian to her stomach, burrowing her face into the angle of her folded arms. A murmured protest at the intrusion of her sleep escaped her, but that was all. Blue Feather drifted back into that netherworld of half-dreams and interrupted slumber.

271

Moments later a cool breeze drifted in through a slash in the canvas tent, wafting over the sleeping couple. Blue Feather lay closest to the side of the tent, and she shivered at the sudden draft. The fur had slipped away when she'd turned over, and goosebumps prickled her bare, chilled flesh, finally penetrating her sleep. Drowsily, she lifted her head and peered through the shadows to discover the source.

Two hands darted through the vertical slash in the tent to grasp Blue Feather, one large palm covering her mouth and effectively silencing her before she could scream. Her heart pounded and she began to struggle, but the copper face looming over her became recognizable in the gloom. Gray Eagle—he had come for her as he'd said.

Swallowing her scream at the warning shake of his head and threatening glance at the still-sleeping Adrian, Blue Feather nodded to indicate her willingness to cooperate. He would not harm Adrian if she did as he wanted. Despair flooded her as Gray Eagle jerked his head to signal that she was to come with him. Though she longed to cry out and wake Adrian, to plead with him to hold her and not let her cousin take her, Blue Feather dared not do it. It was too risky, for Gray Eagle might very well kill Adrian without a thought. And she knew that Adrian would not let her go without a fight.

So she nodded silently and motioned with one hand toward her clothes lying in a tumbled heap. She did not miss the sudden narrowing of Gray Eagle's eyes, or the scornful glance he raked over her as he gave a short jerk of his head. Fully aware of her nudity, Blue Feather reached for the soft doeskin dress Adrian had given her, and she fought against the weakness of tears. Her trembling hands pulled it over her head, twisting to work it down over the thrust of her breasts. It was still bunched around her waist when Gray Eagle impatiently pulled her through the slash he had cut into the tent with his knife.

Pulling her with him into the deep shadows of the trees behind their tent, Gray Eagle did not speak until they reached the horses waiting in a small clearing well beyond the campground.

"We ride now" was all he said as he motioned her onto a paint pony.

Blue Feather did as he bade her, though her heart ached and her throat was tight with unshed tears. She was bitterly aware that once more she was being abducted without regard to her own desires. Only this time it was as kinsman, and he would not understand or tolerate her wishes to remain with a white man, especially a white man who knew so little about the land.

Mounted and impatient, Gray Eagle reached out for her mount's bridle and gave it a jerk so that the paint followed him. Blue Feather sat numbly, only turning around once to gaze back in the direction of the tent where Adrian lay. She could not know that he stirred and reached for her in his sleep, secure in his dreams that she was there by his side.

Dawn filled the eastern sky with a pearly mist as they rode away from the Green River. The wind began to blow, bringing the promise of rain.

Chapter 15
The Magician

Rolling over, Adrian fought his way to wakefulness. It was cold in the tent, and the fur covering him was not keeping out a draft. He reached out, one hand fumbling for Blue Feather, and encountered only an empty blanket. Slowly opening his eyes, he had the vague thought that she must be outside the tent with Harry, cooking the morning meal, perhaps, or helping to pack. A faint smile slanted his mouth, and he wished she had not been so energetic this particular morning. It would have been nice to hold her awhile longer, to feel her tawny curves nestled close to his body, to hold and caress her . . . ah, enough of that, Adrian scolded himself. There would be plenty of time for that later. They had the rest of their lives before them, a lifetime of love to share.

Blinking against the slice of gray light filtering through the tent, Adrian slowly realized that it was not coming from the open door of the tent. A soft flapping as cool air whisked through the tent drew his attention to a long slash in the canvas, and his heart lurched. The torn edges of the gash blew with the wind, holding his gaze for several agonizing minutes as his brain struggled to absorb the implications.

Then he was surging to his feet, ignoring his nudity

as he bent and stumbled outside. His eyes raked the area in front of the tent even as he was demanding from Harry, "Where's Blue Feather?"

"Margarethe?" Harry asked in surprise, looking up from the fire he was feeding small limbs. "Why, I had supposed—do you mean she's not with you?"

"No," Adrian answered tersely. "Have you seen her this morning?"

"No, my lord. Perhaps she had to step into the woods."

"I hardly think she would hack her way out of the tent to do so," Adrian shot back as he bent and reentered the canvas shelter.

"Do you mean to say she is gone?" Harry called after him, forgetting the fire and rising hastily to his feet. "But who—oh, dear me, I just don't know what could have happened to her."

"Neither do I," Adrian said from inside the tent, and Harry could hear him jerking on his clothes and swearing under his breath. A minute later Adrian emerged fully-dressed and with a grim expression on his face. "But I may have a good idea what happened, Harry," he said. "Do you recall her cousin's name?"

"Gray Eagle?"

"Ah yes—Gray Eagle. I think maybe he came for her after all."

"But . . . but why did she not cry out? Do you think he—dear God, I do hope he hasn't *murdered* her!" Harry ended, his face paling.

"I don't think he has. It could only have been someone she knew who could have coaxed—or abducted— her from the tent last night." Frowning as he automatically checked and loaded the rifles and his pistols, Adrian continued, "It had to have been much later, though . . . perhaps just before dawn. And dammit!—I was so tired, so sleepy that I just slept through it! I never heard a thing, Harry."

"You can't blame yourself, my lord," Harry comforted, though his expression was so woebegone Adrian thought he might burst into tears at any moment.

"But I do. Broken Arm has cautioned me often enough not to trust anyone. I knew her kinsman wanted to come for her, yet I did not keep up my guard. I was too complacent, too filled with my own desires to exercise proper caution. And for my lack of caution she has been taken."

"Are you certain it was her cousin and not Ramone Jardin who took her?" Harry asked. "After all, Jardin made no secret of the fact he wanted her."

"No, I am convinced it was not that Frenchman. He would take her when all could see, so that he could boast of having won her from the Englishman," Adrian said. "Besides, if it had been Jardin, he would have likely have slit my throat while I slept."

"Ah, that's true," Harry agreed thoughtfully. "What shall we do, my lord?"

"I intend to go after her," Adrian said briskly.

"Go after her?" Harry echoed. "How are we to do that?"

"Who said anything about 'we'? This will be dangerous, Harry, and I cannot expect you to—"

Drawing himself up to his full height, Harry gazed at Adrian with offended dignity. "My lord, if you think me a coward who would cry off going after such a lovely young woman as Margarethe—of whom I've grown quite fond—I will be most displeased! I am not unaware of the attending dangers, and believe that I am quite capable of confronting them admirably."

"Harry," Adrian said gently, "Blue Feather and I discussed your future last night, and we both agreed

276

that it might be best if you were to return to England. I would feel better knowing you were safe."

"And I would be most offended, sir!" Harry shot back.

"There may be no return from where we might have to go," Adrian warned, but the older man was adamant.

"I will go with you," he insisted firmly.

Adrian grinned. "Good. And you shall be the first to know that I have asked Blue Feather to marry me, Harry!"

"May I admit that I have expected just such an announcement, my lord," Harry replied imperturbably.

"Well?" Adrian demanded after another silence. "Why don't you tell me if you approve?"

"Are you searching for support in your decision, my lord?" Harry asked with arched brows.

"No, dammit!" Adrian replied with some exasperation. "I just thought you might be happy for me."

"I didn't need that announcement to know that you would be happy with Margarethe," Harry replied with a smile.

Tucking two pistols into the waistband of his trousers and hefting a rifle, Adrian stood up. He just looked at Harry for a moment, realizing that he *had* wanted the old man's approval for his decision. So many doubts assailed him. The most troubling doubt was if he could successfully protect Blue Feather against the many dangers in this harsh new world where he knew so little. His love for her transcended any other emotion.

"Get packed while I find Broken Arm," Adrian said after a moment. "We need to move out as quickly as possible."

Harry began throwing supplies into the leather

packs as Adrian strode swiftly away. He stepped around men sprawled on the ground, noting that the camp was beginning to stir in the gray light of early morning. It was hard to distinguish Everett Bowie's tipi from the other makeshift dwellings cluttering the huge campground, but Adrian finally found the right one.

Broken Arm had fallen asleep propped against a wooden crate, the empty stone jug of rye cradled lovingly in his arms as he slept. Adrian noted Bowie slumped in a corner snoring loudly, and shook his head. It was obvious both men had drank until they passed out. The sour smell of the rye whiskey hung in the air with stale smoke and the smoking remnants of the oil lamp.

Moving across the littered space, Adrian reached down and gave Broken Arm a sharp shake. "Broken Arm, get up!" he said urgently.

Broken Arm mumbled a protest and slid farther down. His wolf hat slumped over his head until it completely covered one eye. Smacking his lips once or twice, his grip tightened on the stone jug as if protecting it.

Exasperated now, Adrian gave the old trapper a quick, hard thrust with the heel of his hand, demanding, "Get up, Broken Arm! Blue Feather is gone! We have to find her!"

Still the old trapper just rolled with the blow, his hat sliding still farther over his face. "Wha'dya want?" a muffled voice inquired from the folds of the furry wolftail. It flapped with the motion of his lips as if it were alive and wagging, and Adrian rolled his eyes.

"Enough of this!" he muttered, scanning the contents of the tipi. His gaze settled upon a small wooden bucket of water, and he didn't hesitate. Reaching over, he lifted it and emptied the chilly contents over Broken Arm's head.

This action had the desired effect of jerking the old trapper upright. His eyes flew open, and he clawed at the drenched fur hat on his head, gasping for breath as the water streamed over his face.

"Aagh! Wha'. . . damme, wha's happened?" he managed to gasp. He flopped about as if a landed fish, squishing in the puddle of water surrounding him. His hat now hung at a comical angle on his head, and beads of water adorned the gray beard on his jaw. "Wha' happened?" he repeated.

"I poured water on you," Adrian said patiently.

Broken Arm squinted up at him. "Duke?" he asked in a vaguely incredulous tone. *"You* did that?"

"I did. It's Blue Feather. She's been taken by her kinsman."

Blinking away the water in his eyes, Broken Arm heaved himself to his feet, teetering precariously for a moment until he got his balance. Now he was at eye-level with Adrian, and he asked in an injured voice, "Why did you pour water on me?"

"I told you!" Adrian shot back. "Blue Feather is gone!"

"I heard that," the old trapper said. "But I still don't know why you went to such extremes — oh, you don't *want* her to go with her kinsman."

"No," Adrian said, "I don't."

Raking a hand through the sparse tufts of gray hair on his head, Broken Arm started to replace the wolf hat. He noted that it was dripping wet and wrung it out before doing so. Then, with a much stronger voice than Adrian had believed him capable of, he said, "Then let's go after her, Duke."

Relief flooded Adrian's features, and he said, "I was

hoping you'd feel that way!"

Gray Eagle's and Blue Feather's trail led north into the mountains—toward Wind River. The three men rode furiously for a day and a half, and Adrian's hopes of finding Blue Feather were dimming as they crested a rocky ridge and paused to rest the horses. His mare blew softly and hung her weary head to crop listlessly at harsh blades of grass alongside the trail, and Adrian leaned forward to gaze intently at Broken Arm.

"How far ahead are they?" he asked.

Broken Arm didn't answer for a moment. He pushed back his bedraggled wolf hat and squinted into the distance, his eyes skimming over the empty horizon. There was nothing moving, not even a hawk or eagle. Only the wind whistled down through the mountain ridges and towering trees, making an eerie moaning sound that seemed to mock the three men.

"I don't know," Broken Arm said finally. His weathered face was creased in an unhappy frown, and he made his strange, piercing moan as he admitted, "The rain obliterated their tracks last night. I can't seem to pick it up again. . . ."

"Lost the trail!" Adrian said. "What are you talking about? How could you lose it?"

Shrugging, Broken Arm sucked in a deep breath before he replied, "The Shoshoni are very clever, Duke. I imagine Gray Eagle knows more tricks than the white man ever thought about knowing."

"But that doesn't help me!" Adrian cut in. "We have to find her, Broken Arm. We have to!"

Nodding unhappily again, the old trapper said, "I know, Duke. Look," he added, waving away Adrian's frustrated protest, "Gray Eagle knows you want the girl. He also knows that you will try to find them. He is doing his best to leave you behind. If Gray Eagle doesn't want you to find his trail, you can bet your beaver you won't!"

Determination thinned Adrian's mouth to a taut line as he muttered between clenched teeth, "But I *will* find them!"

"We'll find them" — Broken Arm surprised him by agreeing — "but it won't be soon. See — I know where they're headed."

"Are you certain?" Harry asked as he removed his derby and mopped his forehead with a linen handkerchief.

"No. I'm not certain of anything in this land," the old trapper retorted. "The only thing you can be certain of is death, and even then you don't know when."

Straightening in his saddle, Adrian gave a short jerk of his head, then looked past Broken Arm to stare at the seemingly impenetrable wall of trees and mountain peaks ahead of them. It was hopeless. He would never find her. His fingers tightened on the leather reins, and he swallowed the sudden lump in his throat.

Taking pity on Adrian's obvious misery, Broken Arm said, "Look, Duke, let's camp for the night. It's almost dark and we can't see the trail much longer anyway, so we might as well rest."

Harry immediately seized on the trapper's suggestion. He swung down from his horse, groaned and put one hand to the small of his back. "Surely man will invent another method of travel one day," he mused aloud as he hobbled to a nearby log and perched upon its curved surface. "I find this manner decidedly uncomfortable at times."

Adrian smiled as he gazed at Harry. The older man

was leaning forward with his hands on his knees, his hat tilted at an angle and his jacket coated with dust. Harry's face was weary, but his mouth curved in a resigned smile as he returned Adrian's gaze.

Swinging down from his mare, Adrian said, "Broken Arm's right. A good night's rest should refresh us all, I think."

"But not here," the old trapper put in as he scanned the area with a sharp eye. "Let's move just over that ridge where the trees are even thicker. It's safer there."

Once they were camped, with a fire built from the limbs of a tamarack so there would be no tell-tale smoke, Adrian asked Broken Arm the question that had been on his mind for several hours. "Do you think her people will harm Blue Feather?"

For a moment Broken Arm concentrated on the strip of meat he held over the flames on a stick. Gray brows were furrowed in a frown as he regarded his dinner critically, and his lips pursed. "Well," he answered as Adrian began to shift impatiently, "I don't rightly know. I don't *think* so, but you never can tell about Shoshoni. They're a lot more moral than most white men give them credit for being, and they frown on their women being loose. It reflects badly on the whole tribe, see. If this Gray Eagle had been watching you all day—which you and Harry think he was— then, he's figured out that you and Blue Feather are a little more than friends." At Adrian's expression of dismay, Broken Arm added quickly, "Not that he'll put all the blame on her! He knows she was kidnapped by the Crow, and he knows that she was rescued by us. She's smart enough to have told him that right in the beginning, so he's not liable to hold her responsible for something she couldn't help. But you've got to see his side of it, Duke. This is his kinswoman, a girl whose grandfather is the chief. A white man just wouldn't be good enough for her in his eyes."

"Are you forgetting that Margarethe's father is French?" Harry asked.

Shaking his head, the old trapper said, "No, but that is a different case altogether. Pierre Duvalle is not a white man who came to this country for a little adventure that he can go home and tell his friends about. Duvalle is something of a legend himself up here, and respected by the Shoshoni. In his eyes, Gray Eagle is saving his cousin from being degraded. And remember, Duke," he added when Adrian's head jerked up and his eyes narrowed, "that Gray Eagle could have easily slit your throat while you were sleeping, but he didn't. He just took the girl, and now he's going to make damn sure we don't follow him." Pausing, he sighed and said, "There's just one more thing . . ."

"What?"

"If Gray Eagle thinks you may actually succeed in finding Blue Feather, he might take her so far up into the mountains that we can never find them. He might just take her to Duvalle. . . ."

"But what would be wonderful!" Adrian exclaimed. "Duvalle will surely have more empathy for a white man than do the Shoshoni."

Broken Arm carefully regarded his dinner again, then pulled it from the stick and bit off a chunk. Dragging a sleeve across his mouth to wipe off the grease, he gestured with the stick as he said, "Think again. Duvalle is well hidden in those mountains for a *reason,* Duke."

"Why?"

"I can't tell you that—" Broken Arm began, and Adrian cut in harshly.

"You mean you *won't* tell me."

283

Shrugging, Broken Arm said, "Suit yourself on that point, but the outcome's the same."

Frustrated, Adrian leaned back against the rough bark of a tree and watched the trapper. He had the distinct feeling Broken Arm knew much more than he was telling him, much more than he'd even hinted in past conversations. But he also knew that the old trapper would not divulge any information he didn't want to divulge, so there was no point in badgering him.

"Do you think we can find the Shoshoni camp?" Adrian asked after a moment.

"We will—sooner or later," Broken Arm said. He reached out to lift the blackened coffee pot from the flames. It tilted slightly, and strong coffee hissed against the hot stones ringing the fire.

"Shall I pour you some coffee, my lord?" Harry asked Adrian. "Or some tea, perhaps?"

"No . . ."

"Shall I prepare you some dinner?" Harry asked then, but Adrian shook his head.

Watching them, Broken Arm reflected on the relationship of servant and master with wry amusement. Harry was so anxious to please, and Adrian nonchalantly accepting. Of course, it was the way things were done in certain levels of English society, but he couldn't help but wonder for a moment if a man like Adrian Herenton could survive on his own. Though he'd shown some initiative and certainly didn't lack courage, Adrian wasn't accustomed to caring for himself. Sipping his hot coffee, Broken Arm peered at Adrian over the rim of his battered tin cup.

The evening breeze blew over the ridge, stirring leaves on the trees and pushing Adrian's hair into his eyes. He shoved it back impatiently, his mind preoccupied with Blue Feather. Where was she? Did she know that he would come after her, or did she think he would simply allow her to disappear from his life? And most importantly—was she all right?

Pushing abruptly to his feet, Adrian took several steps away before Broken Arm motioned for him to halt. "What is it?" he asked the old trapper, noting his suddenly alert posture.

"I hear something."

"What?"

"Shhh!"

Harry and Adrian exchanged glances, then both looked back at Broken Arm. He was still sitting beside the fire, his head tilted to one side as he listened. A moment later he dropped to his hands and knees on the ground and put one ear against a patch of ground bare of dead leaves.

"What the—?" Adrian began, but Broken Arm motioned him quiet again. Several minutes passed as the old trapper remained motionless with his ear pressed close to the ground, then he sat back on his heels. This time Adrian waited for him to speak first.

"Someone's following us," Broken Arm said at last. "I think several men, maybe more."

"How can you tell that?" Harry wanted to know.

"By listening. If you put your ear on the ground you can hear the vibrations. They're not close yet, but I know they're back there."

"Do you think it means danger?" Adrian asked. "Or could it simply be someone who's also travelling this trail? Or even a herd of antelope or horses, or something."

Broken Arm flicked him a weary glance. "I don't have to see or hear them to know someone's following us, Duke. I've known it all day. I just didn't realize they were this close yet."

285

"Well, if you knew why didn't you say something about it earlier? Harry and I could have been on our guard—"

"No need until now. It's a feeling a man gets out here, something he knows without knowing how or why, Duke. I didn't want to worry you until I knew they were still behind us."

"Do you suppose it might be—" Harry swallowed hard—"savages?"

Shrugging, Broken Arm said, "I don't know. I only know we need to watch over our shoulders now."

Adrian looked around him. Trees towered on both sides of them, seeming to reach as high as the mountain peaks. There was an eerie silence in the forest, a quiet that seemed to hang from the tree branches blotting out the sky. No birds chirped, and the tethered horses were whickering softly as they faced the wind.

"They smell something," Adrian guessed, and the trapper nodded.

"More than likely. We sleep with one eye open and our rifles in our hands, gentlemen—loaded and ready!"

Sleep was scarce and restless that night. Every sound pricked their attention, looming even louder in the shadows surrounding them. When morning finally dawned, daylight slowly filtering through the thick canopy of leaves overhead to dapple the ground, Adrian breathed a sigh of relief. Everything seemed more normal in the daylight, safer somehow, but when Harry remarked upon that fact to Broken Arm, the trapper laughed.

"Don't you remember the last time we waited through the night?" he asked. "If I recollect rightly, the morning sun also brought a screaming horde of Blackfeet down on our heads!"

Crestfallen, Harry said, "Oh. I hadn't thought of that. Do you suppose . . ."

"No. Let's ride," Broken Arm said shortly. "We can chew on jerky for breakfast."

Not stopping to build a fire or cook anything for their morning meal, they saddled up and rode on. Having missed his dinner the night before, Adrian was acutely aware of the rumblings of his stomach as he chewed on the tough strip of buffalo jerky. It tasted similar to what he imagined shoe leather to taste like, and he grimaced as he tried to swallow. A glance at Harry showed him that he was having the same problem, and Adrian sighed as he nudged his mare closer behind Broken Arm's gelding.

By noon they had crossed the ridge and were in a low valley between steeply rising mountain slopes. A meadow stretched in front of them, and Broken Arm halted at the edge. A worried frown knit his brows as he studied the open expanse of beargrass that was belly-high to their horses. A jumble of huge rocks were scattered at one side, and on the other side a deep ravine yawned dangerously. The safety of the trees waited across the meadow, dark and beckoning.

Sensing Broken Arm's caution, Adrian asked softly, "Is anything the matter?"

"Nothing I can see" came the slow reply, "but a whole hell of a lot I can feel."

Adrian waited for him to say more, but the old trapper just waited there at the edge of the meadow, his senses tuned to the area around him. He seemed to be watching for something as he sat his broad-backed gelding, his rifle cocked and slung under one arm. They must have stood there without moving for twenty minutes or more, until finally Broken Arm gave a silent signal and they moved cautiously forward. Tall grasses rubbed the horses' undersides as they advanced in a slow walk. Even the animals seemed to feel the tension, and they walked with ears pricked forward and nostrils flaring.

Adrian grasped his rifle tightly, aware of the sun beating down on his head and the absence of a breeze. He thought that odd, for the wind had been constant. Shifting in his saddle, he looked from right to left. Sweat trickled down his back and sides, and he began to wish he wasn't wearing his vest and coat. Perhaps it would be more practical to dress differently, he thought, then sliced a glance at Harry on his left. Harry was sitting stiffly, his immaculate hat perched atop his head and a clean though dingy cravat swaddling his throat. What a sight they must be, Adrian thought distractedly. He could hear the buzzing of bees, the creak of saddle leather and jangle of metal bits on the bridles, but the rest of the world seemed ominously silent and waiting.

They were halfway across the meadow when it came. A shrill whoop and the thunder of hooves burst over the ridge behind them.

"Piegans!" Broken Arm yelled as he lifted his rifle and fired over one shoulder.

Both Harry and Adrian spurred their mounts, bounding forward and racing behind Broken Arm as he galloped toward the jumble of rocks at one side. Adrian fired his rifle, desperately aware that he had hit nothing, then leaned low over his mare's neck. She ran gamely, stretching out so low that Adrian could almost feel the whip of the beargrass against his shoulders. He was vaguely aware of Harry close beside him, and acutely aware of the pursuing Indians.

They screamed wildly, their howls rising when the three men reached the comparatively safety of the rocks. Sliding from his mare, Adrian grabbed the packs and threw his reins over the animal's head. Their horses bolted in fright, hooves loudly clattering over the rocky shale. As their last hope faded with the horses disappearing into the trees, Adrian flung himself to the heated surface of a rock and peered over the top. His eyes widened.

"There must be fifty of them!" he exclaimed in horror.

"No, more like thirty, but still too damned many," Broken Arm observed laconically. He was reloading his rifle, pouring powder and ramming the ball into the muzzle with swift, practised movements.

Adrian and Harry followed suit, loading their weapons with shaking hands. Precious powder spilled as fingers trembled, and Harry moaned softly.

"I can't do this, my lord!"

"You have to," Adrian said practically. "We may not get another opportunity." As he voiced his fear, his head lifted and he thought about Blue Feather. Blue Feather. He would never see her again, never again feel her satiny skin beneath his hands or taste her honeyed lips. Sparing a prayer for her safety, Adrian turned his attention back to the business at hand. Memories of his mother flashed through his mind, and for an instant he saw the faces of his father and Richard; then it was gone and the shooting had begun in earnest.

Rifle fire ricocheted all around him, and as the balls hit the rocks, pieces of granite splintered in the air like angry bees. Adrian fired automatically, shooting until his weapon was empty then lifting another, taking aim and slowly thumbing the hammer, feeling the recoil against his shoulder and firing again. His mind was blank now, his reactions coming without thinking.

They might have held off the Blackfeet for some time, but several enterprising braves managed to sneak around and attack from the rear, and it was all over. Trapped, they conceded defeat. Slowly lifting their arms over their heads to indicate surrender, they waited apprehensively as the Blackfeet bounded gleefully over the rocks and began to plunder their packs.

"What happens now?" Adrian asked the trapper curtly, and Broken Arm shook his head.

"Depends on their mood. We might be used for target practice, or maybe just hung upside down by our ankles and roasted over a slow fire until our brains are cooked. And then again, we might be given a chance to die fighting if they're in a generous mood," Broken Arm ended as a painted warrior approached.

The time for talking was over, it seemed. The Indians were much amused by Harry's and Adrian's clothes, and with the help of sign language and Broken Arm's translation, they divested Harry of everything but his smallclothes. If not for the desperate situation Adrian might have laughed to see Harry's immaculate derby perched atop the head of a painted Blackfoot warrior. He seemed proud of his prize, for he paraded up and down on the rocks, crowing like a rooster as he flaunted the hat. One brave soon wore Harry's linen cravat, and another his vest, while Harry stood still and terrified.

Then the interest shifted to Adrian. A brave who was almost as tall as the Englishman looked him over carefully. He reached out and tested the size of Adrian's muscles with one hand, then gave him a quick jab in the solar plexus. Adrian had steeled himself when he realized the brave's intentions, so he did not even flinch. This seemed to impress the Blackfoot, and he turned and said a few words to his companion. They both laughed, and Broken Arm swore lightly under his breath.

"What are they saying?" Adrian started to ask, but the brave who had first approached him lashed out with the butt of his rifle to knock Adrian to the ground. Lights exploded in front of his eyes as his head snapped backward, and Adrian landed on his elbows and shoulders. His hat sailed through the air to be immediately claimed by a stocky brave who happened to catch it, and he was left sprawling on the rocks.

Groaning, Adrian rolled to his side, holding his jaw as he worked it back and forth to see if it was broken. It seemed to be intact, and he blinked to clear his vision. By this time the braves had decided that he was to participate in a game of sorts, and they hauled him to his feet and stripped him of his clothes.

Almost frantic with distress, Harry turned his pained gaze to Broken Arm, who silently shook his head at him to remain quiet. The mystery of the Blackfeet's intention was soon solved, however, for they enlisted Broken Arm to interpret their desires.

"They want to know if you can run fast," Broken Arm asked Adrian somberly.

Swaying on his bare feet, Adrian was only vaguely aware of the warning in the trapper's eyes, but he managed to give his head a slight shake. "No," he mumbled, "I can't."

While Broken Arm translated this, Adrian let his gaze shift to Harry's agonized face. The ghost of a smile that was meant to be reassuring flickered for a moment, then faded as Broken Arm began translating again.

"This is the deal, Duke. You're to run for your life,

291

they say. They're probably going to give you sixty seconds head start since you're an obvious tenderfoot, then they'll be chasing you with everything they've got. They intend to hack you to pieces, Duke, so don't look back. Keep running, and about three or four miles north you'll come to a fork in a river. It's your only chance. Try to get downstream, and maybe—"

A frowning Blackfoot growled something, and Broken Arm quieted immediately. Adrian could see from the corners of his eyes that his clothes had already been distributed, and he noted that his vest adorned the bare chest of a grinning warrior.

"Has anyone ever outrun them?" he had to ask Broken Arm, and the trapper hesitated before nodding.

"Yes, but he was an experienced mountain man and guide, Duke. *Just don't look back.*"

That was all there was time to say before the Blackfeet were pushing Adrian through the rocks toward the meadow.

"Good-bye, Harry!" Adrian yelled over his shoulder as he was propelled forward, and he dimly heard Harry's answering call of "Godspeed, my lord!"

Adrian's heart was pounding and his throat was dry as he was pushed to the edge of the meadow and held for a moment, and he had a brief fear that they would decide to just kill him. Suddenly shoved roughly forward, he began to run. His legs pumped up and down, and he tried not to notice the sharp stones that tore at the soles of his bare feet as he ran.

The rough edges of the beargrass slashed like razors at his unprotected body as he surged through the tall grass, but he didn't slow. He ran faster and faster, dodging thorn bushes as best he could. The meadow seemed endless, stretching for miles, and it seemed as if he would never reach the trees so far ahead. If he could just reach the trees, could just make it that far before they started after him, then perhaps he would have a chance, he thought.

But even before the thought had faded he heard a wild whoop and knew they had begun. That realization lent speed to his pumping legs, and he raced even faster to the line of trees ahead.

The forest became a blur of dizzying colors, green and brown and gray mixing with deeper shadows. Adrian's heart drummed loudly, and his leg muscles ached as he made it to the trees; but he never faltered. Still he ran, pushing himself harder as the sounds behind him grew louder.

A fallen log lay in his path, and he leaped it, stumbling and almost falling before he caught himself, then surging on. Sharp thorns scraped his side and flayed his hands, but he ignored them. The breath rasped harshly in his throat, and he clenched his teeth against the driving pain in his lungs. Behind him he could hear the frenzied howls of his pursuers, and he imagined they were almost upon him, could almost feel their hot breath on his bare back. Sweat rolled down the sides of his face and over his brow into his eyes, but he never paused to wipe it away. Still he ran, pushing on and on, and concentrating only upon what lay just ahead, dodging any obstacle he could and plowing through what he could not.

Enraged that their quarry was outdistancing them, the chasing Blackfeet redoubled their efforts, and Adrian could hear their high-pitched voices lift in what sounded like a chant. Aware that the Indians often chanted war songs, love songs and death songs, Adrian had the vague thought that they must be chanting *his* death song. An arrow whizzed past his head, barely missing him as it struck a tree trunk with a solid thunk and quivered ominously. Another arrow zipped over his head, then another, and a war hatchet clipped leaves from a bush as it, too, missed him. Thank God they weren't using their rifles, Adrian thought as he ducked and dodged the flying missiles. Sucking in a deep breath he forced his aching legs higher and higher.

Branches crashed behind him, sounding too close, and remembering Broken Arm's warning not to look back, Adrian tucked his chin into his chest and ran. He leaped a wide ditch, half-falling on the other side, recovered his balance and kept running. The trees were thicker here, soaring toward the sky in serene majesty, ignorant of the life and death struggle being fought in their shadows. Mud coated Adrian's feet and legs, and dead leaves clung to his sweaty body as he propelled himself forward. It occurred to him to wonder why it was muddy even as he slipped and slid down a thorny slope and climbed the opposite bank.

The cries of the Blackfeet were growing stronger, but in spite of them Adrian could distinguish another, faintly familiar sound. It was like a whisper of the wind through the trees, faint at first then growing louder as he kept running. *Dear God,* Adrian prayed silently, *let it be the river. . . .*

His prayers were answered, for as he puffed up the next incline and staggered on the crest he saw it. It glittered below him, bright and surging with promise. Barely pausing in his stride, Adrian half-slid, half-ran down the slope to the muddy banks. He never hesitated as he neared the foamy, swiftly running currents but plunged into the icy water in a desperate dive.

Immediately engulfed by icy water, he sank to the bottom. It was easier to let the fast-moving current carry him downstream than it was to fight it, and

Adrian offered no resistance for the moment. He could feel rocks on the bottom of the river tearing at his skin as he skimmed over them, rolling along, then his lungs began to ache from lack of air. Finally breaking the surface of the water, Adrian gave his head a shake, gulping in the sweet air in huge gasps. His arms automatically began to reach out, his legs churning as he began to tread water. The current swept him onward, and behind him he could hear the muffled cries of the Blackfeet as they stubbornly pursued their prey.

Dismay flooded him as Adrian realized they had not given up, and he was tempted to let his exhausted body rest, to just give up. Then thoughts of Blue Feather flickered for a moment, and he knew he couldn't do it. He had to live, had to find her.

Renewed energy surged through his veins, and he glanced around him for a possible place to hide. As he floated downstream, he noted the changing shoreline and saw an offshoot to one side of the swiftly moving river. It was only a matter of time before they found him, and he grasped this detour immediately, hoping to stall detection. It took great effort and several minutes to maneuver his way through the water and into the slower stream that curved along wooded banks. Then Adrian bumped into a breastwork of limbs and mud that had been built across a narrow portion of the waterway. The pressure of the water behind him had built up, and he realized suddenly that he had somehow found a beaver dam. This triggered a memory, and he thought of Broken Arm and Everett Bowie, and how Bowie had claimed to have once been inside a beaver lodge.

Lifting his head, Adrian squinted through a mist of foamy water as he searched for the turtleback-shaped lodge that should be close by. It should be farther downstream, he rationalized, and made his way around the dam. Behind him the Blackfeet were loudly voicing their rage at their elusive quarry, and he slid as far down as he could, keeping just his eyes and nose out of the water. Perhaps it wasn't as farfetched as it sounded, Adrian thought swiftly, and wondered just how one went about finding the entrance to this misshapen hump of mud, stones and sticks. Frantically feeling his way around the circumference of the stick shelter, he could not discover the entrance and began to despair. The Blackfeet were growing closer and might soon realize that he had taken the offshoot. Then it would only be a matter of minutes before they were upon him. His imagination supplied every grisly detail to what they would do to their captive.

The icy chill of the water had also taken its toll upon Adrian, and he found his arms and hands were clumsy in the water as he tried to move. They felt like huge paws slapping at the surface, and his feet were numb as he tried to tread water. A movement on the shore caught his attention, and he saw a huge beaver approaching the lodge, dragging a tree that seemed much too large for the size of the animal. As the curious, web-footed creature cautiously reached the bank, it lifted its head and sniffed the air. Beady little eyes seemed to look directly at Adrian, and as he stared back he heard a loud smacking noise.

Another beaver had spotted the intruder and was sounding the alarm by slapping the water with its tail. The beaver on shore immediately hit the water and swam furiously toward the lodge, then dove beneath the surface. Sensing his chance, Adrian filled his lungs with air and did the same. If this beaver was headed for the entrance to his lodge, then so was Adrian.

Fumbling in the murky waters of the stream, Adrian reached the underwater shaft of the lodge and swam upward, bursting into a musky smelling air pocket just as his lungs began to ache. The odor was rancid, but the air had never seemed so sweet. He shook the water from his eyes and grasped a muddy shelf just over his head. Dragging his bruised, scratched and bleeding body up onto the narrow shelf of mud and stone, Adrian buried his face in his hands and shuddered. He could hear the Blackfeet clearly now and knew they had found him. Perhaps the beaver had alerted them to his presence in their lodge, or perhaps they had seen him dive underwater.

Helpless to escape, and almost too weary to care, Adrian sat numbly and waited. A shaft of sunlight pierced the murky gloom of the lodge from an airhole overhead, and he watched in idle fascination as light chips danced on the surface of the water. There were no beavers in the lodge, no young kits or their parents, and Adrian waited for death in solitude.

Vague memories crowded him, and he thought sadly of his uncle, his father and his brother. They might never know what had happened to him. After all, the Blackfeet would hardly treat poor Harry and Broken Arm with kindness either, he reflected. Then, as usual, his thoughts turned to Blue Feather, and he wondered if her people were treating her well and if her grandfather was still alive to protect her. Perhaps she had been taken to her father, and that might be the best thing. She would eventually hear about the white man who had been pursued and killed by the Piegan, would know that he was dead and would grieve for a time, but then she would go on. In this land there was not much time for grieving, only survival.

Survival. His death would prove Madame du Jessupe wrong, would prove that her prediction for his future had been pure theatrics. She had simply enter-tained her hosts on a stormy evening, and he had been gullible enough to attach some importance to her silly predictions. Well, it seemed as if the last laugh was really on him, Adrian mused ruefully.

He didn't know how long he'd sat there before he realized that the sounds of the Blackfeet had faded. There was nothing to disturb the slapping sound of water against the lodge. He could clearly hear the cheerful chatter of birds and imagined that he even heard the piercing cry of a hawk circling overhead. Then silence again.

The silence was finally broken by the angry chatter of a beaver as it emerged from the water, its brown furry face indignant as it scolded the intruder. Tilting back his head, Adrian saw that the light from the air shaft had grown dim. It must be almost dark. Dark. In the cover of night he could swim downstream per-haps, could make his way to safety. It was worth a try.

Sliding from the dryer shelf to the icy water again, Adrian shivered. It didn't seem possible; but the water had grown even colder, and he had to grit his teeth as he ducked beneath the surface and made his way out the narrow shaft. Feeling his way along, he could see nothing beneath the dark surface, but had to find his way by touch.

Only when he finally rose to the top and took a deep breath of air did he feel safe. As he wiped the water from his eyes, Adrian realized that now he was totally alone in a land that he knew nothing about. His stom-ach rumbled, and he remembered that he had had nothing to eat all day except a strip of buffalo jerky. Even that sounded good at this moment. As he made his way downstream close to the shore, Adrian won-dered if he would survive. It seemed that he had managed to escape one fate only to plunge into worse circumstances.

It was shallow close to the bank, and he walked slowly through the water, listening for any sound of the returning Blackfeet. There was no sign of them. When he had gone several hundred yards downstream, he finally allowed himself to pull up on the muddy banks. He lay there for a long time, letting his mind assimilate all that had happened to him.

He was alone, hundreds of miles from civilization and possibly even another civilized human being. He'd been pursued by Indians intent upon killing him, and had left behind not only Harry and Broken Arm, but the woman he loved. He had no clothes, no food, no weapon and no way to even start a fire to warm himself. He had no idea where he was or which direction to take, and as the adrenaline that had sustained him in his flight slowly ebbed, he was becoming painfully aware of the abrasions and bruises covering his naked body. It was not a heartening situation.

Closing his eyes, Adrian let his tense muscles relax. He listened to the sleepy murmur of nightbirds in the trees overhead and heard the chilling hoot of an owl as it soared in search of easy prey. A cool breeze had sprung up, and his flesh prickled with the chill. The cushioning mud had grown cold beneath his back, and he began to shiver uncontrollably. His teeth chattered, and Adrian sat up and clasped his arms around his knees. His stomach growled again, and he knew he would have to get up and push on or die.

Staggering to his feet, Adrian climbed up the bank to stand in the thick fringe of trees that had once seemed so hospitable and now offered no sign of comfort. The soles of his feet were shredded from the day's efforts, and he limped slowly into the dense underbrush and towering trees.

There was no hope of finding food in the dark, so he contented himself with making a bed of dry leaves and pine needles, shivering as he pulled them over his aching body. Cradled within the knobby knees of the roots sticking up from the ground, Adrian lay at the foot of a huge oak that must have been six feet around. A wolf howled in the distance, its wail lingering in the night air, and another one answered. Adrian lay in his bed and thought of the dangers surrounding him, wondering if he would ever live to see his family or Blue Feather again.

Sunlight pricked gently at Adrian's eyelids, urging him awake, and he was surprised to discover that he had slept at all. Yawning, he sat up and leaves showered down around him. The bed had been warmer than he'd thought, and he had slept deeply and dreamlessly. Now he blinked the sleep away, and when he focused his gaze on his surroundings, he froze.

A shadow lurked just behind the thick branches of a pine, and he was suddenly aware that he was not alone. His first thought was of the Blackfeet, then he realized that they would not have remained hidden. Adrian's heart was pounding loudly, and he swallowed hard as the branches rustled and moved.

"Who are you?" came a rasping call in English, and Adrian started.

"Friend or foe?" he demanded loudly, deciding to bluff his way out if he could. "I've a pistol with me. . . ."

A laugh floated from behind the pine needles, and the voice rasped, "I heard the Piegan and saw the race, my friend. You have only your courage as a weapon."

300

There was a brief pause while Adrian absorbed this fact, then the voice demanded again, "Who are you?"

"Lord Adrian Herenton, Viscount of Montagu," Adrian answered. "Who are *you?*"

A lengthy pause developed, and Adrian could see the dull sheen of a gun barrel glinting in the morning sunlight dappling the woods. Left with little choice, he waited for the man to speak again.

"There are no viscounts out here," the voice finally observed. "Just God, man and the animals. And sometimes it's hard to tell the difference a'twixt the last two."

The pine branches swayed and danced, and an old man stepped from behind the shiny green needles. He was garbed in buckskin from head to toe, and had a long white beard and the most piercing blue eyes Adrian had ever seen. He was grinning, but his rifle was pointed directly at Adrian.

"Who *are* you?" Adrian asked again, and the old man chuckled.

"Cheney. . . ."

Chapter 16
The Strength

Harry and Broken Arm stood like stone statues, listening to the shrill cries of the Blackfeet pursuing Adrian. The sun seared down on them as they stood in the middle of the rocky clearing with their backs to the granite bluff behind them. Their hands were tied tightly behind their backs with rawhide cords, and two of their captors had been left as guards. Even if untied, escape would have been difficult because of the ring of boulders surrounding them. To their left was a steep descent that plummeted to a rocky ravine, and beyond that an open stretch that would have been impossible to cross without horses to get them away quickly. A bad situation, Broken Arm reflected gravely as he shifted position on the hard rock floor. And poor Harry seemed about to faint as he braced his bare feet on the sharp rocks, wearing only his smallclothes and squinting against the glare of the sun.

As the two Blackfeet seemed more interested in the race than they were their captives, Harry sidled closer to Broken Arm. They watched with heavy hearts as Adrian ran gamely, and silently rejoiced when he made the safety of the trees. Perhaps he would have a chance, Broken Arm thought, and slanted a glance at Harry. The stocky Englishman was gazing at the spot in the trees where he had last seen Adrian, and his face reflected his misery. There was pain shadowing his eyes, and his mouth worked silently as he struggled to hold back his tears. Broken Arm looked away so he would not embarrass Harry in his grief.

"I never thought it would end like this," Harry choked out. "His lordship is a good and gentle man, undeserving of such a cruel fate. He never took advantage of anyone, even those who would have taken advantage of him, and he was a firm believer in justice. . . ."

"Don't sing his eulogy yet," Broken Arm advised. "He still has a chance."

Harry eagerly turned his head toward the trapper. "Oh, do you think so?"

Clearing his throat softly, Broken Arm hesitated. He didn't want to admit that he had little hope of such a miracle happening, but he knew that the Englishman needed to hang on to even the slimmest possibility of Adrian's making it alive.

"I think he's got a fair chance," Broken Arm compromised. "He's young and strong, and in pretty good shape for a tenderfoot. He just might make it. . . ." Saying it aloud lent credence to his words, and suddenly Broken Arm began to believe what he was saying. His head lifted, and he gazed out over the broad meadow fringed by trees and the rocky slopes they had travelled. He could barely hear the Piegan now, and they sounded very far away. "He just might make it," Broken Arm repeated more firmly. "He seems to be giving our friends the run of a lifetime!"

Harry brightened and lifted to his toes to peer

over the rocks and across the meadow. The sun beat down on his bare head with a vengeance, and even though he squinted, he could not see a sign of either Adrian or the pursuing Blackfeet.

"How can you tell?" Harry asked anxiously. One of their guards chose that moment to turn around and, seeing Harry on his toes, sent the butt of his rifle crashing into the older man's stomach. Gasping and retching, Harry fell to his knees on the rocky slope.

Waiting until the guard turned back to his perusal of the meadow, Broken Arm said softly, "Look at those two guards, Harry! They're worried! The others aren't back yet, and usually a kill has been made by now. If they'd caught Adrian, they would be bringing back his body or his scalp."

"Then they haven't caught him?" Harry wheezed. He was still bent over, his face close to the ground as he coughed and moaned.

"No, I'm sure they haven't," Broken Arm murmured. He shifted uneasily then tensed, the back of his neck prickling in warning as he sensed a movement behind him. Before he could move or say anything, he felt a sharp tug on his bound wrists and the cold slide of steel along his skin.

"Say nothing," a low voice ordered in Shoshoni, and the old trapper nodded as he continued staring straight ahead.

Broken Arm was standing with his feet spread apart, balanced and waiting, and when he felt his bonds slip away and the weight of a knife being placed in his palm, he began to plan his attack. Harry was still kneeling on the ground, oblivious to what was going on behind him, and the two Blackfeet warriors were intent on the race. There was little time to act, for at any moment the warriors could become bored with the fading sounds of their companions.

There was a nudge at his back, and Broken Arm understood and nodded. Shifting the knife from his left hand to his right, the trapper rose to the balls of his feet, and with a final hope that he had correctly interpreted his rescuer's intentions, he surged forward silently. One of the Piegan never heard him, only felt the cold blade entering his back. His body arched, his weapons falling to the ground, and he collapsed in the trapper's arms. The other guard whirled, his face diffused with color as he realized what was happening, but it was too late. The Shoshoni's knife found his heart, and he collapsed atop his companion.

Broken Arm looked up at the tall Shoshoni warrior and said, "You must be Gray Eagle."

The handsome warrior just nodded and indicated Harry with a jerk of his thumb. "Bring him along," he said in his own language. "I will catch your horses."

Nodding, Broken Arm helped the dazed Harry to his feet. The Englishman still didn't quite understand what had happened, that they were being rescued and that they must hurry before the others returned. Broken Arm patiently helped him scramble down the steep rocky slope to the grassy area where Gray Eagle waited with their horses.

"But my clothes," Harry kept insisting with an expression of dismay. He looked down at his bare legs and feet, repeating, "But my clothes —"

"What you got on will do just fine!" Broken Arm snapped back. "At least you're wearing more than Duke. . . ."

This reminder served to silence Harry, and in just a few minutes they were astride the horses and following the Shoshoni warrior along a narrow trail that led in the opposite direction from the Blackfeet.

The Shoshoni kept up a fast pace on the rocky lip of a trail Broken Arm wouldn't have thought existed. On one side of them was a sheer drop, on the other side a steeply rising granite slope. Then Gray Eagle swerved into an opening that appeared to be no larger than a man's hand and disappeared. Lifting his brows, Broken Arm followed and discovered a narrow passageway cut deep into the mountain. It must have been there since time began, for there were strange carvings and crude paintings on the rock walls, but there was no time to stop and investigate. Hooves clattered noisily on the hard surface, the sound spiralling up to the top of the crevice several hundred feet above them.

When they emerged they were in the midst of a forest, a dense wood of vine-draped trees and thick underbrush. The silence shrouded them, and all Broken Arm could hear was the wheezing of the winded horses and Harry's heavy breathing. The Englishman seemed ready to fall from his mount. He was leaning over his mare's neck and holding on for dear life, but Broken Arm sensed that Harry was about to slide to the ground. Gray Eagle watched impassively as the trapper leaped from his mount to catch Harry, and it was a soft cry that first alerted Broken Arm to the presence of someone else.

"Harry! Oh, is he wounded?" Blue Feather cried as she ran from behind a gnarled, twisted tree trunk.

"Margarethe?" Harry moaned, lifting his head to peer around him. "Oh, dear me! I'm not properly dressed for a young lady . . . I'm not dressed at all . . . oh, dear!" he ended on a long, wailing note.

Kneeling beside Harry as Broken Arm lowered him to the ground, Blue Feather asked anxiously, "Adrian? *Qu'est-ce que lui est arrivé?*"

Broken Arm and Harry exchanged reluctant glances, a fact Blue Feather immediately noted as she demanded again, "What happened to him?"

"Piegan," Gray Eagle interrupted in Shoshoni from atop his horse. "They are running him."

Sitting back on her heels, Blue Feather looked at Harry for a long moment. "This is true?" she asked huskily, bowing her head when he nodded.

"He might have a chance," Broken Arm offered. "He was outrunning them when your cousin showed up to rescue us."

"Then we shall go after him," Blue Feather decided immediately.

"And tempt the Piegan to do the same to us?" Gray Eagle demanded contemptuously. "This white man has deranged you, my cousin. I have helped those you wished me to help, and it is not my fault that your chosen man was not among them. We shall go now—"

"No!" Blue Feather cried out angrily. "Adrian rescued me when I was in danger of being killed, and I shall not let him die because you are afraid! I shall go after him myself if you will not go—"

"Enough!" Gray Eagle warned with narrowed eyes.

Broken Arm, who easily understood their dialect, spoke quietly. "It is possible that he has reached the river and gone downstream. Maybe we could follow

307

his tracks."

"When the Piegan could not?" Gray Eagle demanded scornfully. "Are you so much better at reading sign, old one?"

Irritated by Gray Eagle's reference to him as old, Broken Arm nodded tersely. "I am. And so are you."

Harry—who could not understand a single word they were saying—slowly sat up. Though mortified that Margarethe had seen him in his smallclothes, he rationalized that most of the Indians he had seen wore a lot less, so it could not have shocked her sensibilities nearly as much as it had his. They were all talking in that strange, guttural tongue that made absolutely no sense to him, so he cleared his throat and asked quietly, "Does anyone mind translating this argument for me? I'm afraid I'm a bit at sea as to what is going on."

"*Ai*," Blue Feather said, "I will tell you. My cousin is afraid to look for Adrian, and he might still be alive. . . ."

Gray Eagle snorted. "I am not afraid, little cousin, just not a fool. The Piegan will not have let him escape them so easily."

"Can we not look?" Blue Feather pleaded tearfully. "I do not feel I can face our grandfather without knowing the fate of the man I love."

Broken Arm looked from the distraught girl to the man sitting astride his painted horse. Gray Eagle was a fine figure of a man, copper-skinned and muscular, with the fine features of his race, high cheekbones and aquiline nose, deep-set sharp eyes, and a full, mobile mouth that was now curved in an expression of irritation. Gleaming wings of black hair framed his face, and he shook them back impatiently as he glared at his small cousin.

"Do not attempt to barter with me, Blue Feather!" he said harshly. "I have done as you asked, now you must do as I tell you."

Facing him boldly, Blue Feather shook her head. "No, my esteemed cousin. I cannot. I must follow my heart and do all I can to save Adrian. I could never stay in the village of my people if I did not know his fate. . . ."

"Then it would satisfy you to see what is left of his body?" Gray Eagle demanded cruelly. "For I tell you that is all that you will find of your beloved!"

A spasm of pain creased her features for a moment, but Blue Feather nodded. "*Ai*. That is what will satisfy me."

"Then you shall have your wish, my foolish one," Gray Eagle said, and motioned for Broken Arm and Harry to mount their horses. "Go in peace," he began, but Broken Arm shook his head.

"No, great warrior. We wish to go with you."

Exasperated, and obviously wishing he had not yielded to his cousin's pleas to rescue them, Gray Eagle barked, "I do not wish to be burdened with two old men! I have already saved you from the Piegan, now go your own paths!"

"Oh, but they must go with us," Blue Feather said, earning a dark glance from her cousin. "They must . . ."

Stiffening atop his fine, prancing horse, Gray Eagle gave a curt nod of his head and shrugged. "Do as you wish, but if they draw the attention of the Piegan I will leave them behind."

"Fair enough," Broken Arm put in. He bent to the task of lifting Harry to his feet and helping him back on his horse. "We are looking for Duke," Broken Arm told him, and Harry nodded that he understood.

"I will endeavor to be no burden to you," he assured the trapper. "It is important to me to see Lord Adrian safe at last."

Broken Arm did not voice his fear that the fair-haired Englishman was dead, but merely nodded as he snatched up the trailing reins of his gelding and swung into the saddle. He waited, watching the regal Shoshoni warrior as he brought his small cousin her horse. Though gruff, it was evident that Gray Eagle cared a great deal for Blue Feather. It was not the Shoshoni way to pamper their women, and Broken Arm understood that. Women were servile and should be obedient to the men of the tribe, but little Blue Feather seemed to have mastered the art of coaxing this austere warrior into doing her wishes. Broken Arm hid a smile. It would not do to allow Gray Eagle to know that he understood the situation. That would shame him, and he would demand satisfaction. So Broken Arm said nothing as they kicked their horses into a trot.

Blue Feather's tawny legs tightly gripped her mount as she rode, and her blue-black hair whipped behind her in a flowing ribbon. The buckskin dress was pushed up above her knees, but she didn't care. All that mattered now was Adrian. She had to find him. Somehow she could not think of him as being dead or even injured. There was a driving sense of urgency that spurred her on and made her so determined, determined enough to defy her forbidding cousin and risk Gray Eagle's wrath.

Tree branches lashed her bare legs and arms, whipping at her face as she rode through the thick trees and bushes, but Blue Feather never made a

310

murmur of protest. She kept her mind trained on Adrian as Gray Eagle led them through the forest. He seemed to be following a trail that was parallel with that Adrian and the Blackfeet had used, and it wound deeper and deeper into the dense forest. They travelled for what seemed like hours to Blue Feather. The insects were thick and worrisome, clouds of them swarming at times until she could hardly see ahead of her. Time dragged slowly, and the barely visible sun had begun its descent in the west when they drew near the spot where Adrian had entered the woods. Gray Eagle lifted his hand in a silent warning to halt.

They reined in and waited. In the distance they could hear the faint shouts of the Blackfeet, reminding Harry of hounds chasing a fox. And like the hounds, he could tell by the sound of their lifted voices that they had lost the scent of their prey. Harry smiled broadly and looked over at Gray Eagle. The Shoshoni warrior had come to the same conclusion, and he motioned for them to remain silent.

Purple shadows began to deepen, and there was the rustling sound of the forest settling in for the night. When the day creatures scurried to the safety of their burrows, the night predators began to rouse. Harry shifted uneasily in his saddle and shivered. The breeze was cool against his bare arms and legs, and he wished for what must have been the hundredth time that he could retrieve his clothes.

Finally Gray Eagle gave the signal, and they nudged their horses forward. It was quiet now, but for the sounds of the forest around them. Though there were no shouts or howls from the Blackfeet, Gray Eagle motioned for them to move cautiously.

311

It was a difficult trail, little more than a slight break in the thick undergrowth. Branches constantly slapped them in the face or scratched their arms and legs, but Gray Eagle gave no sign that he even noticed.

When he abruptly reined his horse to a halt and pointed ahead of them, Broken Arm stood up in his stirrups to look. There were footprints imprinted in the dirt and mud of a slope. Broken limbs and crushed twigs were evident signs that many feet had trampled the area. The infuriated Blackfeet had been careless in their anger at their prey, and had probably destroyed any signs of Adrian.

Gray Eagle nudged his mount forward. His black eyes scanned the ground, and he leaned from his horse to study the turn of a rock or bend of a branch. When he urged his horse up the slope, Broken Arm felt a new wave of respect. Most Indians were good trackers out of necessity, but Gray Eagle seemed to be a master of the art. He followed a trail with dogged persistence, sometimes through places where his horse could not go, sometimes where even the others had difficulty following, but when he emerged from the forest at the top of a ridge, he pointed downstream and said, "The fair-haired one went this way."

Blue Feather's throat closed, and her heart began to pound loudly in her chest. Adrian had run so far! How had he done it when he was not accustomed to a life of constant walking or running as were the Shoshoni? He must have great stamina to perform such a feat, and she felt a sudden wash of admiration for her beloved. He was fair, yes, and more handsome than any man she had ever seen; he was kind and gentle and considerate, but she had never thought he might be so courageous as well. Perhaps she'd sensed it when he had rescued her from the Piegan, but until now she had never dwelled on that particular quality. And Adrian had shown great courage in his race against death, she mused as she saw the deep-cut footprints leading directly into the river. The water came down from the mountain peaks and was as icy as the snow run-off from which it came. Her heart ached with sympathy for what he must be suffering, but she didn't doubt he had survived. She couldn't let her thoughts drift in that direction. . . .

Blue Feather's legs gripped the mare more tightly as it began to slide down the slope to the banks of the rushing river. She was slightly behind the others and nudged the horse into a trot to catch up.

Gray Eagle was following the edge of the bank with his eyes skimming the tracks cut deep into the mud. They rode for a mile or more, and the fading light made it difficult to see. When the Shoshoni warrior took a detour from the main bed of the river, Harry's voice lifted in protest.

"I say! Shouldn't we be following this main body of water instead of a stream that leads nowhere? I hardly think his lordship could plan on finding a settlement by choosing such an indirect route. . . ."

"Gray Eagle looks like he knows what he's doing" was Broken Arm's reply. "And from the looks of those tracks he's following, I'd say Duke was forced to hide instead of run. He'd have a better chance that way."

They were a half-mile along the winding stream when the tracks suddenly stopped. Pausing, Gray Eagle studied the area for a moment before announcing that the Piegan had given up and climbed the opposite bank to go back through the forest the way they had come.

"Does it look like they caught up with him?" Broken Arm asked, and the Shoshoni warrior shook his dark head.

"I see no sign of such a thing. There would have been a struggle . . . and blood. I see none."

Relaxing in his saddle, Broken Arm turned to Harry and repeated what Gray Eagle had said. The Englishman broke into a happy smile, then asked, "Then where is he?"

"Now, that we don't know," Broken Arm admitted. "If the Piegan couldn't find him, I doubt we will, either."

"Perhaps if we call out?" Harry began, but Blue Feather shook her head quickly.

"Oh, no! The Piegan may hear us if we do!"

Dismayed, Harry let his gaze skim over the deserted banks of the stream. Lord Adrian was so close, he could sense it, but there was little he could do. The spot was lovely, a veritable paradise of lush growth and sparkling water, with various species of wildlife scurrying away from the intruders in their domain. A beaver tail slapped the water in warning and a hawk circled overhead, its piercing cry spiralling down in a lonely echo. Harry's shoulders slumped as he reflected that even paradise had its demons.

Gray Eagle had circled his horse and approached Blue Feather. His obsidian eyes were hard as he looked at her and said, "I have done as you wished. The fair-haired one is gone. If we linger we may also die. . . ."

"He is not dead!" Blue Feather flashed. "I feel it!"

"No matter. We shall not stay here any longer," her cousin answered imperturbably. "If you refuse to come willingly, I shall regard you as my captive instead of my kinswoman."

Hot tears stung her eyelids, but Blue Feather slowly nodded. There was little choice. She had pushed Gray Eagle as far as she dared and must now yield to his decision. "*Ai,*" she whispered hoarsely. "I will go."

"And you?" Gray Eagle turned to ask Broken Arm. "What will you do?"

After a thoughtful pause Broken Arm said, "I've never wanted to leave my scalp on some Piegan's lance, so I reckon I'll have to give it up for now, too. If Duke did manage to escape, he'll find some way of letting us know."

Harry, flustered and apprehensive, asked, "What are you discussing?" When Broken Arm explained, Harry added, "But where shall we go, Mr. Broken Arm?"

Saddle leather creaked as Broken Arm shifted to gaze at Harry. "I was headed for the Wind River range, myself, but I don't think you'd like it up there."

"If you could just escort me to a nearby post, perhaps I could wait on his lordship there," Harry began hopefully, but the trapper was shaking his head.

The dangling wolf tail bobbed against his cheek as Broken Arm replied, "I need to be riding on, I'm afraid. I have to be in the Wind River range soon."

Blue Feather leaned forward and put her hand on Harry's arm. "Come with me," she said softly. "My grandfather will treat you well. And if Adrian is nearby, my people can search for him."

"But what if we don't find his lordship soon?" Harry asked worriedly. "What shall become of me?"

"I shall see that someone takes you down the mountain to a trading post where you can find another guide," Blue Feather reassured him.

Indicating Gray Eagle with a nod of his head, Harry asked, "And what of your formidable relative? Will he be displeased at such a solution?"

Turning, Blue Feather spoke rapidly to Gray Eagle in her own tongue, and he gave a noncommittal shrug of his bronzed shoulders and a brief reply. She turned back to Harry. "He sees no difficulty in such a thing. Will you come?"

"I don't see that I have many alternatives," Harry said with a sigh. "Lead on, Mr. Gray Eagle!"

As the horses trotted back up the banks toward the river, Blue Feather turned to look back. Her eyes scanned the area as if waiting for Adrian to emerge from behind a tree or rock. There was a huge lump in her throat and unshed tears burned her eyes, but she managed to keep her face impassive. Hadn't she yet learned that life could be bitter? One had to accept what one could not change. One stored up memories of the happy times whenever possible, retrieving them at the dark times in life to cherish them over and over, like stored sunbeams.

Adrian was such a memory, a cherished memory that would lighten the darkest days. If she closed her eyes, she could still see him, his fair hair and crooked smile, the silvery light in his pale eyes when she came to him on his pallets at night. . . .

Straightening her shoulders, Blue Feather sat stiffly on her horse as they turned in the direction of the Wind River range.

* * *

Wind River lay high in the mountains of Wyoming Territory, winding through majestic peaks and magnificent valleys. Seeing it again, Broken Arm thought of years before when he had last seen it with Duvalle and others. He had travelled to Canada since then, been down to the city and seen many things, but Wind River had always remained in the back of his mind. The memory of high mountain peaks where only eagles dared to soar had been buried under years of neglect, but now he remembered why he had come back. This was his home, his destiny.

Taking a deep breath of brisk mountain air, Broken Arm followed Gray Eagle down a hidden valley into the camp of the Shoshoni. Even Harry—who was wrapped in animal skins and near exhaustion—expressed admiration for the beauty surrounding him.

"I must say, that though the past five days of travel have been dreadfully debilitating, this is the most lovely site I have yet seen!"

"I've always thought so," Broken Arm murmured as his gaze rested on Blue Feather. She was sitting her horse and staring straight ahead, hardly seeming to notice that she was home at last. In the past five days she had spoken very little and had not mentioned Adrian Herenton at all. It had occurred to Broken Arm that perhaps she had accepted his probable death, for the Shoshoni never spoke of their dead.

Blue Feather's reticence had not gone unnoticed by Harry, either. Filled with his own misery, it had been hard for him to cope with hers also, and his conscience stung smartly. Now he could only watch sadly as she sat in a daze and ignored her surroundings.

There were close to twenty tipis scattered about the valley along the Wind River, and Harry examined them as they passed. These were larger than those he'd seen at the rendezvous, with long slender poles emerging from the top of the cone-shaped dwelling.

"Why do they call them tee-pees?" Harry wondered aloud, and Broken Arm grinned.

"It comes from the Dakota words *ti,* for 'dwelling,' and *pi,* which, roughly translated, means 'used for.' Simple enough description, I think."

Harry agreed, "Yes, I suppose it is. Do you speak all Indian dialects, Mr. Broken Arm?"

"No, but I tried to learn a little of as many as I could in case I ever needed to know them," the trapper replied. "It's come in handy a few times."

"As with the Blackfeet?"

"Ah, those Piegan can get pretty nasty sometimes, and it's always best to know what your enemy is saying," Broken Arm said. He nodded his head in the direction of Gray Eagle, who had halted in front of a large tipi. "I think we are about to meet the old chief. . . ."

But Broken Arm was mistaken. Instead they were shown to another tipi several yards away, while Blue Feather was escorted into her grandfather's dwelling. Food was brought to the weary travelers, and a skin of fresh water was laid beside the steaming bowls.

"Might I inquire as to what we are about to eat?" Harry asked he peered dubiously into his wooden bowl. "I do not believe I am up to eating a dog, as

I've heard some tribes consider a delicacy."

Broken Arm laughed softly. "Don't insult our hosts by refusing to eat," he said. "And I don't think this is dog. It smells more like elk to me, with some herbs thrown in for seasoning."

"And this?" Harry asked, referring to the skin. "What sort of leather is this waterpouch made of?"

"That's not leather," Broken Arm answered between mouthfuls of food. "That's a buffalo bladder. It works better than leather."

Harry blanched and turned his attention back to his food. "I *was* hungry," he murmured miserably, "and now I do not believe I can take a single bite of this concoction."

"It's only elk stew," Broken Arm admonished. "And it's the best I've had in a long time."

Harry would have offered a comment on what he considered quality when it concerned food, but at that moment the tipi flap fluttered back and Gray Eagle stooped to enter. He came to squat companionably by the fire in the center, his eyes dark and unreadable as he regarded them both for a moment.

"I have seen your kindness to my cousin," Gray Eagle began at last, speaking in Shoshoni to Broken Arm. "I am to thank you for saving her life and taking her from the Piegan. Our grandfather wishes you to know that he regards you kindly. You are to be honored among our people for your deeds, and will be allowed to stay in our camp for as long as you wish."

Broken Arm nodded. "I am honored to stay in the lodge of such a great warrior as Gray Eagle. The reputation of such a warrior is famed throughout the land, and I speak for both Harry and myself when I thank you for allowing us to stay."

319

Gray Eagle's eyes moved to the round-faced Englishman, who was staring at him with something akin to awe in his pale eyes. "Why do you call him hairy when he is not?" the warrior surprised Broken Arm by asking. "Is it a jest? He has no hair on his head or his body."

Nonplussed, and not wanting to laugh and perhaps offend the Shoshoni warrior, Broken Arm struggled for composure. "It is just a name," he finally replied. "The English do not necessarily name their children for any reason."

"Ahhh." Gray Eagle nodded, perfectly willing to accept that the English were a bit peculiar. In his dealings with the white man, he had learned that most of them were quite different and quite strange. Only a few had escaped that last judgement, and this old trapper was one of them.

"What is he saying?" Harry whispered to Broken Arm.

"He's just said that we could stay here as long as we like," Broken Arm answered, then grinned and added, "and he thinks you have a most peculiar name!"

"Peculiar . . . well, of all the preposterous, most . . . *my* name is peculiar?" Harry sputtered.

"Tut-tut. Don't offend him," Broken Arm warned with a straight face.

"Ask him about Margarethe," Harry said stiffly. "Is she all right?"

After a moment's discussion Broken Arm turned back to translate, "She is well and resting. Her grandfather was very glad to see her, and Gray Eagle extends the chief's regards to you. It seems that Blue Feather has told him you are brave, loyal and strong. He respects your loyalty and courage, and says that you are welcome in his tipi. It seems that you are also allowed to converse with Blue Feather whenever you wish."

"Tell him I am overwhelmed by his generosity," Harry said, then paused before adding, "and ask him for one last kindness, if you please."

Warily, Broken Arm asked, "What is that?"

"Ask him how quickly we may begin the search for his lordship. I fear we may wait too long."

"Harry—"

"Ask him!" the stout Englishman firmly demanded, and the trapper reluctantly complied.

Gray Eagle just stared blankly at Harry for a moment, his dark eyes reflecting the flickering flames of the fire in the center of the tipi. Then he shrugged, his words rapid as he gave Broken Arm his answer. Rising gracefully to his feet, Gray Eagle did not give the trapper an opportunity to say more. He ducked and stepped through the open flap of the tipi, disappearing into the night.

"What did he say?" Harry asked anxiously when Broken Arm remained silent. "Is he angry?"

"No, he's not angry. He just thinks you are lacking in wits, and I'm beginning to agree with him."

"Then he refused?"

Broken Arm shook his head. "No, he said he would tell his people to look for sign of him whenever they could, but he will not go back to look for Duke."

Harry sighed. "I suppose I shall have to be satisfied with that for now. I daresay his lordship could not have travelled this far by himself, and would not know where to look for Margarethe and myself anyway, but there you have it. One can not always have everything one wants."

"Well, don't give up yet," Broken Arm advised. "I have a notion that little Blue Feather is not about to let time go on too long before she insists that someone search for Duke. And she strikes me as a woman who can get her way. . . ."

Harry smiled at last. "I believe you are right, sir! It is a comforting thought."

"Not to her relatives, I'll bet!"

"Perhaps not. I had always assumed that Indians were a primitive, rather dishonest people. It seems that I was gravely mistaken in my opinion. Gray Eagle is a man of honor, I believe."

"Well, Indians are like everyone else, Harry. There's the honest ones, and then there's the ones who'd cut your throat for a jug of whisky, just like in London or Paris or New York."

"And Gray Eagle?" Harry asked.

"You're right. He's a man of honor."

Harry looked down at his cooling bowl of stew, then gingerly lifted a bite to his mouth. To his surprise it was good, and he smiled. "Perhaps it will not be so bad being here," he commented.

Broken Arm leaned back against a pile of furs and blankets and smiled. "Wind River range is the most beautiful spot I know of, Harry. This is where I intend to die."

Book Three

1836
Prophecy Fulfilled

From the prairies to the mountains, the storm raged . . . bringing tears and laughter, love and hate, hell and finally paradise. . . .

Chapter 17
Rendezvous

Summer 1836, Green River

Blue Feather's sleep was strange. When she closed her eyes, in moments the dreams were vivid, confusing and took a great deal of energy. She felt that, each time she awoke. Over and over she awoke unrested, hot, drained. She felt the dreams had meaning, that a spirit power was pawing her: There was a snake that followed her through the long, strange streets of a silent village of pale white tipis; a bear seemed to fly as she fled through rolling and endless fields of parched corn. . . .

She awoke and forced her eyes open for a long time. She fought against sleep for so long that she didn't realize she'd slipped into it again: It seemed natural to be walking on a steep green slope under blue-green pine trees illuminated by a brilliant sky. It made sense to be following the tall, lean mountain man in raw buckskins, with an amazingly long rifle tilted over his shoulder. She believed he was hunting the flying — or floating — bear. She sensed the bear was near. She had no memory of the snake.

The man stopped and put the gun down, then turned. She knew him. He was tanned, with a wild beard, but the nose and the eyes told her it was

Adrian. But what an Adrian! He was strong, sure and wild. She felt the wildness. She was a little afraid, but her fear was a tremendous desire, too. He smiled slightly. His hide shirt was open to the waist, and his chest was sunburnt, the hairs coppery gold glints in the fierce sunlight.

"Oh," she said.

"Come to me," he responded.

"I thought you were dead."

He smiled.

"The old Adrian is dead," he told her.

Then the need was too much to bear, and she fell into his arms and found herself kissing his chest and sighing. She bit and kissed. Her feelings were immense, and she felt sweet and wicked, tender and wonderful.

His hands went over her body, and she moved deliciously as they effortlessly discovered the secrets under her clothes. She kissed his neck, the rough beard prickling at her face as she found his lips and opened her mouth to him as if to breathe her soul into him. . . .

Then, somehow, they melted apart, and she felt the dream tiredness again. She was blinking, almost awake, seeing him standing there, and she knew he was alive. She knew it. And behind him—as if it had been there all along—was the bear, except it had a human face. She stared and realized they were Cheney's features.

As her eyes opened again, she murmured:

"He lives . . . the spirit-man Cheney has taken him. Oh, he lives . . . he lives. . . ."

A large caravan drew up on the crest of a ridge and surveyed the scene below them. The two men at the head of the caravan were both tall and muscular, one of them with fair hair and the other with hair of a flaming red. The red-haired man smiled broadly and gestured at the panorama spread before them.

"There it is, Your Grace, just as I promised!"

"Yes," his companion agreed in an awestruck tone, "just as you promised, William!"

Rising in his stirrups, William Drummond Stewart—second son of Sir George Stewart, seventeenth Lord of Grantully and fifth Baronet of Murthly, veteran of the Napoleonic wars and an avowed big-game hunter—gave the signal to proceed. He was a Scottish patrician who had been lured to the West by the promise of adventure and big trophies, and had acquired along the way a worthy companion in this endeavor. His Grace, Lord Richard Clarence Herenton, Duke of Hertfield in his own right, had joined Stewart's cavalcade in St. Louis. It had been a chance meeting, suggested by Lord Hertfield's second wife, Lady Josette. It seemed that the duke was searching for a long-lost brother who had been reported to have gone to the rendezvous at Green River the year before, and Lady Hertfield—being somewhat prophetic—had said Stewart was the man to help her husband. This fit in perfectly with William's plans, and the two had gotten along famously.

Now His Grace scanned the horizon before him and finally understood why his brother had lingered in this wild, primitive country. It was awe-inspiring and majestic, and left him feeling humbled. Turning to Stewart, Richard said, "I know now why Adrian has not returned to England."

William nodded. "It has all the raw beauty of the Scottish crags, yet retains the wildness that our settled lands have lost. I understand that Prince Maximilian brought along an artist to capture these scenes on canvas. As I have decided that whatever a German prince can do, I can do, I have done likewise, Your Grace."

"An excellent notion," Richard approved. "Josette was correct in her conjecture that I would be quite taken with this area. She is the one who really encouraged me to come alone, you see. I had wanted her to accompany me, but she felt that she would only be a burden, and so insisted upon remaining in New Orleans."

"Her Grace is not only beautiful, but understanding," William observed, and Richard nodded.

"Yes," he agreed, "she is."

"And I cannot help but think how aghast Her Grace might have been if she had attended the rendezvous," William added. "It would not have been wise for Her Grace to be in such a situation, even with us as protectors. But you, Your Grace, will be quite taken with the rendezvous, I think! If you are to locate your missing brother at all, you will find no better place to begin than a gathering of mountain men and Indians, who together know every square foot of the area as well as all the local gossip!"

Richard said wryly, "It will be a large improvement over the men I hired to find Adrian. They refused to look farther than the Dakotas, where he was said to have joined up with another group. It seems that those worthies found the American wilderness a bit too 'wild' for their liking!"

Laughing, Stewart pointed ahead to where the steep slope narrowed to a path navigable by only one horseman at a time. "I suppose I can understand that! But I find it exhilarating instead of terrifying."

"So do I," Richard said, "but I am not as athletic as you are reputed to be, William. I understand that you are a superb shot, as well as excellent in all manner of blood sports."

"I *have* been reputed to excel at emptying a stone jug of whisky," Stewart replied with a broad grin.

Richard grinned back. "I've been known to take a pull myself, William! My brother and I used to compete when we were younger."

Stewart slanted him a sympathetic glance. The duke had said very little about his reasons for finding his brother, but there was a sense of urgency about him that made William curious.

"If you don't mind my asking, Your Grace, why is it so urgent that you find your brother?" he asked.

Pausing, Richard thought for a moment, wondering how to explain something he wasn't quite certain he understood himself. It was a difficult situation. He was consumed with guilt for inadvertantly wronging Adrian, filled with anger at his father for sending his brother away, and chagrined because he had not had the courage to stand up and insist that the matter be righted at once. And Eleanor—cruel, greedy Eleanor—had been the spark to light the fire of rebellion.

"We did not part company on good terms," he answered Stewart a few moments later. "I wish to rectify that."

The Scotsman nodded in understanding. Such things often happened in large families where a title and great wealth were at stake. Wasn't his own older brother successor to the family baronetcy? It made

329

perfect sense that there had been a family squabble among the Herentons.

"Just another few miles and we will have reached Green River!" Stewart said cheerfully, dragging Richard's morose thoughts back to their surroundings.

Richard took a deep breath as he gazed out over the Green River. It was a placid, serene setting, marred only by the revelry and riotous men who inhabited it. Gentle spurs of sand cradled the waters of the slow-moving river, and densely-wooded humps of land embroidered the river's edges. Low-lying mists often shrouded the blue-green water, and the distant scoops of hills slowly melded into high mountain peaks with snowy crests. It was a beautiful place, but he was restless to move on.

The mountain men were rough-and-tumble as Stewart had promised, but Richard found them too loud, too raucous and too crude. He had been horrified by the drunken orgies, the bloody fights that sometimes ended in death for one of the combatants, and the blatant selling of Indian girls into carnal slavery. He shuddered to think of human beings as mere barter and wondered if Adrian had experienced similar feelings. Adrian. His younger brother seemed to have disappeared from the face of the earth, for no one at the rendezvous had seen or heard of a fair-haired Englishman by the name of Adrian Herenton.

"Your Grace!" a voice called, and Richard turned to see William Stewart approaching. A fur-clad trapper was at his side, appearing as disreputable as the rest of the lot in his buckskins and animal-head hat.

Richard smiled and waited for the breathless Scotsman to reach him. Flaming-haired Stewart seemed to always greet life at a run, whether in work or play, and his energy and enthusiasm were boundless. Richard was glad he had met him.

"Your Grace," Stewart said when he drew abreast, "I want someone to meet you . . . Everett Bowie, this is His Grace, Lord Herenton, the Duke of Hertfield. Your Grace, Mr. Bowie, as you can possibly tell, is a fur trapper."

Richard's lips twitched. "I *have* noticed an abundance of fur trappers at this occasion, William."

The irrepressible Stewart grinned boyishly. "Just so. However, this particular fur trapper might interest you."

Richard's gaze skimmed over the fur-clad man who seemed rather uncomfortable. His eyes narrowed thoughtfully as he realized that Stewart must have finally found a man who knew Adrian.

"How may I help you, Mr. Bowie?" he asked.

Shifting from one foot to another, Bowie said, "It's me who can help you, your dukeship—"

Stewart quickly hissed, "Your Grace!" into Bowie's ear, and the man shrugged.

"Your Grace," he amended. "See, I saw him last year. Only, his name was Duke then."

"Duke?" Richard's eyebrows rose. "He was calling himself a duke?"

"No, not that I recollect, but Broken Arm was."

Thoroughly confused, Richard parroted, "Broken arm? Do you mean my brother was injured?"

"No, no," Stewart hastily intervened. "There is a trapper by the name of Broken Arm, and it seems that your brother Adrian was with him. This trapper called him Duke, probably as a nickname because of his heritage. Mr. Bowie recalls him because your brother was dressed similarly to you, Your Grace."

"That's not the only reason," Bowie asserted. "Me and Duke and Broken Arm all sat in my tent and pulled a cork together."

Richard blinked. "Pulled a cork. . . ?"

"Drank some whisky," Stewart translated.

A wide smile slanted Richard's mouth as he suggested, "Why do we not all repair to my tent and partake of a bit of brandy, gentlemen? I feel that this is to be an auspicious occasion and cause for celebration!"

Bowie blinked just as Richard had a moment before. "Wha'?" he said.

"He asked us if we wanted to pull a cork," Stewart explained, enjoying himself immensely. This was his idea of high adventure and great entertainment, and he meant to do it all before he left the rendezvous. If the Duke of Hertfield did not care to join in all the festivities, that was his own decision, but the Scotsman fully intended to participate in every mountain man activity possible.

Bowie was grinning, pleased at the way things were going. "Let's go partake!" he agreed happily.

Once seated in Richard's well-constructed tent, the three men gazed with appreciation at the bottle of fine French brandy. Richard opened it and motioned for Bowie to lift his cup, which that gentleman did immediately.

"Tell me about my brother," Richard asked as he poured a liberal portion of brandy into Bowie's tin cup. "Was he well?"

"Looked fine to me . . . say! This here stuff just

332

slides down nice and easy, don't it?" Bowie remarked with great admiration as he gulped the amber liquor.

Wincing at such abuse of fine brandy, Richard refrained from telling the fur trapper that it was intended to be sipped, not gulped. He merely nodded and poured the same amount into the grinning Stewart's cup.

"His brother?" William prompted, and Bowie nodded.

"Oh yeah . . . he was here in thirty-five with Broken Arm and some others. They came in from the north, as I recollect, and old Broken Arm had been their guide."

"This Broken Arm," Richard said, "tell me about him."

"Not much to tell. Just an old man who's trapped this country since right after Lewis and Clark came through. He had a Frenchman by the name of Ramone Jardin with him when he first came down. You could always ask that one a lil' more, or mebbe one of the Stanfill brothers."

"Is this Ramone Jardin here this year?" Richard asked.

Bowie nodded. "Yeah, he's here, but I don' know how much he'll tell. I got the feelin' he didn't get along with Duke too well."

"Do you know where my brother went after the rendezvous was over?"

"Over? Hell, they didn' even stay two days!"

"Are you certain of this?" Richard asked. "Do you know why Adrian would leave? Did he leave with anyone?"

Holding out his empty cup, Bowie waited patiently while Richard filled it, then leaned back and settled deeper into the folded blankets upon which he sat.

"All I know is," he said after taking another healthy swig of brandy, "that he came to my tent all upset and tryin' to sober up Broken Arm. He was blabbering something about his Injun woman bein' taken, and he wanted to go after her."

"Woman?" Richard sat back, stunned by this, then realized that of course Adrian would take a female companion for comfort in this wilderness. But to be upset because she was gone? "An Indian woman?" he asked carefully.

Bowie nodded. "A real beauty, too! Shoshoni, and those women are all pretty if'n you ask me. 'Course, Duke shoulda known that her bein' the cousin of Gray Eagle would cause a bit of trouble . . ."

"What do you mean?" Richard asked quickly.

"Well, ol' Gray Eagle is grandson to the chief, and pretty powerful in his tribe. The girl is his cousin, and he didn't much like her being the casual woman of a white man, y'see."

"So this Gray Eagle took his cousin and Adrian followed them?"

"That's purty much the way of it," Bowie agreed.

Thinking aloud, Richard murmured, "So, Adrian must now be in some Shoshoni encampment, and I must discover which one he is—"

"No," Bowie interrupted, "that ain't right."

Struggling for control of his temper, Richard managed to ask politely, "Then what *is* correct, Mr. Bowie?"

"D'ya mind if I have another partake of brandy 'fore I answer?" Bowie asked as he held out his cup. "My throat's gettin' awful dry from all this

334

talkin'. . . ."

"By all means," Richard grated, and splashed another liberal amount into the tin cup. "Do go on, Mr. Bowie."

"Well, when yer brother and ol' Broken Arm lit out after that gal, they got tangled up with the Piegan—or Blackfeet. Them Injuns are bad news, and I heard that Duke got hisself kilt. Don't rightly know if that's true or not, but that's what I heard."

Richard just stared at Bowie for a moment, his throat tightening with dread. This was his worst nightmare, his worst fear, that Adrian would be dead before he could find him, and now it seemed that it was true.

"Are you certain of this?" he asked gruffly.

"Naw, I ain't certain of nothin' except what I see in front of me!" Bowie replied. "And then I ain't so sure of that sometimes. . . ."

"Then he might still live?"

"Well, I don't want to get yer hopes up, but Jardin said as how the Blackfeet had captured him. If'n that is true, he'd be dead, but I've know those Injuns to like playin' games sometimes. There's a chance Duke could have outwitted 'em."

"Was this Broken Arm with him?" Richard asked.

"Yeah."

"And is he dead?"

Bowie shook his head. "No, he's livin' up in the Wind River range, the way I hear it. Livin' with the Shoshoni tribe what that girl belonged to."

"Then Adrian could very well be with them!" Richard exclaimed hopefully, and looked at Stewart. The Scotsman was frowning, and Richard's hopes dimmed. "You don't think that possible, William?"

"I didn't say that, Your Grace. . . ."

335

"No, but your face is very expressive, my friend."

Stewart turned to Bowie. "Do you know how to find this Shoshoni camp?"

"Might. Then again, it's a long way go before it starts gittin' cold in those mountains. Winter hits 'round early October, you know."

"This is July."

"Yeah, but . . ." Bowie scratched at his bearded chin as he reflected, then his jaw dropped and his eyes widened as Richard offered him money equal to a year's wages in pelts to take him to the Shoshoni camp. "A year's wages in pelts?" Bowie spluttered in astonishment.

"And I expect loyalty for those sort of wages," Richard stated. "If we safely return, another bonus."

Bowie gazed at him craftily. "And if'n we don't get back?"

"I hardly think you'll be worried about money then," Richard returned coolly.

"No, but I got me a wife now," Bowie said. "I'd hate ta leave her without nuthin'."

"Half now, half when we return," Richard said promptly.

"You got yerself a guide!" Bowie said happily.

Glancing at Stewart, Richard asked, "Should I be able to make this trip before winter sets in?"

"Yes."

"Can you wait for me here?"

"I'll wait as long as I can, Your Grace, but you had best gather your provisions as soon as possible and start out. If an early snow hits, you may find yourself battling nature as well as enemies."

Richard nodded, stood up and looked at Everett Bowie. "We leave before first light tomorrow," he said.

That night was spent in a flurry of letter writing as Richard penned notes to his wife Josette and his Uncle Timothy, a favorite relative. Richard smiled. Uncle Timothy was probably the most understanding member of his family, a true believer in following one's beliefs. *Thank God for Uncle Timothy and Josette,* Richard thought as he blotted the wet ink on his letters and sealed them with hot wax.

A thick mist lay like a blanket on the encampment when they rode away the next morning, shrouding the shores and muffling the sounds of revelry. Everett Bowie had brought along his Indian wife — apologetically explaining that she had refused to be left behind — and another man who was to help. At first Richard had frowned at the notion of a woman being along on such a dangerous mission, but Bowie had insisted that she would be no trouble and a great help.

"She's a half-breed, see, and I bought her from this bully by the name of Shumar. He'd killed her husband in a fair fight and took her as his woman, but I saw her and knew I wanted her." His chest had puffed with pride as he continued, "Named her Charlotte, after my mother. She cost me my .60 caliber Hawken, but she's been worth it."

So Richard found himself riding along with a mountain man who seemed like a character out of a book. He vaguely recalled reading an account written by one James Isham, a Hudson's Bay trader who in 1743 had made an earnest attempt to satisfy European curiosity about beaver trapping. Mr. Isham had faithfully reproduced all the details entailed in hunting the beaver, and had included a description of the men who hunted them. Everett

337

Bowie could have stepped out of the pages of his epistle.

He wore buckskins with fringed seams, and footwear cut from a buffalo hide. His waist was encircled with a leather belt that held a sheathed knife and two pistols, and suspended around his neck was a bullet-pouch which was securely fastened to his belt in the front. Beneath Bowie's right arm hung a powder-horn, held by a strap that crossed his chest to his opposite shoulder, and was there attached with his bullet mould, ball-screw, wiper and an awl. He carried a homemade ramrod cut from hickory wood next to his .50 caliber Hawken rifle, which he declared to be the best buffalo or grizzly rifle in existence. Not one to be caught unprepared, Bowie also brought along an extra set of leggings, several knives, a pipe, tobacco and a tattered Bible for idle moments. Packed on the back of a horse were spare locks and flints, twenty pounds of gunpowder, almost a hundred pounds of lead and a very small amount of food. Except for a small sack of flour, some coffee, tea and salt, Bowie found no use for other provisions.

"But what will you eat?" Richard asked in amazement, and was met with an equally amazed stare.

"Why, there's plenny of elk, deer and rabbit!" Bowie finally replied. "And if'n ya git tired of that, there's wild plums and nuts fer variety. Ya cain't go hungry out here unless yer crippled or stupid."

"I see," Richard said lamely.

"And my woman kin do ennything," Bowie boasted. "She kin cook, cut wood, blaze a trail and even trap beaver."

Charlotte proved herself to be as adept as Bowie claimed over the next few days. Speculating upon his brother's reasons for pursuing his Shoshoni companion, Richard decided that she must have proven as invaluable to Adrian as Bowie's woman was to him. That conclusion courted another question. Once Adrian was found, would he wish to return to England with him? For the first time, Richard faced the very real possibility that his younger brother had changed a great deal.

Another day passed, and for the first time they encountered a party of Indians. Richard was admittedly nervous, but Bowie soothed him with the remark that he knew them.

"Arapaho," he explained. "I used to trade with 'em some." The trapper rode forward to speak with them in their own language and hand signs, while Richard waited.

"Will they let us pass without trouble?" Richard asked Charlotte when he could no longer stand the suspense.

She nodded, replying in broken English, "Yes . . . my people not bad to we. Bowie, he ask for your lost one." She smiled encouragingly, her round face beaming. "Arapaho hear many things. Arapaho talk much. Like presents."

"Ah," Richard said speculatively, "then they can be bribed, perhaps."

Not understanding his meaning, Charlotte just nodded vigorously, wanting this oddly dressed man to be pleased with her husband. "Arapaho not like Shoshoni," she offered. "Arapaho like presents. Shoshoni like alone."

As it turned out, the party of Arapaho did not request gifts. They freely told Bowie what he asked, and the trapper rode back to Richard wearing a big smile.

"Good news!" he crowed. "It seems that Ramone Jardin came this way not too long ago, and he was asking the same questions I asked. Mebbe we are not the only ones looking for your brother, heh?"

Frowning, Richard asked, "What do you mean? I thought you said Jardin was at the rendezvous. . . ."

"Seems like he musta left right after I saw him."

"Do you view Jardin as a help or a threat?"

Shrugging, Bowie said, "Jardin is no man's friend. If he asks about your brother or Broken Arm, I kinda get to wonderin' why. It makes me think, now why would a Frenchie like Jardin be int'rested in a old man like Broken Arm and a worthless—beggin' yer pardon—tenderfoot like Duke."

"And your conclusions?" Richard asked when Bowie paused.

"My conclusion is that Jardin cain't be trusted, and that you might better find yer brother first."

"Did your acquaintances have any other comments that might be of assistance to us?" Richard asked.

"Well, they did say somethin' kinda odd, but I don't know that it has anything to do with your brother."

There was a strange expression on Bowie's face, and he scratched at his head as he contemplated, which left Richard wondering.

"Tell me," he insisted, and Bowie complied reluctantly.

"Seems like they've got some funny story about Cheney," he said, and cut his eyes at Charlotte when she gasped.

"Who's Cheney?" Richard wanted to know.

"Cheney . . . evil spirit! Cheney bad!" Charlotte wailed, and her high-pitched voice grated on Richard's raw nerves.

"Be still!" he commanded sharply, and when she had hushed he turned back to Bowie. "Who is this Cheney?"

"Some folks aren't sure if he's a who or a what," Bowie muttered. "These fellows were kinda shook-up by what they'd heard, and were in a hurry to get to their summer hunting grounds far away. They told me old Cheney's spirit flew away from his ancient body and found a new body. He's s'posed to be roamin' around up there somewhere, all new and ready to live for another hunnerd years."

"Tripe," Richard pronounced firmly, "Pure, unadulterated tripe! Foolish nonsense!"

"Mebbe," Bowie conceded, "but you cain't tell that to them Arapaho. They think he's come back in a new body."

"You still haven't answered my question, Mr. Bowie. Just who is this Cheney, and why does he have such a significance to the Indian?"

"Cheney seems to have been here forever. He rode out years ago with Lewis and Clark's expedition, and just kinda stayed. After Lewis shot a Blackfoot, things got real hot for the white man in this country. A lone white man just couldn't survive, but Cheney did. The Blackfeet tried to kill him again and again, but they never could. They lost good braves tryin', but Cheney always lived. He musta kilt a hunnerd or more of 'em; it didn' matter what tribe. Ute, Pawnee, Cheyenne, Arapaho or Piegan—it just didn't matter. Legends grew up

341

around him, I guess, made him out to be more than he was. A Cheyenne warrior once claimed that he stabbed Cheney through the heart and it kept right on beatin', blood gushin' out like a freshwater spring. Cheney is s'posed to be bad medicine."

"Do you believe this?" Richard couldn't help asking.

"I know that some of it's true. Cheney used to trap with the Frenchman, Pierre Duvalle. Then he just up and went crazy, ran off into the mountains and didn't come down again. No one but the Indians saw or heard from him since." There was a lengthy pause, and when Richard shifted in his saddle, Bowie said quietly, "Until now."

"Until now?" A chill shivered down Richard's spine.

"This new body of Cheney's is said to be that of a white man with hair and beard like the sun."

It took a moment for Richard to speak as possibilities crowded his mind, but he finally said, "Do you think it could be my brother?"

"I ain't fer sure," Bowie said, "but it's possible. I know one thing—Cheney ain't died and come back as a young man, *that's* fer sure!"

"Does this Jardin know?"

"Probably, but if he does he ain't worried about it. The Arapaho said he headed northwest to the Wind River range. He seems real interested in Gray Eagle. It appears that the old chief died this past winter, and Gray Eagle is chief now."

"Well! You learned quite a lot in that short conversation," Richard approved, and Bowie held up his hand.

"There's another thing," he said uneasily. "I don't know what it might mean to you, but it's said there's two white men in the Shoshoni camp, one of 'em bein' Broken Arm, and the other bein' a kinda nurse to two golden babies belongin' to a Shoshoni gal. . . ."

"Golden babies?" Richard stared at him blankly.

"Golden babies born to the chief's granddaughter . . ."

"They must be Adrian's," Richard said slowly, not quite able to believe such a thing. "So what do I do now?"

Grinning, Bowie suggested, "Look for your brother. I know where this ghost was last seen."

"Lead on!" Richard said with a dramatic flourish of one arm, and followed Bowie, Charlotte and the taciturn Indian in a northeasterly direction.

There was the solid, thunking sound of an axe hitting a log, then a crack as it split in two. A muscular, bearded man bent, lifted another log onto the thick slab, positioned it carefully and repeated the act. Another loud crack, and he bent to reach for another log. This time his eyes caught a flicker of movement, and he straightened cautiously, reaching for the rifle propped against a nearby tree stump. Riders.

When the riders drew close, they were met by a hard-eyed woodsman bristling with weapons. Though bare-chested, the man had a long, wicked knife strapped to his left leg, a pair of pistols tucked into the waistband of his buckskin trousers, and a lethal rifle cocked and aimed at them.

"Wait a minute!" Bowie protested, reining his horse in sharply. "We come as friends!"

"Speak your piece," the man began, his granite

eyes locked on Bowie. It was only when his gaze shifted slightly that he paused, and the muzzle of his rifle lowered. His eyes softened, and the trace of an astonished smile flickered for a moment on his hard mouth. "Richard," he murmured.

Stiffening in shock, Richard Herenton could not believe his eyes. This . . . this man could not be Adrian! Not this lean muscled man with no trace of the former softness about him, no trace of the gentle brother he remembered so well. In Adrian's place was a hard-eyed man with a barrel-chest and a thick, golden beard. His hair was long, brushing over his shoulders, and he wore the fringed buckskin trousers and knee-high moccasins that mountain men wore. No, this could not be Adrian Herenton. . . .

"Don't you know me?" Adrian was asking as he strode swiftly forward. "It's me, Richard—Adrian!"

"I . . . I can't quite believe I've finally found you," Richard replied awkwardly, his natural English reticence keeping him from throwing himself at his brother. Then, as realization sank in, Richard abandoned his notions of what was proper and was off his horse, striding toward Adrian at a near run.

Brother clasped brother, arms circling one another as they struggled for composure.

"Adrian . . ."

"Richard . . ."

Finally pushing away, they stood close and smiled. It was a shock to each of them to find one another in this untamed land, hundreds of miles from civilization.

"I should have recognized Bowie," Adrian said at last, awkwardly, as if he could think of nothing else to say.

Richard grinned. "You should have recognized *me,* you dolt!"

Adrian grinned back at him. "I suppose I should have," he agreed.

Bowie came forward, greeting Adrian with a smile. "How's the hunting, Duke?"

"Fair, Bowie, just fair," Adrian replied.

Bowie nudged him with an elbow. "You don' look like you lost no weight to me, Duke! You gotta partner?"

Adrian's smile faded, and he shook his shaggy head. "No, he's dead."

"Cheney?" Bowie guessed, and Adrian nodded. "I kinda thought it musta been him who found you when I heard reports that he'd died and come back as a golden-haired youth," Bowie observed.

Grimacing, Adrian said, "Youth?"

"Well, to them Injuns you are!"

"I certainly don't feel like a youth anymore," Adrian said, and Richard had the fleeting thought that he didn't resemble one, either. "What's the matter with your woman?" Adrian asked as he spied Charlotte cowering on her mount. Her voice quavered in a high-pitched keening as she begged the spirits to deliver her from harm.

Without turning his head, Bowie answered, "Aw, she thinks yer Cheney's spirit. It's the Indian in her. I'll explain it later, and she'll be all right."

Turning to his brother, Adrian gazed at him quizzically for a moment, then asked gently, "Why are you here, Richard?"

"Adrian," Richard said, "I came all this way to fetch you home with me. I wanted to put an end to our quarrel, and unite our broken house."

Startled by the familiar echo of his words, Adrian

just stared at his brother for a moment, recalling a long-ago prophecy. *A house divided . . . a house united. . . .*

"Adrian?" Richard prompted, and his brother's distant gaze focused again. "Adrian, Father died. . . ."

Adrian flinched, and his fingers tightened on the rifle he still held. "When?"

"Almost two years ago."

Nodding, Adrian said heavily, "Come to my lodge and tell me about it, Richard." His voice rose to include Bowie and the others. "You are all welcome."

They followed Adrian to his lodge, a shelter made of slender curved poles and covered with skins. It was built beneath an overhang of rocks, hidden by granite slopes and a natural screen of thick brush. A stream trickled nearby, and a fire slumbered near the entrance of the hut. A stout wooden frame was built close by for the purpose of stretching dressed skins, and a graining block rested at the edge of the frame.

"You built all this?" Richard asked in amazement, but Adrian shook his head.

"No, Cheney did this. I was his guest, and after his death, it was my inheritance." His mouth twisted in a bitter, self-mocking smile, and Richard put a hand on his arm.

"Adrian, I know where your woman is. . . ."

He jerked to an abrupt halt. A light flared in Adrian's eyes, and his nostrils flared as he searched his brother's face. "You . . . you know where Blue Feather is?"

"Blue Feather . . . yes, if she is your Shoshoni woman, I know where she is. Bowie has agreed to

346

guide us there if you like."

"If I like . . . if . . . dear God, how I have dreamed these many months of being able to find her!" Adrian burst out. "She is the reason for my being here, the reason for . . . Cheney was too old, too weak to take me. When he found me I was too weak to go in search of her, and he nursed me back to health. He gave me all he had, then he grew too ill. I couldn't leave him. He died a fortnight ago. In truth, Richard, if I did not think you would raise your hand to me, I would kiss you!" Adrian ended with a wild laugh.

"Spare me" was Richard's dry response. "I shudder to think what your reaction will be when I give you the rest of my news, dear brother."

"Try me and see," Adrian advised with a grin.

"I am of the opinion that you have two golden-haired babes. Unless your woman has chanced upon another fair-haired man in these mountains—which could happen, I suppose. . . ."

Stunned, Adrian gaped at Richard. "Two . . . but that is not possible, Richard!"

"Have you never heard of twins?"

"Oh . . . oh, yes!"

"Then, shall I congratulate you?" Richard returned.

Adrian's eyes were shuttered as he said slowly, "I do not know. Tell me, have you heard anything of Broken Arm, Bowie?" he asked, turning to the trapper.

Everett Bowie, who was busily trying to convince the leery Charlotte that Adrian was really an Englishman and not a transformed spirit, turned his brief attention to him. "He's said to be in the Shoshoni camp with your woman and an old man who

347

plays nurse to babies," he said before turning back to the gibbering Charlotte.

Now Adrian laughed aloud, saying softly, "Dear Harry! I must truly be a father, then!"

Clapping him on the back, Richard said plaintively, "I am delighted to be the bearer of such glad tidings, dear brother, but as I am about to expire from hunger, I find it most difficult to be truly enthusiastic."

"I have a stew that you might find appetizing," Adrian assured him. "And while you eat, we will talk. I have a lot of questions."

Chapter 18
A New House

It was a bright summer day, with the sun smiling gently down on the Shoshoni encampment. Life went on as normal, filled with the sounds of laughing children at play and women chattering as they performed their daily tasks. Looking up from the softened strip of elkhide that she was fashioning into a dress, Blue Feather smiled. She sat cross-legged in front of her tipi, enjoying the soft day. Two naked babies curled up next to one another on a nearby blanket, their pudgy arms waving in the air as they played together. Sturdy limbs wobbled as they crawled across the blanket, and pale golden curls waved over their foreheads. Sighing wistfully, Blue Feather gazed at her daughters and wished once more that their father could have seen his children. He would have thought them beautiful. Twins. She had been more shocked than the midwife when two infant daughters had been given her, but had furiously foiled the superstitious midwife's attempts to leave one out to die, as was the custom.

"Two babies—and girls!" the Indian woman had spat. "It is foolish to keep both."

Blue Feather's howls of rage and Harry's intervention had prevented the midwife from carrying out what she saw as her duty, and both babies had grown strong and happy. Their names had come to Blue Feather as she cradled them close that starlit night, thinking of their father and yearning for him. Memories had tugged at her, and she'd recalled the first night they had come together, that soft night on the banks of a stream when the sky had been full of stars and the moon had beamed approval. Now White Star and Blue Moon were almost six months old, and she saw traces of their handsome father in the color of their golden hair and their good natures.

Smiling, Blue Feather reached out to caress a dimpled child as she thought of Harry. Though struggling gamefully to hide his dismay at first, Harry had soon become a staunch defender of the children. They were frowned upon by many in the camp because they were children of a white man and bore his mark in the color of their hair. Blue Feather was ostracized by most of the women in her tribe for having borne a white man's children. This incensed Harry, and he was often seen toting the babies in a huge grass basket as proudly as if he was the father. Of course, this elicited more snickers from the tribe, yet Blue Feather held her head high and ignored them. Even the chief's cousin was not immune to ridicule and slander, it seemed.

A noise at the edge of camp drew her attention, and Blue Feather glanced up with mild interest as the camp dogs barked furiously. Children scampered through the tipis in abandon, and women's voices lifted in shrill conjecture as a group of horsemen approached.

Blue Feather thought little of it. After all, many

riders passed through their camp this time of year when the buffalo were hunted. She wiped away a sheen of moisture from her forehead, then lifted one of her daughters into her arms as the child began to fret. It was White Star, called Star by her loving mother and doting nursemaid, Harry. Star had been born first and was usually the first to cry, the first to demand maternal attention. Now the chubby girl gazed up at her mother with wide, liquid eyes, and Blue Feather smiled as she attended the hungry child. Well-pounded deer meat was mixed with a thin cereal of wild oats for both girls, for by the time Star had quieted, Blue Moon was fussing. Her mother replaced one child with another. Blue was less demanding, more docile and patient than her sibling, but equally as hungry. Blue Feather was relieved when she could put them both on their pallet for a nap. Though she preferred the cradle boards more commonly used, Harry insisted upon the blankets.

"Cradle boards restrict their movements," he'd reproved her, "and I consider them unusually cruel." Harry had also protested the fact that Indian babies wore no clothing—saying that it was barbaric—but had soon been convinced of the practicality. In the heat of summer, light swaddling was infinitely more comfortable than several layers of clothing that would have to be frequently changed, and so he had yielded on that point though remaining adamant about the use of cradle boards.

So a large grass basket became the girls' common method of transportation, and Harry was satisfied. Now Blue Feather arranged their pallets in the shade of the tipi and settled back to her sewing, threading a bone needle with thin strands of sinew. She squinted at the needle as she poked at the tiny hole with her thread, and was concentrating so intently she didn't hear Harry's call at first.

"Margarethe!" he called again, and this time his urgent tone penetrated her concentration.

Looking up, she gazed inquiringly at the pudgy man approaching the tipi. He looked disheveled, standing out among the others in his garb of trousers, vest and jacket as he had always worn. The only item missing from his wardrobe was his hat, which he had not been able to replace.

"*Ai,* Harry?" she asked softly. "What is it?"

"Riders," he said a bit breathlessly, paused and added, "white men!"

"Who are they?" Blue Feather asked, warily this time, as she recalled only too well the Frenchman, Jardin.

"I cannot tell yet, Margarethe, but I do know that it is not that pig of a Frenchman returning." Harry harbored the ever-present hope that he would someday learn news of Adrian, though he dared not mention his name aloud. She became upset so easily when his name was mentioned, a fault of her Shoshoni upbringing and their ridiculous belief that speaking the name of the dead would bring ill fortune.

Pushing to her feet, Blue Feather smoothed back stray wisps of dark hair from her eyes as she gazed anxiously up the wide path running through the middle of the village. A cloud of dust wafted in the air, but she could not yet make out individual forms.

"I shall go look at them," she decided, and

Harry nodded as he scooped up a grass basket and placed the children inside.

"They halted at Gray Eagle's tipi," he informed her as he scurried along behind. "Perhaps we can learn something if we just go and listen."

"Is Broken Arm in camp?" Blue Feather asked, and Harry shook his head.

"No, he is still hunting."

"Then Gray Eagle may need me to interpret for him," she said as she moved quickly forward. "He does not speak the language as well as I do."

But when they arrived at the large tipi belonging to Gray Eagle, all thoughts of interpretation vanished. Harry skidded to a stunned halt, his eyes wide as he viewed the party of men and one woman waiting before the chief's tipi.

"My word!" the Englishman breathed softly as he recognized the fair-haired man sitting astride a sorrel mare. It was Lord Richard Herenton, a bit dustier and older than when Harry had last seen him, but otherwise the same. Harry's first impulse to rush forward was checked as his gaze shifted to Richard's left and he saw the vaguely familiar man sitting with easy grace atop a paint gelding. Thick flaxen hair fell to the man's shoulders, and a bushy beard covered half his face. His chest was broad, and he wore fringed buckskins and knee-high moccasins, and a long, sheathed knife was strapped to his left leg. There was an air of quiet confidence about the man as well as tantalizingly familiar gestures. It was only when the man turned slightly and Harry saw his face that he knew.

Falling to his knees and still gripping the heavy basket, Harry murmured, "Lord Adrian . . ."

If he had thought to worry about Blue Feather's reaction when she heard her beloved's name spoken aloud, he would have been relieved. She didn't even hear Harry as she moved forward, shuffling through the dust in a daze. It was another dream, and she would soon wake and find her arms achingly empty again. It could not be her beloved. Oh, how cruel that his memory should still be so vivid. . . .

But when she drew close and he had not yet faded away into wakefulness, when she was able to reach out and touch the hem of his shirt, Blue Feather knew that it was Adrian. A sob escaped her, and Adrian turned to look down, seeing at last the woman who had tormented his every waking moment for the past year.

"Blue Feather!" he cried hoarsely at the same instant that she called out his name.

"Adrian! Oh, my beloved!"

Adrian was off his horse and sweeping her into his arms in a single, fierce motion, holding her so tightly she couldn't breathe. He kissed her hungrily, her eyes, her nose, her parted lips, over and over again while she sobbed helplessly.

Those gathered around whispered among themselves, speculating on this strange occurrence until the chief made a sign that they should depart. Gray Eagle stepped forward and stood quietly, waiting with arms folded across his chest until the proper moment to speak to his cousin.

Blue Feather clung to Adrian, her arms around his neck and her feet lifted from the ground to barely graze the dust as he clasped her against his chest. Her tears wet his face and neck, and he could taste the salt as he kissed her repeatedly. Finally Adrian lowered her gently to the ground and held her as she swayed against him.

"It's been so long," she managed to choke out, and he nodded.

"Yes, it has, my sweet, shining star," he whispered huskily. "And you are more beautiful than ever. . . ."

His words prompted Blue Feather to draw back and gaze at him shyly, wondering how he would react to her news. "I have something to show you," she said, and took one of his calloused hands in hers. She marveled at the rough-hewn look of her man, at his new-found poise and the air of assurance he wore like a fur cloak. Even the calluses on his palms were new, different from the soft hands he'd had before.

Blue Feather guided him through the thinning crowd of curious onlookers to where Harry knelt in the dust, and Adrian's voice cracked slightly as he greeted his servant and beloved friend.

"Harry . . ."

"My lord," Harry returned in a whisper, unable to rise and greet him, unable to do more than gesture to the large basket at his side. "We have a surprise for you, my lord," Harry said then, his eyes meeting Blue Feather's smiling gaze.

Reaching down, Adrian pulled back the light blanket that covered two sleeping bundles and stared at them silently. So it was true. He did have two children, two sturdy girls who bore his color of hair but not his name. That was an oversight he intended to rectify as soon as possible, Adrian promised himself, and straightened.

"Do you like them?" Blue Feather asked anxiously, and Adrian grinned.

"They seem awfully fat," he said, and watched her expression grow indignant.

"They are not fat! They are beautiful, and I . . . oh, you are teasing me!" she cried out as he laughed aloud and scooped her into his arms again.

"They are the most beautiful children I have ever seen," he answered truthfully. "I am more proud than I had ever thought I would be. . . ."

"And they are quite bright too, my lord," Harry put in with a fatherly pride. "Why, Star is well advanced for her age."

"Star?" Adrian echoed, turning to Blue Feather. "Is that what you named her?"

Nodding, Blue Feather said, "White Star was born first, and then came Blue Moon."

"Lovely names, don't you agree, my lord?" Harry asked as he straightened the blanket lying over the sleeping girls. "I approved Margarethe's choice, though my preference was something a bit less tantalizing, such as Blanche, Daisy or even Sarah."

"I remembered the time we first lay together, and they were born on just such a night," Blue Feather told Adrian.

His fingertips caressed her cheek as he said, "I am sad that I could not have been with you, that you were alone."

Grasping his fingers, Blue Feather said, "But I was not alone. I had Harry to comfort me."

Turning to his servant again, Adrian gazed at the older man's tear-streaked face with such a loving expression Harry was taken aback. "There are not enough words to express how dear you are to me,

356

Harry," he said at last. "How can I ever thank you for your loyalty and courage?"

"Perhaps you could shave, my lord," Harry offered after a moment's contemplation. "I am quite undone at the sight of you, and feel that you have been sorely neglected."

A loud laugh burst from Adrian's throat. "For you, Harry, I shall cheerfully comply with your heartfelt request!"

"Shhh! My lord, you might wake them," Harry reproved, "and they are absolutely insufferable when they have not had their proper rest."

Grinning, Adrian reached down to wrap an arm around Harry's shoulders and lift him to his feet. "I have sorely missed you, my dear friend," he said. "Your wit has always cheered me."

"Shall we repair to a tipi, my lord? I am most anxious to get out of the sun and learn how you escaped those wretched Blackfeet, as well as to learn your whereabouts for the past year."

"We have a lot of catching up to do," Adrian agreed.

Campfires burned brightly, beacons against the indigo backdrop of the night. A waterfall tumbled noisily in the distance, visible in daylight and heard as a musical serenade when the village grew quiet at night.

Now, however, the village was riotous with laughter and celebration. Adrian relaxed, content to watch Blue Feather dance as his return from the dead was celebrated in Shoshoni fashion. There was a feast and dancing and drums, and Gray Eagle had ordered that Adrian was to be honored. Adrian was certain it must be a true concession on the part of

357

the Shoshoni chief, instigated by Gray Eagle's affection for his cousin. But to refuse such an honor would be an insult, even if Adrian had stated his true desire to be alone with Blue Feather.

She was garbed in the doeskin dress he had given her at the rendezvous. Her soft, shining hair framed her radiant face as she gazed at him lovingly, and her supple body twisted in the steps of the dance. Teasing him, she tossed back her sable hair and lifted her arms as she joined the lines of females dancing in a circle around the fire. Adrian's loins ached with the need for her, and his heart yearned to hold her close and whisper the tender words he had longed to say for so long. Leaning forward, he stared at her intently.

Sensing Adrian's impatience, Broken Arm leaned close and murmured, "The old Duke would have demanded immediate gratification. I see you have learned patience in the past year, my friend."

Smiling wryly, Adrian commented, "I had little choice."

Broken Arm nodded. "I must admit that I never thought you would survive, Duke. I remember thinking that you would find it difficult to get along without Harry to care for you, and the next thing I know you're on your own. Then you turn up alive and healthy after all that happened!"

Shrugging, Adrian narrowed his eyes. "I had help," he said shortly. His gaze had moved from the dancers to the shadowed mountain peaks in the distance as if he could see them in the dark. "It was bad at first," he said slowly, so quietly that Broken Arm had to lean close to hear, and it seemed as if Adrian was speaking to himself rather than his friend. "I don't think I've ever been quite so shocked or felt quite so alone . . . if it hadn't been for the old man, I would have died. But I didn't die, and as it turned out, he needed me in the end. Perhaps he'd somehow known he would, as he suggested when he made excuses for rescuing me after the race."

"Cheney?" Broken Arm asked, and Adrian nodded. A long silence stretched between them, then the old trapper said, "There is something I must mention to you about Blue Feather, Duke."

Adrian's gaze shifted back to the trapper. "What is it?"

"You must remember that she is a cousin to the chief. Her grandfather was considered a great man, and her father is also well-respected in the tribe. If need be, they would give their lives for Duvalle."

"Yes, I know all that," Adrian pointed out.

"But you must know that even though Blue Feather is the mother of your children you are not considered her husband, Duke."

Adrian's brows lifted as he stared at Broken Arm in disbelief. "Surely that cannot be! Why, what sort of ceremony do the Shoshoni have that will ensure—"

"No ceremony, Duke, not like you mean. It's all protocol here. Usually a maiden is promised to a man when still an infant, and that betrothal is secured by a gift of some sort."

"A gift? You mean, I must buy her?" Adrian asked, his tension easing. "Why, that should be no problem!"

"No? What do you have that her cousin would want? Six fine horses, perhaps? Luxurious robes or fur pelts? She is the granddaughter of a chief, and now cousin to the present chief. She will not go cheaply, Duke!"

A dull flush spread up Adrian's neck to his face, and he growled, "I did not mean to say that she would! She is worth more to me than a hundred horses! More than a castle full or ermine robes and beaver pelts—"

"I know, I know," Broken Arm soothed quickly, "but I am not too sure that her cousin will know that. You will not be allowed to . . . to be with her, Duke, until you have satisfied certain requirements. I just wanted you to understand that."

Collapsing back against the pole behind him, Adrian shook his head dolefully. "One more obstacle to overcome," he muttered.

"Gray Eagle is sitting just a few feet away," Broken Arm observed. "Shall I negotiate for you?"

A wry smile twisted Adrian's mouth, and he gave a short nod of his head. "It appears that I greatly need a mediator in this area. But what can you offer that will interest the chief?"

"Let me feel him out first. Mebbe I can get some kind of idea as to what he wants. He does expect something to be offered, though, you can bet on that," Broken Arm said.

Lurching to his feet, Broken Arm crossed to where Gray Eagle sat cross-legged, his eyes on the dancers. The old trapper greeted the chief and was invited to sit down, and after a few moments Adrian was motioned to join them.

"Gray Eagle is honored that you wish to marry his cousin," Broken Arm began formally when Adrian was seated. "He considers Blue Feather to

360

be a worthy prize."

Gray Eagle spoke in his own language, and Broken Arm listened attentively. The handsome Shoshoni chief motioned with his hands, and Adrian could not help but think he must be demanding a great deal as barter. Despair flooded through him, and he wondered what he had of great worth that would interest the crafty chief. His only horse was a borrowed one, and it was not exactly a magnificent specimen. All his supplies were long gone, of course, as was anything else of value he might have. His only hope was that Richard may have something Gray Eagle would desire, but even that could be an awkward situation if the chief was insulted that it had come from another. It was a deuced awkward situation anyway, Adrian thought with frustration. The only word he recognized in the conversation between Broken Arm and Gray Eagle was *taiva-vone,* and that was not reassuring. He had no desire to be thought of as a stranger or outsider.

Finally Broken Arm turned back to Adrian. "It don't look good, Duke," he said. "Chief Gray Eagle here seems to think that his little cousin is special and, even though she is burdened with girl babies, should bring more than you seem to have. He did mention guns, but I'm not too sure you have enough to—"

"Guns!" Adrian said quickly, startling Broken Arm. "I may not have very many guns," he explained, "but I have a very special one." He leaned forward to look at Gray Eagle as he spoke. "Tell him I have the rifle that belonged to Cheney, Broken Arm. Tell him it has powerful medicine."

361

Gray Eagle recognized the name Cheney, and his eyes sharpened as he waited for the trapper to translate. He listened carefully as Adrian waited in silence, and at last he gave a short nod of his head. A slight smile curved the thin lips as Gray Eagle made a quick gesture and one of his warriors went to fetch Blue Feather. A rapid torrent of words accompanied quick, graceful gestures, and finally the old trapper nodded.

"He approves," Broken Arm said. "You seem to have just what he wants. He says Cheney's rifle will be powerful medicine, that his spirit will make Gray Eagle stronger."

"Then Blue Feather is mine?"

"Not yet," Broken Arm said with a grin. "Don't be so hasty, Duke! I said there wasn't a big ceremony, but that don't mean there's *no* ceremony!"

By this time Blue Feather had been brought to her cousin, and was standing before him with downcast eyes. She sensed what was about to happen and stood nervously waiting for Gray Eagle's words. Her breath caught in her throat, and she tensed though she tried not to show it. Once joined with Adrian in the Shoshoni way, there would be none who would separate them. A wife owed allegiance to her husband forever. It was the Shoshoni way.

Gray Eagle looked at her as he rose slowly to his feet. "You are to be married to this white man, my cousin. It is a good thing, for you already have his children. As his wife, perhaps you will be blessed with sons." He paused and looked past her, his back ramrod straight and his head held high. "Your path is different, my cousin," he said softly. "You

362

have not chosen the path of The People."

"Am I to be sent away?" Blue Feather asked anxiously.

"No. But your man will not want to stay here. He is white, and the white man is rarely content with such a life as we live." A faint smile touched the corners of his mouth as he said kindly, "Be happy, my cousin. Go now, and dance the dance of the blanket with your beloved."

A delighted smile curved Blue Feather's mouth, and her sapphire eyes glowed with happiness. "Thank you, Great Chief," she returned, then backed away.

At Broken Arm's suggestion, Harry had gone to fetch the Hawken rifle that had once belonged to Cheney. It was now presented to Chief Gray Eagle with a ceremonious flourish, and all the tribe crowded eagerly around to see the rifle that had once belonged to the spirit-man Cheney. Gray Eagle held it proudly, then lifted it over his head so that all might see. Firelight glinted from the bluish barrel, and he turned slowly with it held high as he began to speak to his people.

"What now?" Adrian asked Broken Arm in a low voice. "I don't see Blue Feather."

"Can you dance, Duke?" the trapper asked with an impish smile.

"Dance?"

Drums began to pound again, and there was a thin wail of music from reed and bone pipes. The rhythm pounded as Adrian was motioned to sit again, and this he did with a rather peevish frown. He had completed his bargain and was now expected to participate in some sort of ceremony!

After all the months of waiting, it was just one more obstacle to overcome, and he felt his patience ebbing.

Richard sidled close to his brother, asking what was going on. "Is this another native ritual?" he added as he eyed the women who had begun dancing with blankets thrown over their backs.

Adrian grinned. "I guess you could say that, Richard."

"How fascinating. Any particular reason for this display of delight?"

"It's a marriage celebration," Adrian answered casually.

"You don't say! Where are the bride and groom?"

"You're sitting next to the groom" was Adrian's reply, and he felt Richard's recoil.

"Adrian! But . . . are you . . . is this necessary?" he stuttered in horror.

"No, of course not. But it is what I want, Richard."

"But what about England? Uncle Timothy? The life you have always known?"

Adrian shook his head. "I've been thinking . . . I prefer life here, Richard. This is my life. Blue Feather is my life."

"I can understand your feeling that way after all that has happened, but perhaps I should finally explain a few things to you, Adrian. You might change your mind," Richard said after a moment of shocked silence.

"I don't think there's anything you can say that will change my mind," Adrian said gently. "But right now is not the time for you to try. This is my wedding night, and I have every intention of taking my beautiful bride to a remote spot."

Richard's attention was unwillingly drawn from his brother to the dancers as they came closer and closer, their bare feet stamping and shifting in time to the music. Their movements were graceful as they swayed like willow limbs in the wind, bending and turning. There was nothing overtly sexual in their dance. These young women were prim and proper as they dipped and swayed. Richard recognized Blue Feather as she approached, and he had to admit that she was quite lovely in an exotic sort of way. Her dark hair and dusky skin only made her eyes seem bluer and brighter, and her form curved temptingly as she danced up to Adrian.

Then, bending swiftly, Blue Feather threw her blanket over Adrian's head. It was the signal for the tempo of the drums to change, and they began to beat with a throbbing force as Adrian stood and took her hands. Blue Feather's heart was beating as rapidly as the drums. She would be wed to the father of her children, a man who was becoming a legend among The People because he had lived with Cheney. Now she would be a respectable married woman and would be accepted by the women of her tribe.

Moving provocatively now, Blue Feather deliberately let the blanket slip from his shoulders as she held it by two corners, seeming to let it drop to the ground then snatching it up. It sailed in an arc and settled over her shoulders as well, encompassing both of them within its soft folds. He was hers, and she was his. He had given her male relative a great dowry, and she was his wife. Blue Feather slanted

Adrian a breathless smile, her eyes darkening with the same desire she saw in his gaze.

There was laughter, giggles, and much conjecture as the pair retreated from the campfires. They went to Blue Feather's tipi, the dwelling her cousin had given her for herself and her children. It was at the edge of the village near the water, and Adrian could hear the rush of the waterfall cascading into the placid pool upon which the camp stood.

This was his wedding night, and he gently took Blue Feather in his arms.

Chapter 19
The Lovers

Trembling with longing for the man who had haunted her dreams for over a year, Blue Feather closed her eyes and tilted back her head. Long dark hair fell in a silken cape over her shoulders, dark against the pale doeskin dress Adrian had given her the year before. A pulse fluttered wildly in the golden hollow of her throat, and when Adrian pressed his lips to the madly beating spot, she shuddered. It was so sweet, so poignant a moment, that she wanted it to last forever. This coming together was not only ripe with suppressed desire, but rich with tender emotions.

There had been no man for her in the past year, nor even the suggestion of a man. It was forbidden to lie with a man while nursing children. When her milk had inexplicably dried up, the babies had been weaned, and Gray Eagle had begun to cast his eyes about for a suitable mate for his disgraced cousin. This suggestion had been met with rage and fury, and the chief had bided his time. Now there was no need. Adrian had been restored to her. Adrian . . . no longer a pale white man from a strange place, but someone transformed by the spirit of Cheney. Now he could understand her as he had seen much of the Indian way in his time in the wilderness. She would never doubt him again.

"My love," he was saying as he cradled her in his arms.

He kissed her closed eyelids, the straight line of her nose, and then her half-parted lips, letting his mouth linger lovingly, sweetly, tasting and teasing. It was torture for him, sweet torture, and he loved every moment of it. Adrian's palms slid from cupping Blue Feather's face to her throat, then her shoulders. His fingers were strong and caressing as they moved sensuously over her back, feeling the mature curves beneath the doeskin dress.

Pausing with his hands resting on her slender hips, Adrian wondered if he had forgotten how rich her curves had been or if they had changed. Was it his imagination, or did the press of her breasts against him feel fuller somehow? He recalled small, firm breasts like ripe apples, filling his palms perfectly. He had dreamed of them at night, recalling the dusky peaks that had tempted him to wild passion, and imagined Blue Feather was in his arms again with her pert body swaying above him. Adrian's hands moved to the hem of Blue Feather's dress, and he pulled it slowly over her head.

Light from the fire flickering outside lent a rosy glow to the interior of the tipi, filtering through the lifted flaps at the bottom and illuminating Blue Feather's body. She wore nothing beneath the dress, and she stood before him in unabashed splendor, enjoying the appreciation in his eyes.

There was a glow in the gray eyes drifting over

her body that made Blue Feather's heart lurch. He truly loved her. She didn't need to hear him say it as long as he continued to look at her with such soft eyes that expressed his love. Where there had been only gentleness in her man before, there was now something else. The past year had given Adrian a hardness somehow, a sense of his own strength that was even more apparent in his gentleness.

When Adrian lifted her into his arms, cradling her nude body against his broad chest, Blue Feather sighed. She let her fingers trace the smooth line of his clean-shaven jaw as he held her, then ran her hands through his thick golden mane of hair. Bending, Adrian lay her gently on a spread blanket and knelt beside her, his eyes skimming every inch of her.

Blue Feather waited silently, a burning ache spreading inside her as she observed Adrian's subtle change of expression. Squirming, she shifted slightly on the blanket and shivered.

"Cold, love?" Adrian asked immediately, and she shook her head.

"No, just weary of waiting. . . ."

Fires of passion flamed in his eyes at her words, and he lowered his body over hers, holding her in his arms. His buckskin garments rubbed roughly on her skin, chafing her, but Blue Feather did not mind. Indeed, she welcomed the distracting sensations as Adrian's hands dragged slowly over her soft curves, touching and caressing. Her eyes shut tightly as he teased her with his fingers, provoking fiery reactions. It was sweet torment, and Blue Feather writhed beneath his touch. When she moaned and

369

reached out for him, he drew back. Thick lashes fluttered open as she gazed up at him with mounting frustration that turned to expectation when she saw Adrian tug off his shirt.

Sitting up, she reached out for him greedily. Giving a sharp yank, Blue Feather soon divested Adrian of his trousers, baring his lean-muscled body. Her hands explored him as he had explored her, touching tenderly, stroking the ridges of his muscles, the hollows and angles that held such mystery for her still. On her knees beside his reclining body, she bent forward. A fresh, clean fragrance wafted from his skin, the scent of sage and clear mountain water. Breathing deeply, Blue Feather inhaled the faint scent of tobacco and the good French brandy Adrian had drank earlier in the day. Her senses were attuned to every aspect of her husband's body—the smooth feel of his skin, the ripple of his taut muscles beneath her palm, and the thickness of golden hair like cornsilk.

Her hands moved lower over the flat plane of his stomach, light as a summer butterfly, skimming over his contracting muscles. At his groan of pleasure, she smiled. She was pleasing him. Lowering her head, Blue Feather let her mouth follow the path her hands had taken, heard Adrian's harsh, irregular breathing and could feel the erratic thump of his heart. A feeling of triumph swept through her as his passion rose, and she held him tenderly between her hands.

Finally unable to stand any more of her gentle ministrations, Adrian's muscular arms flexed, dragging her up his body until she lay half atop him, her face only inches from his.

"Enough, sweet love!" he whispered.

"Enough . . ?"

"Enough for now . . . let me love you. . . ."

His mouth covered hers then, plundering with a fierce intensity. He ravaged her senses with his ardor, sweeping her up heights she had never scaled before, carrying her with him on his rush to fulfillment. With a quick twist of his body she was beneath him, straining closer, her hips arching to receive him. Shutting her eyes, Blue Feather was swept along in a mist of passion. A coiling fire curled upward from the pit of her stomach, burning hot and wild like the dry summer grasses that often blazed on the plains. She could feel the surge of blood scorching through her veins, felt Adrian's urgent thrust and cried out.

Adrian's arms tightened as her velvety warmth surrounded him. They were one being, one flesh, one beating heart, one soul sharing the mysteries of love and life. A soaring exultation filled him as he grew closer and closer to his goal, nearer to that final touching of the clouds that often eluded mortal man. This was the closest a man could come to experiencing heaven, he thought vaguely, aware of Blue Feather beneath him, her dusky face radiant with her love. Then there was no more thinking, only the rush of ecstasy that was almost agonizing.

Release left them both spent and drained, lying in each others arms wordlessly. There was no need to talk, no need to express the feelings that both sensed. This was the magic of their love, the knowing. . . .

Asleep in Adrian's arms, Blue Feather only awoke when she sensed her children needed her. Harry had taken them with him, and with a mother's instinct, she knew they needed her. It was early morning. The faint flush of dawn pinkened the eastern sky, dappling the crystal waterfall with sunlight. A low-lying mist shrouded the placid pool nestled in the shadow of high mountain peaks and dense forests. Birds chirped sleepily as Blue Feather scurried across the few yards separating her tipi from Harry's.

It was not common for a woman to have her own dwelling, for females needed a protector and provider. At first Blue Feather had lived with her cousin in his lodge, but as he already had two wives and five children to feed, Gray Eagle had been only too happy to allow Broken Arm and Harry to provide for Blue Feather. She had made her own tipi from the buffalo Broken Arm killed, and Harry had helped her to sew together the long strips of hide that formed the coverings. As it would not have been proper for her to share a lodge with Harry unless they were married, he was given his own.

The Englishman inhabited a tipi given him by Gray Eagle in his appreciation for the kindness shown his cousin. In typical English fashion, Harry had cleaned and scoured the buffalo-hide dwelling and planted flowers about the door. A few of the men in the village considered Harry a *berdache,* or one who had chosen the woman's way of life instead of a man's. He was laughed at by the men, but Gray Eagle would not allow them to harm him. Harry endured his trials with a stoic patience that eventually impressed his tormentors, so they finally left him in peace.

The flap to Harry's tipi was open, indicating that he was awake, and she knelt and called his name.

"Harry! Harry, I have come for Star and Blue. . . ."

Harry's face appeared in the opening. "I am glad," he said with a sigh of relief. "Blue has been terribly fussy, I'm afraid, and will not allow me to comfort her. Do you suppose she is becoming spoiled?"

Shoshoni mothers did not believe in such a thing as spoiled children, so this question was absurd to Blue Feather. She gazed blankly at Harry as she entered and took Blue in her arms, laughing and nuzzling the fretting infant.

"I do not understand this 'spoiled,' Harry. Do you mean like rotten meat?" she asked after a moment.

Taken aback, Harry shook his head. "No, but I suppose that could apply in some cases I've seen. Never mind, Margarethe. Blue seems perfectly content now."

And the child did. She had ceased fussing and was curled in her mother's arms, happily toying with a strand of beads on the front of the doeskin dress. The bright beads seemed to fascinate her, and she shook them in her small fist.

"Is his lordship still asleep?" Harry asked after a moment, and Blue Feather nodded.

"*Ai.* He still rests in shadows. I did not want to wake him."

There was a lengthy pause, then Harry observed idly, "Broken Arm is bringing in more meat today. I

373

told him to look for deer instead of more of those stringy buffalo carcasses he's brought us."

"One should not be too critical," Blue Feather pointed out, smiling at Harry's pained expression.

"Do *you* like stringy buffalo meat?" he asked, and she laughed softly, careful not to wake the drowsy child now dozing in her arms.

"No, I do not."

"Neither do I. I've told him and told him to try and pick out a nice, plump rabbit or some sort of wild turkey, or anything but meat that's almost too tough to chew."

"Perhaps Broken Arm is getting too old to hunt," Blue Feather suggested with a frown. "I have noticed this past winter that his step has slowed, and he is not as tall as he once was. . . ."

"Age catches up with all of us, my dear." Harry sighed. "Only the young refuse to consider such a calamity."

Considering the fact that it was due to Broken Arm's and Harry's hard work that she had survived the winter without a male protector, Blue Feather found it difficult to fault either of them.

"Perhaps you are right," she compromised, and gently laid her sleeping daughter back on the blanket next to her sister. She sat gazing at them a moment, at their wild mops of tangled golden curls and dusky skin. Silky eyelashes shadowed healthily flushed cheeks, and their rosy lips were slightly parted in sleep. They were beautiful children, and she sighed contentedly. It was not safe to be so happy, she mused as she gazed at her children and thought of their father asleep in her tipi. To tempt the gods by being happy was to tempt them into burdening one with trials and thus making one a better person. Still, it was hard not to be happy. Adrian was with her at last. . . .

When she crept back into her tipi, she knelt beside him for several minutes, just gazing at his sleeping face. He shifted slightly in his sleep, mumbling to himself, and when she reached out and would have touched him, he jerked awake, his hand flashing out to grab her wrist. He was instantly alert, his muscles tensed and ready as if for danger.

"Oh," he murmured when his eyes focused upon Blue Feather's startled face. "I didn't know it was you."

"I'm sorry—I didn't mean to wake you, my husband," Blue Feather apologized, but he shook his head.

"No, don't apologize. It's me. For the past year I've had to sleep with one eye open, and I guess I forgot that I was safe now." His mouth curved into a warm smile, and his fingers loosened on her wrist, beginning to stroke her forearm in lazy circles. Then, lifting the edge of the fur blanket in an inviting gesture, he arched a brow and murmured, "Care to join me, sweet wife?"

"Lazy dog," she teased. "Would you lie on your blankets all day? I have already tended to our children, and the sun is—"

"Does that mean no?" Adrian asked so plaintively that Blue Feather laughed.

"I never said *that,* my husband!"

"Then take off your dress and lie with me," Adrian whispered. A warm glow flickered in his gray eyes, and Blue Feather needed no more urging to remove her doeskin dress and slide beneath the thick fur covers with him.

Her breath warmed his cheek as she snuggled close, and he held her lovingly. "Umm," Adrian murmured, "this is nice and cozy."

"I agree," Blue Feather breathed softly, secure in his strong embrace. She ran her fingertip lightly over the faint stubble of his night's growth of beard. "Adrian?" she murmured after a moment, and when he lifted a quizzical brow, she continued, "Your brother—why did he come to find you?"

There was a short pause before Adrian answered, "Would you not go to look for a brother you thought lost?"

"*Ai,* but I think there is another reason he came so far to find you. Is there?"

"Yes." A smile crooked his mouth as he regarded her for a moment, then he observed, "You are quite perceptive, my lovely little wife."

Blue Feather kissed him on the chin, then doggedly pursued her questions. "What are his reasons? I sense that he does not find favor with me."

"No, that is not so," Adrian disagreed. "It is not you, but his own desires that Richard is considering. He thinks highly of you, Blue Feather."

"Yet he would take you with him?" she persisted.

"I am certain he would like for me to go back to England, yes," Adrian said heavily. "But that is another matter entirely, and I have not yet thought it all out."

"There was bad blood between you?"

After another pause, Adrian nodded. "Yes, there was. I left angry, but things seem to have changed. I do not know all the details yet because Richard has not told me everything that happened after I left England. For some reason, he has preferred to remain silent, and I have not pressed him. It does not really matter anymore, especially now that I have learned our father is dead." A frown puckered Adrian's brow as he mused aloud, "But I am curious as to why Richard married Josette du Jessupe instead of—"

"Instead of who?" Blue Feather asked when he halted and did not continue. "Someone you knew well?"

Adrian's bitterness startled her when he said, "No, someone I *thought* I knew well! Ah, how easy I must have been to deceive! But . . . that is all behind me now."

Blue Feather was silent for a moment, then said, "There is something you are not telling me, Adrian. I sense it."

A wry smile twisted Adrian's mouth as he pulled away and looked at her in the dim morning light. "As I just mentioned, my sweet, you are very perceptive! Yes, there is something I have not told you. There was a woman in England that I was to marry. I thought she loved me, and I thought I loved her. But events changed, and she was to marry my brother Richard instead. I suppose that situation changed after I left, though I do not know how or why."

"Perhaps your brother put her behind him," Blue Feather suggested, dreading the thought that a woman Adrian had loved might want him back. What if he went with his brother to England and she was there, waiting on Adrian? The unknown woman would be all pink and fair, with the elegant clothing that white women wore, and fine manners

377

and small hands that were soft and white instead of brown and calloused like hers ... Blue Feather quailed at the thought, knowing how she would appear in a strange land among strange people and customs. The woman would laugh at her, and Adrian would see his Shoshoni wife through the eyes of ridicule then instead of love. Blue Feather buried her face in his shoulder, and he gave her a gentle squeeze as if sensing her fears.

"No, I don't think Richard would have put Nell behind him, but it doesn't matter now anyway. Lovely Nell more than likely found a richer man to suit her tastes, one with a grander title perhaps." Blue Feather could feel the shrug of his shoulders, and then he was saying softly in her ear, "But I have all I need here, in you, sweet wife!"

She lifted her head to gaze searchingly into his face. "This is true?"

"This is true," he assured her solemnly. "Do not doubt it?"

She shook her head. "I do not dare," she whispered. "I might tempt the gods to prove me right."

Laughing, Adrian kissed her fiercely, over and over until she was out of breath and laughing also. They began to wrestle on the blankets, rolling over the floor of the tipi and creating chaos of the neatly stacked items along the buffalo-hide walls. Waterskins, wooden bowls and utensils, beaded parfleches, robes, moccasins and leggings — all were scattered about during their play. Finally pausing, the two breathless wrestlers regarded each other's flushed faces.

Lying on his stomach, Adrian had pinned Blue Feather to the blankets with an arm on each side of

378

her, his weight holding her down. "Cry uncle," he told her in a mock-fierce tone. "Cry uncle or I shall tickle you until you plead with me to stop!"

Wriggling, Blue Feather shook her head, silky whisps of hair tangling beneath her as she refused. "No, my warrior! I will not surrender!" she said with a lilting laugh. "I am Shoshoni, and we *never* surrender to the white man!"

"Not even when I do this . . . or this?" Adrian asked slyly, drawing his fingers along her bare, pointed breasts until she shivered. Still holding her down, he lowered his head to tease a rosy peak, his gaze on her face. He felt the sharp inhalation of her breath, the subtle writhing of her hips beneath him, and sensed triumph just ahead. "Never?" he mocked, and her moan was his answer.

Play turned to passion, and the interior of the tipi soon echoed with the soft words of love and ecstasy. It grew warm and steamy, with heated breathing and the rapid pounding of two heartbeats. Blue Feather cried out when he lunged forward, her arms clutching him as together they rode the crests to fulfillment.

Later, lying exhausted and satiated, Adrian smiled at his new wife, pushing back a damp strand of her hair. "We have made a mess of your neat tipi," he said. "I'll help you put it in order."

Blue eyes gazed at him mistily, and she shook her head. "It is not seemly for a man to do woman's work. I shall do it alone, my husband."

"You don't object to Harry doing woman's work," Adrian pointed out.

Shifting uneasily, Blue Feather searched for the right words to explain Harry's position to him, then

379

compromised with "Harry has said he considers himself a 'nanny' to the children. Do you wish to be known as a nanny?"

"A nanny?" Adrian echoed, then laughed. "Dear God, how did that come about here in the Wyoming Territory?"

"Because he wished it so. He told me that in England all young children have a nanny. . . ."

"And so Harry chose to be a nanny!" Adrian said with an amused shake of his head. "How droll. I shall have to remind him of that the next time he wishes to shave me or choose my clothes!"

"I would think you would know it is because he cares so much for you that he cherishes your children," Blue Feather reminded gently.

Taken aback, Adrian said, "Yes . . . I suppose that is quite true. I should have thought of that." He touched the end of her nose with his forefinger and said, "And Harry cherishes you as well, my sweet."

Blue Feather smiled. "I know."

"Modesty is not your most *crowning* virtue, I see," Adrian returned with a teasing smile. "Perhaps I should be jealous of Harry's affection for you! I see that he has given you some gifts, or did Gray Eagle present you with that impressive necklace I see on the floor?"

Blue Feather did not need to turn her head to know what necklace Adrian referred to, and she bit her bottom lip and sat up. It should have been thrown away, but she had been too vain to do so and now . . . now he would know and there would be trouble between them because of her foolishness and vanity.

When Blue Feather did not immediately answer, Adrian looked at her averted face curiously. "Well?" he prompted. "Was it old Harry who gave you such a gift? I know you did not purchase such an item for yourself, nor would you hunt the bear who provided such magnificent teeth."

Shaking her head, Blue Feather said, "No, I did not hunt the bear-necklace. But it was not Harry who gave it to me."

"Gray Eagle, then," Adrian stated, and his eyes dared her to disagree.

His gaze darkened from slate to nearly black when she shook her head again and whispered, "It was Ramone Jardin who brought me the necklace."

"Jardin!" he exploded. Adrian stared at her narrowly. "I do not believe you would accept a gift from that man!"

Bowing her head, Blue Feather could not meet his gaze. "But I did," she whispered so softly he could barely hear. "I took it because he would not go away otherwise, and then I . . . I kept it."

"Why would Jardin bring you gifts?" Adrian demanded.

"I do not wish to speak of it."

Adrian's fingers bit into her arm as he grabbed her. "I wish for you to speak of it! When was he here? What are you hiding from me, Blue Feather?"

Halfway sitting up, his face was close to hers, and Adrian's eyes snapped with anger. Blue Feather flinched from the fury she saw in his face. He was no longer the soft-spoken Adrian, but a furious warrior. "He was here in the village a few weeks ago!" she blurted.

"Why? Did he harm you?"

She shook her head quickly. "No, no, he did not dare do that, Adrian. My cousin would have killed him, even though he came with the sign of peace from another chieftain."

"What did he want? Why did you speak to him after all that has happened? I should have known better than to trust you or any woman. When you thought I was gone did you go to him thinking he'd take you to your father? That he knew where to look?" Adrian grabbed her arm fiercely.

"You are hurting me, great warrior," Blue Feather moaned, tears streaming down her face at the thought that he could trust her so little, angry that she kept the necklace, cursing her own stupid vanity. "No! No! He wanted to *find* my father. He would not say why, except to say that he had something important for him. My father could never wish for anything from a man such as Jardin."

"So? Did you help him?" He held her tighter.

A scornful smile curved her lips as Blue Feather spat, "No! None of The People would tell him anything, and I think he became angry and left. I heard Otter Woman say that she saw him take the trail of the wild horses, which will not help the Frenchman at all. Didn't you learn anything in the woods or will you always just be a white man?"

Grabbing the necklace, he tossed it away. Beads smashed as they hit, shocking them both into silence.

"I'm sorry," he said, releasing her.

"So am I," she replied as she knelt to pick up the glass before the children got hurt playing with the beads.

"There's a yellow one there," he said lamely.

"I see it."

He bent down to help her and his hand reached out to stroke her face. Kissing her he said, "old lessons die hard."

"Jardin could never bring me anything that would make me tell him what he wanted to know."

Adrian sat back on his heels. "Jardin means trouble. I should have killed him when I had the chance. . . ."

Alarmed, Blue Feather blurted, "Do not think such a thing! I would not have you harmed, and I do not trust such a one as Jardin!" She took a deep breath, then said, "Promise me you will not fight Jardin should you see him again!"

"You've not told me everything," Adrian said flatly. "What are you keeping from me?"

Slowly, reluctantly, she answered, "He will come back. He has said he will bring many gifts to buy me for his wife, and Gray Eagle did not refuse."

"Then you were promised to Jardin?" Adrian asked incredulously.

"Oh, no! Gray Eagle did not refuse, but he did not agree to such a thing, either. It's just that I know the Frenchman will return, and I cannot bear to think of what will happen when he does."

At last Adrian smiled. "Do not worry, love. Before, I may have been in danger, but I have not spent the past year alone without gaining some knowledge and skill. I can deal with a man of Jardin's caliber." Holding out his arms he said, "Come here, Blue Feather."

"I should not have kept the necklace," she confessed.

"And I should not have behaved so badly."

Snuggling close, Blue Feather sighed. "If you say so," she murmured.

Adrian pressed his cheek against the top of her head. "Ah, you would be a delight in England," he observed, then lapsed into silence before adding, "I think I shall relent and accompany Richard on his return. What do you think? Do you think you would like to go to England, Blue Feather?"

"We would take Star and Blue?" she asked after a moment's frozen hesitation. Terror gripped her at the thought of leaving the land she had always known, and she dreaded the unknown future.

"Of course!" Adrian's voice reflected his astonishment that she would ask such a question. "I would not dream of leaving them behind, and I am certain Harry would not allow such a circumstance, either! We shall all go. I think a short visit would be satisfactory, then we could return to your people, if you like."

Because she was more afraid of losing Adrian than she was of crossing the Great Water and facing a land peopled with strangers, Blue Feather agreed. Nothing could be too bad if she was with Adrian.

"When will we go?" she asked, and her hopes for more time were dashed at his reply.

"Richard said something about meeting a Scotsman back at the Green River before the first snow flies. I suppose we should leave within a few days."

Nodding, Blue Feather whispered around the lump in her throat, "I shall be ready."

A lone rider cautiously approached, slowly riding along the outskirts of the Shoshoni village. Here and there a camp dog barked, but no Shoshoni came out to greet him. He was known in the camp, and there were few who wished to see him again. Only one man marked his arrival with interest, and he stepped out to meet him with a rifle.

"What are you doing back, Jardin?" Broken Arm asked sharply. "I thought you understood you aren't welcome here any longer."

A caustic grin slid across the burly Frenchman's face. "I don't recall the chief saying that, old man! *Sacre Bleu!* The chief, he seemed glad enough to parley with me about horses and guns—"

"Forget it," Broken Arm said flatly. "I told you that you will never take Blue Feather with you."

Leaning forward to gaze narrowly at the fur-clad trapper barring his way, Jardin sneered. "You may have his ear now, *mon ami,* but you shall not be heard when I show him what I have brought!"

Broken Arm shifted his rifle in a casual, careless movement and spat on the ground. Then he looked up at Jardin with a curious smile. "I don't think so, Frenchman. And I ain't your friend," he added.

Jardin frowned. The old trapper seemed too confident and he wondered what had happened in his absence. Gray Eagle knew that he, Ramone Jardin, was a formidable man and a good trapper. He would gladly give his cousin to him for the furs and rifles he had brought as barter. Making a quick, irritated gesture, Jardin dismissed Broken Arm's words from his mind. It was inconceivable to him that he would not get the girl. He *had* to have her or he could not get to Pierre Duvalle. And getting to Duvalle was essential. . . .

"Get out of my way, old man!" Jardin said

roughly, and Broken Arm shrugged and stepped aside.

"Fine with me," he said to Jardin's back, "but you're in for one hell of a surprise, Frenchman!"

Unable to imagine what that could be, Jardin rode forward at a brisk trot, his mount stirring up clouds of dust as he passed down the wide path running through the middle of the village. He was so intent on his own plans and purpose that Jardin did not notice the strange horses at first, nor the white trapper and his half-breed woman. It was only when he'd pulled his horse to a halt and dismounted at Gray Eagle's tipi that he saw them, and he turned with a puzzled frown. His words were blunt and clipped as he eyed the fur-clad man nearest him.

"I know you," he said, and Everett Bowie gave a sage nod of his head.

"That you do, Jardin, that you do," he agreed.

Jardin's gaze sliced to the fair-haired man standing close by. "But I do not know this man."

Staring back at him, Richard said, "No, I do not believe you do."

Jardin might have made further comments, but his attention was distracted by a movement on his right. Swirling, he stiffened as a tall, muscular form emerged from a tipi. Then the swarthy Frenchman blanched. "You!" he rasped.

Chapter 20
Temperance

Staring at Ramone Jardin, Adrian felt the old twist of hatred. Much time had passed since he had seen the Frenchman, and still there was that hatred between them. It was as fresh as it had ever been.

"Surprised, Jardin?" Adrian mocked, successfully hiding his own surprise at seeing the Frenchman.

Recovering from the shock with an effort, Jardin gave a shrug of his wide shoulders. "I thought the Piegan had done you in," he said.

"Did you?" Adrian smiled. "As you can see, they were not successful in that endeavor."

"Too bad . . ."

"For you, perhaps," Adrian agreed.

"Non, non! Je suis content que vous soyez arrive!" Jardin protested.

Adrian's smile widened. "I find it quite difficult to believe that you are glad I am here, Jardin!" he said.

Again a shrug of the Frenchman's shoulders as he said, "But why not? It is always wise to know where one's enemies are."

"I must agree with that," Adrian replied with a lift of his eyebrow. "And I must remember not to turn my back on you, also."

"Pah! Do you think me so craven I would attack from behind you?" Jardin sneered. "It is not so! You, I would fight from any angle, English!"

"Perhaps we can arrange that," Adrian began, but Broken Arm intervened.

"I do not think now is the time or place to settle your differences, Duke," he said softly. "After all, Gray Eagle considers Jardin to be a guest just as he does you."

"With a big difference," Adrian pointed out. "Blue Feather."

"Ahh," Jardin purred smoothly, overhearing their conversation, "and how is the lovely Blue Feather?" He kissed the tips of his fingers with a loud smacking noise, and Broken Arm was forced to grab Adrian by one arm to keep him from plowing into the smirking Frenchman.

"Don't be sully her name with your Gallic tongue!" Adrian spat, and Jardin laughed aloud.

"Do you imagine I shall deign to argue with you over the girl, English? Well, I tell you that I shall not! It is foolish to do so, when we all know that the half-breed girl is not a one for you. You, you will go back to your stuffy country with the prim matrons and pompous old men who think they are so much better than the rest of the world, and what will you do with one dark Indian girl, heh? She would only scandalize your family, and she would know it. Who would talk to her over there—your precious English aristocrats? Hoo-hoo! You don't even talk to each other!"

Adrian's hands clenched at his sides. Jardin had cleverly managed to hit upon just the point that had been nagging him since he had decided to return to England. Would Blue Feather be cruelly snubbed, even as his wife? Of course, she would, and he knew it. So did Ramone Jardin, damn him!

"Who said I was taking her with me? Or even that I am going back?" Adrian blustered, but Jardin knew it was a bluff.

"Oh, so you will leave her here without a man to protect her, English? Do you not know that the Shoshoni do not believe in charity? *Non,* it is true! They would cast her from the tribe to fend for herself if she did not have a man to hunt for her and her *jeune filles.* It is the way of survival."

"Don't concern yourself," Adrian cut in scathingly. "She is my wife and my problem."

Obviously stunned by this news, Jardin took a step back. "Your *wife?* But I . . . you are such a fool, English!" he snarled in frustration. "You come to this land and just take what you want with no regard. You do not love the land, and you do not want to stay here. You just come as a despoiler, an invader who wants only to satisfy a whim!"

Adrian's voice was cool as he repeated, "As I said, do not concern yourself with my wife."

Dismissing Adrian's words with a contemptuous wave of his hand, Jardin said, "She will be only an Indian whore when you tire of her, English!"

Without pausing to consider the results, Adrian swung a balled fist into the Frenchman's face, smashing his nose. Blood spurted, and Jardin gave a howl like an enraged bull. He staggered, and when he rocked forward again, he held a long knife in one hand, the tip slashing at Adrian.

A thin scream distracted both men, and they paused when Blue Feather flung herself at them.

"Do not do this!" she stormed. "It is foolish!"

Adrian put her gently away from him, but she snatched wildly at the sleeves of his buckskin shirt. "No, no, do not fight with him!" she pleaded.

Glancing into her azure eyes, Adrian said, "Stand back, Blue Feather."

Half-sobbing, she looked to Broken Arm for help, and the old trapper stepped forward. "She's right, Duke. There is no sense in killing over this. The girl is yours, and that should be all there is to it." He slanted a hard look at Jardin. "Put away your knife, Frenchman. There will be no killing today."

After a swift glance at the men surrounding him, Jardin shrugged and sheathed the wicked blade. "Perhaps not today, old man, but soon," he promised. "Soon!"

When Jardin had stomped back to his horse, Blue Feather felt her knees give way with relief. She sagged, and Adrian put an arm around her to hold her up.

"Are you all right?" he asked, and she managed a nod and smile.

"Ai," she whispered. "I am well."

Glancing over at his brother, Adrian saw that Richard was lowering a rifle, and he smiled. It seemed that his brother had been prepared to defend him.

"I say, Richard, who were you going to shoot?" he jested, and Richard managed a wan smile that closely matched the one Blue Feather wore.

"I'm not entirely sure, but my intentions were good," Richard replied. "Why, the man would have stabbed you with that lethal blade, Adrian!"

"He might have tried" was Adrian's careless response. "I do not have as high an opinion of Jardin's abilities as he does, I'm afraid."

"Well, you should, Duke," Broken Arm put in soberly. "I think he'd just as soon sneak up behind you as not."

Adrian shrugged, and Blue Feather looked up at him with a frown. "Do you not think he would?" she asked.

"Oh, yes, I think he would if he got the chance. I do not intend to give him an opportunity, however. This only reaffirms my earlier decision," he added, and turned back to his brother. "Richard, I have decided that we shall go with you to England after all."

Richard's face lit up, and he was so delighted that he did not fully comprehend what Adrian meant. "Wonderful! I cannot tell you how much this means to me, Adrian! Josette told me to have faith, that matters would work out, but I did not listen, I'm afraid. I should have known better than to question her judgement in such things. . . ."

Frowning, Adrian said, "That reminds me, Richard. I should like very much to talk to you—in private, please."

Richard grew silent, then nodded. "Very well, though I am certain I know why you wish to talk to me."

Sensing that she was not to join in this conversation, Blue Feather murmured an excuse about seeing to the girls, and turned and fled. Adrian flicked a glance at her, then turned his attention back to his brother.

"Shall we?" he suggested, and indicated the tipi

Richard had been sharing with Bowie and his half-breed wife Charlotte.

When they entered, Charlotte was crouching by the fire in the center. She slanted Adrian a fearful glance and began to moan. He sighed, thinking of the week's journey from his hut to the Shoshoni village. Charlotte had acted as if he was a spirit instead of a man, jumping when he came near and behaving as skittish as a new colt.

"Your man is outside," Adrian said in obvious invitation, and she scooted around the fringes of the tipi and out the flap he held invitingly open.

Richard chuckled. "The poor woman is frightened to death of you!" he remarked.

"Yes, it's superstition, of course, but one can't get that through to a woman who has been brought up to believe in such things."

"No, I suppose not." Richard knelt on the pallet of folded blankets and waited expectantly as Adrian did the same.

"How did Father die?" Adrian asked bluntly, taking Richard by surprise. "Was it an accident or illness?"

Shifting uneasily, Richard groped for the right words. "I haven't wanted to tell you, old boy," he began slowly. "It's been deuced awkward, but . . . it's still rather painful to tell, you know."

"Of course I know. You know how *I* must feel, then," Adrian said.

Wincing, Richard murmured, "Oh, yes, of course. Well, I don't know how to say this gently, so I shall just say it—Father was murdered, Adrian."

Of all the things he'd expected, this was one event

that had never occurred to Adrian. He stared at his brother in open amazement. "Murder, you say!" he finally blurted. "I don't believe it! Who would want to murder Father?"

Richard's voice was faintly mocking as he said, "Who, indeed. Who coveted the title so badly that he—or she—would commit murder, I wonder?"

"But that doesn't make sense," Adrian protested. "You would have the title sooner or later, Richard, why would you—"

"Not me, you dolt! And do you think I would be fool enough to travel all this way and tell you about it if I had? Gather your wits, Adrian, old boy."

"Then . . . who?"

"Who else stood to gain by Father's death? Who could parade around in the family jewels and preen under the title of duchess? Who, Adrian?"

There was a loud buzzing in Adrian's ears, and he said slowly, "You don't mean . . . Nell?"

"Ah yes, lovely, sweet-faced Nell! My wife, my pure bride who was *not* a virgin. The woman who swore to love and obey, to be faithful—and who did none of those things." Richard's voice was bitter, his mouth twisting with remembered pain and hatred. "Ah, how I would have liked to put my hands around her slender white neck and snap it in two like a twig!"

"But . . . *murder!*"

"Ah, our lovely Nell was not above that, dear fellow. No, not she! Oh, and she could be sly as well as bold, I grant her that. She may not have flaunted her indiscretions in my face, but she did make one mistake. That little error gave her away to Father, and when he confronted her, why our little

Nell just decided to do away with him. She dared not risk my finding out and putting her aside, not before she became a duchess!" Shaking his head, Richard steadied his voice as he continued, "She tried poison first, and when that failed, a stone gargoyle was mysteriously loosened from over the doorway and narrowly missed Father. It fell from the roof and crashed inches from him. Unfortunately, the first attempt had claimed another victim by this time, and so she grew even bolder. I suppose it's easier to kill the second time . . . do you suppose that?"

Steeling himself, Adrian asked, "Who did she kill the first time?"

A shudder racked his body as Richard replied softly, "Madame du Jessupe . . ."

"Madame du . . . but how horrible, Richard!"

"Yes, wasn't it?" Richard said tonelessly. His face was carefully blank as he looked at his brother. "Do you wish to know the worst of it, Adrian? The worst of it," he continued without waiting for a reply, "was that I didn't even suspect her. It never occurred to me that Nell would commit such horrible crimes. It was so . . . so *unthinkable,* that I didn't see what was right in front of me. And then poor Father went riding with her one day. It wasn't his idea, I discovered later, but Nell had insisted. She was trying to make amends for her earlier indiscretions, she told him. They found him at the bottom of a cliff with his horse — do you remember the Barbary stallion? That one. It seemed that Father had carelessly ridden too close to the edge, if Nell's story was to be believed. What she did not count on was the fact that Father was stronger than

394

she had thought. He was still alive when they found him, still able to name his murderer. . . ."

"Dear God!" Adrian whispered hoarsely.

"Dear God, indeed."

"And Nell? Was she hanged for her crimes?"

"No, she fled justice. But before you cry foul, let me tell you that justice found her. . . ." A smile curved Richard's mouth as he reflected, then said softly, "She fled through the woods on her favorite mare, and in the twilight could not see the low-hanging branch across the path. Her neck was broken as cleanly as I would have liked to do," he said dreamily.

There was a long silence. The back of Adrian's neck prickled with horror, and he could feel the erratic thumping of his heart. He swallowed hard.

"So, as you can imagine," Richard began, breaking the brooding silence and startling Adrian, "you will be welcomed back at Hertfield with open, loving arms."

Adrian nodded. "I will be glad to return with you, Richard. I had no idea so much tragedy had befallen in my absence. Perhaps Blue Feather and the children can help to lift some of the gloom. . . ."

"Blue Feather?" Richard echoed blankly. "What do you mean?"

"What do you think I mean?" Adrian returned. "She will go with me, of course."

"But Adrian, think! How will she be received? I had not considered that you might wish to actually take her back with you," Richard said.

"Richard, I married her," Adrian pointed out in a reasonable tone.

"But I thought that was just for the sake of expediency, you know—her cousin the chief and all that."

"You thought wrong."

"But think, old boy! She would not be received in any of the best homes, and would only be snubbed there. Can you not just leave her here and return now and again to visit with her?"

"Really, Richard! Do you hear what you're saying?"

When Adrian made an impatient gesture, Richard reached out to touch his arm. "I know you're fond of her, and I admit that she is a most lovely young girl, but you must consider your position in life, Adrian. A wife such as this one would only be a burden to you. And the children—do you think they would enjoy the snubs they would receive?"

Adrian sat thoughtfully. Richard was confirming his worst fears, and somehow they sounded so much worse spoken aloud. Hadn't he worried about this same thing when he'd considered going back to England? Perhaps he should not go, or at the least, only for a short time.

"Adrian?" Richard prompted.

Looking up, Adrian said heavily, "I agree that Blue Feather and the children may cause problems for me, but I do not see how I can explain that to her. She has no malice in her, Richard. And the girls are just innocent children."

"Be that as it may," Richard said firmly, "if you take them with you, you will soon regret it."

"You may be right. . . ."

Standing just outside the half-open flap of the tipi, Blue Feather froze with one hand outstretched.

She had been about to summon Adrian, but the sound of their voices had stopped her. Adrian would regret taking her and their children with him! She had heard him admit it! Gasping with dismay, she whirled and ran blindly away from the tipi.

Hot tears scalded her eyes, blurring her vision so that she did not see the burly form in front of her until she had run into him. Harsh fingers gripped her tightly by the arms, ignoring her struggles to free herself.

"Oho!" a hated voice said. "Do you run to me already, little one?"

Blue Feather tried to pull away, but her efforts were futile. Glaring up at Ramone Jardin through a mist of tears, she spat, "Let me go, evil one!"

"Ah, does your husband not know how to treat his wife? I could be gentle with you. I could show you how a real man treats his woman, *cherie*. . . ."

Aiming a kick at his shins, Blue Feather snarled, "You do not know about men, you French dog! You run like the cur with its tail between its legs!"

"Do I?" Jardin said softly. "I do not think so. I came back for you like I said I would, did I not? Listen to me, *cherie,* that one is not for you. You call him a man and look after him with big eyes, but he does not feel the same way about you. He belongs with his own kind, not here where you run with the wind and sleep under the stars. His world is one with high ceilings, and his stone tipi is so big it would swallow this camp in one gulp . . . so like a big fish swallowing a little fish!" He made a descriptive motion with his hands, releasing Blue Feather as he did.

Taking several rapid steps away from him, she

stood poised for flight but did not flee. Indecision flickered on her expressive features as she gazed at the Frenchman, and he sensed her doubt. Pressing home his advantage, Jardin smiled winningly.

"You see the truth in my words, eh *cherie?*"

"Your tongue is always crooked, Frenchman," she returned, but her voice held none of the conviction of earlier. After a brief pause, she ventured, "Tell me more about the tipis of my husband's people. Do all have such dwellings?"

"Ah no, *cherie,* they do not? In his own land your husband is a prince, a chief among his people. He is privileged, with many who look after him, like the man you call Harry. There are those who cook, those who put out clean clothes, those who put the clean clothes on for one, those who take care of the children, those who—"

"Enough!" she said. "I understand. What do . . . what do the women of these men do in such big tipis?"

"Do? Ah, *cherie,* they do nothing!" Jardin spread his arms expansively and added, "They sit and smell the flowers in the garden, perhaps."

Blue Feather stared at him blankly, unable to comprehend such a life. Sit and smell the flowers? But that was no life for someone accustomed to working all day! It seemed empty and useless, and she doubted the Great Spirit would smile upon such a worthless one who did nothing to contribute to life but sit.

"But me, *cherie,*" he was continuing, "me I would give you my blankets, my care, my protection. This is my land, your land, the land we hold dear. Would you really be content in a strange land?"

398

His smooth voice flowed over her like oil, smothering her valid arguments. Dejected, Blue Feather's shoulders slumped forward and her head bent, ebony wings of hair falling forward to hide her face. She knew Ramone Jardin was speaking the truth, for he was repeating her private fears aloud.

Taking a deep breath, her chin lifted, and she faced him. "I will be happy with my husband, wherever he may be."

Jardin sneered. "Do you think so? We shall see." His gaze followed Blue Feather as she pivoted on a bare heel and stalked silently away. The sneer still curled his lips as Ramone Jardin reflected that the Shoshoni maid would soon see he was right about the faithless Englishman.

Dust rose in small puffs as Blue Feather scuffed down the wide path back to her tipi. The Frenchman had given her much to think about, but it was the memory of Adrian's words to his brother that still haunted her. *Blue Feather and the girls may cause problems for me . . . may regret it. . . .* over and over the words whirled in her head.

Even the sight of Harry and her children did little to comfort Blue Feather when she ducked inside her tipi. She paused, then moved to sit down on a blanket and draw Star and Blue onto her lap. Pressing her cheek against the top of Blue's silky curls, she took a deep breath and tried to concentrate on what Harry was saying. He was giving her a recital of the girls' activities during the morning, and how they had enjoyed their daily baths.

"You know," he was saying, "I believe that if allowed to, Star would swim. She is so energetic, yet they are both such proper English ladies. Yes, I believe that—"

"That's nice," Blue Feather said with a wan smile, and her quiet penetrated to Harry at last. Pausing, he gazed at her with a perplexed frown.

"Is there something the matter?"

She shook her head, thinking of the fact that he was right. Her children could be 'young English ladies' but for the fact that their mother was Shoshoni. After all, they could pass for English with their fair hair and pale eyes, while she—she would always look Shoshoni, would always *be* Shoshoni in her way of thinking and her beliefs. Perhaps her children should be given an opportunity to live in the white man's world, to see and do things they could never do here in the Wind River range where the winters were harsh and enemies abounded. Perhaps they should be given a chance to live in a stone tipi and have servants like Harry who would bring them their every need. Talents like the ones she possessed were necessary for survival, but her children could grow in a tranquil land where luxury was normal.

Blue Feather's imagination could not conceive of the things Jardin had told her, and she tried to recall little details Adrian had related, stories of long tables heavy with cooked geese, cows, chickens, and all manner of fowl and strange-sounding dishes. There were soft clothes to wear and huge fireplaces capable of burning entire trees. There were fine horses, green lawns and beautiful flowers. And the women were pale-skinned and fair-haired. Shivering, Blue Feather felt suddenly inadequate. It did not matter that she could hunt and cook wild game, that she could fashion garments out of animal skins and put up and take down a tipi. Those things would not make her satisfactory in the land called England.

"Blue Feather?" Harry prompted, dragging her attention back to him. "Are you sick?"

"Only in my heart," she whispered.

As the morning hours dragged by, Blue Feather waited for Adrian to return to her tipi. He did not. Instead she spent the time with Harry and the girls, her eyes and ears straining for the welcome sign of his approach. Perhaps he would not return to her, she thought with a sense of panic, perhaps he would go with his brother back to that land called England. Hadn't she heard him say he had regrets? But in the next instant she was telling herself that he would not leave her, or at least, that he would not leave without saying farewell.

Several hours passed as she fretted, then, donning a clean cotton skirt and her prettiest blouse, Blue Feather left her tipi. She would find Adrian, find him and ask him about what she had heard. The skirt clung softly to her slender legs as she knelt at the opening to the tipi the man Bowie was sharing with the Englishman.

"Adrian?" she called, observing the proper etiquette of announcing oneself. If the flap was not open, it was proper to call out and announce one's presence. The occupant was given the option of asking you to come in, or of coming out. She waited and, when she heard Adrian's voice, ducked into the tipi.

He looked up with a distracted smile, and Blue

Feather noted the strange objects he held in his lap. She tried not to stare, but politely averted her face, asking if he was well.

"Yes, I am fine," he answered, and motioned for her to sit close to him.

Blue Feather happily complied, relieved to see that he didn't seem too remote from her. Perhaps she had worried for nothing. As she sat with her legs tucked beneath her under the cotton skirt, her gaze was drawn to the small objects he held. They were strange, like nothing she had ever seen before, and she leaned closer.

"What do you have, my husband?"

"These? Oh, these are miniatures of my family. Richard brought them with him. He thought I might like seeing them. See?" He held them up, and Blue Feather peered at them closely.

"Miniatures? What does that mean?"

"Oh, these are the likeness of my mother and my father." He held one higher. "This was done when my mother was quite young. Wasn't she lovely? Here, take it and look at it. I believe I see traces of Star and Blue in my mother's face . . . perhaps the chin or the shape of the eyes. What do you think?"

Shifting uneasily, Blue Feather took the tiny portrait and looked at it. "*Ai,* but . . . but Adrian, I thought your mother had gone to the Land of Everfeasting."

"Land of . . . ? Oh, oh yes. She died many years ago . . . hey! What's the matter?"

Blue Feather dropped the portrait as if it had burned her fingers, letting it fall to the blanket bunched up around her knees. There was a horrified expression on her face as she turned her head

402

away from the miniature.

"Blue Feather?" Adrian pressed. His brow was creased in an irritated frown as he reached down to lift the portrait. "What is the matter?"

She covered her face with her hands. "Do not show it to me again! Put it away!"

Nonplussed, Adrian did as she asked, laying the miniatures facedown on the blanket. "All right. I have done as you asked. Now tell me what frightened you."

"It is not right that one should have images of the dead. It is disrespectful," she whispered.

"Ah, I see." Adrian paused for a moment, then said, "In my country, we have many such portraits of our ancestors. We hang them on the walls of our homes, and when we look at them we are comforted."

"Comforted?" Blue Feather shook her head at such a notion. "I do not understand."

"It's simple enough, really. These are images that are only painted, but remind us of the person we loved, so that when another child is born, one is able to look back and say, 'Ah, she must have her nose, or her chin.' Now do you understand?"

Blue Feather's hair shimmered as she shook her head. "No. I do not. Why would it matter if Star's nose looked like that of someone else? She is her own person, not that person."

"Well, it . . . it . . ." Adrian stumbled to a halt and stared helplessly at Blue Feather's averted profile. How could he explain such a vast difference in cultures to her? More than miles separated the English from the Shoshoni, and he was at a loss to explain. Reaching out, he took her by both shoulders and turned her gently around. "Blue Feather. Look at me. Up here," he coaxed, tilting her chin with his thumb and smiling. "That's better. If it bothers you to look at the portraits, then I won't force you to do so. It doesn't matter that much, but I want you to know that in my land, it is not wrong to do so. It does not mean bad medicine in my land like it does here. Do you understand?"

Blue Feather's head dipped sharply, and her gaze rested on his face. "I understand."

"Good." His hands fell away from her, and he smiled again. "Good. I should hate for you to be distressed by seeing them in the halls of my home."

The breath caught in Blue Feather's throat. "Do you mean I am . . . I am to go to your land with you?"

"I thought we had already settled that. Didn't you say earlier that you would?"

"*Ai,* but then I heard . . . I heard you talk to your brother, and I heard him say that I should not go," she blurted, half-afraid he would be angry with her for eavesdropping. "I should not have listened, but I did. Do you have regrets about such a thing?"

Gray eyes widened thoughtfully, and Adrian strained to recall his conversation with Richard. Had he voiced regrets about taking her? Perhaps he had, but not for the reasons she obviously thought.

"Oh, my love," he said, shaking his head. "You did not fully understand what I meant. What you heard was taken out of context . . . I mean, it was not meant in that way. I only regret that there will be problems you will encounter, and that I am powerless to prevent them. There will be people there — like people here — who will judge you on your

404

appearance instead of your actions. They will think you strange because your skin is darker and your customs different. They may not be kind."

"I understand that, for I understand how the Shoshoni laughs at the white man sometimes," she said.

"Laughs at the white man?" Adrian repeated. "But why?"

"Why? Because the white man thinks his way is so much better, yet he cannot survive as does the Shoshoni. The white man must have guns, must have warm coverings in the winter, must have soft furs upon which to lie. The Shoshoni can go out naked in the snow and not feel the cold; The People can kill and prepare food without guns, and often lie upon the bare ground with no cover at all. Until the white man came and killed so many buffalo, the Shoshoni did not need guns. Now there are not so many beaver or otter or buffalo, and we must have guns to survive. Now the white man says we must have the firewater and bright shiny beads instead of the beaver. We must live as he lives, and believe as he believes, and do as he says, or he will push us from our land and take it for himself. We are not respected nor feared. We are the enemy in our own land." Shaking her head, Blue Feather said, "I see why my father went so high into the mountains. He said he found it difficult to watch The People die."

"And you think that is what the white man is doing?"

Her voice was almost a whisper. *"Ai."*

"You may be right," Adrian said after a moment. He put a hand upon her gleaming hair. "It makes my heart ache to think it, but you may be right."

405

Blue Feather looked up at him. "You are different than the others, my husband. You do not covet our lands or think we should believe in your gods, your ways."

A guilty pang struck Adrian as he realized that he had just expected that very thing of her, and he made a silent vow to let her make her own decisions. Gathering her close, he brushed his lips against the top of her silky head.

They sat together for a moment, with only the sound of their heartbeats in their ears. Then Blue Feather shifted slightly away and asked, "Is it important that you go home to this England, my husband?"

He nodded. "Yes, it is. My brother Richard has brought grave news to me. It seems that my father is dead—killed by the woman whom Richard married. . . ."

"The woman you loved?" Blue Feather asked, startling Adrian.

"Oh, you remember that, do you? Yes, that woman. But she is dead now, also."

"She was killed for her wickedness?"

"In a way, I suppose you could say that," Adrian said in a reflective tone. "Anyway, there are necessary details to be attended, papers to be signed, legal matters to see about—all of which mean nothing to you, I suppose. But I must see to them, and so we shall leave in a day or two."

Blue Feather shook her head. "No, I shall not go with you."

There was a moment of shocked silence before Adrian pushed her away and said, "What do you mean?"

"I mean that I shall stay here with The People. You may take Star and Blue if you wish, for Harry will care for them and teach them the ways of their ancestors, as you desire. It is good that they learn, for soon there will be no more ways of the Shoshoni. They will be accepted because they have fair hair and light eyes."

"But Blue Feather . . . but that is preposterous! I do not intend to leave without you!"

She lifted her head and gazed into his eyes. "I would not be happy there. I would long for the rivers and mountains and streams, for the eagles that soar on the wind."

"Would you not long for me?" Adrian asked, his tone husky as he looked down at her.

Swallowing the sudden lump in her throat, Blue Feather nodded. *"Ai,* I would."

"Then don't say you will not go with me. . . ."

Blue Feather could not halt the tears that spurted from her eyes, and when Adrian pulled her close to hold her in his arms, it seemed only natural that she raise her mouth for his kiss. He kissed her tenderly at first, his lips moving over hers in a light caress, then more hungrily as his arms tightened. Adrian was kissing her with an urgency that he could not deny, fiercely, almost bruising her lips as his mouth slanted across hers.

Breathlessly, she began, "Adrian . . ." but he ignored her as his mouth moved along the sweep of her jaw to her ear. He was pushing her back against the folded blankets beneath them, his hands tangling in her hair as his lean body lay across her.

"Say we'll never part," he murmured a moment later, his lips worrying that vulnerable spot just below her ear. "Say it, Blue Feather. . . ."

But she couldn't say anything then, as his mouth covered hers in hot, smothering kisses. It was light and dark all at once, a steamy prison of flesh and desire, and they undressed and clasped one another with painful ferocity.

Bare breasts pressed against the smooth, hard plane of muscles on his chest, flattening as he gripped her tightly and lunged forward with swift urgency. A sweet fire surged through their veins, pounding and pulsing with each motion of their bodies. Only when they lay quietly, with the ebb of passion leaving them weak, did Blue Feather voice her fears.

"Do not leave me," she whispered against his ear, and he turned to face her.

"I shall not leave you," he promised. "This act of love sealed our commitment to one another. Now our problems no longer matter."

A tender smile curved her mouth, and Blue Feather rubbed her forehead against his jaw. "Our love is the most precious possession we have."

"Have you forgotten Star and Blue?" Adrian teased.

"Forgotten them? No, how could I?"

"They are precious possessions also, my love."

"Oh, no, my husband. They do not belong to us. They are only gifts to be cherished for a time. We nurture and care for them, then send them into the world with all the weapons they need to survive. One can never possess such a special thing as a child."

"Your wisdom never ceases to amaze me," Adrian said. "I wonder if I am the only one who has noticed how wise you are?"

"I only repeat the teachings of my people. This is not my wisdom, but that taught to The People long ago."

"Perhaps your teachings will impress those in England who would think you uneducated," Adrian remarked. "I recall an old professor of mine who would be delighted by them. And Uncle Timothy! — why he will be absolutely enthralled with you and the children, I am certain, Blue — "

Jerking away, Blue Feather drew back and stared at Adrian with hot, stormy eyes. "You said you would not leave me!"

"And did I say differently? I don't intend to leave you at all. What is the matter?"

"You said you would not leave me," she repeated.

"Yes, I said that. I intend for you and the children to accompany me to England. I told you that." Adrian's eyes narrowed when she shook her head. "Have you changed your mind again? A few moments ago you said we would never part! Now you are saying nay?"

"I told you my reasons! Are you like the other white men — so intent on your own purposes that you neither listen nor care about what another says to you?" Blue Feather demanded.

Adrian's lips thinned to a taut line, and his own eyes grew dark and stormy with anger. "Blue Feather, you know that is not the truth. Is it so wrong to want my wife with me? I think not, and I think you are worrying too much about what will not happen. After all, we will not stay in England forever."

When she shook her head again, he snapped.

"Dammit, Blue Feather! You *will* go with me!"

Hot tears spilled from her eyes down her dusky cheeks, and she snatched up her skirt and blouse and struggled furiously into them. Her movements were quick and jerky, and once dressed, she stumbled to her feet. Adrian grabbed her arm, but she pulled away and flung over her shoulder, "You say you love me, but you do not listen to my pain! You lie!"

When she had flown from the tipi, Adrian sat staring after her for a long time.

Chapter 21
The Hermit

Blue Feather held back her sobs until she had reached the banks of the icy pool beneath the waterfall. Then tears fell, streaming over her cheeks as freely as the water cascaded over the high slabs of rock and into the pool. Her gentle features showed the ravages of the pain that racked her, and she bowed her head as she perched upon the flat, warm surface of a rock hanging over the edge. How could Adrian think that she would be happy among people who would laugh and jeer at her? Didn't he know how her pride and dignity would suffer?

A hand descended upon her shoulder, startling Blue Feather so that she whirled, gasping. It was Broken Arm, and he came to sit beside her on the rock. "Why do you cry?" he asked after a moment of silence, then guessed, "Duke?"

Her eyes widened slightly, and she nodded. *"Ai.* But it is not what you may think. . . ."

"Then what is it? Has Duke done something he shouldn't have done?"

"Oh, no!" Sunlight glinted in her blue-black tresses as she gave her head a vigorous shake. "No, he has done nothing bad, only what he feels is right." Her hands twisted in her lap, then she blurted, "I wish I had someone to talk to about it — someone old and wise who would understand what I am feeling!"

Withdrawing slightly, Broken Arm gave her a reproachful gaze. "I won't do?"

Again her hair shimmered in the sunlight as she shook her head. "No, you are a man."

A slight chuckle escaped him as Broken Arm allowed that this was, indeed, true, then added, "But I've been known to be helpful at times."

When she still hesitated, looking up at him almost shyly, Broken Arm sensed her inner turmoil. Clapping his hands upon his knees, he lifted his shaggy head and gazed across the pool. The water's surface mirrored the sky, a translucent blue that was as soft and pale as the wind that blew down through the mountain crevices. His eyes grew distant, and his imagination saw other things mirrored in the pool, the eternal struggle between life and death and love and loneliness. He had made his choice between love and loneliness long ago, and had made a more recent choice in returning to his beloved Wind River range. There was so little time left to a man to do the things he wanted to do, to smell the wind, the sharp scent of the pines, and to feel the sunshine on his face. Ah, it had been a good life, and if he could do something for this lovely, gentle girl in the time he had left, he would do it. One never knew when the time would come that it would be impossible to rise from the sleeping mat.

"Come with me to my tipi," he told her. "We will talk, and you can tell me what is making your heart so heavy."

This time Blue Feather did not argue, but rose obediently and followed the old trapper to his buffalo-hide tipi. She knelt on the fur blankets he indicated, and accepted the cup of clover tea he gave her. Arranging her cotton skirts around her legs and feet, she waited expectantly.

"You are afraid of England," Broken Arm stated when she looked up at him. "Is this so?"

"*Ai*, this is so."

"And Duke expects you to go with him."

Again she nodded and whispered, "*Ai*."

"This frightens you? Is it the thought of England being so far away?"

"Oh, no, that is not it at all. I feel that . . . that if I went with him to this England, that I would be shamed. And I could not bear seeing *him* look at me with the fires of shame in his eyes. . . ."

"Shame? Because you are different from the English?" Broken Arm nodded slowly. "Yes, of course that is it. They would stare at you, treat you as a curiosity instead of a woman with feelings. I have seen that happen often enough." He drew in a deep breath. "It has been said that England is a lovely land, with bright green hills and magnificent stone castles. Duke is a great man there. You would have an important position as his wife."

Blue Feather gazed at him steadily, then said, "You know that I would not be accepted by his people. They would never allow me to be his wife."

"Perhaps it would not be so bad," Broken Arm began, then paused. "I know Duke loves you," he said after a moment.

"*Ai*, but would his love remain when he saw that I was not accepted? Our differences would be too great in his land. Here in the mountains it matters little. One tries only to survive. But there, in a land where the women sit and smell the flowers all day — no. I would only make him unhappy, and our love would die."

Broken Arm's weathered face creased into a deep frown, and he sighed heavily. "You understand much for a woman who has so few years. I had hoped that Duke would not want to return to England, but I see that I was mistaken. Somehow, I thought that he would change after his time with Cheney . . . ah, but it seems I was wrong."

"No, you are not wrong. He has changed. He is stronger and more like you," Blue Feather said. "I see it in him, in the way he walks and in his words, yet I also see that he is torn between two worlds."

Nodding in agreement, Broken Arm observed, "I once felt the same way. I was torn between civilization and the things I could find there, yet longed for the peace and contentment I could find in the mountains."

"And now you are at peace?"

"Yes, most of the time."

Pondering this for a moment, Blue Feather stared out of the tipi's flap, across to the lake and its shimmering tumble of water falling from the rocks. It made a loud noise in her ears, a rhythmic sound that reminded her of forever. It was said that the waterfall had always been there, had always cascaded into the lake. The Shoshoni had built their village along its shores, filled with the security that it would always be there. There was a feeling of peace in that knowledge, and she thought of Adrian, and how he felt no peace at being in this land.

Perhaps he would find it in England. Or perhaps, once there, he would realize that it was behind him.

"Adrian is not at peace with himself," she said at last, softly, reflectively. "He longs for one thing, yet is drawn to another. He loves me, but he also loves the past, the dreams he once held dear. They battle inside him."

Broken Arm remained silent, puffing on a pipe and letting her work it out herself. He had learned long ago that true wisdom was knowing what to do next.

"There is no easy solution," she said. "I will not leave my land, and he feels he must go."

Rubbing at his grizzled jaw, Broken Arm nodded, then said, "I kinda know how Duke feels. I've got unfinished business myself, and it's been pulling at me lately. I don't want to wait until it's too late, but I've put it off as long as I can."

Blue Feather waited politely, feeling that if the old trapper wanted her to know his business, he would tell her. But her head jerked up when he said, "I have to find Pierre Duvalle. . . ."

"Pierre Duvalle—my father?" she asked.

"Yes. I know he never mentioned it to you, but Pierre and I were friends a long time ago."

Her brows knit into a frown and she murmured, "It is strange that my father never mentioned you to me."

"Not so strange if you know all the facts," Broken Arm returned with a brooding sigh. "Let me start at the beginning, so maybe it will be a little clearer. You see, Pierre ran with Cheney for a time. By the time I met Duvalle, he and Cheney had already parted company. Then Cheney went kinda crazy, and after he and Pierre had a big fight, he took off by himself. Your father and I hunted together for years. Anyway, things took a bad turn between your father and myself sometime after that. We parted enemies, and I have not been back since that time."

"Parted enemies? But . . . it seems that my father should have mentioned such a bad thing around the lodge fires on the few nights he came to visit our camp . . . you know how the men talk about such things when they smoke the pipe. Yet no one ever hinted at bad blood between my father and any other man."

"Didn't really think Pierre would tell anyone. He was always pretty close-mouthed about things, and besides, he had his reasons for not telling about it."

"Why did my father and Cheney quarrel?" Blue Feather asked curiously.

"They quarreled over a woman and gold, the woman being your mother," Broken Arm answered. "The gold—pah! *I* never found it, and believe me—I looked. Only Pierre Duvalle knows where that gold lies. He and Cheney fought long and hard over that, but Pierre said the gold was worthless and would only bring many men to the mountains, men who would not respect the land but destroy it. He refused to ever tell where it was hidden. And then, after your mother went with Pierre, old Cheney just kinda went crazy and took off into the mountains. Until Duke ran into him, I thought he musta been dead."

"And now you wish to make peace between my father and yourself?"

Sighing heavily, the old trapper said, "I'm an old

man, Blue Feather. I've lived long and well, but there are things I cannot leave unsettled when I die. Pierre Duvalle was a good friend. I would not have him think of me as an enemy when I am gone."

"So you go into the mountains to search for him?" Blue Feather shook her head. "You will not find him unless he wishes it. No one can find him if he does not wish it."

"I've got a pretty good idea where he is. I can camp, and sit and wait until he comes to me. If he's anywhere around, he'll come to me. If for no other reason than to kill me," he added.

"But what did you do to anger my father so?"

Broken Arm's face was bleak as he looked up at Blue Feather. "I was married to his sister, Lilith—and I killed her."

Rocking back, Blue Feather stared at him uncomprehendingly. Her father's sister—her aunt. Pierre Duvalle had never mentioned her, never indicated that he had even had a sister. It seemed unbelievable that this gentle man would kill a woman. "Why did you kill her?" she asked bluntly.

"We lived in Canada then. She would stay in the town while I hunted and trapped the furs, and I would go home sometimes to see her. I came home earlier than usual one time, and I found her with another man. I shot him right there. Ah, I was young and hot-blooded, and so was Lilith!" Broken Arm's eyes narrowed with the memory, and his big hands clenched around his pipe as he continued. "We argued violently. She was half-crazy with anger and so was I. When she picked up a knife as if to use it on me, I broke her neck. . . ." His voice faltered, and he stared past Blue Feather as if seeing

417

the past reenacted before his eyes. "I didn't really mean to, but I was so angry with her, and it just happened. She was so pretty, so young and wild and full of life—I suppose it was hard on her being alone all those months. . . ." Jerking as if just realizing he was not alone, Broken Arm finished, "I fled Canada, of course. I came back to the Wind River mountains, the valleys I loved and hunted. I had to tell Pierre what had happened to his sister. That was when we quarrelled, and I knew one of us had to leave these mountains. I traveled to the Dakotas and trapped for a while, then acted as guide for a time before I went back to Canada. Now I have come back."

"It is right that you have come back. My father should walk with more understanding now. Perhaps it is not too late to end this bitterness between you."

"I hope not," Broken Arm said. "I would like to end my days in peace with all men."

"*Ai,* all men must find peace," Blue Feather said. "If my husband does not return to his land, I fear he will not find his peace. I know that he will not be happy until he does, just as you will not be happy until you are at peace with my father."

"That's true," Broken Arm agreed. "But I don't think Duke will go without you, little one."

"I think you are right. That is why he is not to know that I will stay behind when he leaves. You will not tell him?" she asked anxiously.

Slowly, he shook his head. "No, I will not tell him, but I cannot agree with your decision. He should be told."

"If he is told, he will not go. It must be kept from him until it is too late."

418

"I will keep your secret as long as I can," Broken Arm agreed, but his brow was furrowed in a deep frown.

"Then that is all I can ask of you."

Returning to her tipi, Blue Feather found Adrian and Harry there. She paused in the opening, recalling how she had run away from Adrian a short time before. Would he be angry with her? But no, he was smiling, and she smiled back at him.

"Hello, my husband."

"Hello, my wife," he returned.

Harry, seeing the glance between them, decided he would only be in the way if he remained. Leaning down, he picked up the twins, one in each arm, and announced his decision to take them for a walk.

"They love their walks," he added, backing toward the open flap of the tipi. The girls struggled in his grip, and he juggled them carefully as he ducked and left.

"They are growing," Adrian remarked, and Blue Feather nodded.

"*Ai,* they will soon be grown."

Silence fell, and Blue Feather shifted from one foot to another, then sighed. "I did not mean to argue with you," she began at the same time as Adrian said, "I'm sorry we quarrelled," then both halted and laughed.

"You first," Adrian said.

"I am sorry. I do not wish to argue with you. Can we not forget my angry words?"

Gray eyes crinkled at the corners as he smiled,

and Adrian said softly, "They are already forgotten. Gone—phfft! Like a feather on the wind!"

Throwing herself into his arms, Blue Feather buried her face in his chest and took a deep breath. "I am so glad, my husband!"

"Just how glad are you?" He wanted to know, his tone teasing.

Tilting back her head, Blue Feather looked up into Adrian's laughing eyes, and her smile dimmed. "Very glad." She laid her head against his chest again, feeling the regular thud of his heart against her cheek, and thought of the long, lonely winters ahead of her, winters without Adrian. He would be gone from her, far away in that place called England, and she would not see him. Perhaps he would never come back to her. Steeling her weakening resolve, she vowed to remain strong, not to let herself yield to her desire to stay with him.

"You know," he was musing aloud, his breath stirring her hair, "I remember when I stayed with Cheney, and how he used to say the land was the only thing that mattered. I would begin to think he may be right, but then I would recall you and I would think, 'No, not to me. I must find her.' We would have quite lively discussions on that point, Cheney and I." Adrian gave her a quick squeeze and added, "I always won."

Blue Feather laughed dutifully, though her heart wrenched at what she intended to do. He must not know until it was too late. . . .

"Anyway," Adrian was saying, pushing her slightly away as he bent to retrieve some papers from the small writing desk resting on a blanket, "I have much to do when I get back to England. It will be some time before I can devote the proper amount of attention to you, if Richard has his way, but then I shall be *most* attentive! I intend to show you things you've never dreamed of, my sweet! You will be enchanted by them, I'm certain." Adrian's voice trailed off as he frowned down at the papers in his hand, and he gave a sigh of dismay. "So much to do, so much to do," he murmured, then tossed them back to the writing desk.

"Do you have many in your family?" she asked him. "Or is Richard your only kinsman?"

"Oh, no, I've got an uncle still alive and thriving, and a multitude of various cousins. Oh, that reminds me—did you know that your father may be a distant relative of Richard's wife? Yes, it's true. Lady du Jessupe had mentioned him long ago, and Richard reminded me of it this morning. Odd, isn't it? As large as the world is, one is still likely to encounter such strange coincidences!"

"Yes, it is odd," Blue Feather agreed. Her brows puckered in a frown. "Does that mean we are somehow related also?"

"No, no. But you may be related to Lady Josette. See? That would give you a kinsman in England!"

Swallowing the lump in her throat, Blue Feather managed a smile. Her mood seesawed up and down, from hope to dismay and back, but she could not see that she would be accepted in England. She snuggled close when Adrian folded her in his embrace again. He could sense her uncertainty, and wrongly interpreted it to the journey ahead of her. This time their kiss held a sense of urgency. . . .

Dusty light streamed through the flaps of buffalo hide that had been lifted to provide ventilation in the tipi, and dust motes danced lightly over Adrian's bare body as he lay drowsing on his blanket. It was late afternoon, and the sun would soon be setting in the west. Blue Feather lay on her stomach, chin propped in the cradle formed by her palms as she watched the sunlight bathe her husband's body in a golden glow. He was like the golden-haired god of an ancient Cheyenne legend, she thought lazily, all pale and perfect. She would miss him terribly. . . .

Shifting at the thought, she swung to a sitting position and flipped back her long fall of hair over one shoulder. It was too painful to think about, too painful to consider. She—who had once thought she was inured to pain and broken promises—was finding it most difficult to deal with this constant ache. The future hung like a dark cloud over her, shading any momentary happiness she might feel.

"Where are you going, love?" Adrian asked in a throaty murmur, one hand reaching out for her. His fingers stroked the bare skin of her thigh, sliding upward in a sensuous motion that brought a sigh from her.

"I am going nowhere," she returned in a breathless little whisper. "I intend to stay here with you as long as I can. . . ."

He pulled her down into his arms, and nuzzled her neck. "Good."

Much later, when the evening meal had been eaten and the dishes scraped clean and scoured with sand, Richard appeared at the open flap to their tipi.

"May I come in?" he called.

"Come in, Richard," Adrian answered. He was in a jovial mood, with his stomach full and his wife and children around him, and he was feeling as if he had the world at his feet. He smiled at Richard as he ducked into the tipi and sat on a folded blanket.

"It's rather warm today, don't you think?" Richard observed, wiping at the beads of perspiration dotting his forehead.

"Yes, it is. Warm weather never lasts long enough up here, though. It will be winter much sooner than in the valley. When the snow flies, the camp will move down to the valley."

"The entire camp?" Richard asked, surprised that all of the village would move.

Adrian nodded, then stretched out a hand and offered his brother a pipe. "It's fairly good tobacco."

"No, thank you. I had experience with this kind of tobacco at the rendezvous. It's very bitter."

"It's kinnikinnick—tobacco with aromatic herbs. Sure you won't try it again?"

Richard gave an adamant shake of his head. "No, it makes my head ache." He looked over at the small girls playing happily and quietly on their blanket. They had been given a few shells and some large rocks, and were busily pushing them around. "Beautiful children," he remarked with a smile at Blue Feather. "They are quite arresting, with their golden curls and dusky skin."

"Yes," Adrian answered before Blue Feather could respond, "they are as lovely as their mother in

423

their own way, don't you think?"

"It's yet too early to tell if they will be as lovely as she, old boy, but I guarantee it will be quite close!"

A light blush stained Blue Feather's high cheekbones, and she bent her head and toyed with a fold of her skirt. It still made her uncomfortable to be with Adrian's brother. Perhaps it was because of what she had overheard, or even because she knew he wanted Adrian to return with him.

Adrian stretched lazily, and his smile was easy as he gazed at his wife. "I am a fortunate man to have such a lovely wife and two beautiful daughters."

"And it is indeed time that good fortune finds you, Adrian." Richard cleared his throat, then continued, "That is part of what I wished to speak to you about. As you are aware from the papers I gave you, Father was quite generous in his settlement with you. It was only what you deserved, of course, since the title and manor passed to me. However, there is a lot of work to be done on some of the properties, and I am depending upon you to help me. It entails lands that you now own, and I am not at liberty to make any disposal of them now that you have been found."

Adrian, who was toying with the ends of Blue Feather's raven hair, looked up at his brother. "I intend to take care of any business that is left to me, Richard."

"I know you will, old boy. I brought over a paper that I especially wanted to discuss with you—oh, drat it! I must have left it in the tipi . . . would you mind fetching it for me, Adrian? I shall take the opportunity to chat with your lovely wife while you are gone. . . ."

"Remember that she is married," Adrian said mockingly, rising to his feet in a smooth, easy motion. "What am I to search for?"

"A paper bound with a black ribbon, and it has *Executor* written on it."

"You just want my wife to yourself," Adrian accused with a laugh, and Richard readily agreed.

"Of course, I do! Can you blame me?"

"Not a bit. I shan't be long, however."

Blue Feather watched Adrian leave, her face composed so that Richard would not know her thoughts. It was never wise to allow an enemy—should he be one—to know too much about what one was feeling. But inside, her heart was hammering, and her throat was suddenly dry. This man had a purpose in being here, she knew it. Perhaps in his way, this Richard was just as sly as Ramone Jardin.

Richard broke the silence that fell on Adrian's heels, leaning forward to face Blue Feather solemnly. "I do hope that you will not be offended by what I have to say to you," he began, "but I fear it must be said. Not just for Adrian's sake, but yours."

Blue Feather's face was carefully blank as she nodded. "Say what you feel you must."

He sat back and looked at her. "Very well. Adrian has always—since childhood—been intense, emotional, impulsive and ruled by his feelings. He was always one who would leap before he looked, which was often to his detriment. Oh, his feelings were usually noble and just, but rarely realistic. Do you understand what I am trying to say?"

Though she didn't understand some of the words

he used, Blue Feather recognized the tone, and she nodded. *"Ai.* You are worried what will happen if Adrian takes me to England with him."

Nonplussed, Richard just gazed at her for a moment. "Yes," he said when he recovered, "you have hit upon my sentiments exactly. It appears that you are much more perceptive than I had considered."

"If that means that I can see what lies ahead, then you are right. I am no fool. I know that I would never be accepted by the people in my husband's land." Blue Feather leaned forward to gaze at him intently, and her voice was quick and urgent. "But my children—they look almost English, do they not? I think they would do well in this England, in a land where there is plenty to eat and the winters are not so harsh as here. The buffalo will be gone one day, and even now the food in the mountains is less and less. The People are hungry much of the time, and I want more than that for my children—for Adrian's children. Do you understand me, brother of my husband?"

Richard's eyes were pale like Adrian's, and they gazed at her as he nodded. "By Jove, I think I do! If I can promise that your children will be well cared for, then you will remain here, am I right?"

She sat back. *"Ai,* you are right."

Shaking his fair head, Richard said, "I have rarely felt respect for a woman as I do you, Blue Feather. I must admit that I also feel regret that things are the way they are. You would be a fine addition to English society were it not for the strict social demands."

"Thank you."

Putting his hands on his knees, Richard said, "I

assure you that I will care for your children as I would my own. My wife will be quite pleased to have them with us."

Swallowing hard to remove the lump in her throat, Blue Feather inclined her head slightly. "Again, I thank you. You are receiving my greatest gifts—my children. And before my husband returns, I must tell you that if he discovers I am not going, he may refuse to go. It will be wiser if you do not say anything to him about this."

Rather startled, Richard just nodded. "If you wish . . ."

"It is not what I wish. None of this is what I wish. It is what must be," she answered, then looked toward the open flap of the tipi. "I hear his step on the path. Do you think Star has the bluest eyes, or is it Blue?"

Fires of admiration glowed in Richard Herenton's eyes as he took Blue Feather's cue and began to loudly admire the girls playing on their pallet. An odd feeling crept over him, the feeling that he had just witnessed the supreme sacrifice of true love.

Chapter 22
The Devil

Tossing in restless slumber, Adrian and Blue Feather spent a fitful night. The slightest sound awoke them, and several times Adrian lifted his head to look at his children as they slept. Though drowsy, Blue Feather felt his movements beside her, and smiled. She had worried about Adrian's response to his daughters. Now she need not worry if he would feel responsible for them. He was obviously quite willing to care for them, and that thought made it easier for her to bear what lay ahead. With Adrian and Harry caring for them, Star and Blue should not want for anything.

Heralding the dawn, tiny rays of sunlight filtered through the open ventilation flaps of the tipi, and Blue Feather rose from her nest of blankets. She flicked a brief glance at Adrian and resisted the urge to touch him, to caress the damp tendrils of hair curling over the back of his neck and onto his shoulders. He would wake, and she knew what would follow. A smile curved her mouth as she slipped quietly into her skirt and blouse and lifted the wakening twins into her arms. She shushed them gently when they protested, then left the tipi without awakening Adrian.

Harry greeted her at the open flap of his tipi, gladly taking the girls from her arms. "They look as if they have missed me," he announced as he cradled them close.

Blue Feather smiled. "You mean that you have missed them."

"Perhaps that is more correct," Harry agreed with an answering smile. "I was restless the entire night, wondering if they needed me."

Her voice was gentle as she said, "You love White Star and Blue Moon very much, don't you?"

Rather surprised by such a question, Harry looked up at her with lifted brows. "Of course, I do! What a thing to say, Margarethe! Are you beginning to doubt my ability to care for them?"

"No, no," she hastily assured him. "I often feel that you are a better mother than I am."

Harry set the girls on a blanket and gave them wooden bowls of a thin cereal. He sat beside them and helped them with their spoons, his brow furrowed. "Is there something amiss, Margarethe?" he asked several minutes later.

"I am only tired."

Nodding, Harry slanted her a quizzical glance. She did have dark circles under her eyes, and her face seemed pinched and strained. Perhaps it was the journey ahead which bothered her, or the long nights she was spending with Adrian. He wondered if he should speak to his lordship and admonish him for keeping her awake at night, then dismissed the thought. Adrian would only be amused.

"Have you packed anything?" Harry asked her then. "I have only a few things packed in the large leather bags. If you need to take one or two of the

429

smaller parfleches, feel free to take them with you."

Blinking, Blue Feather just stared at him for a moment as she gathered her thoughts, then said, "Oh . . . oh yes. I shall need one or two. We have little to pack."

"Yes, most of what I shall be taking along are food supplies. My one suit has gotten quite threadbare, but I intent to take along an entire suit of clothes your illustrious cousin gave me. It should cause a great deal of comment in London."

"*Ai*, it should," she agreed as she pushed to her feet. "I think I shall go now. Are these the parfleches you meant?"

"Yes, those are the ones. Fortunately, Richard and Mr. Bowie brought extras in case they were needed. They were certain we would be found eventually, and wish to accompany them home."

"Does it mean much to you to go back to England, Harry?"

"Why, yes, I suppose it does. I shall enjoy exhibiting my trophies to the kitchen help. There is a certain woman—Gladys Carmichael—who is an absolute harridan. Just because she is the housekeeper and has a ring of keys, she imagines that she knows everything there is to be known. I shall take immense pleasure in showing her up," Harry said with great satisfaction.

Blue Feather had to smile, and she thought how relieved Harry must be to be returning to his home. She thought of her long year away from the Shoshoni, when she had been captured by the Crow and taken away, and she knew how he must feel. It would be good for Harry and Adrian to go home.

"I shall return later to be with the children," she

promised. "I have a matter to discuss with my cousin."

"Certainly. We shall be here—ah-ah, Blue! You must not wear your food, but eat it—like this," he was instructing as Blue Feather left.

Draping the beaded parfleches over one shoulder, Blue Feather crossed the dusty path cutting through the middle of the village. She paused before Gray Eagle's tipi and called out to him. "May I enter, cousin?"

"Enter," he called back, and she ducked through the flap and immediately went to the left as females were supposed to do when entering a tipi. Gray Eagle was sitting cross-legged with his first wife at his side.

"This is a private matter," Blue Feather began, "so if it is inconvenient to Willow Bud, I shall return later."

"No, my cousin, you may stay," Willow Bud responded. "I must go to help Sun Woman gather herbs and tend the children of our husband."

Blue Feather nodded gratefully, glad that Gray Eagle had chosen such an even-tempered woman for his first wife. His second wife, Sun Woman, was not quite as easy-going. When the tipi was empty but for the two of them, she looked Gray Eagle in the face and waited. It was now proper for him to make the first move, as she had already indicated a desire to speak to him about an important matter.

Resting his palms on his knees, Gray Eagle looked at her for several long moments before he spoke. "You are not happy. What is it, my cousin?"

"I must go to my father."

Her blunt statement surprised Gray Eagle, and he

431

said nothing for a moment. His mouth pursed in a frown, and his dark eyes narrowed briefly. "Why?"

Blue Feather's hands moved in an awkward gesture as she searched for the right words. "It is right that I do so. It has been many moons since I have seen him, and I feel that he would like to see me."

Gray Eagle considered this carefully before replying, "That is not your entire reason. Your husband has said he is leaving for the Siskadee, and that you are to go with him. Does this request mean that you do not desire to go?"

Bowing her head, her reply was almost inaudible. *"Ai,* that is true. I do not wish to go to the land across the big water."

"It is your duty. You are his wife. A woman of The People is always loyal to her husband," Gray Eagle said in his sternest voice. "Would you have me go back on my word? You were given in good faith, and taken in good faith."

"Ai, ai, I know. But you don't understand . . . he wishes to take me to a land where I will be surrounded by white men, a land where I would only be a disgrace to him. Because he is a good man and loves me, he does not see this. I wish to spare him his own humiliation."

"Ah, I see." Gray Eagle frowned thoughtfully. "There must be another way to solve this nettlesome problem."

Blue Feather shook her head. "There is none. I have thought of many things, but unless I go away he will insist I go with him."

"And your children?"

This was the hardest, and she had to draw in a deep breath before she could answer without her voice breaking. "They are to go with their father. They have pale hair and eyes, and will not bring shame upon him. There will be enough food in the winter, and they will never go cold with him."

"You have thought much about this?"

"*Ai.* I have given this much thought."

"Then so be it." Gray Eagle's eyes narrowed to dark, glittering slits, and he hesitated before adding, "I cannot go with you to your father's lodge. It is too far, and I cannot leave my people without proper guidance that long. There are too many hunters gone for the buffalo at this time."

"That is all right," she said quickly. "I can find my way. If you will remember, I often strayed far from home when I was a child."

Gray Eagle's thin lips quirked in a smile. "I remember. Many is the time one was sent after you, only to return and find you waiting for him." Rubbing his chin, he sighed and said, "Duvalle's lodge is near Blue Lake. It is well hidden, and on the east bank is a lightning-struck tree that is bent thusly." He made a right angle with his hands. "When you see that, follow the pointing limb south. Walk until you see a path in the rocks, then go straight into the mountain. Duvalle's hut will appear to you."

Blue Feather's lips moved silently as she memorized his instructions, then she nodded once. "I hear, cousin. My thanks to you."

"May your quest be fulfilled and the Great Spirit kind to you," Gray Eagle said gently, lifting one hand palm outward in a gesture of benediction.

Again Blue Feather bowed her head, and she closed her eyes. Then she left Gray Eagle's tipi silently, and made her way back to Harry's tipi. He was waiting for her, and his face lit up when she entered.

"Margarethe! I am glad you are back. His lordship was searching for you not long ago, and I said that I thought you might be back in your tipi. . . ."

"No, I was still with Gray Eagle."

"Ah well, no matter. His lordship left a message for you."

"A message?"

"Yes, he will be gone for a while, as he and His Grace and Mr. Bowie have gone to inspect some horses that Gray Eagle has generously offered to sell them." A smile crooked his mouth as Harry shifted the twins, then placed them back on their blankets. "There . . . they are such precious girls, don't you think?"

Blue Feather's throat tightened. "*Ai, ai,* they are most precious, Harry."

"Well, at any rate, we shall have enough horses for our journey to Green River to meet this person who is waiting to guide us back to St. Louis. Ah, I can hardly wait to see a three-story building again, and perhaps have a mutton pie or hot English muffin. . . ." He gave his head a regretful shake. "It has been far too long without proper tea, you know."

"*Ai,* I know it has been a long time for you." She paused, then asked, "Is Broken Arm to go along?"

"Broken Arm? No, he intends to stay here in the Wind River range, he says. I daresay he will soon miss us, though, and I know I shall miss him."

"Did he go with my husband today?"

"No, I do not believe so, though I have not seen him this morning. He's grown rather fond of fishing, you know. He might be at the waterfall again."

434

"Oh. I had need of him," she mused aloud, and Harry immediately offered to fetch him. "No, you don't have to do that," Blue Feather said. "I can go."

"No, I shall be glad to do it. I need the exercise, and the notion of a short walk sounds delightful."

Looking down at her children, Blue Feather realized she could take this opportunity to hold them closely and whisper her love into their ears without drawing attention. She smiled brightly. "Thank you, Harry. I shall wait here."

"Excellent. If you don't mind, I think I shall take my time and just amble along slowly. The wind is blowing gently for a change. I rather regret that a Piegan infidel stole my best derby. It would keep the sun off my head much better than this wretched piece of animal fur. But, so it is. I shall be back soon, if it pleases you."

"*Ai,* take your time," she returned, and was glad he had offered her such a chance as this. Pulling on his cap, Harry left the tipi, and she heard his footsteps fade away on the dusty path.

Kneeling beside the two little girls, she touched each of their golden heads, then succumbed to emotion and pulled them to her. In spite of their squirming, she held them tightly in her embrace, then lay her cheek against the downy curls atop two heads, each one separately. Hot tears coursed down her cheeks, spilling onto Star's chubby thigh. The infant looked curiously up at her mother, and reached out a stubby finger to touch her cheek.

A frown marred Blue's tiny, perfect features. Her rosebud mouth pursed in distress, and Blue Feather reacted quickly to stop the child from crying.

"Hush, little grasshopper. *Umbea* is not hurt, only sad. You see, I must go away for a while, and I will miss you both very much. But you are to always remember that I loved you, and will love you as long as there is a sun in the sky, and the wind still blows and flowers grow—can you remember that?"

When the children just gazed at her in sorrowful confusion, Blue Feather sighed. They did not understand her words now, but perhaps one day they would recall a loving woman who had held them tightly and poured love onto them.

Sobbing, she rocked back and forth with the children held in her lap, her eyes closed against the pain that was tearing her apart. How could she part with her children? And her husband? What would Adrian say when he found her gone. . . .

"Ah, *cherie,* you are crying again," a husky voice said from the open flap, and Blue Feather's head jerked around. She knew and hated that voice and the man who owned it.

"Get away!" she snapped, glaring at Ramone Jardin. "I thought you were far away from our camp. . . ."

"Oh, I was, but I came back for you, *cherie.*" He stepped closer, and Blue Feather's arms tightened protectively around her daughters.

"Flee, before my husband returns!"

"Non, ma petite. Your husband, he is gone and will not be back for some time. Ramone, he knows this." A toothy grin accompanied this statement, and Jardin came closer. When he reached out for her, she jerked away, scooting back on the blankets, her children clutched in her arms.

436

"Cochon! Stay away from me!" Glaring up at him with wide blue eyes, Blue Feather felt the pounding of her heart like war drums in her chest. Where was Harry? And Broken Arm? Oh, if only Adrian would return early from his horse-buying trip! Then she thought of Gray Eagle not far away in his tent, and opened her mouth to scream. Someone would hear, even if it was some of the women. Shoshoni women could be quite wicked and fierce when they chose. . . .

But when Blue Feather's mouth opened and Jardin recognized her intention, he lifted his knife, holding the tip only inches away from Star's baby face. "If you make a single sound," he hissed, "I shall slice her face to ribbons."

Swallowing the scream, Blue Feather sat still and silent. Perhaps she could trick him somehow, or stall for enough time so that Harry would return to his tipi. But Jardin's next words dashed those hopes, as he snarled a command for her to get up and come with him instantly.

"We have little time to waste, *cherie,* and I intend for you to guide me to your *papa.*"

"My papa? But . . . but I do not know where he is. No one knows!" she stammered.

"Do not lie. I know that you will find him. Pierre Duvalle would not hide from his only daughter. *Al-lez-vouz!"*

Rising reluctantly to her feet, Blue Feather cast her eyes about the tipi as Jardin grasped her by one arm, still holding the knife tip to Star's face. Perhaps she could leave some sign that she had been taken against her will, or perhaps he would allow her to leave her children behind.

"Sil vous plaît," she begged. "Let me leave the little ones behind. They will only slow us down and be in the way while we travel—"

"Non! I will need them for barter, just as I need you, my pretty one."

"But . . . but I don't understand," she said helplessly, watching as he slit a long tear in the back of the tipi. "I do not know why you must find my father."

"Gold, you stupid *jeune fille!* It is for the gold the old man has that I do this! Do you think I would steal one skinny Indian girl and risk Gray Eagle's anger just for love? Hoo-hoo! You are silly and foolish, *cherie!"*

Gold? Blue Feather shook her head in confusion. What gold did this man think her father possessed? Pierre Duvalle had no use for gold.

"You are mistaken," she began, but Jardin slapped her hard across the mouth, splitting her lip and knocking her to the ground to lie in a stunned daze. Too frightened to cry out, the twins began to whimper.

"I know it!" Jardin snarled, spittle flying from his mouth as he glared down at her. "Do not try to fool me about this, or I will kill you!"

"Hey!" a voice boomed from the tipi flap. "Who is to kill whom, Frenchman?"

Jardin whirled to see Broken Arm's silhouette outlined against the half-open flap. As the old trapper straightened and started forward, Jardin flexed his arm in a peculiarly graceful movement. Broken Arm staggered, and an odd sound bubbled from his lips. The hilt of Jardin's knife had magically sprouted from his throat, and blood spurted. One fist still held a knotted string of fish, and they slid to the floor of the tipi as he pitched silently forward.

Lying half-dazed, Blue Feather could still see what was happening and wondered why she did not scream. Perhaps it was instinct that kept her from giving rise to the hysteria that welled in her throat, an instinct for survival that told her Jardin would not hesitate to kill her children if she made so much as a sound.

"Get up, you worthless *femme!*" Jardin was saying, kicking at her and motivating her to action. "We need to go now!"

Wordlessly, with a last, grief-stricken glance at the old man lying on the floor of the tipi, Blue Feather got to her feet and carried her children with her through the long slit in the buffalo hide. Behind the tipi rose a thick mat of bushes and trees, a dense thicket that hid Jardin's horses from view.

"You see?" he sneered. "I planned well, did I not?"

Still unable to answer, Blue Feather just nodded as he motioned for her to mount. The two little girls clung fiercely to her side, and she realized that it would be almost impossible to ride with both of them.

"Please, Jardin . . . I need something to carry one of them in. I cannot manage. . . ."

"Perhaps I should kill one of them and lighten our load!" the Frenchman grated, then paused to reconsider. *"Non,* that would not do. I may need both for barter with Duvalle. Give me a child . . . *give* it to me! I will get a cradle board to carry one." He sneered again. "I do not trust you to wait if I do not take one with me."

Fortunately, Jardin grabbed Blue, who was much more placid of nature than the more rebelious Star. The child merely stared at the bearded Frenchman with wide eyes while he carried her back into the tipi with him. When Jardin returned several moments later with Blue and a cradle board, Blue Feather heaved a sigh of relief.

"These children are too big for a cradle board," she pointed out when Blue was safely in her arms again. "She will not fit."

"Make them fit, or maybe I cut off the feet, heh?"

With that threat hanging over her, Blue Feather worked swiftly to fit the squirming Blue into the leather and wood cradle board that Gray Eagle's wife had given her upon their birth. It had rarely been used, and the baby made a mild protest at being confined. Fortunately, the top was left open so that Blue could have some freedom. The leather straps binding the pouch to the wooden frame were tightly tied, and Blue Feather hung the cradle board over the front of the saddle and pulled Star next to her in the seat.

"It is about time, *femme*," Jardin said with a scowl, and he nudged the horses forward, pulling Blue Feather's mount behind him. They rode at a rapid pace until they were well away from the camp.

Blue Feather barely noticed the path they took. She saw only the bright red spurt of blood and Broken Arm's surprised expression when Jardin's knife blade had sunk into his throat. He had been a good friend, and had died because of her. Blue Feather fought a sudden wave of nausea, then lapsed into dull acceptance. It was life, and death, the endless cycle, over and over.

Star wriggled in her arms, and Blue Feather looked down at her. Her moment of apathy altered to a fierce surge of hatred for Jardin and his threat against her children. She would not give in as she had done when stolen by the Crow, and even the Blackfeet. No, not this time. This time she had more than her own existence to think about. This time she had her children, Adrian's children. She would do whatever she had to do to keep them alive.

Perhaps that was why she didn't hesitate when Jardin paused at the crest of a hill and turned to ask her which way to Duvalle's?

"Blue Lake," she answered immediately.

"Zut alors," Jardin groaned in disgust. "That is four days ride! I thought it was closer—you do not lie? Because if you do, *petite femme,* I will cut out the liver of your oldest child."

"I do not lie," she said calmly. "You will see."

Jardin stared at her for a long moment, then obviously satisfied that she spoke the truth, he turned the horses in the direction of Blue Lake.

Blue Feather gazed straight ahead, her back straight and her mind working frantically. A lot could happen in four days. . . .

Harry was irritable. He had searched every favorite fishing spot he knew about, and Broken Arm was not to be found. At first the walk had been enjoyable, but then the unaccustomed exercise had begun to wear on him. Now he had to return and

441

report to Margarethe that the old trapper was not to be found.

"Probably hidden away with a jug of that dreadful stuff he drinks," Harry muttered to himself. He wiped his forehead and grimaced at the dust coating his face. England with its constant rain and emerald green lawns would be so soothing.

Stooping and removing his otter-skin hat in the same motion, Harry ducked into his tipi and skidded to a halt. A large form was sprawled upon the floor. Cautiously, he nudged it with his foot, then realized it was Broken Arm.

"Just as I thought!" he exclaimed. "Dead-drunk . . . get up, old chap!" he ordered in the next breath, nudging Broken Arm more firmly. "This is just the outside of enough, getting drunk and coming here to—Broken Arm?"

A harsh rattling sound erupted from the old man's throat, and Harry bent and rolled him over. He gasped. A knife hilt protruded from the trapper's throat, and his eyelids were still fluttering.

"Oh, dear God!" Harry rasped. "Dear God—Broken Arm! I don't . . . I don't know what to do . . . who . . . what happened?"

Fumbling weakly with one hand, the old trapper managed to grasp Harry's sleeve. He tried to raise up, but failed, and slumped back to the floor. Ragged wheezes filtered in a whistling sound from his throat, but he managed to utter a weak, "G-arrnnn!" before collapsing. His eyes rolled back in his head, and Harry held him in his arms heedless of the spurting blood.

"Oh, my good old chap," he moaned, rocking to and fro with the slowly relaxing form. Tears ran

442

freely from his eyes, splashing onto the old trapper's face, and the flicker of a smile ghosted Broken Arm's lips as he died.

Harry had never encountered such a situation. This was so totally unexpected, so dreadful, that he sat blankly for several minutes, just holding the trapper in his arms. Then he began to realize that Blue Feather and the girls were gone. He blinked, drifting slowly back to reality, and laid Broken Arm down as gently as possible. He covered the peaceful face with a blanket, then looked around. There was a long rip in the rear of the tipi, and the knife hilt jutting from Broken Arm's throat had a distinctive carving in the shaft. He remembered that carving, had seen it before, and it suddenly came to him what Broken Arm had been trying to say. Not "gone," but "Jardin." Of course. As he had threatened, that dastardly Frenchman had returned for Blue Feather. Rising, Harry left the tipi.

Crossing the wide path with purposeful strides, Harry called out his name before ducking into Gray Eagle's tipi without waiting for an invitation. The chief was sitting with two other men, and he turned with a black scowl.

"One has not been polite!" Gray Eagle snapped.

"Forgive me, Mr. Gray Eagle, but this is an emergency. I believe that your cousin and her children have been taken by Ramone Jardin. And that is not all—"

Gray Eagle waved an impatient hand at the flustered old man. "I know that my cousin has gone. She informed me of this earlier."

"No, no, you don't understand! She has not gone willingly, no matter what she may have said! Jar-

443

din's knife now protrudes from the throat of a dear friend of ours—Broken Arm."

"This is so?" Gray Eagle demanded as he rose in a lithe motion.

"Yes, this is quite so. Broken Arm now lies dead in my tipi—" Here his voice choked, and he could not go on.

Gray Eagle turned to the two men he had been talking with when Harry arrived. He spoke rapidly in Shoshoni, and they nodded and left.

"I have sent for my best horse," the chief said. "I will go after them."

"But how will you know where they have gone?" Harry asked distractedly. "He could have taken her anywhere!"

"I do not think a clumsy Frenchman can leave tracks I cannot follow" was the Shoshoni chief's terse reply.

"His lordship should know about this," Harry said as he followed Gray Eagle from the tipi.

Once Gray Eagle and Harry were mounted, they rode toward the pasture where the prize horses were kept. It was beyond the village, nestled in a small valley with a stream and well-hidden from possible intruders. The Piegan had a bad habit of stealing horses from the Shoshoni, as the animals were well-known for their fine breeding and stamina. These horses were safely guarded, and as they rode over the hill and down into a ragged rock crevice, there was a shouted challenge given by the alert sentry.

Gray Eagle reined in his spotted horse and looked up at the sentry, who now recognized him. They were waved on, and as they approached several men, Harry identified Adrian's tall figure on the fringe of the group.

"Your lordship!" he called, snaring Adrian's attention.

Turning, Adrian saw Harry galloping toward him. A vague feeling of premonition shivered through him as he wondered what Harry was doing in such a remote spot as this grassy canyon.

"By Jove, it's Harry!" Richard remarked. "And Gray Eagle is with him."

"Yes, it is." Adrian squinted against the sunlight as he peered at the approaching horsemen.

Everett Bowie stepped up to stand beside him, his hands resting on his hips as he followed Adrian's gaze. "Trouble's a'comin'," he said. "I kin feel it in my bones. Even the' skin on th' back of my neck is crawlin'."

A thick cloud of dust rose from the grass-studded ground as Gray Eagle and Harry reined in their mounts close to the group. Coughing slightly, Adrian laid a hand on the sweat-drenched neck of Harry's mare.

"What's the trouble, Harry?"

Gray Eagle answered, "Broken Arm is dead."

"Dead?" Adrian repeated slowly. "How?"

Again it was Gray Eagle who answered. "It was the Frenchman who killed him."

Adrian's mouth tightened, deep grooves bracketing his lips as his expression grew hard. "I should have killed Jardin long ago," he muttered.

Harry drew in a deep, shuddering breath, his light eyes full of misery, and Adrian's expression softened slightly as he looked up at him. "My lord," the older man began, then could not continue.

"What is it, Harry?"

Once more it was Gray Eagle who had to answer. His copper face was taut and he bit out the words, "Your wife is gone, and so are your children. Jardin has taken them."

"Dear God!" Richard breathed. "But whatever shall we do about this?"

Adrian was already moving to his horse. "I intend to go after them, of course," he said over one shoulder.

"Oh, of course, of course," Richard replied hastily. "Shall I go with you?"

"No," Gray Eagle cut in. "It will be best if only he and I go. I have an idea where they have gone, and it will be a hard ride."

Swinging into his saddle, Adrian jerked his mount's head around. "Where do you think they have gone?"

"To the lodge of Pierre Duvalle."

"Duvalle?" Nudging his mount forward, Adrian frowned. "Why there? Duvalle is her father. He would not care to see his daughter misused, would he?"

"It is not a matter I can discuss freely, but I will explain to you later," the chief answered.

"Hey, Duke!" Bowie called out, and when Adrian started and turned, the trapper tossed him his prized rifle. "Take this with ya. It don't never miss."

Adrian caught it easily. "Thank you, Bowie. I know this is your favorite weapon, so I shall care for it."

"Jus' kill the scoundrel that killed Broken Arm," Bowie answered grimly. "That's all that needs ta be done."

Adrian nodded. "Will you see to . . . to him? He

446

was a good friend and a great man."

"Ayeh, I'll see to him," Bowie said. "An' me and Charlotte will be waitin' here on ya when ya bring back your woman."

Nodding again, Adrian turned to Gray Eagle. "I'm ready to ride."

"Your lordship," Harry put in, "I am going with you."

"No, Harry, this will be dangerous."

Stiffening, the older man gazed sternly at Adrian. "I will be needed. I have always cared for Star and Blue, and I intend to go with you."

For an instant, Adrian hesitated, then he warned, "We shall be riding hard and fast, Harry. If you cannot keep up with us, we cannot wait for you."

"I understand that fully, my lord. I intend to keep up. I shall do my best not to slow you down."

Making an impatient gesture, Gray Eagle snapped, "Enough talk! Let us go before the trail is too cold!" He gestured to a tall warrior standing close by, and the man vaulted to his horse's back and joined them. There were four of them now, and they rode at a steady pace back up the narrow cut leading from the canyon.

Watching them go, Richard felt a sudden sense of loss. Why was it that Adrian seemed more at home here in this desolate wilderness than in a gray stone castle? But, oddly enough, he did. The tall, fair man dressed in buckskins was more of a man than the brother he had come to find. This Adrian sat a horse easily, and had a bold air of confidence that the other Adrian had never possessed. Richard stirred uneasily. Perhaps he had made a mistake in insisting that his younger brother accompany him

447

back to England. Perhaps he should not have placed such a burden of choice on him.

"Yer dukeship?" Bowie said, drawing Richard from his reverie.

"Yes, Bowie?" Richard answered with a sigh. He had given up on teaching the man the proper form of address, and was just content with anything Bowie chose to call him. It was much easier than teaching the trapper proper English protocol.

"Reckon we should go on back to camp now, and see 'bout the horses later. I'd kinda like to see to Broken Arm."

"Oh, of course! I was just . . . um . . . just lost in thought. Let us return immediately," Richard said, and flicked a glance toward the four horsemen disappearing over the rocky ridge above them.

Two more horses were climbing rocky paths high up in the mountain range. Jardin pushed forward with fevered urgency, knowing that pursuers would not be far behind. Once Blue Feather's disappearance was discovered, the Englishman and the Shoshoni chief would be hot on his trail. He had to reach Duvalle and comparative safety before he allowed them to find him. Then, he thought with grim satisfaction, he would kill the Englishman. This final battle had been inevitable since he had first seen the man.

Glancing behind him, Jardin sneered at the Indian girl who rode with stoic acceptance. She was an important part of his plan, a necessary part. Without the girl and her brats as hostages, he was likely to meet with resistance from old Duvalle. Ah, the gold! His eyes lit as he thought of the rumored gold. There was said to be veins so rich that no one man could spend it all, veins of gold that could be cut from the mountainside with a knife. And it would be his, all his if he could manage it. Of course, he would be forced to share his fortune for a time, as he needed help getting it all down from the mountain. For that he would go back to Green River and show the Stanfill brothers a small amount of the gold to entice them into helping him. Jardin's dark eyes narrowed as he recalled how they had scoffed at his insistence that he knew of a place where gold could be found. They would be sorry, all of them, because he would show them only what he wanted them to see. No one—not even the Shoshoni—would stop him.

Twisting in her saddle, Blue Feather glanced down at the cradle board dangling from the side of her horse. In it little Blue was wailing loudly, having been bounced too vigorously along the trail. They had been riding for hours, and the children were hungry. Star squirmed fitfully in her arms, and she realized that they would need rest soon.

"Jardin! We must rest," she called, but the Frenchman ignored her. Compressing her lips in a tight line, Blue Feather held her tongue for the moment, mentally afflicting Jardin with all kinds of tortures. At that moment she would have gladly inflicted several ingenious methods of torture commonly used only by the cruel Blackfeet. "Jardin!" she called again several minutes later, and this time he jerked his mount to a halt and turned to glare at her.

"What do you want now, *femme?*"

"The children, they are tired and hungry. We must stop and let them rest."

"Non! Vous n'avez pas de chance," he retorted with a scornful glance at the two squalling girls.

"It is only bad luck to be with you!" Blue Feather flared in return. "You have no pity, no compassion for small children. . . ."

Jardin stuck his thumb in his chest. "I have compassion only for me, *femme!* If you talk too much, I shall get bored with listening to you, and put a rag in your mouth."

Smothering her anger, Blue Feather lowered her gaze so that he would not see the fires of hatred in her eyes. It would not do to provoke him. He would be crazy in his rage, and she dared not risk her children. Jardin was already on the edge, filled with the necessity of reaching Duvalle and getting his hands on this gold before he was found by those who would be pursuing him. Briefly closing her eyes, Blue Feather offered a prayer to the Great Spirit that Adrian would follow, and that he would find her and take them away from this crazed Frenchman who raced against time.

As day faded into dusk, Jardin paused to rest the horses and himself. "You may feed your *enfants,* but be quick about it," he ordered Blue Feather. "I do not wait."

When he gave her several strips of deer jerky, she did her best to chew it to a softness the girls could eat, then gave it to them. There were only a few moments of time she could allow them to crawl about, and she spoke to them with softly whispered words of comfort. When Jardin once more gave the order to ride, she had managed to snuggle Star into the cradle board, and had Blue in front of her on the saddle. Perhaps changing them about would ease them a bit, she thought as she nudged her mount forward. At least they seemed drowsy now, with full bellies.

Deep purple and orange shadows shrouded the silhouette of the trees ahead of them as they rode up the steep mountainside, and Blue Feather kept her eyes trained on Jardin's back. There was no thought of escape now. That would come later, when Adrian found them—*if* Adrian found them. . . .

Chapter 23
The Emperor

Blue Lake lay below them, a turquoise jewel set in the midst of emerald shores, glittering in the late sunshine. Ramone Jardin sat his weary mount in triumph, staring down at the lake. He had reached it! He had beaten the odds and reached the lake, and he turned to leer at Blue Feather.

She was slumped in her saddle, dejected and weary, her face lined with strain. One child fretted in her arms while the other wailed in the cradle board. Swaying slightly, Blue Feather barely noticed that they had reached the lake. She was sick with weariness and strain, and the children—sensing their mother's distress—reacted as children often do. They mirrored her anxiety with fretful cries.

"This is Blue Lake," Jardin was saying to her, dragging her attention from the restless children. "Ah, look at it, *cherie!* Have you ever seen a place so beautiful to the eyes? *Non,* you could not. This is a paradise filled with beaver, fat fish, and most important—gold. This Pierre Duvalle is a greedy man to keep it all to himself, no?"

Ignoring him, Blue Feather turned her gaze to the gentle blue waters lying placidly below them. Her father was near. It had been so long since she had seen him—would he recognize her? Would he welcome her as he had done in the past?

Ramone Jardin reined his horse close to hers and gave her a sharp nudge with the toe of his moccasin. *"Femme!* Do you not listen to me? I asked you if this is not a pretty place."* His eyes skimmed the surrounding terrain when Blue Feather merely nodded her dark head. A smile curled his lips at the corners as Jardin reflected that he had at last arrived at the mysterious place he had heard about long ago in Quebec. So this was it—the place where Duvalle and Cheney had discovered gold, then argued over it. *Imbecile!* he thought. Cheney had been an imbecile! He should have killed Duvalle and taken the gold, but no, he had let Duvalle run him off. Old Cheney had lived alone in the woods, mad and forgotten. Now, Pierre Duvalle himself must have gone mad also, for he hid in the mountains with his gold. Any sane man would have taken the gold and gone to Canada, or to St. Louis. Perhaps Duvalle's greed had driven him too mad to bother with the gold.

Another sneer curled his upper lip as he turned back to Blue Feather. He would force Duvalle to give him the gold and reveal the source. If the old man refused, he would threaten to kill his daughter and grandchildren. It was that simple. And if Duvalle still balked, then he would carry out his threat without a qualm.

"Where is Duvalle's lodge?" Jardin asked, nudging Blue Feather again.

She thought for a moment, trying to recall Gray Eagle's instructions. There was no thought of refusing. Her children's lives depended upon Jardin's mood. When Jardin frowned at her, she said, "On the east bank is a lightning-struck tree. Follow the bent branch south, then find the path among the rocks. Walk straight into the mountain and you will find the lodge. . . ."

"Walk straight into . . . hey, what is this, *femme?* You would not lie to Ramone? Because if you do . . ."

"No, no, I do not lie to you. It is what was told to me by Gray Eagle. You will see it is true."

Scowling, Jardin commanded, "Then you ride first, *petite femme.* I will follow."

Blue Feather gathered her reins and nudged her pony down the slope leading to the lake. Dense bushes and thorny brambles almost hid the path, and she went slowly. Already weary and discouraged, Blue Feather knew that the worst was yet to come. Ahead lay her father's lodge, and he did not know that she brought evil with her to his home. He was unaware that his daughter brought death in the form of Ramone Jardin. Yet how could she refuse? How could she warn him? She could not. It was a difficult choice, but the lives to two small girls who had yet to live were of more importance in the grand scheme of life than an old man and herself. Somehow she had to do whatever was necessary to ensure their safety.

Holding Star more tightly to her chest, Blue Feather glanced down at Blue in her cradle board. The child's eyes were screwed tightly shut, and her small mouth was puckered in a bud of protest as the long grasses and thorny branches raked across her little face. Gasping, Blue Feather reached to lift Blue, but found it almost impossible to hold Star and safely haul up the cradle board.

"Jardin! Jardin, I must stop the grass from cutting her face," she called over her shoulder, and he swore softly.

"*Non!* And quiet those brats!" he added in a fierce tone. "We must surprise the old man."

"I cannot. I told you, the grass is cutting her face. We must stop for a moment," she insisted.

An impatient snort accompanied Jardin's forward motion as he reached for Blue in her cradle board. "Give her to me! I will stop her from crying. . . ."

Blue Feather grabbed for the child, but Jardin held her out of reach, dangling her in the cradle board, his smile cruel as he added, "You will be more agreeable now, I think, eh?"

Azure eyes snapped with fury as she faced him boldly. "If you harm her, I shall kill you, Frenchman."

"Oho! Shall you, *petite femme?* That will be a sight to see," Jardin sneered. "No, I think that now you shall do exactly as I say, that is what I think!"

Impotent rage swelled as Blue Feather gave a terse nod of her head. "*Oui,* I shall do as you say. Only do not harm the child."

"Ah, that is much better! Now lead on."

Helpless to rescue Blue—who was quiet now and gazing up at Jardin with curious eyes—Blue Feather nudged her mount forward again. She followed the path to the water's edge, then followed the lake shore to the east bank. The stark bare branches of a dead tree jutted skyward, clacking with a skeletal sound in the wind. The upper half of the tree had crashed to the ground, and a huge limb pointed to the south like a blackened finger. Her horse halted at the edge of a narrow loop of the lake, snorting skittishly, and Blue Feather urged it forward.

Splashing through the shallow fringe of water,

she crossed the small jetty and clambered up onto the opposite bank and waited for Jardin. He was right behind her, cursing his belabored mount in French. His dark eyes narrowed as he demanded, "Do you know where you go, *femme?*"

"*Oui.*"

Leaning forward, balancing the cradle board across his lap, Jardin squinted into the distance. "I see nothing," he said flatly.

"You are not supposed to see it. That is why it is so well hidden," Blue Feather pointed out. "My father would not be so foolish as to have a lodge anyone could find. You must know that, for you have searched for it long enough."

"True." Jardin grinned wickedly. "I should have thought of this long ago. I would not have wasted so much time looking in empty caves. And perhaps you would now be married to me instead of that pale Englishman, eh?"

Giving him a sour glance, Blue Feather drummed her heels against her mare's flanks. "I do not think so," she said as the horse moved forward.

"Then perhaps I shall just take you as my wife now," he replied with a throaty chuckle.

"You would always have to look over your shoulder. My husband would always be behind you, Jardin."

"And so? That might be good for me," Jardin said with a deep laugh. "I have been thinking about this husband of yours, *petite femme.*" He slid a sly glance in her direction and grinned. "If he followes—which he will surely do—then I shall kill him. It is so simple, no?"

"Simple enough to say, but not so simple to do," Blue Feather retorted.

"Ah, and was it not simple enough to kill Broken Arm? It was easy, like taking food from a baby, no?"

Shivering with a sudden chill of premonition, Blue Feather tried not to listen to him. Could this wicked Frenchman kill her beloved Adrian? Nothing in his life was certain but death—perhaps she should not be so confident. Perhaps over-confidence would only tempt the gods to rebuke her for her insolence. Adrian was only a man, and like all men, must one day die. She had thought him lost to her once, and he had been given back. Perhaps that had been just a gift of time from the gods, and now he must face his destiny. Death was so easy. It was the living that was hard, she mused as she urged her horse up the rocky slope of a steep bank.

Ahead of her was a seemingly impenetrable wall of gray slab. It rose not fifty feet from where they now stood on the crest of a ridge, and Jardin began cursing again.

"You stupid *femme!* This is not the way! You have lied to Ramone. . . ."

"*Non, non,*" she assured him. "This is the way. Come."

Still cursing, Jardin followed as Blue Feather led the way, and when it appeared that she would have to ride her horse directly into the mountainside, she veered sharply to the right and disappeared. Mouth agape, Jardin spurred his horse faster, and when he reached the spot where she had vanished, he saw the wide cleft in the rock. It had appeared as no more than a shadow on the face of the wall, yet behind it was a narrow pathway through the mountain. He saw her waiting on him, and he grinned as he followed.

The path was short, and led to a green valley filled with trees and winding streams. When they emerged into the sunshine, Jardin held out the cradle board. "Take your brat. I shall lead now," he said.

Wiling to let him, Blue Feather just nodded as she grabbed Blue and held her tightly.

Sunlight glinted from the blade of an axe as it was lifted high, then flashed down to split a wedge of wood in two. The man hefting the axe paused to wipe his forehead, and he squinted up at the late sunshine. Piercing blue eyes narrowed against the glare, and he pushed back a strand of gray hair still sprinkled with reminders of the blond color it had once been. His lean frame had not bent with age, though his shoulders were slightly stooped, and his arms were stringy with muscle. Though of medium height, he gave the impression of being much taller. His gray beard was neatly trimmed, and his buckskin garments were clean and well-mended. A smile of satisfaction curved his mouth as he bent, lifted another log, and placed it on the thick tree stump serving as a block. The sound of the striking axe rang loudly in the air, echoing across the valley.

It was only when he had once more paused to lift another log that Pierre Duvalle heard the approaching riders. Still holding the axe in one gnarled hand, he reached for his rifle with the other. It was brought up in a smooth, almost careless motion, the deadly eye of the muzzle pointing at the burly man riding lead.

"Comment vous appelez-vous, monsieur?" Pierre rasped out, keeping his rifle aimed as the man drew

close and stopped.

"Ramone Jardin . . ."

"I do not know a Ramone Jardin" came the cool answer, delivered with an equally cool glance. *"Où êtes-vous né?"*

"I am from Quebec, Monsieur Duvalle. . . ."

"Ah, you know me?" Duvalle returned in English. "I do not know you."

Gesturing to the girl half-hidden behind him on the narrow path, Jardin nudged his mount a step closer and said, "No, but perhaps you know your daughter."

Now Duvalle could see around Jardin's thick-set body, and he recognized his daughter. The beginning of a smile curled his lips, but he still did not lower his rifle. He had learned to be wary during the years, and there was something too intent and feral about this Jardin.

"Welcome, my daughter," Duvalle said. "It has been many moons since we have seen one another."

"And do you greet all your children with loaded rifles?" Jardin asked pointedly, but Duvalle ignored him for the moment.

The old French-Canadian was gazing at Blue Feather, noting her strained expression and thin smile, the two children she held, and her drooping mount. They had ridden hard to arrive, and he wondered briefly how she had found him. He flicked a glance from his daughter and grandchildren to Jardin, then back. Her husband? Possibly, though the child he could clearly see bore curls as blond as his had once been. The child in the cradle board was hidden by the wood and leather frame, but he could hear annoyed sounds. A slight smile flickered, then faded. How like her mother Blue

Feather was. Running Moon had been beautiful, a slender half-breed Shoshoni girl with huge doe eyes who had captured his heart so long ago. Their daughter was just as lovely, with eyes the same blue as his own.

The muzzle of his rifle lowered to point at the ground. As Blue Feather met his gaze, he noted a troubled expression in the depths of her azure eyes, and he frowned. She had not yet greeted him, and sat her pony with an air of tense expectancy. A familiar prickle tugged at the hair on the back of his neck, and Duvalle slid his gaze back to Jardin. He wasn't surprised to see a rifle levelled at him.

"You come as an enemy?" Duvalle asked mildly.

"Only if you wish it that way, monsieur."

"Ahh, I see." Duvalle's gaze sliced to his daughter, who was staring at him beseechingly. "You bring this man to my camp, daughter?"

She nodded. *"Ai,* but not willingly. I was forced."

Accepting her obvious explanation, Duvalle gave a short nod of his head. "Then this man is not your husband—"

"No! He is not. He is no one!" Blue Feather blurted. "I am sorry to bring this evil into your camp—"

"Hey!" Jardin protested. He waggled the rifle ominously and scowled. "Enough of this talk, talk, talk! We go and sit by your fire, old man. I have much of importance to discuss with you. Ah-ah! You will leave your rifle here, *s'il vous plaît."* Duvalle's rifle dropped slowly to the ground. *"Merci,"* Jardin said with a wide grin. "We go now."

When Jardin motioned for Blue Feather to follow her father, she nudged the pony forward, still holding tightly to her daughters. Her heart ached as she watched Duvalle walk with his back straight and his head held high. He was too old, and should not have had this evil brought upon him like this. To see his daughter again after so many seasons, and to have her bring such trouble to his lodge, must be hard indeed, Blue Feather thought sadly.

It was even harder for her, for when she reached Pierre Duvalle's sturdy cabin and he motioned for them to enter, she thought of the lodge she had once shared with both of her parents. It had been a brush wickiup full of love, and she remembered winter nights spent before the fire with her parents and brother. There had been laughter and teasing, and long stories told while the snow piled thickly around their snug little shelter. Memories flooded back, and she wondered if her father ever thought of those times. It had been so hard on him when her mother had died, leaving him with two small children, and he had left them with the old women of the tribe and retreated into the mountains with his grief. So many seasons ago, and now it was just Duvalle and herself.

Star and Blue squirmed in her arms, and Blue Feather looked down at the fretful children. No, there were more children now, more to fill another winter lodge with laughter and love. Pierre Duvalle should share in this, should be given the chance to know his daughter and his grandchildren. This thought was still in her mind when they sat down at the crude wooden table dominating the one-room cabin.

"Now, old man," Jardin began, lifting his rifle and holding it across the table's scarred surface. "You will tell me what I wish to know."

Duvalle's lips twisted. "And what do you wish to

know, rude one?"

Ignoring the insult, Jardin leaned forward and licked his lips, his dark eyes glittering. A branch in the low-burning fire snapped in two and sent up a shower of sparks as he said hoarsely, "Gold! I wish to know about the gold."

Gray brows lifted, and Duvalle just stared at him for a moment. "What gold are you speaking about? I know of no gold. . . ."

"*Non!* Do not be fooled into thinking I will hear any stupid talk, old one! I *know* there is gold!" Sitting back in his chair, Jardin regarded Duvalle with a narrowed gaze. "It is useless to think I will not do what I say I will do, and I *will* find out about the gold."

Spreading his hands, Duvalle shrugged. "I cannot help you, monsieur."

Jardin's rifle barrel smashed across the table, startling Blue Feather so that she jumped in spite of herself, and frightening the children into wailing loudly. "I do not have time for your games!" Jardin snarled. "I must have an answer! *Femme,* get me some food while I talk to this stubborn old man."

Conditioned to obey without question, Blue Feather rose and set the children in the chair. The past four days had been harrowing enough without causing more trouble, and she quietly shushed the sniffling girls with words of comfort. While she prepared some food, she could think, could plan on what to do.

"There is rabbit stew in the pot over the fire," Duvalle said without taking his eyes from Jardin. "And I have coffee in the tin on the shelf."

"No, I want whisky," Jardin said, indicating a stone jug atop a shelf. "Bring me that now!"

462

After a brief hesitation, Blue Feather complied. She slammed the heavy jug to the tabletop, keeping a wary eye on the Frenchman.

Jardin was pulling a pistol from his wide leather belt and holding it in one hand while he carefully unloaded the rifle. "A pistol is easier to handle, eh?" he said, looking at Duvalle with a catlike smile. "In such close range, a rifle, it would make such a *big* mess. What do you think?"

"I think you do not care to know my thoughts," Duvalle replied shortly. He folded his arms across his chest with deliberate motions, tucking his hands into his armpits as he regarded Jardin with the expression normally reserved for a skunk.

"Ah, but there you are wrong. I *do* wish to know your thoughts, old man. In fact, I insist upon it." Leaning forward again, he said softly, "If you desire to see your daughter and her brats stay alive, you will tell me what I wish to know."

"And if I do not care?"

"Pah!" Jardin made a disgusted motion with his hands. "Do not think you can fool me, old man! I have seen the look in your eyes when you look at your girl, and at her puling infants, too! You will do as I say."

Busily stirring the stew, Blue Feather recognized the game her father was playing. She studied the bubbling pot and wondered if she would be able to distract Jardin long enough for Duvalle to get his gun. But perhaps her father was too old and slow to be able to do such a thing, she thought in the next instant. Regretfully, she put the idea aside as Jardin demanded his meal.

Putting the wooden bowl of stew in front of him, Blue Feather turned to lift her girls into her arms, but he put out a hand to stop her.

"*Non!* You will go and fetch a rope for me." He gave her a shove with his foot. "Hurry. I will feel better when the old man is tied."

Knotting her hands into tight fists, Blue Feather just nodded as she walked to the door of the cabin. As she reached it Jardin said, "And if you entertain any notions of running away, *cherie,* do not forget my promise to take care of your babies for you, eh?"

A cold chill shivered down her back, and she just nodded as she complied. She was trapped as neatly as a beaver snared in the steel jaws of a vise. The sun was low in the sky, and when she stepped out into the fresh air, she choked on the hot tears clogging her throat. There was nothing she could do to help them, nothing. She was too afraid for her children and her father. *Oh Adrian,* she thought silently, *why do you not come to me? Where are you?*

Ramone Jardin had Blue Feather tie her father's wrists and ankles as he watched. Because she knew he would test the knots, she tied them tightly, her eyes sorrowful as she glanced up and met her father's understanding gaze.

"I am sorry," she said in Shoshoni, and he nodded.

"I understand, daughter. You are only doing what you must."

"Hey!" Jardin demanded. "Speak in French! I do not parley the Shoshoni tongue as well, and I must know what you are saying."

As she knelt before the chair Duvalle sat upon, Blue Feather wound the rope as loosely as possible. Keeping her head bent and her gaze on her clumsy

464

fingers, she murmured as loudly as she dared, "My husband will come soon. He will bring Gray Eagle and save us. . . ."

"Husband?"

"*Ai*. He is white man—English. Broken Arm called him Duke, but his name is—"

Duvalle gave a start. "Broken Arm? He is with them?"

She shook her head. "No. He is dead, killed by that one." Her head jerked toward the Frenchman, and she added bitterly, "He was trying to help me, trying to save me from Jardin, but—"

Sneering, Jardin broke in, *"Oui,* listen well, old man! I killed the old trapper, and I will kill you if you do not heed my words!"

"Broken Arm," Duvalle repeated slowly. His gaze lifted to the swarthy Frenchman who was leaning back in his chair and gloating. "He was once my friend, a brother. . . ."

"Well, now he is a dead friend and brother," Jardin said as he tilted up the stone jug of whisky. He kept an eye on them as he drank, and it spilled from his mouth and onto his shirtfront. Lowering the jug, he belched loudly. "Do not grieve overlong, Duvalle. Your time may be at hand if you do not tell me what I want to hear."

After Blue Feather tied the last knot, she stood up, hiding her trembling hands in her dirty cotton skirts. Duvalle said softly, "Do not despair, my daughter. All will be well."

"Not unless you tell me where to find that gold," Jardin grated as he leaned forward again, propping his elbows on the scarred wooden table.

"Gold, gold, gold! Pah!" Duvalle spat. "Gold is evil; it drives men mad, makes them lust after what

465

they cannot have. I have seen what it does to men, seen what it did to my old friend Cheney, and now you defile my home with your greed and lust for it!" Dragging in a deep breath, Duvalle continued, "Men lie, cheat and die for it, and you come here prepared to kill for it. Ah, so be it! I shall show you tomorrow—"

Rising, Jardin kicked back his chair. *"Non!* I must know now! There is little time to waste!"

"It is too well-hidden to tell you," Duvalle argued reasonably. "I shall have to take you, and it will soon be night. It cannot be found in the dark, *comprenez-vous?"* Steady blue eyes did not waver, even though Jardin raged and blustered, and when the Frenchman finally subsided to low mutters and imprecations, Duvalle added, "We can leave at first light tomorrow, if you like."

"Pah!" Kicking a table leg in his frustration, Jardin snarled, "At first light, old man!"

A feeling of relief washed over Blue Feather, and she kept her gaze averted from Jardin so he would not see. Her father had managed to stall for time, time for Adrian and Gray Eagle to find them. With weak knees and shaking hands, she managed to feed her children and do her best to clean them with the tepid water she found in an old oaken bucket. There was very little protest from the girls. The day's activities had left them exhausted. Once fed, they fell asleep, and she placed them gently on Duvalle's cot at one side of the cabin.

The entire time she was tending her children, Jardin watched her with a brooding gaze. He drank heavily from the stone jug, wiping his mouth with the back of his hand and ignoring the whisky he spilled on his clothes. The pistol lay on the table by his hand, and occasionally he would lift it and point the muzzle at Duvalle to see if he would flinch. The old trapper just stared straight ahead, not letting Jardin guess his thoughts.

The fat fool of a Frenchman! Duvalle raged silently. If Jardin thought he would be rich, he was sadly mistaken. Duvalle wanted to laugh, yet dared not. Let Jardin discover for himself what kind of gold was in the mountain. Let him dig and dig for it, sweat and work and dream, and then see his dreams crumble into dust! It would be such irony, such a sweet irony, that Duvalle almost wished Gray Eagle would not find them before he had shown Jardin the *gold*.

Glowering, Ramone Jardin gulped another burning draught of whiskey, letting it trickle down his throat like liquid fire. Damn Duvalle! Damn the girl, damn them all! His fortune was so close, just out of his reach, and now he must wait—when there might be no more time. The Englishman and the Shoshoni chief would be close behind him. He had almost felt them at his back the entire four days of travel, had stayed awake nights not daring to sleep for fear he would be awakened with a scalping knife. And now that he was here, he had to wait through the long, dark night. It was too much, and he felt as if he would burst with frustration.

"Femme!" he bellowed, startling Blue Feather into jerking up from her seat before the fire. She just looked at him, her pale eyes lit with loathing, and he slammed his meaty fist to the tabletop, jarring the pistol. *"Femme,* you come here to Ramone," he snarled.

Pierre Duvalle watched helplessly, twisting his

hands against his bonds. Blue Feather, whom he had last seen as a young girl, was now a young woman, and he regretted that he could not help her. He regretted the years away from her, years when he could have been with her, and now he might not have another chance. He had been afraid to love, afraid to show love to anyone after the tragedy of his wife's death, and then his son's. So he had not. He had abandoned his only living child, and now he could do nothing to help her. All he could do was grind his teeth and watch.

Moving across the dirt floor of the cabin with silent dignity, Blue Feather paused just out of Jardin's reach. Her chin was lifted proudly, and her eyes were grave as she regarded him with contempt. "What do you want?" she asked.

"Ah, what a question to ask of me, *ma petite chou*," he purred with a leering smile. "I want . . . many things." One hand lifted, and he beckoned her closer. When she did not respond he scowled, demanding, "Come closer!"

Blue Feather took a single step closer, her gaze wary. "What do you want of me?" she asked again. Her lithe body was poised for flight as she sensed Jardin was getting drunk and ugly.

A big hand flashed out with surprising speed, grasping her wrist and jerking her into his arms. His fetid breath wafted across her face as he pressed her against him, holding her squirming body as easily as she held one of her children. "Ah, *petite fleur*, you are so soft, so sweet to hold —"

"And you are a pig!" she raged, pushing hard against him with the heels of her hands. When she realized her efforts were only encouraging him, she raked her fingers across his face, leaving crimson

468

streaks above his scraggly beard. Howling with pain, Jardin released her, his hand crashing across her face as he pushed her from his lap.

Stunned, Blue Feather lay crumpled on the dirt floor of the cabin, only vaguely aware of her father's lunge from his chair. Duvalle surged upward, throwing himself at the Frenchman, only to be sent crashing to the floor close to his daughter.

Holding his face and muttering, Jardin lifted the stone jug for another swallow of whisky, then peered at the pair through narrowed eyes. "You think to fight Ramone, eh? You, an old man and a squaw! Pah! I laugh at you! I am Ramone Jardin, and I will soon be a wealthy man, a man who will travel in gold coaches and have all the women he wants. You refuse me, *femme?* You, a filthy Shoshoni squaw? There will be many who want Ramone Jardin, who beg for my favors, and you dare to refuse me!"

Lifting her aching head, Blue Feather stared at him through bleary eyes. His face was a blur, and his words were echoing loudly in her ears as she shook her head to clear it. She was only vaguely aware of her father's effort to stand, and Jardin once more knocking him to the floor with the butt of his pistol.

"Papa?" she quavered as her vision cleared and she saw the blood on her father's face. "Papa? Are you all right?"

Moaning, Duvalle lay on his side. Blood trickled down his face from the cut inflicted by Jardin's pistol, and he shook his head slowly from side to side.

"Papa!" she screamed as Jardin reached down to lift her from the floor and into his embrace. Pure, murderous fury enveloped her as she felt Jardin's hands pushing up her skirt, tearing at her blouse, and she found a strength she hadn't known she possessed. To try and take her, here, with her father lying wounded on the floor and her babies asleep across the room—it revolted and enraged her, and she reacted with a wildly swinging blow that took Jardin by surprise.

He staggered back, his broad, flat features creased in a ludicrous expression of shock. Blue Feather was half-crouched, her lips drawn back in a feral snarl and her eyes glittering with hatred. *"Cochon!"* she hissed.

"Pig? *Mais oui,* my little Shoshoni squaw, I am a pig indeed! And this pig shall take you whether you like it or not . . . but I think you shall," he added with a leering glance that burned her like hot coals.

Fumbling for a weapon of some kind, Blue Feather crept crablike away from him, scuttling across the floor and groping for one of the logs she had seen earlier. But Jardin was upon her before she could snatch it up. His hands wrapped around her arms and dragged her up. She gagged as his mouth covered hers in a sour kiss, and though she tried to wrench away, she could not. Jardin's hands tore at her clothes, and she dimly heard the rending tear of cloth.

Held tightly against him with her hands pinned between them, Blue Feather's first reflex was to bring her knee jerking up. Though she missed her intended target, she did manage to startle him into relaxing his grip. When she twisted away he reached out to catch her by the back of her blouse, ripping it. A sob tore from her throat as she was yanked backward, and she felt his hands splay across her

470

bared breasts.

Jardin grunted hoarsely, shoving his body against her so hard that she could feel his outline even though her skirts. "And now, *femme,* you will undress for Ramone," he grated in her ear. "If you do not, I will kill first your *pauvre papa,* then your sleeping babies. . . ."

"Jardin!" came a croak from the floor, and the Frenchman turned a contemptuous glance to Duvalle.

"What do you want, old man? Do you want to watch while I—"

"Jardin, the gold . . ." Duvalle coughed weakly, then added, "the gold . . . it is useless. Only fool's gold . . . do not do this for such a worthless—"

"Quiet!" Jardin howled, his grip tightening on Blue Feather. "You lie, old man! Why do you lie to Ramone? There is gold; I know there is gold! You only try to distract me, but I am no fool!"

Furious and raging, Jardin threw Blue Feather across the room and turned to land a swift kick in Duvalle's back. He was filled with fury, and spittle flew from his mouth as he raged. Again and again he kicked Duvalle, until finally Blue Feather threw herself at him with a wild cry. She had grasped the heavy metal spoon from the cooking pot, but Jardin knocked it from her hands with a contemptuous ease. His large hand aimed a careless swipe that sent her staggering, and he turned his attention back to the trussed man lying on the floor. Blue Feather once more flung herself at Jardin, clinging to him with desperate anguish.

"No more! Do not . . . you will kill him!" she cried, half-sobbing and wishing she had a gun, a knife, anything to make him stop. But Jardin had the pistol and knife in his belt, and there was nothing she could do.

"Ah, so you decide you want me after all, *femme?*" Jardin crowed triumphantly. " I knew you would . . . *oui,* I knew you would come to Ramone. . . ."

With a swift movement, he tore her blouse from her body and tossed it aside. The cool air in the cabin washed over her dusky skin and made her shiver and attempt to cross her arms over her chest. Jardin pulled them away, holding her slender arms out to the side as his eyes devoured her quivering breasts. *"Sacre bleu!"* he breathed hoarsely, "it has been so long, and you are a prize to have!" He grinned as she attempted to twist away from him, and his dark, shaggy head slowly lowered.

Tilting back her head, Blue Feather gave a long, despairing cry as Jardin's lips began to explore her bared breasts with hot, greedy kisses.

Chapter 24
Justice

The fading shadows lay softly on Blue Lake, blurring the outline of trees and rocky peaks with gentle colors of rose and purple. Gray Eagle nudged his spotted horse into the shallow waters and splashed across the fringe of the lake. It had been a long time since he had been here, but he still remembered the way. His mind flicked back to the years before, when he had come here with his old friend and cousin, Blue Feather's brother. They had visited Duvalle then, two young boys out for fine hunting and high adventure. He remembered Duvalle as quiet and aloof, a man who was not afraid of man or animal. Duvalle's son had desired to be like him, and perhaps would have been chief one day if he had lived. Instead, he had been killed in a Crow raid, and it was now Gray Eagle who was chief, who led The People. It was a great responsibility.

Now he must find his little cousin, Duvalle's daughter. He knew the trail, had known that the Frenchman must be coming here and had planned on being here before him. If not for the temporary laming of his horse, he would have done so. But his spotted pony had stepped into a hole, and they had been delayed. Now the evil Jardin would have already arrived, and the element of surprise was gone. He must plan a new attack, Gray Eagle thought as he trotted up the steep slope to the crest.

Lifting his head, Gray Eagle gestured for those following to stop, and Adrian, Harry, and the Shoshoni brave known as Never Laughs, came to a halt. "It is just ahead," Gray Eagle said, pointing to the sheer rock wall rising abruptly before them.

Adrian and Harry exchanged glances. "Just ahead?" Adrian repeated, squinting up at the rocky face. "Where?"

Gray Eagle did not answer but drummed moccasined heels into his pony's sides. The animal snorted and surged forward. Watching, Adrian was startled to see Gray Eagle turn right and suddenly disappear from sight.

"My lord?" Harry asked with a gasp. "Did you see that?"

"Yes, Harry, I did," Adrian answered, then nudged his horse forward also. "Perhaps we had better follow."

Never Laughs brought up the rear, his dun prancing nervously behind Harry's small mare. His copper face was impassive, showing no reaction whatsoever, and Harry muttered to himself that the blasted Shoshoni must have stone for faces. Nonetheless, he clung to his mare and doggedly followed Adrian in what seemed to the older man like sheer folly.

"My heavens!" Harry gasped when he saw the narrow crevice cut into the mountain. Hooves clattered over the shale floor as they trotted through the short passageway and into a beautiful green valley that seemed protected from the ravages of time. As dusk lowered deep shadows over the land, the four horsemen emerged into the soft-scented hollow. "What a lovely glen," Harry remarked as he drew his mare to a halt beside Adrian.

"Yes. But it seems deserted," Adrian replied, gazing at the log cabin across the valley. It was nestled beneath a rock overhang and surrounded by towering pines on two sides, and he could see no sign of activity. "What do you think?" he asked Gray Eagle.

"They are here" was the reply as the Shoshoni chief pointed to hoofprints cut into the ground. "Two horses have passed this way."

"Recently?"

Gray Eagle nodded. *"Ai."*

Taking a deep breath, Adrian's eyes narrowed on the cabin. "Then they are in the cabin. Remember that Jardin is mine—*only* mine. I intend to do what I should have already done. If I had, Blue Feather and my children would not be in danger now."

"Do not berate yourself, my lord," Harry said softly. "You could not have known."

"Perhaps not, but I should have listened to Broken Arm," Adrian returned bitterly. "He was much wiser than I was. . . ."

"Again, you cannot chastise yourself for being prudent, my lord. After all, you were not brought up to be savage and brutal."

"No, but I should have remembered that we are in a savage and oftentimes brutal land. There can be little compromise at such times." Adrian glanced at Gray Eagle, who was giving Never Laughs instructions in Shoshoni. "What are our plans?" he asked when Gray Eagle turned back to face him. "Do we rush in, or do you have another plan?"

"To rush in would be effective if it were not for my cousin and her children. Never Laughs will stay

475

here, to guard the only way of escaping the valley. He will kill the Frenchman if we fail." Pausing, Gray Eagle shifted on his pony and gazed consideringly at the cabin again. Thick smoke poured from the rock chimney, but there was no sign of life. "We go in thus," he said after a moment, making motions with his hands to indicate splitting up and approaching from different directions. "I will go in the front way, while you go in from the rear."

"Is there a door in the back?" Adrian asked as he slid from his horse.

"No, but there is a window. It may be latched with a leather thong at the bottom. Do you have a knife?" When Adrian nodded, Gray Eagle gave a grunt of satisfaction. "A knife is always useful should a gun misfire."

The horses were given to Never Laughs, and the three men checked their weapons. Dry powder was poured into the pistols and rifles, and the firing caps were inspected. Adrian unlatched the strap on the beaded sheath of his knife, and Harry tucked his loaded pistol into the waistband of his frayed trousers.

The high mountain peaks surrounding the valley were gilded with golden light, while shadows deepened in the hollow. It was time. Gray Eagle gave the signal, and they moved forward, cautiously keeping to the cover of the thick trees and bushes. The Shoshoni chief swung to the left, and Adrian and Harry to the right. They were to converge on the deceptively peaceful cabin at the same time.

Adrian's throat was dry, and his heart thudded almost painfully in his chest as he wondered if Blue Feather was unharmed. She had to be. He couldn't lose her again. Not again.

Leafy branches whipped against his face as he

crept forward, and he could hear Harry's harsh, rasping breaths behind him. As he drew near the cabin, Adrian lowered to his belly to pull himself forward with his elbows. The bushes had thinned, and he didn't want to risk being seen before Gray Eagle gave the signal. Harry hung slightly back to his left, and Adrian lay there, a knife in one hand and his pistol ready. He would wait for the signal, then move to the rear and go in through the window as planned. But in the next instant his resolve was tested. A high, thin wail cut through the air like the despairing cry of a doomed animal, and he recognized Blue Feather's cry.

Frozen, Adrian felt a cold rage sweep through him, and he half-rose with a growl deep in his throat.

"My lord!" Harry whispered frantically. "Not yet, my lord! Oh, do wait for the signal. . . ."

"That's Blue Feather's voice!" Adrian hissed over his shoulder.

"I know" was the miserable answer. "But we must wait or we may do her even more harm."

Recognizing the sense in what Harry was saying, Adrian glanced across the cabin yard to find Gray Eagle. The chief had paused, having heard the cry, and he could barely be seen behind a huge tree stump used as a block for chopping wood. It appeared that Duvalle had been interrupted in the midst of his work, for an axe was imbedded in a partially hewn log. Clenching his hands, Adrian waited and sweated. His mouth was compressed into a tight line, and his gaze was glacial as he watched the cabin intently.

Finally Gray Eagle moved forward, stealthily, his feet soundlessly crossing the cabin yard. He paused just outside the door and waited, jerking his arm once to indicate that Adrian should act.

It was all the fair Englishman needed. Surging to his feet, he ran across the yard in a half-crouch, his muscles tensed. Brushing against the rough bark of the log walls, he rounded the corner of the cabin and found the window. It was closed, Leather hinges attached it at the top, so that to close it, it had to be swung down and latched from the inside. It was a window obviously meant to keep out only forest creatures, not a man, and Adrian slid his knife under the edge. His fingers groped for the rawhide thong that would be holding it closed, and he cursed softly under his breath when he could not find it.

Gray Eagle gingerly tested the front door and found that it was not barred. A shadow of a smile flickered for a moment on his lips as he placed his palm flat against the rough surface and pushed.

Arching her back, Blue Feather was attempting to push Jardin away with one knee, but he half-turned his body so that her efforts were futile. His mouth was fastened to the peak of her breast, his teeth worrying the tender flesh and making her cry out in pain. Grunting, Jardin's breath fanned hotly across her skin as he hooked one leg behind her ankles and jerked. The movement brought Blue Feather crashing to the floor with Jardin's heavy bulk atop her, crushing the breath from her lungs.

Winded, she struggled for air as he pushed at her skirt, tearing it in his haste to push it aside. Blue Feather's naked shoulder blades pressed against the cold dirt floor as she shrank from him, writhing and twisting helplessly. Dragging in a ragged gulp of air, she screamed out in rage and pain at him, pounding at the Frenchman's back with her knotted fists. Laughing, he ignored her as he fumbled with the wide leather belt holding up his trousers.

"Ah, *cherie*," he muttered hoarsely, "I will have you at last!"

It was at that instant that the door flew open, jerking Jardin's attention upward. His hand was near the long knife in his belt, and he brought it up in a smooth, instinctive reaction.

Though he lunged to one side, Gray Eagle could not avoid the swiftly flung knife. It caught him in the shoulder and he pitched forward onto the dirt floor only inches from where a horrified Blue Feather was lying. She screamed again, a loud, animal wail that echoed in the rafters.

Outside, Adrian heard her scream and renewed his efforts to find and slice the leather thong holding shut the log window. Sweat streamed down his face as he could not find it, and he snarled in frustration, looking up at the sturdy, heavy shutter. Then, with a few quick slashes of his razor-sharp knife blade, he simply sliced the leather hinges in two and the window fell into his arms.

As Adrian clambered through the window, his gaze fell on his nearly nude wife as she cowered on the floor. Rage made him clumsy, and he surged forward only to stumble and drop his pistol. It skittered across the dirt floor out of his reach. As he recovered his balance, Adrian's quick, sweeping gaze flicked to Gray Eagle's still form. His mouth tightened. There was another man who lay inert and quiet, a rope tying his wrists and ankles.

The Frenchman was scrambling for his own pistol, which had somehow fallen to the floor in his struggle with Blue Feather. A triumphant smile curled his mouth as Jardin lifted it and turned in a smooth, easy roll, levelling it at the Englishman.

"Adrian!" Blue Feather screamed in warning. She

lashed out desperately with one bare foot, missing the pistol but striking Jardin's arm so that the bullet plowed harmlessly into the cabin wall.

"Bitch!" Jardin snarled, cuffing her with the back of his hand as he leaped to his feet. Adrian made a flying jump at the Frenchman, catching him around the thick middle and sending them both crashing back to the floor. They grappled, rolling and grunting and cursing one another in French and English. Adrian was still gripping his knife, and he struggled to push the blade into his opponent. The wily Frenchman was more agile than he looked. Though he managed to avoid the lethal plunge of the knife as they wrestled, Jardin was soon criss-crossed with several long scratches from the tip.

Crouched on the floor, half-sobbing as she watched, Blue Feather gathered the tattered shreds of her skirt around her and stumbled to her feet. She cast around wildly for a weapon. Long streamers of tangled hair hung in her eyes, and she pushed it impatiently back as she groped on the floor for a knife or gun. She had seen one, had seen it fall somewhere, but now she could not find it—*Gray Eagle*. Her cousin had held a pistol in his hand when he'd crashed through the door. She whirled, whipping back the curtain of hair that covered her bare breasts, and reached out to her cousin. His pistol was still in his hand, cocked but unfired, and she pried it loose from his warm, unresisting fingers.

But as Blue Feather turned with the gun in her hand, lifting it, Jardin snatched it from her grasp. He had kicked Adrian away, and while the Englishman was rolling back to attack again, Jardin had seen Blue Feather. Now he laughed, a high-pitched, triumphant cackle that seared the air.

"So, English! You think to kill Ramone, *non?* But I kill you instead. . . ." His thumb flicked the cocked hammer, and it fired, exploding in a deafening roar that almost drowned out Blue Feather's scream as Adrian crumpled to a heap on the floor.

Sobbing hysterically, Blue Feather flew to her husband. His eyes were closed, and there was a large, spreading patch of blood on his buckskin shirt. He was still breathing, though it was shallow. Kneeling beside Adrian, she lifted streaming eyes to Jardin. He gloated evilly, his face creased in triumph and hatred as he looked down at her.

"So, *cherie* — what do you think will happen now, eh? Do you think I should kill you, or your brats first?" When her gaze flicked to the twins now huddled wide-awake and sobbing on the narrow cot, Jardin laughed at the expression in her eyes. "Ah, I see you cannot decide! So — shall I decide for you?" The muzzle of the pistol traced a path in the air, moving slowly to point at the little girls. "Do you still think I am a pig, *cherie?*" Jardin asked Blue Feather in a thoughtful tone. "Me? Look what I have done! I have killed your cousin and your husband without help! I — Ramone Jardin — have killed the great Gray Eagle and the man who lived with Cheney, and I shall be the most feared man in all of Wyoming Territory!" Throwing back his head, he laughed loudly.

Slowly rising to her feet, Blue Feather faced him with her chin lifted. She was desperate. She had to stop him from harming her children, and it didn't matter how it was done. Her bare, firm breasts thrust boldly out at him, and Jardin's hot gaze raked over her almost nude body. Filled with blood lust, he now felt a different kind of lust, and she could see it in the subtle change of his gaze. "Do

481

not hurt the children," she said quietly, "and I will go with you."

"Pah! What do I need a *femme* and her brats for?" Jardin demanded.

"We will leave the children," she said quickly. "I will go with you, Jardin, and be your woman."

His eyes narrowed as he looked at her. Sable hair draped over one shoulder and framed the dusky perfection of a breast, and he remembered the taste and feel of her. A smile slanted his mouth, and he licked his lips. The torn skirt hung from her slender hips in tatters, and he could see her rounded thighs and flat belly, the small dark mound that was tantalizingly out of reach. Blue Feather moved slightly, putting one leg provocatively forward, resting a hand on her hip and wetting her lips with the tip of her tongue as if in invitation, and Jardin succumbed. With a low roar of approval, he lunged forward at the same time as the cabin door swung open again.

There was a series of short clicks, then a muttered "dammit!" and the sound of a pistol being thrown to the cabin floor. A short, stocky figure leaped to wrap itself around Jardin, arms and legs flailing wildly, his lifted voice bellowing for Blue Feather to take the children and flee.

"Harry!" she breathed as she recognized the man atop Jardin's madly-circling body. The burly Frenchman would crush Harry, would throw him down and kill him as he had done all the others, and Blue Feather was momentarily paralyzed with fear.

"Run!" Harry shouted again, hanging desperately onto Jardin's broad shoulders, his arms circling the Frenchman's head and temporarily blinding him. "Run, and save the children! I can't hang on much longer. . . ."

Galvanized into action by Harry's plea, Blue Feather scurried across the cabin and snatched up the twins, one under each arm. Without pausing, she vaulted over the bodies on the floor and was out the door, running wildly to the safety of the bushes. There was no time to think, no time to plan. She had to save her children, but she could not let Harry die. What could she do? Her mind worked swiftly, and without pausing in stride, she deposited the girls into a thick copse of bushes and told them to stay until she came for them. They gazed up at her with barely comprehending eyes, and she repeated her command, silently praying that she would be able to return.

Harry was no longer astride Jardin when she returned to the cabin, but he was still struggling gamely. His face was red with strain, and he was panting for breath as the Frenchman slowly bore him to the ground with a strangling grasp of his hands around Harry's neck. Choking sounds emerged from his mouth, and he clawed frantically at the thick fingers circling his neck.

Leaping, Blue Feather was atop Jardin, her slender arms wrapping around his neck as she dug her knees into his back in an attempt to choke him. He bellowed with rage, sounding to Blue Feather like an angry buffalo bull. Stumbling in blind fury, Jardin tightened his grip on Harry's throat until the Englishman went limp. Releasing him, he turned his attention to the girl on his back.

He reached behind and grabbed a handful of long hair and yanked, pulling her over his shoulder and slamming her to the cabin floor. Blue Feather had tried to prepare herself, but it still knocked the wind from her for a moment. Rolling, she barely managed to avoid Jardin's kick. She could feel the wind from his foot as it passed only inches from her face, and she scrambled to her knees. A brief regret for the fate of her children passed through her mind, then she turned her attention back to Jardin. He would kill her now.

Bending, Jardin picked up Adrian's knife from the floor and balanced it in the palm of his hand as he smiled at Blue Feather. "You see, *femme?*" he asked softly. "I am invincible! You cannot kill me."

"I am sorry for that," she answered, tossing back her hair and gazing up at him. "You should be killed like a sick dog, for that is what you are. You are a sickness in this land, Jardin. You should be burned away as one would burn away any rotting, useless stench—"

"Enough!" Jardin roared. "I will hear no more! Now it is time for me to finish what I began, eh? And when I am through with you, you will beg for more," he grated as he stepped forward and pushed her slowly down. Though she resisted, she was powerless against his strength, and Blue Feather clenched her teeth together and prayed that he would finish quickly. A red, hazy mist clouded her brain as he loomed over her, and she thought of the clean blue sky and the green fields, anything but Ramone Jardin.

Then Jardin was gone suddenly, his burly form falling to one side, and Blue Feather blinked in surprise. Who . . . ? She twisted to her side and gazed in stunned amazement at the man straddling the Frenchman. "Adrian . . ."

Ignoring Blue Feather as he concentrated upon his hated enemy, Adrian Herenton gave a powerful kick with one foot, and the knife Jardin held went skittering across the cabin floor. It spun, gleaming in the dim light of the fire, a whirl of deadly steel just out of both men's reach. A grunt burst from Jardin as he lunged for the knife, but Adrian's heel crushed his hand to the floor.

"No, Jardin," he snarled, "it won't be that easy to kill me!"

"I thought you were already dead, English!" Jardin gasped as he tried to wrench away.

"You thought wrong. . . ." The words were softly-spoken, a whisper in the silence, but Jardin understood the message.

Sweat poured freely from him as he struggled, and he half-turned and tried to pull Adrian down with his free hand. Jardin's swarthy complexion was pasty with fear, and when he glanced up and saw the icy calm in Adrian's eyes, he sensed he was looking into the face of death.

"I wouldn't have hurt your woman," he whined as Adrian reached for him. "I only wanted the gold, I swear it!"

"You lie."

"Non! Non, that is the truth." He glanced at Blue Feather and pleaded, "Tell him, *cherie*—tell him I would not have hurt you. . . ."

Blue Feather's gaze was cold and stony, and she said nothing. Her expression changed to disgust as Jardin began weeping, copious tears flowing over his cheeks and wetting his beard, She turned her head away as Adrian released the Frenchman as if he had soiled his hands by touching him.

While Jardin knelt before Adrian with his head bent, tears flowing and his sobs rending the air, Adrian glanced at his wife. Though bruised and scratched, she did not seem hurt, and some of his anger ebbed.

"I cannot kill an unarmed man," he said coldly.

"And it would be too easy for you if I did. No, I shall take you to the nearest magistrate and watch you hang, Jardin. That will be infinitely more satisfying, knowing that you will sit and wait for your death." Adrian took a deliberate step back and reached for a strip of leather hanging from a peg on the wall.

As he did, Jardin lunged for the knife still slowly spinning on the cabin floor. It was the moment Adrian had been waiting for—hoping for. When the Frenchman straightened with the knife in his hand, he met the hard thrust of Adrian's blade in his belly. Jardin's eyes widened, and his fingers loosened on the hilt of the knife he held. Adrian thrust deeper, his gaze locked with Jardin's as he twisted his knife and then jerked upward. The knife Jardin held dropped to the cabin floor, its point stabbing into the dirt and its hilt quivering.

Jardin's mouth opened but no sound came out. His lips worked soundlessly, and his eyes bulged. He was dead while still standing, and his body sagged uselessly against Adrian.

Stunned, Blue Feather recognized the method used by the Blackfeet and wondered where her husband had learned it, then she looked away. She heard the heavy thud of Jardin's body hitting the packed earth of the cabin floor, but still she could not look. It was only when Adrian came to her and knelt beside her that she could look at him. A broken sob escaped from her as he held out his arms. Collapsing into his embrace, Blue Feather hid her face in his shoulder.

"Shh, little one," he soothed. "It is all over now." He held her gently, wincing when she accidentally grasped his wounded shoulder.

Feeling him flinch, she drew back, murmuring,

Oh, I forgot your injury! Let me see. . . ."

"It is nothing. Only a flesh wound. We should see to poor Harry and Gray Eagle first, then your father."

But Gray Eagle was already stirring, grimacing and attempting to push to a sitting position, but failing. Blue Feather flicked him a concerned glance, then turned to her father. Duvalle was alive, though weak, his face battered and bloody from Jardin's punishing blows. Her fingers worked swiftly to loosen the knots in his bonds, and when she had released him, she rubbed his wrists and ankles to restore the circulation in his limbs. His heartbeat was weak but steady, and she held him for a moment.

"Papa?" she whispered, and he looked up at her, his eyes slowly focusing.

"Oui?"

"I'm sorry," she said wretchedly. "I have caused this trouble—"

Duvalle's hand rose slowly, and he put a finger over her mouth. *"Non.* You are a good daughter, and did only what you had to do. I would . . . would have done the same." He grimaced, then added, "I should never have left you alone all those years."

Quickly shaking her head, Blue Feather whispered, "I was never alone, Papa. You were always with me, here in my heart, as you are now."

A weak smile touched his lips, and his eyes closed for a moment. Then they fluttered open again, and he struggled to sit up while she pushed him back down. "You may be right," Duvalle admitted when she insisted that he rest. "I do feel weak. I wasn't lying about the gold, you know. It *is* fool's gold, just shine and no substance. . . ." His voice trailed off, and Blue Feather wadded up a cloth to put beneath his head. Leaving him resting, she moved to attend to her cousin.

"I do not need a woman's help!" Gray Eagle snapped. "I am a warrior—" His words faded into a groan as he tried to sit up again, and Blue Feather pushed him gently back to the floor.

"Do not be so proud. You have a knife in you, foolish one! Shall I tell Sun Woman that you would not allow me to aid you? She will be very cross with you, and you will never hear the end of it."

Another groan escaped him as Gray Eagle's eyelids flickered in pain, and he reached up to grasp the hilt of the knife protruding from his shoulder. "I am cursed with domineering women," he muttered as Blue Feather removed his hand and firmly grasped the knife hilt herself.

"This will hurt," she said practically, then pulled. A brief flicker was the only reaction from the stoic Shoshoni chief, but his pallor paled to an unhealthy gray beneath his normal copper complexion. Staunching the wound with strips of cloth torn from her already ruined skirt, Blue Feather soon had Gray Eagle bandaged.

Gray Eagle's eyes shifted to the empty cot across the room, and he asked, "Where are your children?"

"I have hidden them," she answered. "As soon as I am through with you, I will bring them in."

"Go and get them," Gray Eagle said gently, giving her a slight push. "I do not care to be fussed over and made to feel as a child."

Shrugging, Blue Feather rose and left the cabin. Night shadows had fallen as she crossed to the bushes and parted the branches with her hands. She smiled down at the glimmer of two chubby faces peering anxiously up at her. They were such good

488

girls, and she held out her arms to them. When she had one on each hip, she stepped to the bushes where her father had spread out some of his clothing to dry. A large buckskin shirt was damp with the evening dew, but dry enough for her to wear. She set the children down and shrugged into the shirt. It fell to well above her knees, but the remnants of her cotton skirt still trailed below it in a modest fringe. Warmer now, she turned to the cabin.

Hope surged through her as Blue Feather entered and found Adrian and Gray Eagle talking softly. She turned to her husband with a smile. Perhaps their losses were few. . . .

But Adrian's expression was grave as he knelt beside Harry, cradling the old man's head in his lap. Harry's face was a mottled blue and purple, and he wasn't moving.

Chapter 25
The World

Taking a deep breath, Richard lifted the small satchel that held his important papers. It was his final day in the village of the Shoshoni, a day for farewells. He stepped out of the tipi and straightened. A sharp breeze swept across the land, bringing winter's promise with it.

Looking up at the high mountain ridges, Richard let his gaze drift over the camp with its buffalo-hide tipis, racks of drying meat, naked children running about, and the inevitable camp dogs. It was a beautiful spot to live, and he suddenly understood why the Shoshoni clung so fiercely to their land. Turning his head, he gazed at the shimmering waterfall dropping into the clear pool as it must have done since time began, and he heaved a sigh.

"Richard!" a voice called, and the duke turned to see Adrian approaching. A smile slanted Adrian's mouth, and his lean, tanned face glowed with happiness.

Putting down his heavy leather satchel, Richard waited. "I see that you are faring much better today," he commented when Adrian paused beside him. "Your wound must be healed."

"Yes, I believe it is almost healed. Surprising,

isn't it? I would have been laid up for weeks in England, but here in this sunshine and mountain air, I heal almost overnight."

Richard smiled. "Well, it's been a bit longer than that, Adrian."

Laughing, Adrian agreed, "Perhaps it has!"

Richard's smile faded slightly, and he couldn't help asking one more time, "Do you still intend to stay?"

Adrian's expression sobered, and he nodded. "Yes." He felt no need to add an explanation; all possible explanations had been given long ago.

Shrugging, Richard managed another smile. "Somehow, old boy, I felt that it would turn out this way. I had just hoped . . ." His voice trailed into an awkward silence, and he turned his head so Adrian would not see the distress in his eyes. It would be so difficult to return to England without him, to have to explain—and to have to understand. This might be the last time he would ever see his brother, and it grieved him to think of it. "Uncle Timothy will be quite disappointed," Richard remarked as he strove for composure.

"Richard, I belong here. This is my destiny."

"Destiny?" Richard turned to face his brother. "Destiny is an odd word to use. . . ."

Shaking his head, Adrian said softly, "Don't you recall that night it stormed—the night before Elizabeth died? Madame du Jessupe was there, and she told me of it, only I didn't really pay attention. My thoughts were elsewhere."

Richard's brow furrowed. "Yes, I do recall that night, of course. And Josette has spoken of it several times."

"Of course she would . . . Josette would understand," Adrian mused, then added, "That night, my fortune was told and my destiny predicted. It is uncanny, Richard, but I suppose I was swept away with the wind and the rain beating against the windowpanes, but when I went to bed, I had a dream." He paused for a moment, then gave a half-embarrassed laugh. "I dreamed of a young woman, Richard. This young woman was also being swept away in a storm, and she had long dark hair and was young, very young. I didn't see her face in my dream, of course, but I believe now that it was Blue Feather I dreamed of that night. . . ."

"Adrian," Richard put in with an amused expression, "do not say it!"

"No, I do," Adrian insisted. "And Richard, everything that Madame du Jessupe predicted has come to pass! Only consider—she said I would build a new house, and that must be this house, this land and people."

"One could apply such general predictions to almost anything, old boy!" Richard protested uneasily. "And if you think that her predictions were true, only remember—she said my house would be united. See? That cannot be, as I am leaving you here while I return alone. . . ."

"Don't you see?" Adrian persisted. "This *is* true, Richard! Our house has been reunited by your coming and finding me here. We had quarrelled, and now we are together again, even though far away. We can look at the past and be content. We have survived the storm. . . ."

Startled, Richard stared at his brother for a long moment. Then, slowly nodding his head, he said, "Perhaps you are right, Adrian. Yes . . . I believe I see that now. We were apart in more than just distance, but now we are together again. Yes, you are definitely right, and I should have seen it before." A smile curved his mouth, and he held out his hand to his brother. When Adrian took it, Richard shed his natural reserve and flung his arms around his brother. "I shall miss you dreadfully!" he said in a choked whisper, and Adrian hugged him tightly.

"And I shall miss you, my brother." Struggling with his raw emotions, Adrian could not speak for a time, then he managed a smile as he and Richard stepped apart. "Until we meet again," he said softly, "whether in this life or the next. . . ." He put up a hand in the Shoshoni way of farewell, and Richard returned the gesture.

"I will think of you often," Richard said, clearing his throat.

Standing slightly apart, they stood silently then, staring at the high mountain peaks ringing the camp, and thinking of the future. White clouds scudded across the sky, whipped by the wind, dancing upon mountaintops and then fading. The wind bent the tall pines, cedars and firs, moaning through the branches in a constant song. Sunlight threaded through the leaves in shifting patterns, warming their faces as they stood in companionable silence.

"It *is* beautiful," Richard remarked finally, and Adrian agreed.

"Yes, it is." Adrian paused, then added, "So Bowie is to guide you to the Green River to meet Stewart, I understand?"

"Yes, and then it's on to St. Louis from there. Stewart is a competent traveler. I believe I recounted to you his entourage?"

Laughing, Adrian said, "Yes! It is difficult to

think that he brought his companion Mr. Celam as well as two dogs, three servants, and four extra horses with which to run the buffalo . . . and didn't you say he brought along quite a few mules as well?"

"I did. Oh, make no mistake about it! Stewart is an odd fellow, indeed, but quite likable. The man fairly exudes energy, and I have seen him chase after antelope like a hound, then swear that he could have caught them if he'd had a blooded animal!" Shaking his head with amusement, Richard said, "He's quite a fellow indeed, Adrian."

"So he sounds. Perhaps I shall make his acquaintance at the rendezvous next year."

"You could tag along now. . . ."

"No," Adrian said with only a trace of regret. "I am afraid that after all the turmoil and strain, my little family would find it impossible. And I refuse to go without them."

Richard smiled. "I can understand your reluctance after all the trouble you have had lately." He paused, then asked, "And how is Blue Feather?"

"She is doing well."

"And the children?"

Smiling, Adrian said proudly, "They grow more lovely every day!"

After a brief hesitation, Richard blurted, "Adrian, I never meant to upset Blue Feather, you know. I only thought I was doing what was right for all of us. . . ."

"No need to explain, Richard. I understand and so does she." His gaze grew distant, and he wondered once more why Blue Feather had wanted to leave him. She had confessed that she had intended to do so, that she had intended to flee to her father

494

even before Jardin had abducted her. It was a sore point with Adrian, and he still could not comprehend why she would do such a thing. Didn't she trust him? Couldn't she talk to him?

"I believe Bowie has everything almost packed," Adrian commented, and Richard turned.

"Wait a moment—I have something for you," he said, and ducked back into the tipi he had occupied. When he returned he held out a small leather satchel and said, "Here—this is for you, Adrian."

Adrian paused in the act of reaching out for it, his mind flashing back to a long-ago day on a foggy dock at the shipyard, another time, another man, and the smell of the sea around him.

"Adrian?" Richard prompted, breaking his reverie.

Taking it, Adrian asked, "What is it?"

"Just some things I would like for you to have—letters and portraits, and a few favorite books of mine to pass the long winter nights." He smiled. "I thought Harry might want to teach the girls to read."

Grinning, Adrian nodded. "His convalescence is beginning to wear upon my nerves, so perhaps I can persuade him to start now!"

Richard laughed. "Well, he can never say that I did not give him the opportunity to go back to England with me. I still find it hard to believe that he prefers staying here."

"You find it hard to believe that I prefer staying here also!" Adrian retorted.

"Not as much as you might think—ah, here comes the illustrious Mr. Bowie and his blushing bride, Charlotte! I think my time here is nearing an end, Adrian."

Turning, Adrian watched as Bowie sauntered across the path to them. "Good day, yer dukeship," he greeted Richard, and Adrian grinned broadly.

"Good day, Bowie," Richard returned with weary forebearance. "Are we almost ready?"

"That we are, your dukeship!"

"I quiver with anticipation. Well, Adrian," Richard said, turning once more to his brother, "I suppose this is farewell."

A twinge of pain shot through Adrian, and his gray eyes rested on his brother's face for a long, poignant moment. They both realized that they would probably never see one another again.

Everett Bowie, never one to believe in long, drawn-out farewells, cleared his throat and said, "Me and my woman are lookin' forward to bein' back at the Siskadee, Duke. Thought we might head to Oregon Territory for a while after that. Might see you next year at the rendezvous." He turned to Richard then. "Well, it's time ta go, yer dukeship," he said, and turned on his heel and strode to the horses.

Shrugging, Adrian looked at his brother. "Farewell, Richard."

"Farewell, Adrian."

Watching as Richard mounted his horse and settled into the saddle, Adrian cupped a hand over his eyes. He stood, tall and straight and strong, a sight Richard Herenton, the fifth Duke of Hertfield, would long remember.

"Farewell, Duke!" Richard shouted with a broad grin, removing his hat and waving it in the air as he nudged his horse into a trot. "And farewell to your lovely lady!" This last was accompanied by a half-bow from the waist as he rode past Adrian's tipi.

Turning, Adrian saw Blue Feather standing just outside, waving a farewell, her mouth curved in a smile. Both girls were at her sides, clinging to her skirts as they often did now, their sweet faces smiling. Adrian's heart lurched as he thought of how he had nearly lost them all. It had been so close, such a near thing, and he lay awake nights of late, going over it again and again in his mind. The ordeal would return in detail, and he would hear Blue Feather's scream and Jardin's laughter, then he would feel his own helplessness. And over all of that, was the knowledge that Blue Feather had intended to run away from him.

Still flinching when he thought of it, Adrian walked toward his wife with firm, purposeful strides. This could not continue to lie silent between them. It would grow, a malignancy that would only spawn mistrust and anger, and it needed to be cut away and healed.

Pausing beside Blue Feather, Adrian looked down at her. "We must talk," he said. There was a quick widening of her eyes, then she nodded.

Adrian's tall frame bent as he held open the flap of the tipi for her, but Blue Feather had turned to their daughters. "Go to Harry," she told them. "He needs you now, and I must talk to your father." Giving the children a slight nudge, she shooed them across the six feet separating Harry's tipi from theirs.

As she turned back to face him, Adrian was once more struck with how poised and beautiful she had become. If anything, she was even more lovely than when he had first seen her, and she had greatly matured in the past two years. He gazed at her face, at the curves and hollows that seemed sculpted from the finest clay, and his throat tightened. How could she have wanted to leave him?

"You go in first," he said, and lifted the flap high. Ducking, Blue Feather slid inside and stood in the center, waiting. Adrian entered and let the flap fall. It was dim inside, with only a dusty, hazy shaft of light streaming in from the air hole at the top. Blue Feather waited quietly. She stood in the center of the shaft of light, her dark hair gleaming and her hands folded in front of her. Her chin was lifted and her gaze steady as she returned his stare. Adrian was once more struck with her air of maturity. Gone were the awkward, coltish, frightened movements of the young girl, and in their place were the assured, confident expectations of a woman. The ordeal with Jardin had left its mark on her, and he could not help but wonder if she felt the same toward him that she once had.

"Please sit," he said then, his voice sounding overloud in the cottony silence of the tipi. Blue Feather sat with a graceful movement, spreading her cotton skirts to cover her legs. Again she folded her hands in her lap and waited for him to speak. Adrian sat abruptly, cross-legged and facing her, only inches away. His eyes darkened from silver to slate gray as he regarded her with a steady frown.

Waiting and watching, Blue Feather sensed what he wanted to say, and she did not know how she would respond. How could she explain her reasons, when they had seemed so sensible then and so foolish now? Perhaps the recent danger had reinforced her love for Adrian to the point where she now knew that she could not live without him. He would have felt betrayed without her, and she would have wandered lost and miserable without him. But would he believe her now, after hearing how she had intended to flee from him?

Shifting, Adrian cleared his throat. "You intended to leave me," he stated, and she nodded slowly.

"*Ai, ai,* I did."

"Why?"

Blue eyes darkened with pain as she shook her head. "I do not know how to say it without sounding foolish, but I had thought that you would be happier if I did so. No, it is true!" she added when he snorted derisively. "I never wanted to leave *you,* but I knew I would never be accepted by your people if I went with you to England." Leaning forward, she said earnestly, "I knew our children would be well cared for by you and Harry, and I was willing to give you all up so you would be happy. But then . . . when Jardin came and took me away and it seemed as if I would never see you again, I knew how precious you are to me. I think that if I had been foolish enough to let you go away without me, I would have followed you. I cannot bear the thought of being without you, even if it means being where I am hated. . . ."

"Dear God!" Adrian whispered in a tortured voice. "How could you have ever thought I would subject you to open ridicule? Do you think so little of me?"

She shook her head. "No, of course not. But I am more aware of how the white man feels about the Shoshoni than you are, my kind and good husband. You feel no hatred toward any man, no prejudice but for that which is earned by a man's own character. You would not have expected it, but I have experienced it." A soft smile curved her mouth

499

as she looked up at him. "It is that quality that I most admire about you, my dear husband."

Stunned, Adrian leaned back against a stack of blankets. "What quality—my stupidity?" he asked bitterly. "After talking with Duvalle, I know what you are telling me is right. I just refused to see it when you tried to tell me before, and now you shame me by taking the blame upon yourself. . . ." He surged forward, folding Blue Feather into his arms and laying his cheek against her head. "Ah, sweet love, how I have wronged you! I am the most fortunate man alive that you still love me."

He could feel the shake of her head beneath his cheek, and smiled as she said, "No, it is I who am fortunate!"

Adrian's arms tightened, and for a moment he could not speak. Shutting his eyes, he searched blindly for her lips. It was a sweet kiss, tender and filled with pain, regret and the greatest love he had ever known. As he held her in his arms, kissing her without passion and only love, he knew he had found his future. His future leaned into his embrace, filling him with peace and contentment and a happiness he had never dreamed existed.

"And to think I almost lost you," he muttered minutes later, and she drew back slightly to gaze up at him.

Her fingertips traced the outline of his mouth, the sweep of his jaw, and his high cheekbones. "But we are here together now," she reminded him.

"Yes, here where we both belong," Adrian agreed.

"Do you mean that, my husband? You have no regrets about England and your brother?"

"None about England, though I suppose I shall miss my brother at times. I chose the life I wanted,

Blue Feather. I chose you and my children. This is all I want, all I need for the rest of time."

Snuggling closer, Blue Feather sighed happily. "I am glad to hear you say it, though I would have gone with you if that is what you wished."

Adrian rubbed his chin against the top of her head. "No, this is my home now. This is where I am happy. Even Harry, who could have chosen to go with Richard, chose to stay here."

"I thought it was because he is still too weak to travel," Blue Feather commented with surprise. "He had said many times how he longed for England. . . ."

"That was when he thought you and the girls were going," Adrian pointed out with a dry laugh. "Once he discovered that you were remaining here, his desire to see 'Merrie old England' waned. And, I think that somehow the land caught him as it has caught me."

"The land?" She turned in his arms to stare up at him. "What do you mean?"

Adrian stroked back the soft sable curls that had fallen onto her forehead, his tone distant as he murmured, "It is something that Broken Arm once told me. It was when we were on our way to the rendezvous, before we found you, and I can clearly recall the soft look in his eyes as he gazed around him. His eyes held a reverence I could not understand then, but I do now. We were alone, and Broken Arm told me that it is the land that lasts, the land that is eternal, and when a man can be in harmony with the land, he finds peace." A smile curved his mouth, and he gave a half-embarrassed cough. "He was right, for I have found peace here—peace in my heart and in my mind."

Blue Feather remained quiet, lost in thoughtful memories of the old trapper. He had been a wise man in his way, and she would miss him. Then she was startled to hear Adrian say aloud what she had been thinking, and turned her face to his with a soft smile.

"I was just thinking that, my husband," she said. "I shall never forget him."

"Neither shall I."

"Do not remember him with sadness. He knew his time was near, and he came back to Wind River to die," Blue Feather said, then added so softly that Adrian wasn't quite certain he had heard her say it, "Broken Arm was a good man."

Adrian remained still. The significance of her words struck him, and he knew she was trying to adapt her ingrained beliefs to his. For her to say aloud the name of the dead person was a great step, and he dared not say the wrong thing to diminish her gesture. Clearing his throat, Adrian said simply, "I love you, my wife."

A bright silver moon was mirrored in the surface of the lake, shimmering moonbeams dancing in the dark water. Tall pines bent and swayed with the wind, a gentle lullabye murmuring through the branches over the Shoshoni camp. It was gentle now, but soon the wind would grow stronger, pushing against the sides of tipis and moaning through the tree branches.

"Snow will come soon," Pierre Duvalle observed. His fingers curved over the head of a walking stick he had used since his confrontation with Jardin, and he slanted a glance at the man sitting cross-legged before the fire in the center of the tipi. "It won't stay in her hair," he said then, and Harry frowned.

"Of course it won't. She's too restless, but I still must try. After all, every proper young English lady has ribbons in her hair—sit still, Blue," he added with a sigh as the child squirmed in his lap.

Duvalle snorted. "She's no 'proper young English lady,' my friend! She has the blood of Shoshoni warriors in her veins, as well as good French-Canadian blood!"

"Well, I don't hold that against her," Harry said in an unperturbed tone that didn't fool Duvalle for a moment. "And I shall endeavor to tutor them both in the proper manners and customs, of course."

"That should come in handy on the plains," Duvalle remarked dryly. "I can just see them serving tea from silver pots while shuffling between tipis!"

"You scoff now, but you shall eat your words one day," Harry said with a superior smile.

"Pah! This prediction from a man who has yet to best me at a game of chess?" he retorted with a challenging smile.

"Do you have the board set up and ready?" Harry asked. "I believe the last match was mine. . . ."

"Only because my attention was distracted by Star," Duvalle protested, thoroughly enjoying himself. "Ah, Harry, I shall miss you when I return to my cabin for the winter."

"Why not stay here in the valley where it is warmer?" Harry asked as he finished tying the ribbon in Blue's hair and let her go. She immediately pulled it out and put it in her mouth, and he sighed. "Dear, dear, this is so difficult to accomplish — give it to me, child."

Blue's tiny mouth puckered in a frown as Harry removed the ribbon from her hands and mouth, but when she would have cried Duvalle distracted her. "Come here," he coaxed, and held up a small bear he had carved from soft pine. "Do you want to play with this?"

Happy again, Blue moved to her grandfather and took the toy, which spurred Star to protect. Soon, both children were playing with carved wooden animals.

"You're quite handy with a carving knife," Harry said as he pulled out a chess board and set of figures that Duvalle had carved. "White or black?"

"White, of course."

"Naturally . . . but don't think I shall be easy on you this time, Duvalle! It is a battle to the bitter end," Harry said gaily.

Pierre Duvalle squinted at Harry in the rosy light of the fire. "Even sorry you didn't go back?" he asked casually as he placed his pieces on the board.

"To England, you mean?" Harry shook his head. "No, though I did rather fancy the notion of lording it over that wretched Gladys Carmichael. She's the housekeeper, and a snooty woman if ever I've seen one," he explained at Duvalle's inquiring expression. "Well, I shall have to be content with knowing that she will be amazed to hear of my adventures. Ahh — are you really going to use that opening gambit, Duvalle? How clever of you. . . ."

The silver image of the moon was shattered as slender brown arms thrust through the water's sur-

504

face, breaking the reflection into a thousand pieces. Surging forward with smooth strokes, Blue Feather swam toward a rock at the edge of the waterfall. The water was cold, and the breeze across her exposed body made her flesh prickle. Long hair ribboned behind her as she reached the rock and pulled her body from the water. She perched on the rock's surface. It was still warm from the day's sunshine, and she leaned back on her elbows to wait for Adrian.

A smile curved her mouth, and tossing back her head, she smoothed wet tangles of hair from her eyes. He had been much slower in removing his clothes than she. She had been wearing only a skirt and blouse, while he had worn trousers and shirt, and belt and boots. Giggling to herself, Blue Feather turned to lie on her stomach. The rock was rough beneath her, scratching her tender belly and breasts and thighs. A spray of water from the crashing falls tickled her skin and roared in her ears, and she closed her eyes.

She was content. Life was good. It would change, of course, as life always did, but with Adrian at her side she felt she could meet any obstacle that came her way. Perhaps it would—

Surfacing by the rock, Adrian broke into her thoughts as he pulled himself, dripping and laughing, from the water. "So, you thought you would get away from me?" he asked. "Where did you learn to swim so well, little fish?"

Rolling to her side, Blue Feather held out her arms to him. He stood over her, his body lean and taut, shining wetly in the moonlight. The waterfall roared in her ears and splashed shimmering diamond drops over them as Adrian knelt beside her, his eyes glowing with love and desire.

Swept along on the winds of passion, neither of them noticed the brisk whip of the cool Wyoming wind as it blew across them.

Dear Readers:

We hope you enjoyed reading this ZEBRA romance. As writers we feel that it is important to stay close to our readers. It is the reader that we write for, and hope to please. Contact with you lets us know if we are doing our job properly. Please write and let us know how you feel.

THANKS,
Emma Harrington
(Virginia Brown and Jane Harrison)

Write in care of ZEBRA BOOKS

LOVE'S BRIGHTEST STARS SHINE
WITH ZEBRA BOOKS!

CATALINA'S CARESS   (2202, $3.95)
by Sylvie F. Sommerfield
Catalina Carrington was determined to buy her riverboat back from the handsome gambler who'd beaten her brother at cards. But when dashing Marc Copeland named his price—three days as his mistress—Catalina swore she'd never meet his terms . . . even as she imagined the rapture a night in his arms would bring!

BELOVED EMBRACE   (2135, $3.95)
by Cassie Edwards
Leana Rutherford was terrified when the ship carrying her family from New York to Texas was attacked by savage pirates. But when she gazed upon the bold sea-bandit Brandon Seton, Leana longed to share the ecstasy she was sure sure his passionate caress would ignite!

ELUSIVE SWAN   (2061, $3.95)
by Sylvie F. Sommerfield
Just one glance from the handsome stranger in the dockside tavern in boisterous St. Augustine made Arianne tremble with excitement. But the innocent young woman was already running from one man . . . and no matter how fiercely the flames of desire burned within her, Arianne dared not submit to another!

MOONLIT MAGIC   (1941, $3.95)
by Sylvie F. Sommerfield
When she found the slick railroad negotiator Trace Cord trespassing on her property and bathing in her river, innocent Jenny Graham could barely contain her rage. But when she saw how the setting sun gilded Trace's magnificent physique, Jenny's seething fury was transformed into burning desire!

Available wherever paperbacks are sold, or order direct from the Publisher. Send cover price plus 50¢ per copy for mailing and handling to Zebra Books, Dept. 2504¹, 475 Park Avenue South, New York, N.Y. 10016. Residents of New York, New Jersey and Pennsylvania must include sales tax. DO NOT SEND CASH.